"*I* have one last question to ask of you, Quinton."

"And that is, my dear?" She was so serious, and so amusing.

"When are you going to kiss me again?" Allegra queried him.

"Why right now, my dear," he answered her, pulling her into his lap. Taking her chin between his thumb and his forefinger, his lip met hers in a rather fierce kiss.

She gasped, surprised. His finger caressed her jawline for a brief moment, and then he kissed her again; this time slowly, slowly until she felt as if her bones were melting away. His eyes looked into hers. Allegra felt a wave of heat wash over her and her heart hammered wildly.

"Do you think I kiss well enough for you, my dear?" he asked her wickedly. Actually he had quite enjoyed it himself.

"Quite well enough," she admitted to him. "I will swear that my toes curled, sir."

"You are flattering me, Allegra, and I will quite confess to liking it," he told her.

THE
Duchess

BERTRICE SMALL

BALLANTINE BOOKS • NEW YORK

The Duchess is a work of fiction. Names, places, and incidents either are a product of the author's imagination or are used fictitiously.

An Ivy Book
Published by The Random House Publishing Group
Copyright © 2001 by Bertrice Small

www.ballantinebooks.com

ISBN 0-345-43695-4

Manufactured in the United States of America

First Ballantine Books Trade Paperback Edition: July 2001
First Ballantine Books Mass Market Edition: December 2003

OPM   10 9 8 7 6 5 4 3 2 1

Lovingly dedicated to my late mother's best friend,
Constance MacIntyre of Tryon, North Carolina.
Thank you, Connie.

The Duchess

England 1794

Prologue

"*D*amn me, there is no other way! I shall have to take a wife," Quinton Hunter, the Duke of Sedgwick, announced to his assembled friends. He was a very tall man, standing over six feet in height, with a lean hard body, and a shock of black hair.

"We all do eventually," his friend, Viscount Pickford, replied with a cheerful grin.

"I don't notice you in any great hurry, Ocky," the duke said.

Octavian Baird, Viscount Pickford, grinned again. "I'll tell you what, Quint, we'll do it together. We'll go trolling for brides this coming season, eh?" His blue eyes danced mischievously.

"I think we should all do it," Marcus Bainbridge, the Earl of Aston, announced. "My family would be delighted to have me bring a pretty heiress home."

"By God, Bain, what a splendid idea!" Viscount Pickford laughed.

The three friends looked to their fourth companion, Lord Adrian Walworth.

"Well, Dree?" the duke said.

Lord Walworth shrugged. "If I don't, and you do, I'll not have anyone left to play with," he grumbled somewhat petulantly. "Wives don't like their husbands having single gentlemen friends." He was thoughtful for a brief moment, and then he continued. "We'll not be able to play our little games in France any longer if we take wives. I suppose it is better that we don't. We were almost caught the last time. I don't relish having my head on some Frenchie's pike." He grinned. "If only all the fashionables in London knew that they had us to thank for their favorite dressmaker. We were at our zenith when we rescued Madame Paul and her people," he waxed nostalgically, but then he agreed, "Aye if you three plan to marry then I must out of necessity, or lose your company. It will certainly make my mama happy. All she talks about when I'm down at the hall is her lack of grandchildren."

Viscount Pickford chuckled. "When we appear this season all the mamas will go wild with delight. Frankly I don't know of four more eligible gentlemen in the ten thousand. I hear Lord Morgan's daughter is going to make her bow under the sponsorship of her aunt, the Dowager Marchioness of Rowley. Now there's the girl for you, Quint."

"I shall have a harder time than any of you finding a wife," the duke responded seriously. "While my blood is the bluest in England, even bluer than the king's, my purse is virtually empty. My antecedents had the rather romantic notion of marrying for love, and by God, they did! Far worse, most of them had a passion for gambling. This estate of mine is intact by some miracle, but look around; Hunter's Lair is falling down about my ears. The lady I choose must be wealthy enough to put it all back together again, and bring me enough income so I may get on my feet. Unlike my father, and those before him, I have no desire to gamble, nor necessarily marry for love. I must wed for practical reasons. Then I will put my estate back in order and make it prosper. *If I can find a lady noble enough, and rich enough to have me,*" he concluded.

"Then it's Lord Morgan's daughter for you," Viscount Pickford insisted. "She's quite the heiress."

"Her blood is barely blue," the earl noted. "Her father is only the second to hold his title. The family were London merchants, and he is still involved in business. Her mother, however, was the old Duke of Arley's youngest child. Ran off with some Italian count when the daughter was two, and her brother eight. It was quite a scandal at the time. Lord Morgan divorced her, of course, but has never remarried. Then the son was killed a few years ago. Lord M. has devoted himself to his remaining offspring ever since. She is indeed fearfully rich, Quint, but her pedigree ain't good enough for you."

"Don't be such a snob, Bain," the viscount said. "With a father as rich as Croesus, and a duke for a grandfather, she will surely pass muster. The bluer-blooded gels ain't got dowries big enough to help Quint. This could be a perfect match."

"I knew her brother slightly," Lord Walworth said helpfully. "A nice chap, exquisite manners and always paid his debts promptly."

"Did you ever see her?" the duke asked.

Lord Walworth shook his head. "She's a country mouse, I'm given to understand. Never been up to London although her sire has a big house on Berkley Square."

"I wonder if she's pretty," the duke mused.

"All little kitties purr the same in the dark, Quint," the earl noted practically.

"True, but one must sit opposite them at the dinner table," the duke quickly riposted, and his friend laughed.

"So we are agreed then, gentlemen," the viscount said. "We are to seek suitable brides next season, and marry at long last. Just think, Quint, when Hunter's Lair is in prime condition again, what parties you will give for us all!"

"What parties *his wife* will give," Lord Walworth said gloomily, "and our wives had best be in her favor, or we won't get invited."

"You will always be welcome at Hunter's Lair, Dree; and Ocky and Bain, too. Remember, a man is master of his own house. You are my best friends, and have been since our days at Eton. That is not going to change because of a mere woman. Now," he banged his goblet upon the scarred oak table and shouted, "Crofts! Where is dinner?"

"I'll bring it right in, Your Grace," the manservant said with a bow. "Mrs. Crofts didn't want the venison to be overcooked." He hurried out of the paneled old Great Hall where the dukes and earls of Sedgwick had dined for centuries.

Hunter's Lair was a large house, but it had never been modernized, not even in the Stuart era when almost every great house in England had been redone to include large public dining rooms with marble fireplaces. Quinton Hunter was the ninth Earl and the fourth Duke of Sedgwick. The first duke had been created in 1664, several years after Charles II's restoration. The earldom had come to them in the time of King Henry VIII. Prior to that, fourteen Baron Hunters descended from the year 1143, and before that the heads of the family were baronets; Saxons who had wisely supported William of Normandy over Harold Godwinson only to find their thanedoms turned into baronetcyes, and fair Norman wives in their beds. It was a long and proud heritage.

The present house was built upon the ruins of the original Saxon hall, and a second house which had burned in the reign of Henry VII. The third house had stood in its present incarnation since the year 1500. It was built of red brick, although the stones were generally obscured by the shiny green ivy growing over it. The ancient leaded paned casement windows remained lovely, but had become, with time, very fragile. They were opened rarely, and then most carefully. It was, despite its antiquity, a very elegant house that had been home to many generations of Hunters, and the duke loved it.

It had always been expected that he would marry, although his late father's wishes in the matter seemed to lack a sense of reality. Who was going to marry a blue-blooded pauper? the duke thought to himself; but marry he must if Hunter's Lair was not to fall into further decay. And then there was his younger brother, George. Without a rich wife's monies the duke could not buy his brother a commission in the army, or even a pulpit in some small church.

"I shall have to sell some horses if I am to have a fashionable wardrobe and pocket money," Quinton Hunter said aloud.

"And we shall all stay at my father's London house," the viscount decided. "The old man don't come up for the season anymore. He scarcely goes to Parliament, but he keeps the house open for family and friends from September through June."

"Damned generous," Lord Walworth said.

"Yes, thank you, Ocky," the earl agreed. "We ain't never had a house in town. I hope the lady I find to marry has a family with one."

"I shall be glad to accept your invitation, Ocky," the duke said.

"We have two months to prepare," the viscount said. "Tomorrow we part, and we shall meet again on March fifteenth to travel up to London together, gentlemen."

"Agreed," the earl and Lord Walworth replied simultaneously.

"Agreed," the duke said.

Part One

A.D. 1795
A Very Successful Season

Chapter One

"At best we can bag an earl, or perhaps an earl's heir for Allegra," Lady Olympia Abbott, Dowager Marchioness of Rowley, told her brother-in-law, Lord Septimius Morgan. "Pandora's behavior ain't helped her daughter, but there it is. My sister was always selfish, and do not glower at me, Septimius; it is the truth even if you have never faced it." She sipped her tea from a Wedgwood saucer thoughtfully. "We won't know what opportunities we have until the season begins, and we see what unmarried young men have come; but I can guarantee that Allegra's extraordinary beauty and wealth will attract only the best. The bluest of bloods, of course, will ignore her, but we'll do very well nonetheless. This tea is delicious, Septimius. Who is your importer? I must have some for myself."

"The tea comes from my own plantations, Olympia. I will see you are supplied with it from now on," Lord Morgan said.

"Your own plantations in India? I never knew," his sister-in-law replied, surprised. She slurped from her saucer appreciatively.

"Ceylon. My holdings are quite diverse," he explained. "It is not wise to put all of one's eggs in a single basket, Olympia. I have taught my daughter that lesson."

"I don't know why you bothered," Lady Abbott responded. "Allegra is going to be someone's wife, m'dear. She needs little knowledge other than how to manage a household efficiently, how to direct her servants to live moral lives, how to paint pleasing watercolors, play a musical instrument, sing, dance prettily, and of course give her husband an heir as promptly as she can do so. After that she must raise her children as God-fearing and mannerly, with a strong sense of their English heritage."

"Allegra is my heiress, Olympia. She should know how my many businesses are managed else she lose them one day," Lord Morgan told his sister-in-law, who only shook her head at him.

"Septimius!" said the exasperated lady. "Allegra's husband will be in charge of her inheritance. You know that we women are not capable of such things." She laughed. "How you dote on that girl, but she is still a girl." Then she grew serious. "I know you miss James Lucian, but your son is gone, Septimius. Allegra cannot replace him." The Dowager Marchioness of Rowley's soft blue eyes filled with tears, and she put a comforting hand on her brother-in-law's arm. "He was a great hero, my nephew, God rest him. A hero, and a true gentleman."

"Do not speak on it!" Lord Morgan said harshly. "While Allegra is indeed just a girl, she is extremely intelligent. Whoever her husband is to be he must appreciate that. Until the day I die my daughter will have a personal allowance from me of two hundred and fifty thousand pounds a year. And after I am gone my estates will continue to see Allegra receives those monies. I don't intend my daughter be at the mercy of some charming blue-blooded wastrel who will mistreat her after he has captured her heart, use her dower to pay for his vices and his mistresses, and then drink himself into an early grave leaving her and my grandchildren helpless to his family."

"Septimius!" his sister-in-law cried, shocked. "What kind of men do you think we are offering Allegra to, for mercy's sake?"

"I know the kind of men who inhabit the ten thousand, my dear Olympia. Most of them are useless, and all of them are snobs. As Lord Morgan's daughter, Allegra must of necessity choose one of them for a husband, but I will not leave her unprotected." His fist slammed upon the mahogany side table causing Lady Abbott to start.

"But whatever you give her the law says is her husband's," she protested. "You cannot circumvent the law, Septimius."

He looked at her, amused, thinking that Olympia was a good soul, but entirely too naive for a woman of her years. "Of course I can skirt the law, my dear. That is one of the advantages of being the richest man in all of England." He chuckled. "When I want something there are those only too glad to accommodate me. My occasional gratitude is both known and appreciated. No husband will be able to confiscate Allegra's monies for his own purposes. Now, let us speak on more imminent subjects.

"You will, of course, be staying at the house in town for the season.

"Allegra is to have the finest wardrobe that can be made. She is not to be outshone by lesser lights, Olympia. It is very good of you to take her under your wing, especially considering the youngest of your daughters is also making her entry into society. I hope you will allow me to cover the cost of Lady Sirena's wardrobe as well. It will help you to get Allegra to stand still for the modiste if her favorite cousin is also suffering the same fate." Lord Morgan smiled. "Do not stint on either girl, my dear. Charles Trent, my steward and secretary, will see that they have the proper jewelry. The safe in the London house is full to overflowing."

"You are very kind, Septimius," Lady Abbott said gratefully. Her son, the young Marquis of Rowley, was married. His income was adequate, but hardly allowed for a generous allowance to be expended on his youngest sister. And worse, when she had returned home from Morgan Court, his wife had voiced objections to Sirena having a season at all.

"Augustus," Charlotte had said pettishly to her husband while in his mother's presence, "Sirena's dowry is hardly worth mentioning. I don't know who will have her. Couldn't we find a husband for her here in the country? I understand Squire Roberts has a fine son who is ready to take a wife. It seems foolish to expend *our* monies on a season in London for your sister."

The dowager marchioness had been outraged by her daughter-in-law's mean words. She had always tried to keep a good relationship with Gussie's wife, but this was intolerable. "My dear Charlotte," she said in icy tones that sent a shiver down her only son's spine. "Your dowry was not particularly overgenerous I recall, and yet you managed to attract my son's affections. You are married five years now, and have produced no heir. Still, I do not complain. Sirena's dowry was set aside by her father, God rest my darling husband, as were the monies for Sirena's debut in London. My daughter shall have her season!"

"And where will you reside?" the foolish Charlotte demanded. "*We* may go up for the season."

"I am sponsoring my niece, Allegra Morgan. Lord Morgan has invited us to live in his house on Berkley Square," Lady Abbott replied silkily. "Everything is already arranged, and we shall leave for London on the first of March."

"You could stay at Abbott House, Mama," her son said generously, to his wife's pique.

"Good heavens, Gussie, I should hope not!" Lady Abbott said loftily. "It is much too small, and not on the most fashionable of streets, I fear. We do want Sirena to make a good impression, don't we? Besides, I expect you and Charlotte will be filling the house with all your friends. It will hardly be the place for a young girl." She smiled at the couple.

"The house my father gave us as a wedding gift is on a perfectly good street!" Charlotte burst out, stung.

"Perhaps, my dear," her mother-in-law purred, "but it is not Berkley Square now, is it?" She smiled again, pleased to have put the aggravating chit back in her place. "I'm certain Septimius will invite you to all the parties he is giving for Allegra. After all, she is Gussie's cousin, isn't she?"

"She is a most delightful, but naughty puss," the Marquess of Rowley said with a fond chuckle. "I have always been quite taken with Allegra. But when she and Sirena get together all hell is apt to break loose!" He chuckled again. "You are going to have your hands full, Mama," he said, waggling a finger at her.

"Which is why I shall enjoy a quiet summer back here in the country," his mother said with a smile.

"If the girls bag themselves husbands, Mama, you shall have no peace at all this summer, for you shall be busy planning their weddings. I know that my uncle

Septimius depends upon you in such matters, and when Allegra marries, it will be quite the spectacle, I think."

"Miss Morgan has little hope of making a particularly distinguished match," Charlotte interjected. "She may be rich, but her blood is barely blue, and her mama's disgraceful behavior can hardly recommend her, or be overlooked. Is there not a saying, like mother, like daughter?"

"Allegra's mother, you may recall, Charlotte, was my youngest sister," Lady Abbott said. "Her unfortunate conduct cannot reflect on my niece any more than it can reflect upon me, or any children you might finally bear. What twaddle you babble, my dear!"

"Have you ever heard from Aunt Pandora since she ran away, Mama?" Augustus asked, curious.

"Because you ask me, I shall tell you, Gussie, but it is never to be discussed with Allegra, or anyone else for that matter. Yes, I know where my sister is. She married her count, and they live outside of Rome. They are quite well liked, I am told."

"How could a divorced woman be remarried?" Charlotte asked.

"Pandora's first marriage was not performed in the Roman Catholic faith, and therefore not recognized by that church. My sister was first baptized into the old faith, and then married to her count. Septimius knows, but Allegra has never been told."

"She can hardly remember her mama," Augustus said. "She was only two when Aunt Pandora ran off."

"She doesn't remember her at all, but for the portrait of my sister which hangs at Morgan Court. Septimius has never taken it down because he has never stopped loving Pandora. My sister did not deserve such a good man."

"Why, madame," Charlotte giggled inanely, "you sound as if you had a *tendre* for Lord Morgan." She looked slyly at her mother-in-law, giggling again in a particularly irritating fashion.

What had Augustus seen in this ridiculous girl, Lady Abbott thought. Her dear husband had been dead a year, and Lady Abbott was barely out of mourning when they had met. Charlotte's parents, the earl and his countess, had been delighted with their daughter's prize catch. They certainly should have been! They had rushed the young couple to the altar almost immediately, hosting a large wedding at St. George's on Hanover Square, followed by a wedding breakfast afterward at their rented town house. There had been no time to point out to her son that Charlotte was a featherbrained chit who could be both selfish and mean. Still, she seemed to make Augustus happy, even if she had not yet produced a child. Her son said that Charlotte was afraid of childbirth, having been treated to horror stories from her mother, a brainless creature who had easily managed to produce three offspring despite her alleged fears.

"Will you need the coach to get up to London?" the marquess asked his mother, ignoring his wife's silly outburst as indeed he hoped his mama would. While he loved Charlotte, even he was ofttimes embarrassed by her tactlessness.

Lady Abbott gave her son a small smile, and patted his hand reassuringly. "No, m'dear, I will not. Septimius's traveling coach will convey us all to London in style."

"I hear the fittings on his vehicle are real silver—not gilt," Charlotte said.

"I believe they are," Lady Abbott replied. "Sirena and

I are going to travel to Morgan Court in a few days, and from there up to London. I should appreciate the use of your carriage, Gussie, for that short journey."

"Of course, Mama," the marquess replied dutifully.

"But what if that is the day I wish to go visit my sister?" Charlotte whined.

"If it is," her husband said, "I shall drive you to Lavinia's in the Stanhope gig myself, my precious."

"Oh," Charlotte said, brightening, "I should like that!"

The drawing room door opened at that moment, and Lady Sirena Abbott entered, a packet in her hand. She was a very pretty girl with golden blond hair, and blue eyes with just the hint of gray in them. Her complexion was one of the most favored and in fashion—peaches and cream. "Mama, this has just come for you from Uncle Septimius," she said breathlessly. "I think it must be our traveling schedule." Then remembering her manners she curtsied properly to her sister-in-law, but hugged her brother enthusiastically. "Ohh, Gussie, isn't it exciting? I'm going to London with Allegra! We have both decided that we are going to be Incomparables, and have all the gentlemen at our feet. We shall only consider the men who fight duels over us for husbands!"

He laughed heartily, and hugged the slender girl back. "I certainly hope it will be just as exciting for you as you anticipate, Sirena. And, I hope you will find an excellent husband of good family, and better income to take care of you."

"Will he love me, Gussie?" she asked him anxiously.

"How can he not?" her brother replied. "You are beautiful, Sirena, and sweet-natured. You excel at all the feminine skills, and you are virtuous. No man could ask for more in a wife, little sister."

"But you must not be so trusting of the other girls in London as you are at home," Charlotte interjected. "Remember, they are all on the marriage hunt, Sirena, and will not be charitable toward others if it means they might lose a particularly desirable gentleman."

"That is excellent advice," Lady Abbott noted, surprised by her daughter-in-law's sudden generosity. Then she realized that Charlotte would be far happier having Sirena married and out of the house.

"You make it sound like warfare," the trusting Sirena said.

"It is," Charlotte replied. "You cannot let down your vigil until you are well and truly married. I knew a girl in my season who became engaged to a most desirable gentleman, only to have him turn about and elope to Gretna Green with another. She was ruined, of course, and has not showed her face in London since. She has little chance now of making a successful match."

"Poor thing," Sirena said sympathetically.

"If you were not going with Miss Morgan I should truly fear for you, Sirena," Charlotte responded impatiently. "At least your cousin has good common sense."

Again Lady Abbott was surprised. "I thought you did not like Allegra Morgan," she said to her daughter-in-law.

"I neither like her nor dislike her," was the lofty reply.

Lord Morgan's packet was a brief missive asking that they depart in a week's time. The Rowley coach would not be needed. Lord Morgan was sending his carriage for Lady Abbott and Sirena. They would visit at Morgan Court for a few days, and then go up to London. Lord Morgan would be gone when they reached Morgan Court, but he would await them in London. He had already engaged the town's most important modiste,

Madame Paul, a refugee from the Terror in France, to make the girls' wardrobes, including the court dresses in which they would be presented to the king.

Sirena was beside herself with excitement. "Just imagine, Charlotte! Uncle has said no expense is to be spared, and we will have jewelry to wear from the family safe! Madame Paul is to make our gowns! We will even be presented to His Majesty and the queen."

"All young ladies of good blood are presented," Charlotte replied sourly. "I was, but I am certainly surprised that Miss Morgan is to be. After all, her blood is hardly blue. Well, perhaps a pale, pale shade," she amended.

"Certainly as pale as yours," Lady Abbott replied sharply. "I think a duke and a duchess for grandparents certainly equals an earl and a countess for parents." She arose before her red-faced daughter-in-law could respond, saying, "Sirena dearest, come. We must begin to pack, although you shall certainly need little. Just enough to tide you over until Madame Paul has your new wardrobe ready." She swept from the room, her young daughter in her wake.

"Why does your mama hate me so?" Charlotte wailed to her husband when they had gone.

Augustus put a comforting arm about his wife. "Perhaps, m'dear, if you did not try to be so superior with her it might be better for you. You are surely no match for Mama. She is older, wiser, and a duke's daughter. She is also most fond of Lord Morgan and Allegra. When you denigrate them, she feels bound to defend them. I hope that in the future you will learn to keep your own counsel, for you see, I, too, have a fondness for my uncle and my cousin. My inheritance was not a great one monetarily, but Uncle Septimius took it, and in the few years since my father died, has tripled it with his cleverness. Many of the furbelows and geegaws so dear to your heart, that I so generously bestow upon you, are provided thanks to my uncle. We are debt free, and will have the school fees for our sons when we need them one day." He kissed her cheek tenderly.

"I do dislike it when you scold me, Gussie," Charlotte pouted.

"Then amend your behavior, my darling, and I shall not have to do so," her wise spouse replied, and gave her another kiss.

"I shall be glad when we are *finally* alone," Charlotte told him. "I will enjoy these next few weeks before we go up to town, with just you for company, Gussie. And if we are fortunate your sister, Sirena, will find a proper husband, and not return to Rowley Hall at all." She sighed. "Of course we shall still have your mama in the dower house."

The marquess laughed. Had he not found the sparring between his mother and his wife so damned amusing, he might have been annoyed. They were, however, quite entertaining; his mother trying to adjust to being a dowager; his wife so eager to be lady of the manor. He was concerned that Charlotte had not conceived yet, but the Duchess of Devonshire had been a slow breeder, too. Only the presence of a son and a daughter among his cottagers reassured him that he, himself, was capable of siring children. When his wife was more secure she would certainly give him children.

Lord Morgan's coach appeared at Rowley Hall exactly one week later, just after first light. It was a magnificent vehicle, shiny black with silver fittings, and Lord Morgan's coat of arms—a gold sailing ship upon an azure background, three gold stars and a silver crescent moon above it—painted upon each of the carriage doors. Inside, the seats were fashioned of fawn-colored leather and pale blue velvet. There were crystal and gold oil lamps set on either side of the comfortably padded benches, and small silver floral vases filled with daffodils, fern, and white heather. The coachmen and two grooms wore elegant black and silver livery. Even Charlotte was impressed, if not just a trifle envious.

The luggage was carefully loaded by the grooms. The coachman remained in his place atop the box controlling the four dappled gray horses with the black manes who danced and snorted, obviously impatient to get going again. Lady Abbott and Sirena exited the house, accompanied by their personal maids. Both were garbed in fine fur-collared wool mantles over their gowns.

"Good-bye, my dear," Lady Abbott said to her son, kissing him.

"I shall look forward to seeing you in London, Mama," the young marquess said with a twinkle.

"Do some serious ploughing with Charlotte while you are alone, and have the time," she advised him pithily. "It is past time the wench did her duty by Rowley, Gussie." She kissed him again, and then allowed one of the grooms to help her into the vehicle.

Actually blushing, the marquess quickly turned to his sister, who having heard their mother's remark was hard-pressed not to giggle. "Good-bye, little one," he told her. "Good hunting!"

"Oh, Gussie, you make it sound so . . . so . . . so common!" she replied.

"It will be fun, I promise, but take Charlotte's advice and trust no other maiden except Allegra. The husband hunt is not for the faint of heart, sister." He kissed her on both cheeks, then helped her into the carriage where her mother and the two maids were already seated.

"Good-bye! Good-bye!" the Marquess of Rowley called to his female relations as the vehicle pulled away, and the horses trotted quite smartly down the drive.

"Good-bye! Good-bye!" Sirena called, leaning out the window until her outraged mother yanked her back inside.

"Behave yourself, girl!" the dowager said sharply. "Your hoydenish days are over now, and you must grow up."

"Yes, Mama," Sirena replied, just slightly chastened.

They traveled the twenty miles separating Rowley Hall and Morgan Court, arriving by midday. As their carriage drew to a stop the two grooms jumped down from their outside seat behind the coach, and hurried to open the door and lower the step, allowing the passengers to descend. Charles Trent, Lord Morgan's steward, hurried from the house to welcome them. He was a distinguished gentleman of indeterminate years with a serious demeanor and quietly graying brown hair. He kissed Lady Abbott's hand as he bowed, and then Lady Sirena's.

"Welcome to Morgan Court. His lordship has already returned to London, but he left me behind to see to your comfort. Let us go into the house. I know that Miss Allegra is eagerly awaiting her cousin."

They had no sooner entered the building when Allegra Morgan appeared and threw herself into her cousin's arms with a shriek of delight. "Wait until I tell you!" she said excitedly. "Madame Paul has sent down her chief assistant, Mademoiselle Francine, to take our measurements and show us fabric samples!" Then remembering her manners she detached herself from Sirena's embrace, and curtsied to Lady Abbott. "Good day, Aunt," she said. "I am most pleased to see you have arrived. Papa has asked me to tender his greetings, and say he looks forward to seeing you in London." She kissed the older woman upon the cheek.

"Thank you, m'dear," Lady Abbott said, feeling a warmth in her cheeks, and wondering if the others had noticed.

"Luncheon is served, m'lady," Pearson, the butler, came to announce as the travelers' cloaks were taken away.

"Will you join us, Mr. Trent?" Lady Abbott asked. She knew that such was the steward's high position that he frequently came to table with the family while they were in the country.

"Thank you, madame, but I do have work to be completed today. I will, however, join you at supper. When the young ladies are ready they may go upstairs where Mademoiselle Francine is awaiting them in the Primrose chamber." He bowed politely, and hurried off.

"Such a lovely man," Lady Abbott said. "What a pity he is the fourth son. His parents are the Earl and Countess of Chamberlain, y'know. The eldest son, Francis Trent, will inherit, of course." She allowed Pearson to seat her, and then lowering her voice said, "He gambles, I'm sorry to say. The Earl of Chamberlain is constantly paying off his debts. The second son is out in India with the army, a colonel, I believe I heard. The third has an excellent pulpit in Nottingham. Both of them have married heiresses as they should have and consequently give their parents no trouble. The eldest has such an unsavory reputation that they cannot even find a wife for him. Imagine!

"*And then there is Charles Trent.* Beautifully educated at Harrow, and at Cambridge; a man with exquisite manners, and an instinctive sense of what is correct.

Fortunately your father found him twelve years ago, and employed him. Being steward to Septimius Morgan is an honorable profession for a man of Charles Trent's superior breeding. I do not know what Septimius would do without him. He manages both the London house and this one. He handles the household accounts, engages any new staff, pays the wages, is responsible in fact for the entire staff. And he is your father's personal secretary as well. How he does it, I do not know. A lovely man," she repeated. Then Lady Abbott dipped her spoon into the turtle soup that had just been ladled into her plate, and began to eat.

Allegra looked archly at her cousin, and Sirena had to stifle her giggle. The two girls ate scantily and quickly, in order to be swiftly excused from the table that they might go to Mademoiselle Francine. But Lady Abbott understood their excitement, and released them before the sweet and the cheese were served. They both rose slowly, attempting not to appear too eager. Then they curtsied, and walked carefully from the dining room through the doors the liveried footman held open. As the doors closed behind them Allegra and Sirena looked at each other, and then raced for the stairs. Stepping from his office, Charles Trent saw them, and smiled.

They burst noisily into the Primrose chamber where Mademoiselle Francine was waiting. The Frenchwoman arose, and looked disapprovingly at them, shaking a finger.

"Mademoiselles! Are you horses that you clomp?"

"Forgive us, mademoiselle," Sirena said politely. "We are so anxious to have you measure us so our gowns may be made!"

"Ahh," the lady replied with a small smile. "Well then, come, *mes petites*, and let us get your gowns off so

I may ascertain what we have to work with. You are both very different. Are you related?"

"We are first cousins," Allegra said. "I am Allegra Morgan, and this is Lady Sirena Abbott."

"Thank you, mademoiselle," the Frenchwoman replied.

Allegra walked to the bellpull, and yanked upon it several times. She told the footman who answered her call, "Fetch Honor at once and Lady Sirena's maid, Damaris, as well."

"Yes, Miss Allegra," the footman replied, and hurried off.

"You have samples, Mademoiselle Francine, that you wish to show us? We might look while waiting for our maids," Allegra said.

Well, Mademoiselle Francine thought as she brought forth her box of samples, she has the manner of a duchess for all she is just plain Miss Morgan. "We have just obtained a marvelous selection of silks and satins from France. They shall be quite sought after, you understand, Miss Morgan."

"We shall buy the entire bolts of whatever we choose," Allegra said matter-of-factly. "I should not like to see myself coming and going, nor would my cousin. Ahh," she held up a clear pink striped silk, "this would be perfect for you, Sirena! It favors your coloring."

"The whole bolt of each fabric you choose?" The Frenchwoman was absolutely astounded. These fabrics did not come cheap, for they had to be smuggled into England as France was no longer a civilized country in which to live, or do business.

"Yes," Allegra said. "Is there some difficulty in my request?"

"I must ask Madame Paul, Mademoiselle Morgan. Never have I heard of such a thing!"

"It must be," Allegra said firmly. "I am certain that Papa will make it well worth Madame Paul's while to cooperate, but if she feels she cannot meet our wishes, I can always obtain my fabrics elsewhere. Of course I would want Madame Paul to do our gowns. We will send a message to London to ascertain your employer's desires in the matter. Will that be satisfactory, Mademoiselle Francine?"

The modiste nodded weakly. "Of course, Mademoiselle Morgan," she replied. This innocent-looking girl was going to be a power to be reckoned with one day. She sat silently now as the two young girls pored over her fabric samples, not even daring to make suggestions. The Morgan girl obviously knew what she wanted, and she was not hesitant about telling her pretty cousin what would be suitable for her either. Oddly enough, the country-bred miss had excellent taste.

There was a knock upon the chamber's door, and it opened to admit two young women in maid's garb.

"Ahh," Allegra said smiling, "here are Honor and Damaris. Come, lasses, and help us to disrobe so Mademoiselle Francine can obtain the measurements she will need."

The servants quickly did her bidding. Shortly both Allegra and Sirena were standing in their lawn chemises. The Frenchwoman took her measurements, working quickly for she suspected that Allegra would have difficulty standing still for very long. She carefully wrote each figure down upon a clean sheet of parchment. "Neither of you will need a corset," she told them.

"I wouldn't wear one even if told I had to," Allegra announced.

"You may change your mind one day, Mademoiselle Morgan," the modiste told her with a small smile. "Voilà! It is finished!"

"You will return to London tomorrow?" Allegra asked her.

"*Oui,* mademoiselle, I will," was the polite reply.

"Then you will take my instructions regarding the bolts of fabric from Mr. Trent to your mistress. If she does not wish to cooperate with us, then I must go to the mercers who import through Papa's firm. I should, however, hate to lose that wonderful forest green silk. It will make me a most marvelous riding outfit, don't you think? I can just see the jacket with the gold frogs below my cream silk stock."

The modiste smiled. "You have not only an excellent eye for color, but for style as well, mademoiselle," she told Allegra.

"Thank you," was the quiet reply.

*W*hen Mademoiselle Francine reached London several days later she told Madame Paul of her conversation with Allegra Morgan. Madame laughed to her friend's surprise.

"And what did Monsieur Trent say?" she asked Francine.

"Marie! He said whatever the young mademoiselle wanted she should have! Is Lord Morgan *that* rich? And can you afford to lose all that wonderful fabric so that one girl may not see it made into another gown for someone else? Oh, Marie! It was so difficult to obtain that fabric as it is! Now not to have it to display and offer to our most important customers . . . !" Mademoiselle Francine was near tears.

"Do not weep, Francine," Madame said sharply. "We still have the fabrics that were not chosen, as well as a number of others besides. Actually it makes our season easier. Each bolt of fabric Miss Morgan chose for herself and her cousin would have made two to three

gowns. Now we shall just have to make one gown, but
we shall be paid for the three, plus the cost of the fabric!
Those are Mr. Trent's terms to me. We shall have more
time for our other customers, plus a handsome profit to
bank as well. Now, tell me what the two young ladies
were like. Plain? Beautiful?"

"Miss Morgan is extraordinarily beautiful. She has
skin like a gardenia, Marie. It is quite flawless. Her hair
is the color of that mahogany table you ordered from
Mr. Chippendale last year. Dark, not brown, but not
quite black, and with a faint hint of red to it. Her eyes
are most unique in color. They are violet."

"*Violet?*" Madame queried, disbelieving.

"Violet," her companion repeated firmly. "She has
dark brows, and thick dark lashes. She is taller than is
fashionable, but actually not too tall. Slender with a
tiny waist. Her bosom is not yet full, but pleasingly
rounded. She has a lovely smooth broad chest that will
make a wonderful display for her jewelry. Her hands
and feet are delicately made.

"As for Lady Sirena, she will be an Incomparable
without a doubt. She is dainty and petite. Her hair is
that wonderful pure blond without any darkness to it.
Her eyes are blue-gray with surprisingly long sandy
lashes. She is so recherchée, and the gentlemen will
adore her. Miss Morgan is quite protective of her, for
Lady Sirena is as natural and sweet as a honeycomb.
There is neither malice, nor deceit in her. She is most
charming, and loves her cousin every bit as much as
Miss Morgan loves her. They are an unusual pair."

"Miss Morgan then is not quite so helpless,"
Madame noted.

"Not that one!" Mademoiselle Francine said. "She is
charming and obviously educated, perhaps too educated
for a young lady of breeding and fashion. She does not

tolerate fools, and speaks her mind. She is fully aware of the power and the status of her father's wealth, and the fact she is his heiress, confers upon her. If she wants something, she wants it! I wonder if the gentlemen will like her despite her great beauty and fortune."

"She will have a titled husband before the season's end," Madame said cynically. "Her family will seek out the best title they can find, and Miss Morgan will wed it, mark my words, Francine. They will not settle for a mere baronet, or petty lordling. It will be a gentleman of some consequence, and her father's wealth will obtain him."

"But what of l'amour?" Mademoiselle Francine asked, plaintively.

Madame laughed. "These English make their marriages like shopkeepers making the best bargains. There is little sentiment involved, I fear. It is all about status and wealth."

"*Pauvres petites,*" Mademoiselle said.

"Do not weep for these girls, Francine," Madame replied. "They will get exactly what they seek, and deserve. And strangely, most will be very happy. They are odd people, these English. Home and hearth are what matter most to them. They have no sense of adventure."

"But everyone should have love," Mademoiselle persisted.

Madame laughed again. "You are a romantic, Francine," she said. "Now give me the measurements you took, and we will begin designing."

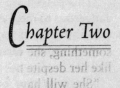

Chapter Two

On their arrival in London Allegra found a number of invitations awaiting Sirena and herself. The envelopes were piled upon a silver tray in the order in which they had been received.

"Gracious!" she exclaimed. "What am I to do with all of these?"

Charles Trent took the ornate salver from the butler, Mr. Marker. "I shall go through these myself, Miss Allegra, and arrange for them to be answered properly. Ahh, I see the Bellingham crest. She usually gives the first ball of the season. That will be an acceptance. Some will be invitations from those seeking to improve their social standing by inviting you. Then there will be those from very important people, and some events that are certainly not suitable for young ladies in their first season."

"Such as?" Allegra demanded.

Charles Trent smiled. "Certain card parties where the wagering is fast and deep, Miss Allegra. Why the Duchess of Devonshire has been known to lose hundreds of thousands in a single night. You don't want to get caught up in anything like that, but of course, there will be those only too eager to lure you into their gaming hells. Your father would not approve."

"This season we are to join sounds more and more dangerous to me," Allegra said. "I wish Papa had let me remain home. If I must marry I could have wed with Rupert Tanner. He has asked me, you know, but Papa will not hear of it."

"A second son? I should hope not!" Lady Abbott declared.

"His father was in favor of it," Allegra said.

"I don't doubt it. Having a second son wed with the greatest heiress in all of England would have been quite a coup," her aunt replied. "The old Earl of Ackerly is a sly dog, and always was. Besides, his countess is not someone your father would have you related to, even by marriage. She is his second wife, and her background is quite shadowy."

"Besides, you don't love Rupert," Sirena said. "You've always said he was like a brother to you."

"Yes, but I am comfortable with him, and he does whatever I tell him," Allegra admitted frankly.

Mr. Trent swallowed a guffaw at this remark.

"Upstairs with you both!" Lady Abbott ordered. Then she turned to the butler. "Marker, send a footman to Madame Paul's to say we have arrived and would like a fitting on the girls' gowns as soon as possible. They certainly cannot be seen in public in such old-fashioned country clothing."

"Yes, m'lady," the butler replied with a bow.

They easily settled into the house on Berkley Square, but late that same afternoon they had a visitor as they sat in the gardens enjoying the sunshine. Marker came with the card, and offered it to Lady Abbott.

"Good gracious!" she exclaimed, paling. Then, "Of course I *am* at home to Lady Bellingham. Show her out here at once! Girls, your very best behavior, *please!*

Clarice Bellingham is one of the arbiters of both fashion and society in London. If she approves of you, you will be given entry to everywhere that is important."

"And if she does not?" Allegra inquired.

"Your season will be a total failure, my dear child," Lady Bellingham said, coming into the garden. She was a tall, handsome woman dressed in the height of fashion. "They all listen to me, although frankly I do not know why, but there it is. How do you do, Olympia? It has been four years since you brought a daughter to London." Lady Bellingham plunked her ample frame onto a marble bench, looking about her as she did so. "Septimius has the finest gardener in all of London. I don't know anyone else's garden that looks so beautiful." She stopped speaking for a moment to catch her breath and gaze sharply at the two young girls in her view.

"I-it is good to see you, Clarice," Lady Abbott said, regaining her composure. "No, I haven't been up to London since Amanda made her bow. I am a country-woman at heart, I fear. And then, too, London is not the same without my dear husband. Marker, tea, please."

"I suppose I should miss Bellingham if he went and died on me," Lady Bellingham remarked dryly. "I shouldn't like to take a backseat to that featherbrain my son is married to, but fortunately my good husband seems to be in grand health, praise God! How are Augustus and his Charlotte? That marriage was executed quickly, and we were all quite certain . . ." She paused, and then continued, "Well, you know what everyone was thinking, Olympia. Yet here it is several years later, and she has not produced."

"We continue to hope, and pray," Lady Abbott said weakly. She had forgotten what a whirlwind Clarice Bellingham could be.

"Now introduce me to these two fetching young creatures. Who is the outspoken one, and who is the gentle one, as if I didn't already know," she chuckled.

"This is Miss Allegra Morgan, my niece."

Allegra curtsied politely, although her cheeks were still warm from having been overheard; and now to be called outspoken was most embarrassing.

"*Not Pandora's gel?* Well, she's certainly a rare beauty. I suppose as her father's heiress we can expect she will be a great success," Lady Bellingham pronounced quite candidly. "How d'do, Miss Morgan."

"How do you do, madame," Allegra replied as another rush of heat suffused her face. Lady Bellingham had called her *Pandora's girl*. Did they all have such sharp memories? She supposed so. It was interesting that they could remember her mother when she could not.

"And this is my youngest, Lady Sirena Abbott."

Sirena made her curtsy to Lady Bellingham, giving her a shy smile as she did so.

"How d'do, my dear," the formidable lady said. Then she turned to Lady Abbott. "She will certainly be an Incomparable, Olympia. She is the loveliest of your three gels," and then seeing Sirena flush with pleasure, Lady Bellingham said, "Why, child, has no one ever told you that?"

"No, madame," Sirena replied.

"Well, you are, and I have seen both Caroline and Amanda. The elder has shoulders a bit too broad, and the other's nose was a bit too retroussé, I fear. Still, they did well in the husband hunt, but you, I suspect, will do better." She turned her attention back to Lady Abbott. "She has a respectable dowry? I know how selfish Charlotte is, and how she must begrudge this lovely child."

"Fortunately Arthur left monies in his will for both Sirena's season and her dowry. It is identical to that of my two elder daughters, and more than adequate," Lady Abbott said proudly.

"And being in the company of her cousin won't hurt either," the redoubtable lady replied. "I assume Septimius is giving them both a ball? What a house this is for entertaining! What a pity it is only used by Lord Morgan when he is in town managing his many affairs."

"My father does not cheesepare, madame," Allegra spoke up boldly. "Of course he will give a ball for both of us. Sirena's will be at the beginning of May, and mine at the end of that month. If you wish to know the dates, I can call Mr. Trent. He keeps track of such matters for us."

"*Allegra!*" Lady Abbott's voice was anguished.

"Bless me, the gel is hardly shy," Lady Bellingham chuckled. "Don't scold her, Olympia. I like her. She is not the usual simpering miss I meet each season." Her gaze swung about to Allegra. "Have Charles Trent check with me regarding the dates of your balls, my dear. You don't want to find out when it is too late that there is a more important event those nights. And you will want Prinny at your balls. Nothing adds the stamp of success to a gel's own ball than having Prinny there."

"Tea, m'lady?" Marker asked, prepared to pour from the silver pot.

"Gracious, yes!" Lady Bellingham replied. "Septimius keeps the best store of tea in town, I am told." She sniffed the steam arising from the cup that Marker had handed her. "Ohh, yes!" she approved and, spilling some into her deep saucer, sipped. "Ah, indeed!"

Lady Abbott felt weak with relief. Clarice Bellingham had approved both of the girls despite Allegra's quick tongue. Their entry into society was therefore assured. She sipped her own tea, and once fortified said, "It is so nice of you to call on us, Clarice. I cannot take the girls out until their new wardrobes are ready. We must not make a bad impression, or give rise to jealous gossip from the other mamas."

"Rightly so!" Lady Bellingham responded. "When Miss Allegra and Lady Sirena first appear, they must be seen as the height of fashion. I assume Madame Paul is doing the gowns."

"She sent her assistant down to Morgan Court to measure," Lady Abbott divulged proudly. "A footman has already been sent to her shop to inform her we are here, and ready for fittings."

Lady Bellingham nodded. "Have you obtained a date for your gels to be presented at court yet?"

"Clarice! We are just arrived several hours ago," Lady Abbott protested, half laughing.

"I will have Bellingham arrange it for them immediately. They should be presented in the first wave of young ladies. Make certain that Madame Paul has their court gowns ready first. I will send to you when a date has been obtained."

"Are court gowns different from the others, madame?" Allegra asked the older woman.

"Indeed they are, my dear. Hooped skirts are still required at court, not to mention elaborate wigs with ridiculous decor atop them."

"I have never worn a wig," Allegra told her.

Lady Bellingham smiled. "And you are unlikely to after you have been presented at court. It is such a needless yet necessary expense, for it is required, although I do not know why."

"Gracious! I have forgotten the wig maker!" Lady Abbott cried.

"Have Mr. Trent make an appointment with Monsieur Dupont, and say that I recommended you to him.

Charles knows how to handle it," Lady Bellingham replied with a smile.

"Your faith in me is deeply appreciated," Mr. Trent said as he came into the garden. Taking Lady Bellingham's hand up, he kissed it, smiling. "You are as magnificent as ever, madame," he told her.

Lady Bellingham chuckled. It was a deep, rich sound. "What a pity you are the youngest, Charles," she said. "You have the bearing of an earl, but you are still a rogue. Since your father yet survives, it is to be hoped that your eldest brother will either gain some sense before his demise, or die himself from the drink so your brother out in India can inherit. He probably will one day, anyway," she finished frankly.

A shadow of a smile passed over Charles Trent's face. Then he said, "The first of May for Lady Sirena, and the thirtieth of the month for Miss Allegra?"

Lady Bellingham thought a moment. "Yes," she finally said. "There are some unimportant events being given by some unimportant people those nights. Get your invitations out immediately, Charles."

"They are already written," he replied, now smiling openly.

"Rogue!" she repeated with a chuckle. "Then why did you ask if you already knew?"

"Because, madame, you know more than I do, and usually before I do," he explained. "Besides, I value your approval." He bowed to her. "You ladies will excuse me," he said, and hurried off.

"Clever of Septimius to engage him," Lady Bellingham said. "He is utterly invaluable, but I do not believe for one moment that I know anything before he does. What a flattering devil he is." She chuckled again. Then she grew serious. "I understand there will be an unusual number of young eligible gentlemen this season, and fewer ladies than is usual. Both of you should have husbands before it is all over." Then she thought a moment before she spoke again. "Olympia! My ball is in ten days' time. It is always considered the official opening of the season. Do not accept any invitations before then for your gels. Those silly chits, just out of their schoolrooms, are even now parading themselves about the park, giggling behind their hands at the gentlemen. There isn't one of them that I've yet seen who can hold a candle to either of your two gels. Of course everyone knows they have come to town, but keep them out of sight until the night of the ball. It will make their first appearance and entry into society spectacular!" She chortled wickedly. "All the men will want to meet them that evening. The doting mamas will be absolutely furious."

"What a wonderful idea, Clarice!" Lady Abbott agreed. "And as you have assured me that there are plenty of gentlemen to go around this year, I need not feel a bit guilty about using such a tactic."

"Zounds, Aunt, is that not devilishly wicked of you?" Allegra teased.

"My child, do not use language like that," Lady Abbott replied. "It is so common. There is nothing wrong with you and Sirena making a unique entrance into this world you are going to inhabit for the rest of your lives. It is really the best way to get you noticed immediately."

"*Oyez! Oyez!* Two prime young virgins with proper dowries, ready to wed. What am I bid, gentlemen?" Allegra mocked.

"*Allegra!*" her aunt cried, distressed, but Sirena giggled.

Lady Bellingham, however, burst out laughing. "She's absolutely right, Olympia." Then she turned to

Allegra. "Yet, m'dear, how else are you to meet proper gentlemen?"

"I am not certain I want a proper gentleman, madame," Allegra responded, half seriously, half mischievously.

"The naughty ones are more fun, I will agree, and I speak from experience," Lady Bellingham said with a twinkle in her eye, "but it is the proper ones we marry. For our sakes. And for our families'. Sometimes you will find a unique gentleman with both naughty *and* proper qualities. However, they are very rare, m'dear. Do not fear, Allegra Morgan. I will be your guide. I will advise you myself, for I know all about the ten thousand, or the ton as some are now calling us. Trust me, and I will bring you safely through your first season. Hopefully your *only* season."

"I fear I shall need a pilot to traverse the choppy waters of society, madame. I cannot simper, or be coy. I think those attributes ridiculous. A gentleman with no more on his mind than cards and racing is as much of a featherbrain as a girl who thinks about nothing but gowns and balls," Allegra said. "I shall be a difficult match, I fear."

Lady Bellingham reached out, and patted the girl's hand with her own plump white one, which sported three beautiful rings. "There, there, my child," she said. "There is someone for everyone. Of that I am certain." Then she heaved her ample bulk from the bench, saying as she did so, "I have surely overstayed my welcome. Olympia, walk with me. Good-bye, my dear gels. I shall look forward to seeing you at my ball."

When the two older women left the garden Sirena spoke. "Mama says she is a power to be reckoned with in London society."

"She will be a good friend to us, and I suspect that we are fortunate in that," Allegra noted shrewdly.

"Do you think that she is right?" Sirena asked her cousin.

"About what in particular?" Allegra replied.

"That there is someone for everyone," Sirena answered. "What if we go through the entire season, and do not find husbands?"

"We will come back next year," Allegra said practically. "Not everyone, I am told, bags a husband their first time out."

"But we will be eighteen in December," Sirena said.

"And we are seventeen now," Allegra responded laughing. "Oh, sweet coz, I am not sure I am ready to be married yet. We are just out of the schoolroom. I should like to see something of life and the world before I am settled down into a dull married existence."

"But I want to be married!" Sirena said plaintively. "Mama won't move into the dower house until I am safely settled with a husband. I hate living at the hall now. Charlotte so obviously dislikes us. She begrudges Mama and me every mouthful we eat or drink."

"Marrying to escape your sister-in-law is a rather bad idea," Allegra said. "If we do not find husbands this season, sweet coz, then you shall spend the summer with me, and in the autumn I shall have Papa take us abroad for the winter months. We will return next season refreshed and most sophisticated from our travels. It will make us far more interesting than the schoolroom chits joining us next year. We shall be utterly fascinating to the gentlemen."

"Oh, Allegra, you are so sensible! I wish I could be more like you, but I really do want to find the man of my dreams, and have my own home."

"If that is what you wish," Allegra responded, "then

it is what I want for you, too, Sirena. You will not have a difficult time in finding suitors. Your background is impeccable. Mine, however, is not. Papa's title is not very old, and my mother's behavior will surely lead the gossips to believe I am like her."

"But you are so *rich*!" Sirena said frankly. "Mama says all else will be forgotten regarding your background because of your papa's wealth."

"Oh, yes, my status as Papa's heiress. But I don't want a man marrying me just because I am my father's daughter," Allegra said.

"You cannot escape what is fact," Sirena replied.

"I suppose I cannot," was the thoughtful answer, "but I can certainly judge a man's sincerity, I hope, which may keep me from an unhappy misalliance. My mother married Papa for his wealth when she did not really love him. If she had loved him she could not have fallen in love with her count and run away with him, could she?"

"I suppose not," Sirena said softly. Her mother had always cautioned her to avoid any prolonged discussion of Allegra's mama. Pandora had, Lady Abbott told her daughter, been the youngest of their father's children. Beautiful, winning when she chose to be, and utterly selfish from her birth, Lady Abbott said. Her divorce from Lord Morgan had been all her fault, not his; and as she would not allow Allegra to suffer because of her mother's bad behavior, Sirena must avoid all conversation leading in that direction with anyone, including Allegra.

It was at that moment that Lady Abbott hurried back into the garden. "Oh, my dears, you have made such a good impression upon Clarice Bellingham! She will lead you both through the season, she has assured me. Her approval is a guarantee of your success!" the good lady burbled. Then she hugged them both. "And Madame Paul, herself, has arrived with her assistants to personally oversee your fittings. I have explained to her that you must each have a ball gown ready for the Bellingham ball, and your court dresses almost immediately. Come along, now!"

"Do you think Madame Paul will be as sparrowlike as Mademoiselle Francine?" Allegra whispered to her cousin as they hurried back indoors and up the main staircase of the house to their shared bedchamber suite.

"I don't know," Sirena whispered back. "She is probably more formidable, for Mademoiselle was very deferential when she spoke of her."

Madame Paul turned out to be a tall, gaunt woman with iron gray hair, black eyes, and a commanding nature. When the girls entered the room set aside for the fittings she immediately cried, "Off with your gowns, mademoiselles. *Vite! Vite!* The time, it is precious!"

Madame's two little assistants quickly stripped them down to their chemises. Madame clucked and fussed with seemingly shapeless piles of material while Lady Abbott sat expectantly in a high-back tapestried chair.

"Mademoiselle Morgan," Madame said, beckoning Allegra with a bony finger. "*Ici, s'il vous plaît.* Bess! The cream gown!"

The garment, high waisted with a gently bouffant skirt, a gathered bodice, and short, tight sleeves with exquisite silver lace that hung just to above her elbow, was fitted on Allegra. The skirt's hemline came just off the ground, and had a delicate silver lace overskirt. The rounded neckline was lower than any gown she had ever worn, and seeing her young breasts swelling above the gown's fabric made Allegra blush. She struggled to pull the silk up.

Madame yanked it down with a severe look at her client. "It is the fashion, mademoiselle," she said in a stern voice.

"Even for such a young girl?" Lady Abbott ventured hesitantly.

"Madame," the modiste said, "you are offering a new product. Do you not wish it to be seen to its best advantage? Necklines are low this year. Your niece has a pretty bosom, unlike some my studio is dressing, who will need certain . . . um, aids to show their wares."

"The gown is indeed lovely," Lady Abbott said softly.

"Of course it is," Madame Paul responded. "No one takes the measurements like Francine. Come, mademoiselle, to the looking glass. I would have your opinion, for you are to wear the gown."

Allegra stared at herself in the mirror. How grown-up she looked. The faintly cream-colored silk with its silver lace overskirt was certainly the most beautiful gown she had ever possessed. She turned her head this way and that, admiring the image reflected back at her. The color of the gown brought out the translucence in her skin. Her mahogany hair looked richer, her eyes more violet. "Yes," she said. Nothing more, but Madame Paul understood perfectly.

"You will have a shawl, silver and cream, woven as if by spiders themselves, cream kid gloves that will come to the elbow, a very small reticule made from cloth of silver, and silver kid dancing slippers. You must wear only pearls with this gown, Mademoiselle Morgan. The impression you will give is that of elegance and utmost purity."

"Yes," Allegra answered the modiste, unable to take her eyes off her image. What would Rupert think if he could see her in this gown, she wondered. Then, smiling, she turned to her aunt, questioningly.

Lady Abbott nodded her approval.

The gown was removed, and set aside to be returned to madame's studio for the final finishing. Now it was Sirena's turn. The dress for her cousin was equally wonderful. In the same style, it was of palest sky blue silk brocade with a narrow sapphire blue velvet ribbon belting the waist. The lace on the sleeves of Sirena's garment was cream color, but there was no overskirt, making the dress quite different. The bottom three inches of the hem were pleated tightly. Sirena squealed with delight when she saw herself in the glass.

"A cream lace shawl and elbow length gloves, a reticule and slippers the color of your belt, and for you also, pearls, Lady Sirena. The effect is delicate and fragile as is your blond beauty. Your mama will have to fend the gentlemen off, m'lady."

Both girls laughed at this pronouncement, and even Lady Abbott could not restrain a smile.

"Ohh, Madame," Sirena said, "if the rest of the wardrobes are as wonderful as these two gowns, we shall be the envy of London!"

The modiste smiled archly. "And they will be, and you will be," she replied.

"What of the court gowns?" Lady Abbott asked.

"Cecile, bring the hoops," Madame said. "They are so awkward. I do not understand why your King George is so insistent upon them. Most young girls do not know how to wear hoops, and they certainly dare not sit in them."

"It is his custom, and he is a man who doesn't move easily with change," Lady Abbott said.

"Are not all men like that?" Madame Paul responded with a shrug of her narrow shoulders. "Why should a king be any different? They bleed like any other as we discovered when they lopped poor King Louis's head off his shoulders." She shuddered. "Praise *le bon Dieu* that I had the presence of mind to escape France before that happened!"

"Surely a respectable modiste woman would not be harassed," Allegra said.

"Mademoiselle, I created *only* for the aristocracy," Madame Paul explained. "I worked with my sister and my niece. Francine came with me, but Hortense refused to leave France. She was killed along with many other innocents whose only crime was that they toiled for the nobility."

"I am sorry, madame," Allegra replied.

"As am I, Mademoiselle Morgan. I miss my sister." Then the modiste was all business again.

"These gowns must be ready for the Bellingham ball," Lady Abbott told the Frenchwoman again.

"Both wardrobes in their entirety will be ready two days before," she promised Lady Abbott. "Your young ladies can then put on their new day dresses and parade about the park with the other misses."

"My daughter and my niece will not appear until the night of the ball," Lady Abbott responded.

"Ahh, how clever!" Madame Paul chuckled, looking with new respect upon Lady Abbott. The dowager marchioness was obviously not such a fool as she might appear. She chuckled again.

True to her word, the girls' new collection of wearing apparel arrived exactly when madame had promised them. They were brought by Mademoiselle Francine, who, having directed the footmen in unloading her carriage and the accompanying cart, presented her bill to Mr. Trent. She was mightily surprised to be paid immediately, and in full. Usually it took the rest of the season, and sometimes months afterwards to collect all that was owed them. Often her aunt would withhold the court presentation dress from each collection in order to obtain at least something of what was owed her. Mademoiselle departed smiling, and was distinctly heard to be humming beneath her breath.

Allegra and Sirena could scarce contain themselves. Everything from the skin out was new and fresh. There were chemise dresses, and tunic dresses in fine cotton fabrics, striped and watered silks. There were shawls from India, velvet mantles, bonnets, a dozen ball gowns for each of them, matching shoes and gloves. There were silk petticoats, and fine lawn chemises as well as both silk stockings and tights. Honor and Damaris were kept busy the entire day putting away their mistresses' new wardrobes.

Lady Abbott encouraged her charges to rest until the night of their first ball. "You'll get little rest once you have entered into society. You are already invited to a number of other balls, card parties, picnics, and teas. Mr. Trent has been kept quite busy going over all your invitations. Do you not find it amusing that although no one has yet seen either of you, you are already quite popular?"

"I find it terrifying," Allegra told her aunt. "My invitations are based upon my wealth. I could be as ugly as sin, Aunt, and with a face covered in warts, yet I should still be a succès fou among the gentlemen. They don't know me. They don't want to know me. They just want to marry my father's heiress. Is it possible, given my circumstances, to find a man who will love me? I think not. Whatever match I make must be made for practical reasons. But I vow that while I must go to the highest bidder, he will have to be a man with whom I can get along."

"Oh, Allegra, do not say such awful things!" Sirena begged.

Lady Abbott, however, sighed. Her niece was absolutely right in her assessment of her situation. "I am glad you are so prudent, and cognizant of your situation, Allegra," she told her. "It is possible, however, to make a match with a good man in spite of your circumstances. Often, in time, love enters such a marriage, but if it doesn't, at least affection and respect will do nicely, I think."

"That is terrible!" Sirena cried. "To go through life unloved by one's mate? I could not survive it!"

"You had best become more practical, daughter," Lady Abbott said. "Once the bloom is off the rose, and you have filled the nursery with a new generation, your husband is, in all likelihood, going to return to London, and to the little mistress he has kept hidden away in a house near the park. That is the way of the world, Sirena. Not all men are like your late father or your Uncle Septimius."

Sirena's eyes filled with tears, and her lower lip trembled, but she said nothing more. She was going to find a man who would love her forever. There was no use arguing with her mama about it. Mama just didn't understand at all. She never had.

The night of the Bellingham ball came, and at a quarter to ten o'clock in the evening Lord Morgan's town carriage drew up before the door of his house. Lord Morgan and Charles Trent emerged dressed in fawn knee breeches with three silver buttons at each side of their legs, dark double-breasted tailcoats which were left open to reveal elegant waistcoats, ruffled shirt fronts, and beautifully tied white silk cravats. Their hose were striped black and white, and their black kid pumps sported silver buckles. They were followed by Lady Abbott who was wearing a rich plum-colored watered silk gown, a large powdered wig upon her head decorated with several white plumes sprinkled with gold dust and a diamond hair ornament. Lastly came Allegra and Sirena in their new gowns. The ladies entered the coach first, followed by Lord Morgan and Mister Trent. The vehicle then moved off.

When they reached the Bellingham mansion on Traleigh Square, they found themselves in a long queue of carriages slowly snaking their way to the town house's front door. As each coach reached its destination, footmen quickly opened the door, lowered the steps, and aided the passengers in disembarking the vehicle. Once inside there were more footmen to take the gentlemen's cloaks, and maids to take the ladies' mantles. The house, Allegra noted, was quite fine, but smaller than her father's. Ascending the stairs they reached the ballroom where they again joined a queue waiting to be announced. As they reached the majordomo, Charles Trent leaned over, and murmured in his ear.

"Olympia, Dowager Marchioness of Rowley, Lady Sirena Abbott," the majordomo boomed, and then as Sirena and her mother entered the ballroom he announced, "Lord Septimius Morgan, Miss Allegra Morgan, Mr. Charles Trent."

Zounds! Allegra thought to herself as her father escorted her to the reception line to greet her hosts, I have actually arrived. She was suddenly very aware of the many eyes upon her, then she caught herself, and curtsying said, "Good evening, Lady Bellingham."

"Good evening, m'dear," her hostess replied, and then introduced her spouse, who smiled at Allegra.

"Pandora's gel, eh? But more your gel, I'm thinking, Septimius," Lord Bellingham said frankly.

"Indeed she is," Lord Morgan replied proudly, and then with a bow moved on with his daughter to join Lady Abbott and Sirena.

Allegra didn't know where to look next. The ballroom was utterly magnificent. It seemed hardly possible that a house of this size could contain such a large chamber. The woodwork was all gold and white rococo. The chandeliers were sparkling crystal with gold fittings. The beeswax tapers burning in them were scented with honeysuckle. At one end of the room was an ornate gold baroque balcony thrusting out from the wall. Musicians, garbed in dark blue velvet knee breeches and matching coats, were seated on the balcony playing. The walls were covered in pale blue silk brocade and paneled with mirrors. Before each mirror was a gilded pedestal upon which rested a large blue Wedgwood urn filled with multicolored flowers. The floors were of polished wood. About the room were rose velvet settees and small gold chairs with sky blue velvet seats. Looking up, Allegra saw the ceiling of the ballroom was filled with gamboling cherubs.

Lady Abbott led her daughter and her niece to a settee, and sat down. "Now," she said softly, "we await the bees to come to the flowers displayed so prettily before them."

"Where did Papa and Charles go?" Allegra asked.

"To drink or play at cards with other like-minded gentlemen," Lady Abbott replied. "Balls are for you young people." She smiled.

About them the other mothers and guardians viewed

with discreet side glances the two young women who were said to be the season's greatest beauties, even though neither had been seen until tonight.

"Well, what do you think?" Viscount Pickford asked the Duke of Sedgwick.

"Which one is she? I was not looking when they were announced," the duke replied. "The fragile little blonde?"

"No, the brunette with the pale skin, and the arrogant tilt to her head. God, she really is a great beauty, Quint! She'll wear the family jewels with elegance," the viscount finished.

Quinton Hunter laughed. "We have not yet met. I may need a rich wife, Ocky, but we must suit."

"Come on!" the viscount said enthusiastically. "The dowager and my mother were friends in their youth. I can use that as an entrée. You get the heiress, but I want to be introduced to that delicious thing who is the dowager's youngest daughter."

"You haven't stopped gathering gossip since we got to London," the duke teased his friend as they walked around the crowded ballroom.

"Good evening, Lady Abbott," Octavian Baird said. "I am Viscount Pickford. I believe you knew my mother, Laura Beauley, when you were girls together in Hereford." He bowed politely.

"Of course," Lady Abbott gushed. "May I introduce my niece, Miss Allegra Morgan. Allegra, this is Viscount Pickford. And of course, my daughter, Lady Sirena."

"And may I introduce my friend, Quinton Hunter, the Duke of Sedgwick," the viscount continued. Then he turned to Sirena. "Have you room on your dance card for me, Lady Sirena?"

Sirena blushed, and perused her card, which until

now was empty. "I believe I have the third dance open, sir," she said, quickly writing his name down. "Thank you for asking."

"No," he quickly responded. "Thank you."

"*Sedgwick*," Lady Abbott said thoughtfully. "Your father was Charles Hunter, wasn't he? And your mother Vanessa Tarleton?"

"Yes, Lady Abbott," the duke answered.

"Your mother and I were distant cousins. We shared a great-grandparent, although I don't know which one," she told him.

"Indeed, madame," he replied. Then he turned to Allegra. "Would you have a dance available for me, Miss Morgan?"

"Alas, Your Grace," she quickly replied, "but my card is full tonight. If we meet again during the season, I shall promise you the last dance on my card." She gave him a faint smile.

He bowed, and without another word walked away with Viscount Pickford.

"Are you mad?" her aunt demanded. "No one at all has asked you to dance yet. *He is a duke!* At least Sirena pretended that while she was engaged, she could still fit Viscount Pickford onto her card."

"I did not like the way he looked at me, Aunt. As if I were a horse and he were judging my points," Allegra said.

"Perhaps he is shortsighted," her aunt replied. "I can only hope you haven't insulted him so badly that he will not dance with you next time. You are just suffering from nerves, m'dear."

Across the ballroom the Duke of Sedgwick watched Allegra and her aunt in their spirited conversation, a sardonic smile upon his face. "She had not yet accepted a single dance," he said to his friend, Viscount Pickford.

"But she said her card was full," Ocky replied.

"She lied," the duke answered him. "Her open card was in full view." Nonetheless he was amused more than insulted. This beautiful girl with her fabulous wealth and unimportant background had sent him away. She would, of course, pay for insulting him; and she would be aware she was being punished. He murmured something to Ocky.

The viscount chuckled. "Do you really want to do that, Quint?"

"Miss Allegra Morgan and I must understand each other right from the beginning, Ocky," the Duke of Sedgwick responded.

Allegra sat next to her aunt, waiting to be asked to dance. Sirena's card was shortly filled, but still no one had asked Allegra by the time the dancing had begun. She sat like stone in her beautiful gown as the other young women about her danced the night away. She refused to move when her aunt suggested they go into the banqueting room to visit the buffet. "You may go if you wish," she said, her head held high despite her embarrassment.

"I don't understand it," moaned Lady Abbott helplessly.

"Why is Allegra not dancing?" demanded Lady Bellingham of Lady Abbott, once the situation had been brought to her attention.

"Someone started the rumor that her card was full," Sirena said as her current partner brought her back to her seat.

"When I find out the mother who did this," Lady Bellingham said furiously, "I will ruin her! 'Tis cruel! Cruel beyond imagining!"

The musicians on the balcony began tuning up their instruments for the minuet, the last dance of the evening. Suddenly the Duke of Sedgwick was standing before Allegra. He bowed politely, his face a mask of civility.

"I believe, Miss Morgan, that this is our dance," he said.

Allegra's eyes widened but she could not under the circumstances refuse him. She arose stiffly, and gave him her hand. Her silence was very eloquent.

"Hasn't a crumb to his name, thanks to his father, and grandfather," Lady Bellingham said as the couple disappeared onto the dance floor. "The estate is completely intact, I am told, but the house is in bad repair. Still," her gray eyes narrowed thoughtfully, "I suspect if Allegra wanted to be a duchess, she could have him. What a coup for you all, Olympia! We must look into the possibilities."

"He is said to be very proud of his bloodline, Clarice. Allegra can't match him there," Lady Abbott replied.

"But he is as poor as a church mouse, Olympia. His blue blood will dry up, and his line be gone if he doesn't find a rich wife. There isn't another girl here this season whose fortune can even come near to Allegra's. Her wealth can buy her a duke."

"She doesn't like him," Lady Abbott said. "She said he looked her over as if she were a horse he was contemplating buying."

Lady Bellingham laughed heartily. "I am sure he did, but then he has rescued her from oblivion by dancing the last dance with her, Olympia. She will be grateful for that."

"I think it is he who started the rumor her dance card was full," Lady Abbott told her friend. "He asked her to dance before, and she claimed her card was full when in reality no one had asked her yet. I think he played a jest on her to teach her a lesson."

"Why the devil!" Lady Bellingham chuckled. "I shall have to talk to him about playing such wicked tricks."

"Allegra will be furious," Lady Abbott replied. "She will find a way to repay him in kind, I am certain."

"Then they are indeed well matched," Lady Bellingham answered. "Quinton Hunter is overproud with regard to his heritage, and your niece, being the richest young lady in England, will not allow anyone to lord it over her. I see a wonderful match in the making, Olympia! It is up to us to nurture it along. There isn't a mother in the room tonight who would give their daughter over to this penniless duke. This is a great opportunity! What did you hope for at best?"

"A viscount, or an earl," Lady Abbott responded.

"But we have the chance of a duke, m'dear," Lady Bellingham said. "Ohh, it will be the talk of the season, and to think it all happened at my ball!"

Chapter Three

April passed, and as the lilacs in Lord Morgan's London garden came into bloom, it was obvious that despite Allegra's best efforts to discourage the Duke of Sedgwick, Quinton Hunter could not be dissuaded from paying her his court. At each ball he took up more and more of her dance card until it became the subject of much gossip. Allegra was furious, but there was little she could do about the situation. There was no other gentleman in whom she had the slightest interest at all. Worse, it had become quite obvious that young Viscount Pickford and Sirena had fallen in love. Sirena had little time now for her cousin, and wasn't in the least bit sympathetic regarding the duke's behavior. She thought Allegra mad not to encourage the duke.

Knowing the two girls were going on a picnic up the river one afternoon, Lady Abbott, with her brother-in-law's approval, invited the duke to tea. When he was shown into the garden she thought again what a very handsome man he was. The duke kissed her hand, and at her behest sat down opposite her.

Lady Abbott got right to the point. "You have spent the last month taking up a great deal of my niece's time, Your Grace. I have been authorized by Lord Morgan to inquire of you regarding your intentions toward Allegra."

"Do you consider me a fortune hunter then, madame?" he asked, his tone cold.

"No! No!" Lady Abbott quickly reassured him. "We are well aware of your circumstances, Your Grace. A man of your breeding could hardly be called a fortune hunter, but I have it on the best authority that you are seeking a wife. Is this so?"

He nodded, a small smile playing at the corners of his lips.

"Would you consider a match between yourself and my niece?" Lady Abbott asked him bluntly.

"Yes," the duke replied as frankly. It pleased his vanity that he had not had to come to them on bended knee. They had come to him, which was as it should be. Allegra Morgan would be marrying into the finest family in England. She would be the mother of its next generation of sons.

"Do you love her?" Lady Abbott queried him.

"No," he responded. "I do not believe love should be a factor in arranging a good match. My antecedents married for love. You see the result of their foolishness in my situation."

"Your antecedents were also quite famous gamblers," Lady Abbott reminded him, wondering briefly if she was really doing the right thing.

"I do not gamble. I have, in fact, an abhorrence of it as you may well understand. If a match can be arranged between Miss Morgan and myself, I promise you I will treat her with dignity and respect. We may even in the years to come gain an affection for each other," the duke said. "And, of course, she will be the Duchess of Sedgwick."

Lord Morgan entered the garden, followed by Marker with a large silver tea tray.

"Put the tray on the table, Marker," Lord Morgan said. "Lady Abbott will pour today."

"Very good, my lord," Marker responded, setting the tray down, bowing, and departing back into the house.

Lord Morgan looked to his sister-in-law.

"His Grace has indicated, if I understand him correctly, that he would like to offer for Allegra," Lady Abbott said tactfully.

"There are conditions, sir," Lord Morgan said. "Conditions you may not accept."

"And they are?" the duke responded.

"Allegra is my heiress. When I die she inherits everything. This house, Morgan Court with its two thousand acres, my tea plantations, my trading shares, my ships, my companies, *everything*. I ain't ready to die by a long shot, however, so until I do I intend giving her an allowance of two hundred and fifty thousand pounds a year. It will be hers, and you can't touch it. You'll sign a paper to that effect, although no one has to know of our transaction. I'll also give you an equal allowance each year of two hundred and fifty thousand pounds. And I want your word that you'll treat my daughter with kindness. She ain't like any girl you'll ever meet. Got her mother's beauty and my intellect. If I know Allegra she'll take her allowance and invest much of it. She'll turn a profit, too. I've taught her well. And she can also do all those other female things Olympia thinks are so important, although maybe not well, but that's what servants are for, eh?"

"Your wife had but two children," the duke said, voicing his only concern.

"Pandora didn't like children. After she had given me my son she decided her duties were done. When she deserted me I learned she had purposefully aborted three children before Allegra was born. Why she did not destroy my daughter I'll never know. Be assured, my daughter will be a good breeder for you."

The duke nodded. It was obvious that his future father-in-law was an honest man. It had taken courage to expose his former wife's shortcomings. He obviously loved his daughter very much.

"Your daughter and I have not had the best of beginnings. She is still angry at me, I fear," the duke said candidly.

Lord Morgan's stern face softened, and he chuckled. "It was a wicked trick you played on her at the Bellingham ball. She fumed for a week, and has been considering ever since how best to repay you. She is a sensible girl, however, and will see the advantage to such a fine match as you propose. I will explain it to her when she returns later this afternoon."

"When do you propose we set a wedding date?" the duke said.

"I understand that Hunter's Lair is not in the best of condition to receive a bride," Lord Morgan told him. "Your home must be modernized and renovated, sir, before you wed Allegra. However, I would advise a formal announcement be made at my daughter's ball at the end of this month. In the meantime you and Allegra might attempt a détente between yourselves," he finished with a smile.

"The tea will get cold if I do not pour it now," Lady Abbott said. "Oh, look! Cook has made those delightful little salmon and cucumber sandwiches you so like, Septimius!"

"Your niece's ball was lovely," the duke said sociably. "The decorations were as delicate as Lady Sirena herself. She is a charming girl. My friend, Viscount Pickford, is going to offer for her, Lady Abbott. I do not believe I speak out of turn by telling you this. You will know soon enough. Ocky has already spoken to his father, and the old earl is absolutely delighted by the possibility of such a match."

"Ohh, I am so glad!" Lady Abbott said. "Sirena has always wanted to be a June bride. We shall hold the wedding at St. George's on Hanover Square just as the season ends. I imagine they will leave London immediately afterward. Then I shall return home to my dower house." She smiled. "It's small, but at least I shall not have my daughter-in-law, Charlotte, glaring if I take a second piece of toast."

They sat talking over their tea, and finally the duke arose.

"I had best depart before the picnickers return," he said. "You will want to speak with your daughter before we meet again."

"We are going to Almack's tonight," Lady Abbott volunteered.

"I will be there," the duke promised her as he bowed over her hand. "I hope Allegra will be." Then he departed the garden.

Lady Abbott put a hand over her mouth, her eyes wide with what had just happened. Then, her hand falling away, she said, "We have done it, Septimius! *We have made Allegra a duchess!* There hasn't been such a marriage coup since the Gunning sisters came over from Ireland with their father forty-four years ago! And Sirena, too! My baby will be a countess one day when old Pickford dies. It has certainly proved to be a very successful season so far, hasn't it?"

"Neither of them is at the altar yet, and Sirena will be far easier to get there than Allegra. She is in love. I am not sure that I do not feel a certain guilt about sending Allegra into a loveless union with the duke. Still, I cannot disagree with him regarding love. Look what love has brought me, too," Lord Morgan said sadly. "He seems a good man though. I have never heard anything untoward regarding his character. I believe he will be kind to my daughter."

"We must get Allegra to be kind to him," Lady Abbott replied with a small twinkle in her eye. "I do not envy you your duty, Septimius. You will have to tell her immediately."

"I know," he answered. "As soon as she returns we shall speak. Who was she with today?"

"Sirena and Pickford, of course, and young Rupert Tanner," Lady Abbott answered.

"I wasn't aware Rupert was in London," Lord Morgan said. "You know he had the cheek to ask for Allegra before we came to London. I don't like it that he's come sniffing about. His father cannot get the idea out of his head of marrying his second son to my daughter."

The day had suddenly grown overcast as spring weather was apt to do. Lord Morgan and Lady Abbott repaired indoors.

"When my daughter returns," Lord Morgan told Marker, "tell her I want to see her immediately in my library."

"Very good, my lord," the butler said with a bow.

"And you may tell my daughter I am in my rooms," Lady Abbott said.

"Yes, my lady," Marker replied.

Making himself comfortable in his study, Lord Morgan poured himself a whiskey and sat in an upholstered chair by the blazing fire. He considered how to best approach his daughter, but he knew there would be no easy way. A woman needed to be married in their society. Allegra had been raised to understand that. He knew of few love matches. Families arranged marriages to best suit themselves. The bride and the groom knew they had to make the best of it, and usually did. He had been foolish enough to fall in love with his wife, Pandora. It had made her betrayal all the more difficult.

He had told the duke he did not know why Pandora had not aborted the baby who had grown up to be Allegra. He had lied. He knew very well why Allegra had been born because he had overheard a conversation between Pandora and Olympia that he had not been meant to hear. It had been Olympia Abbott who had threatened her younger sister with exposure if she did not have the baby she was carrying.

"You have destroyed three of Septimius's children," Olympia said angrily. "I will not allow you to destroy this child."

"I have given him a son," Pandora whined. "What more is expected of me?"

"What if something happens to James Lucian?" Olympia asked. "You must give Septimius another child, and you are already ripening with this one. I do not understand how you could allow that awful woman to tear three of your babies from your body."

"Oh, Olympia, do not be so dramatic. She gave me some revolting potion to swallow and several hours later I passed those miserable little inconveniences with painful difficulty. I would never let old Mother Diggums put her hands on me. The creature is disgusting."

"You will have this child," Olympia said stonily. "If you do not I shall tell Septimius what you have done, Pandora. He will have every right to divorce you, and I shall encourage him to it, I swear! And do not think you can cozen me by pretending a miscarriage."

"I shall miss the hunting season," Pandora said irritably.

"We shall both miss it," Olympia replied. "I, too, am

with child. Our children will grow up together, Pandora. They shall be friends, and you will be glad you didn't do away with this little one."

"Oh, very well," Pandora finally agreed. "Honestly, Olympia, the care you have for my husband. If I didn't know how much you loved your own, I should be very suspicious of you." Then she laughed.

"It is a tragedy you do not love Septimius," had been the response.

"But he loves me," Pandora said, a hint of triumph in her voice. "He will always love me no matter what, Olympia. I will agree to have this last child for him. *But no more!* I gained over an inch in my waist with our son. I don't want to look like those fat old sows who sit around the room at the local balls. I never want to grow old!"

The knowledge of his wife's perfidy had been a knife to his heart. He had known Pandora didn't love him. As far as he could see she loved no one except herself. But Allegra had been born. Then when his daughter was not quite two, Pandora had run away with her lover, an Italian count, Giancarlo di Rossi. Septimius had divorced her. The permission to do so hadn't been difficult to obtain. To his surprise she had written him afterward thanking him for making it possible to marry her lover. He had never heard from her again, although he suspected Olympia did now and again; but then Olympia had always had a good heart.

He heard the rain suddenly beating against the windows of his library and laughter in the foyer of the house. Then the library door opened and Allegra came in with young Rupert Tanner at her heels.

"Ohh, Papa! The most exciting thing has happened. Ocky has asked Sirena to marry him! They have gone to tell Aunt. And here is Rupert up from the country. What did you want to see me about?"

"I wish to speak with you in private, Allegra," Lord Morgan said. "Rupert, where are you staying?"

"Allegra invited me to stay here, my lord," he answered.

"I regret that will not be convenient. I'm certain that young Pickford will put you up. That house of his father's is more like a men's club right now. Actually you will be much more comfortable there."

"*Papa!*"

"Sit down, Allegra," her father said.

"Thank you, sir, for the suggestion," Rupert said politely. "Shall I see you tonight at Almack's? You do have tickets, don't you?"

"Yes," Lord Morgan replied. Nothing more.

"Then I bid you good day until the evening," the young man responded and departed, shutting the door firmly behind him.

"How could you refuse Rupert your hospitality, Papa?" Allegra demanded angrily. "He is our neighbor, and I have known him my whole life."

"It would not be appropriate for him to visit with us now, Allegra," her father said quietly.

"Why not?" Allegra's violet eyes were stormy with her disapproval.

"Because this afternoon I contracted a match for you with the Duke of Sedgwick," came the startling answer.

"*No!*"

"He has agreed to all my terms without a quiver—remarkable for a gentleman who is so prideful," Lord Morgan noted.

"*And so poor!*" Allegra snapped back. "He is a fortune hunter, Papa. Surely you must know it."

"Any man who looks to wed you is a fortune hunter, my dear daughter," Lord Morgan said. "I am, after all, the richest man in England. At least Quinton Hunter has something to offer in exchange for a fortune. His is the bluest blood in England, and he is going to make you a duchess, Allegra. *His duchess.* Your children will from their birth be at the pinnacle of society."

"The family are notorious gamblers, Papa," Allegra said.

"He has never gambled, my dear, and has an intense dislike of it, for it has brought him to the brink of poverty."

"And so he is forced by his circumstances to wed me. A young lady of less than peerless social standing and background. *No!* I will not do it, Papa. I shall marry Rupert Tanner, who at least likes me," Allegra declared defiantly.

"Do not be foolish, Allegra. I have already refused young Lord Ackerly's suit. I will not permit you to throw yourself away on a second son. You don't love Rupert in any event."

"We shall elope to Gretna Green," Allegra insisted.

"If you do I shall disinherit you, my dear, and I shall make certain both young Rupert and his father know it. You will not appear very attractive in their eyes without your fortune, Allegra. This is the harsh reality of your situation. Have I not taught you that marriages are arranged to better each family involved? In this instance you will take a huge step up the social ladder. The duke, on the other hand, will regain a comfortable income in exchange. It is not a difficult task to marry this man. You are merely required to behave like the lady you are, be a gracious hostess, and produce a nursery for your husband. He has given me his word you will be treated with kindness."

Allegra burst into tears. *"I hate him!"* she sobbed piteously. *"And he hates me."* She sniffed.

"You started off badly, I will agree," Lord Morgan said, "but that was your fault, Allegra. When he asked you for a dance at Lady Bellingham's ball and you refused him, he saw the empty dance card. He punished you by making certain everyone thought your card was full so you danced with no one except him. You are still angry that you have been unable to repay him in kind, but I know how you can revenge yourself," her father finished with a twinkle.

Allegra's look was distinctly interested. *"How, Papa?"* she asked her father.

"By marrying him, my dear. While I trust Quinton Hunter to keep his word to me regarding his behavior toward you, I know that it chafes him that he must take a wife to save his estates. Worse, that bride is not, he believes, his equal socially. *That* is your not so subtle revenge upon this man. Whatever he may believe, you are most certainly his equal, for his bloodline and your wealth balance each other out. You know it. He may never accept it, and that, my dear daughter, will give you an advantage over this man. But one day when you know each other better, you will, I suspect, soothe his pride so that he believes he has at long last won the battle between you."

The realization of Lord Morgan's words sank into her conscience. Suddenly Allegra smiled. "Ohh, Papa, how clever you are! I have been so angry I have not been thinking straight."

"The duke will meet us tonight at Almack's Rooms," Lord Morgan told his daughter. "I thought we would announce your engagement the night of your ball."

"When will we be married?" Allegra asked her father.

"Not until the autumn. Your new home needs a great

deal of renovation. I shall arrange to hire an architect and send him down to Hunter's Lair with a party of workmen next week. I think you will have to spend part of your summer overseeing the work and choosing your decorations. Where would you like to go on a honeymoon trip?"

"I must think about it, Papa. Just getting used to the idea of marrying the Duke of Sedgwick is enough for me now." She arose from her chair and kissed his cheek. "Forgive my earlier outburst," she said. "May I tell Sirena?"

"Not quite yet, my dear. Let your cousin have her moment in the sun. Hers is the more unusual of the two matches for she and young Pickford are genuinely in love. They are most fortunate."

"Am I not fortunate also, Papa?" Allegra asked him. "After all, I am to be a duchess, the wife of the man with the bluest blood in all of England."

"You are fortunate, Allegra," Lord Morgan assured his daughter. "Quinton Hunter has no stain upon his reputation. He will be a good husband to you, my dear. See that you are as good a wife."

"I will be, Papa. *After I get used to the idea of it,*" she amended her promise.

"Wear one of your prettiest dresses tonight," Lord Morgan advised her. "And, I shall see that both you and Sirena have beautiful wedding gowns and trousseaux. You have both done very well for your families and I am proud of my pair of girls."

"Ohh, Papa, what will you do without me?" Allegra wondered. Then she brightened. "Why, Papa, you must marry Aunt Olympia!"

Lord Morgan flushed beet red. "God's mercy, Allegra, whatever made you say a thing like that?"

Allegra looked hard at her father whose features bore

a distinctly guilty look of sorts. "Perhaps," she said, "I say it because I realize that you and my aunt suit. She is a respectable widow, and you the injured party in a divorce settled years ago. Do you really want her to go back to that tiny dower house at Rowley? Would she not grace your table once I am gone, Papa? Be a most amenable companion?"

"You are too clever by far, you minx," he replied. "I will admit to you that I have considered marrying again. Do you not think, Allegra, that if I choose your aunt there might be gossip?"

"If I have learned one thing this season, Papa, it is that there will always be gossip, even of the most innocent situation. You and my aunt are perfect for one another. I shall, of course, say nothing of our conversation, Papa, but I should not be unhappy if you wed Aunt Olympia one day."

"It pleases me that I have your blessing," he replied dryly.

Allegra laughed. "I had best decide what to wear to Almack's this evening," she said, kissing his brow. Then she hurried from the room and ran upstairs to her aunt's rooms where she knew Sirena and Ocky would now be. "Are you pleased, Aunt?" she asked as she entered Lady Abbott's apartment. "Sirena has bagged herself a lovely viscount."

"*Allegra!*" her aunt cried, flushing, for that was exactly what she had been thinking. She could barely wait to tell Augustus.

"Do you really think I'm *lovely*?" Viscount Pickford asked, chuckling. "I don't think I've ever been called *lovely* before."

"Definitely lovely," Allegra responded. "I think my cousin most fortunate, as are you, Ocky. May you have many happy years."

Sirena burst into tears. "Ohh, if only you would find the same happiness that I have found," she sobbed.

"The richest girl in England must settle, dearest coz, for a splendid title, and I will. True love is most rare as we all know, Sirena. You and Ocky are among the more fortunate." Then Allegra turned to Viscount Pickford. "Ocky, will you allow Rupert Tanner to stay with you? Papa feels gossip might ensue if he remained here, especially as Papa turned down Lord Ackerly's proposal for my hand. He's a very nice fellow as I am certain you have already ascertained."

"Of course he may stay with us," Viscount Pickford replied.

"Thank you, Lovely," Allegra responded mischievously. "I must go and choose a gown for Almack's tonight. Lord, for all their pretensions it is a dreary place. The rooms are quite unattractive, and the dance floor dreadful. As for the supper, we shall not even mention it, but then one does not go to Almack's to eat, but to be seen." Blowing them all a kiss she departed her aunt's chamber.

"She can be so outrageous," Lady Abbott said weakly. "I don't know what you must think of her, Octavian."

"I think she is charming, madame," the viscount responded. "And as Sirena loves her so dearly, that is good enough for me."

The subject of their conversation hurried to her own rooms where her maid, Honor, was sitting, sewing the hem on a gown that had been torn. "What shall we wear tonight?" Allegra said as she entered.

"Is it important?" Honor asked her mistress.

"Yes," Allegra said, "I believe it is."

"Ohh, miss, tell me, do!" Honor begged.

"Not yet," Allegra said, "but soon, Honor."

Putting her sewing aside, the maid arose. "There is a lovely gown you haven't yet worn." She ran to the wardrobe, and drew a garment out. "Here it is!" She held it out for Allegra's perusal.

Allegra nodded her approval. The high-waisted gown was striped with broad bands of pink and cream watered silk. The elbow-length sleeves dripped lace. The rounded neckline was fashionably low.

"We can pick some of them beautiful pink roses from the garden for your hair, miss," Honor said. "And you can wear that sweet pink cameo on the gold chain your pa just bought you, and pearl earbobs."

"I will want a bath," Allegra replied.

"Is it true Lady Sirena is marrying that handsome viscount she's been keeping company with all season?" Honor hung the gown out.

"How do you servants learn all the gossip so quickly?" Allegra laughed. "That has always fascinated me."

"Damaris was there when Lady Sirena and her beau come up to her mother's rooms," Honor said. "She came to tell me right away. To brag was more likely," Honor told her mistress a trifle sourly. "She sometimes gets above herself, does Damaris."

"I'll make you proud soon enough," Allegra promised her maid.

They left for Almack's Assembly Rooms in King Street just before ten o'clock that evening. As Allegra had noted earlier the rooms were not particularly distinguished, but Almack's was considered *the place* to be and be seen in London society. Founded in 1765 by Mr. McCall, exclusivity was its trademark. Balls were held each Wednesday during the season. Low-level gambling was allowed.

One did not simply go to Almack's. Its patronesses issued vouchers to the chosen, and that voucher allowed one to purchase a ticket into the social heaven. Rank and wealth were important, but not a guarantee of acceptance by the patronesses, of whom Lady Bellingham was currently one.

It was at the Bellingham ball that the season's crop of young ladies were observed by the patronesses. They then met to decide who would be allowed into Almack's that season and who would not. It was a near thing for Allegra despite her father's wealth, for the patronesses had noted she danced only one dance. *The last dance.* Gaining their sworn agreement that they would not tell the tale, Lady Bellingham explained that the Duke of Sedgwick had been the first to ask Allegra for a dance, and shy, she had said her card was full, when indeed it was not. The duke, however, had seen the empty card, and played a wicked trick on poor Miss Morgan, for he had taken umbrage at her refusal.

"Poor child," Lady Markham, one of the other patronesses said sympathetically. "Sedgwick is as handsome as the devil himself, but overproud. Of course an inexperienced girl would have been terrified."

The other ladies murmured in agreement as Lady Bellingham continued her story. And when she had finished they all assented that dear Miss Morgan must certainly be issued a voucher, along with her pretty little cousin, Lady Sirena Abbott. Olympia Abbott knew that it was thanks to her friend that both her daughter and her niece were admitted to the sacred circle that Almack's was acknowledged to be. She was quite deeply in Lady Bellingham's debt now.

The dances deemed acceptable by the patronesses of Almack's were English country dances, Scotch reels, the contredanse, the écossaise, the cotillion, and the minuet. While the popularity of the minuet had waned in France with the revolution, each ball at Almack's opened and closed with one. And after each dance, the young lady was promptly returned to her mama or her chaperone by her gentleman, who bowed politely to the older lady; and if interested, or encouraged, remained to chat.

After her first disastrous ball Allegra found herself most popular, to her amusement. She knew it was her fortune that attracted the gentlemen to her like flies to a honeypot. Some were genuinely pleasant young men, and several she grew to like for their clever repartee and quick wit. Others were outright fortune hunters, and not at all subtle about it. After all, a girl with a rich father and a barely new title should be delighted that men of family and background were paying attention to her. Allegra was not. Her suitors were at first confused, then horrified, and at last insulted when Allegra, who had little patience with pretensions, cheerfully sent them packing.

They arrived at the King Street assembly rooms and were admitted by the concierge, who greeted them by name, bowing as he did so. Once inside they found seats, and sat waiting for the ball to begin. Lord Morgan hurried off to find the gambling. The Marquess of Rowley and his wife arrived, and approached Lady Abbott.

"Sirena, darling! Such wonderful news!" Charlotte gushed. "Have you decided upon a date?"

"Lower your voice, Charlotte," Lady Abbott said angrily. "There has not yet been a formal announcement. You will embarrass us all."

"I have not yet thought about a wedding date," Sirena said softly. "I suppose Ocky and I should discuss it as we have his father's approval."

"June!" Charlotte enthused. "You will make the most

divine June bride, Sirena. At St. George's in Hanover Square, of course. Gussie and I will host a wedding breakfast at the house for you afterward."

"*If* Sirena decides upon June," Lady Abbott said, "I am certain Septimius will have the wedding breakfast. After all, dear, his home is better suited to such an affair than your *tiny* house."

The smile disappeared from Charlotte's face. She turned to Allegra. "Still no luck, Miss Morgan?" she murmured with false sympathy. "Well, they do say that money cannot buy everything."

Allegra laughed. "Do not be ridiculous, Lady Charlotte. Of course it can. By season's end I quite expect to be betrothed." She smiled sweetly at her cousin's wife.

"I cannot imagine to whom," Charlotte said softly.

"Good evening, Lady Abbott, Lady Sirena, Miss Morgan," the Duke of Sedgwick said. "Gussie, Lady Charlotte." He bowed elegantly.

"Good evening, Your Grace," they all chorused but Allegra. She was far too busy really looking for the first time at the man she was to marry. Impressive, she decided silently, but a snob.

"I understand from my friend, Viscount Pickford, that congratulations are in order, Lady Sirena."

Sirena blushed becomingly and half whispered, "Yes, Your Grace." She looked about. "Is not Ocky with you?"

"But a few steps behind, Lady Sirena," the duke assured her. Then he turned to Allegra. "Miss Morgan, if you will allow me." He took her dance card from her, and wrote his name in the first and last slots with the tiny quill provided. "And you will, of course, allow me to escort you into supper afterward."

"Of course, Your Grace," Allegra replied meekly, and she curtsied.

He looked sharply at her, and seeing the deviltry in

her violet eyes, laughed. Taking her hand up he kissed it, then bowed, and walked away.

"Well," Charlotte said meanly, "I'm not surprised that a man like *that* would be paying Miss Morgan attention." She sniffed audibly.

"*Like what, madame?*" Allegra responded in icy tones.

"Well, my dear Miss Morgan, the man hasn't a ha'penny to his name. Everyone knows that. He only pays you court because of your father's wealth. Surely you harbor no girlish illusions about him. For all his pretensions I think him rather rough looking. Not at all handsome or refined. They say he lives in one room, for the rest of his house is falling down about him."

"But a rich wife would certainly correct that situation for him, don't you think, madame?" Allegra said sweetly.

"He would marry you for your wealth, if indeed he could even bring himself to make such an alliance," Charlotte went on.

"And I will marry for the grandest title I can obtain in exchange for my father's wealth," Allegra replied.

"To say such a thing is most indelicate and ungenteel," Charlotte responded, shocked by Allegra's frankness.

"Nonsense, madame! Did you not marry my cousin Gussie for his title? After all, a marquess certainly outranks your papa. As the Marchioness of Rowley you outrank your mama, your sister-in-law, and your sisters. What a coup your marriage was for you. Why should I not contract an alliance offering me similar advantages?" Allegra smiled.

Sirena stared openmouthed at her cousin's forthrightness. Lady Abbott was considering swooning. Charlotte had finally been rendered speechless, and the Marquess of Rowley burst out laughing.

"What is so funny?" Viscount Pickford inquired as he joined them.

"Allegra has just given my wife a most proper dressing-down," Gussie answered him plainly. "Too confusing to explain. Ahh, the musicians are tuning up. We'll be dancing soon enough. Congratulations, my dear Ocky, and you most certainly have my blessings. My little sister will make you a splendid wife. You'll be good to her, I know."

"I will, Gussie," Viscount Pickford assured his future brother-in-law. "I will."

The strains of the minuet began, and the Duke of Sedgwick was suddenly there, taking Allegra's hand to lead her off into the figure. They danced well together, but silently. Charlotte was wrong, Allegra considered to herself. Quinton Hunter was extremely handsome, and then realizing he was looking at her, she lowered her gaze. Wealth and beauty, he thought to himself as they danced. It was certainly a better fate than he had antici- pated. *And he would be able to buy his horses back.*

As he led her back to her aunt, he said softly, "Your father has spoken to you, Miss Morgan?"

"He has, and under the circumstances I think you are permitted to call me by my Christian name," Allegra responded.

"I shall come for you at supper, *Allegra*," he told her. Then he bowed, and turned away.

She danced with a succession of young men, most of whom mouthed inanities at her in an effort to gain her favor. She smiled at some, ignored others. She was sud- denly impatient to know more about this man she was suddenly told she was to marry. She almost cheered when the midnight interval came and the Duke of Sedg- wick returned to claim her company. "I want nothing more than a lemonade," she told him. "The lemonade is passable."

"The wine is not," he replied dryly, "but we drink it anyhow."

The refreshments obtained, they repaired to a secluded bench in a small alcove. Seated, Allegra took the silver cup of lemonade from his hand, and invited him to sit also. They each sipped their cups in relative silence, and then he finally spoke.

"Are you content to be the Duchess of Sedgwick, Allegra?"

"If you are content to have me be," she replied.

"You are practical," he said. Or was she cold, he wondered?

Allegra sighed. "My father loved my mother. She wed him only for his money, and then one day she did fall in love. She ran away, leaving him, my brother, and me. I do not remember her, although my brother did. He said she was very beautiful, but cold. It was from my father I learned about love, but his love is that of a parent for his child. I know nothing of the love a man and a woman share. I have been told my whole life that while my mother's behavior was shocking and quite unforgivable, it was out of the ordinary. I have been told that marriages are arranged between families for the purpose of bettering each family involved.

"In our case you will marry me for my money, and the great inheritance my father will bequeath upon me one day. I will marry you because you will elevate me socially. The reasoning behind our match is sensible and pragmatic. Unlike my mother, I like children, and shall be happy to bear them for you. I will respect you as my husband, and be faithful always. Deceit is not in my nature, Your Grace."

He was astounded by her candid words. She had been honest with him to a fault, and he could be no less so with her. "I come," he said, "from a family of romantic men and women. My father, my grandfather, my antecedents before them, all married for love, and were very happy. Sadly, however, the men in my family were also unrepentant gamblers. Worse, when they lost the women they loved through death, they drank. I have one of the oldest names in England, and certainly it is said of me, the bluest blood. But, Allegra, I haven't a shilling to my name. I am taking a wife to restore my family's fortunes. I had to sell two of my best breeding mares in order to afford my sortie into London this season. I am indeed marrying you for your wealth, but I promise you that I will be a good husband to you. I am no tyrant."

"Then, Your Grace, we understand each other perfectly," Allegra replied. She took a sip of her lemonade for her throat was dry with a nervousness she hid well.

"My name is Quinton," he said quietly.

"*Quinton,*" she responded softly.

A shiver rippled down his back, at once both startling and confusing.

"I thought," Allegra continued, "that we might be married in the autumn; but with your permission I shall come to Hunter's Lair this summer to oversee its renovations. If we are wed in early October, we can be prepared to host your friends in November at a hunt."

"How do you know we hunt?" he asked her.

"Everyone knows that Hunter's Lair, despite being in Hereford, is famous for its hunting. I do not hunt, however. I dislike killing animals, Quinton, so while I will see to our guests and their other entertainments, I will not go careening about the countryside chasing after some poor fox or deer, while clinging to a horse in a voluminous skirt. When I ride, I do so in breeches. I hope you are not shocked. Aunt Olympia claims that gentlemen are shocked by ladies astride."

"Do you have pretty legs, Allegra?" he asked teasingly.

"You shall be the judge of that eventually, Quinton," she answered pertly, "but whether I do or not, I will still ride astride."

He was forced to laugh. "You are very forthright," he told her.

"I do not know how to be any other way," she said.

"Good," he replied. "Then we shall have no secrets from each other, Allegra. Tell me about Rupert Tanner."

"We grew up together," she responded, surprised by the question.

"He says he wants to marry you," the duke said.

"Oh, that is his papa's idea," Allegra told the duke with a small smile. "He is a second son. When my papa said I had to come to London to find a husband, Rupert and I decided we would tell Papa we wanted to wed. That way I should be married to someone I knew, and wouldn't have to leave my home. Of course his papa was delighted by such a suggestion, while mine was not. I do not love Rupert, nor does he love me. There was no arrangement between us, formal, or informal," Allegra finished.

"Then your father may announce our betrothal at your ball in two weeks' time. You are to be presented at court next week, I am told," the duke said to her.

"Yes. I have to wear that awful dress with its huge hoop, and that absurd headdress. I shall be decked out in diamonds and other magnificent jewels like some pagan idol, I fear. I don't dare eat or drink a thing for hours before. It is, I have been told, impossible to use the necessary in such a garment. Is the old king really worth such effort, Quinton?"

"Your cousin will be with you, and as my future wife it is most important you make your debut before King George and Queen Charlotte," the duke responded quietly.

"But no one will know until my ball that we are to be wed," Allegra sighed. "I don't want to tell anyone so Sirena may have her day in the sun with Ocky. We both know any mention of our betrothal would overshadow them greatly, and I don't think that's fair."

"I agree," the duke replied, thinking that this girl for all her pride and wealth had a kind heart. He felt strangely relieved by the knowledge. They would, he decided, get on very well. "When will you come to Hunter's Lair?" he asked.

"I must go home first, but I should be able to come in early July. As I realize you will hardly be ready to host guests, I shall come with only my maid, Honor. There will be a certain amount of gossip about it, I am sure, but as our engagement will have already been announced and our wedding date set, I will not mind, if you do not."

"You are a sensible girl," he complimented her. Then taking her hand in his he looked into the violet eyes. "As I have your father's permission, Allegra, now I ask yours. Will you marry me?"

"Yes, Quinton, I will," she responded quietly, happy he could not know how quickly her heart was beating. "I will be honored to be your wife."

Chapter Four

On the night of the thirty-first of May every tree in Berkley Square was festooned with paper lanterns that glittered and lit up the area, making it a fairyland. Carriage after carriage slowly entered the square from the side streets, each waiting its turn to disembark its passengers before Lord Septimius Morgan's house. Once at their destination Lord Morgan's guests were greeted and helped from their vehicles by a seemingly endless stream of black and silver liveried footmen. A stately butler welcomed them at the door to the house as they entered. More footmen ushered them to the second floor where the ladies were invited to freshen themselves in a large windowed cloakroom with several screened necessaries, while the gentlemen in their separate facility did the same. There was much approval of this disposition for usually the sanitary arrangements were set in the corners of the ballroom behind their painted screens, and by evening's end the chamber stank.

Exiting the cloakrooms the guests were guided to the ballroom. They greeted their host and his daughter at its entrance, and were then announced to the company by a barrel-chested majordomo whose stentorian voice echoed throughout the entire area. Moving down two steps they entered Lord Morgan's ballroom into a crowd of London's most fashionable denizens.

No one had refused the invitation to Miss Morgan's ball. Prinny was coming, and just a few days ago a fascinating rumor had begun making the rounds that Miss Morgan's betrothal would be announced tonight, although to whom, no one had the faintest idea. She was always seen in the company of her cousin, Lady Sirena Abbott, Viscount Pickford, and their friends. She certainly hadn't seemed to have favored any one gentleman. It was a mystery, if indeed the rumor was even true.

Lady Bellingham sat smugly in her most fashionable silver and midnight blue ballgown. She and her husband had been the only invited guests to the dinner that preceded the ball. Of course the Dowager Marchioness of Rowley, her daughter, Viscount Pickford, the Marquess of Rowley, and his silly wife were there, but they were family. *And then there had been the Duke of Sedgwick*. Her interest was immediately engaged for she, too, had heard the rumors swirling about Allegra Morgan.

"*Septimius?*" she demanded questioningly. Her look went to Quinton Hunter, and then back again to her host.

"You will be the first to know, Clarice," he said softly, a twinkle in his eye. "Not even the family has been told yet. This dinner is for that purpose. Are you pleased?"

"Indeed I am," Lady Bellingham said. "Quinton's mother was my cousin, Vanessa Tarleton. She was the eldest daughter of the Marquess of Rufford. Had a dowry that would have embarrassed a farmer's gel, but of course Charles Hunter fell in love with her. She was a lovely creature. Died when Quinton was eleven, and his brother, George, six. She gave birth to a tiny girl, and then gave up the ghost. The child died several hours later. It was buried in her arms. A great tragedy. Charles drank himself to death after he had gambled away what little he had left. Old Rufford saw his grandsons were educated, but it was a strain on his finances, and most of his own estate was entailed upon his eldest son and heir. My mother was Rufford's younger sister. Quinton is a very proud man, but he is honorable, Septimius."

"So I have gathered by his conduct towards Allegra, Clarice. He has behaved with the utmost delicacy and kindness. Allegra would never admit to it, of course, but she is very concerned about doing the right thing once she is the Duchess of Sedgwick."

"Nothing the matter with your gel, Septimius. She will do very well, and I can promise you she is going to be an outstanding duchess," Lady Bellingham said with a reassuring smile. "What a coup, Septimius! All of London will be talking about it come tomorrow." She chuckled.

Clarice Bellingham smiled a smugly satisfied smile as she looked out over the ballroom. Oh yes, they would all be mightily surprised by Miss Morgan's catch. There would be some, of course, who would sneer that it was her money, and indeed it was. Her money, and his title. But Allegra Morgan would be a duchess. Wife to the man with the bluest blood in all of England. Without much hope Quinton had come to London seeking a wife; and by God he had landed the prize of this or any other season. And his friends had not done so badly either. Young Pickford and sweet Sirena. The Earl of Aston who had found a wife in the current Marquess of Rufford's middle daughter, Eunice; and Lord Walworth, who to his surprise, had been snapped up by her own niece, Caroline Bellingham. Oh, yes, it had indeed been a most successful season!

The orchestra on its dais suddenly struck up a ruffle and flourish. Escorted by his host, Prinny entered the room, followed by Allegra. Lord Morgan nodded to the musicians, and the strains of the minuet began. The prince bowed to Allegra, who curtsied beautifully, and together they danced most gracefully. When they had finished the ballroom was filled with the thunder of clapping. Prince George, better known as Prinny, was a handsome man of thirty, with blond hair, blue eyes, and a pink complexion. He and Allegra had made a most attractive couple. Escorting her back to her father, he bowed to them both.

"Thank you, Your Highness," Allegra said, and she curtsied again.

"If Your Highness will allow me," Lord Morgan said, "I have an announcement to make."

"Is it *her* betrothal?" Prinny said excitedly.

Lord Morgan nodded with a smile. The prince was a bit childish and loved secrets. "To the Duke of Sedgwick," he told Prinny softly, satisfying his overweening curiosity.

"I say!" the prince replied. "A fine catch for you, Miss Morgan, and an even better one for Sedgwick. You both have my congratulations. Sedgwick," he spoke to the duke who had now joined them, "you really ought to gamble for you seem to have the damndest good fortune. Not only a beautiful gel, but a rich one as well!" He chuckled, well pleased, as if he had been responsible for the whole situation. "Well, Morgan, make your announcement so I can go and gamble," Prinny said with another chuckle.

Lord Morgan nodded again to the musicians who played an elegant tah-rah. Stepping up upon the dais he said, "My lords, ladies and gentlemen, I have the honor, and the pleasure to announce my daughter, Allegra's, betrothal to Quinton Hunter, the Duke of Sedgwick."

A burst of excited applause broke out, but before the couple might be overwhelmed by congratulations, the musicians began to play a country reel. The guests were forced to begin dancing once again. Sirena, however, managed to evade the dancers, and take her cousin aside.

"Why didn't you tell me?" she demanded, outraged. "We have never before kept secrets from each other."

"Because I wanted you and Ocky to enjoy all the attention generated from *your* betrothal. If I had told you that the duke and I were also betrothed, it would have hardly remained a secret, Sirena."

"When did he ask you?" Sirena asked, excitedly.

"He and Papa came to an arrangement several weeks ago, and then he asked me," Allegra answered her cousin.

"Do you love him?" Sirena's pretty face was anxious.

"I barely know him," Allegra replied.

"Then how can you marry him?" Sirena almost wailed.

"Sirena, my dearest romantic little cousin, he is the Duke of Sedgwick. *How can I not marry him?*" Allegra replied.

"That is so cold!" Sirena cried, her blue eyes filling with tears.

"No, it is being practical," Allegra told her quietly. "I must be married, dearest one. Whoever I wed marries me for my money. How can I ever believe otherwise? You and Ocky marry for love, but few in our class have that luxury, sweeting. I am quite satisfied with this arrangement, I assure you."

"As am I," the duke said, joining them. "Please do

not fret yourself, Lady Sirena. I intend taking good care of your cousin."

"Come, sweetheart, I want to dance," Viscount Pickford said as he also joined them. "People will talk if we do not, Sirena. Then all those husband-hunting gels will be after me again, and it will be all your fault, my darling," he teased her, leading her away.

"She loves you very much," the duke remarked.

"I love her," Allegra replied. She slipped her hand through his arm. "Should we not also dance, my lord?"

"I dislike dancing," he replied.

"So do I," she admitted, "but it is my ball, and tongues will wag if we are not seen together tripping the light fantastic."

He laughed. "What a fine sense of propriety you have, Allegra. You really are a very sensible young woman. More like your father than your mother, I think. You will not fall in love with someone else and leave me."

"But you might fall in love one day and leave me," she countered.

"I do not believe in love," he said truthfully. "Love is the cause of more difficulties on this earth than even money, or the lack of it. Since by marrying you I become a rich man, and since I don't hold with the chimera of love, there is little likelihood that I will ever leave you, Allegra."

"You may change your mind when I begin restoring Hunter's Lair, Quinton," she teased him. "From what I have been told, I shall need to expend a small fortune on it."

He laughed again. "I love the old place," he admitted, "but I know it could use a bit of sprucing up. It is yours to do with as you will, my dear. Just leave the Great Hall for my hunting parties."

"I agree," she told him with a smile. "Now escort me

back to the dance floor, and let us make everyone here tonight envious of us."

"Why, Miss Morgan," he teased back, "what a naughty girl you are. I did not expect it from such a proper young woman, but it is not an unwelcome side of you, I am thinking."

"We shall have the summer to know each other better," she replied. "I hope we shall still like each other when the summer ends. It will make for a much better marriage if we like one another, Quinton."

He thought about her last remark afterward. She was a practical girl, but he sensed in her a vulnerability that he would wager even she wasn't aware of in herself. For all her intelligence, and a season in London, she was still an innocent at heart. He found that he wanted to protect Allegra from any hurt. Then he smiled to himself. It would seem that no man could be free of a woman's charms. When earlier that evening he had given her an amethyst ring set round with diamonds as a token of their pledge, she had almost squealed, catching herself in midcry. It had both touched and amused him.

"It is beautiful. How could you afford such a ring?" she demanded.

"It is a family piece," he told her. "One of the few that did not go to pay gambling debts. I chose it because its deep color reminded me of your eyes, Allegra."

Her mouth fell open in surprise. Then catching herself she closed it, saying, "What a lovely thing to say, my lord." She held out her hand, admiring the ring some more.

He took her hand, and kissed it. "I may not love you, Allegra, but it is not difficult to say lovely things to you, my dear."

"I am sorry I didn't have this ring when I made my bow at court. All the other girls, especially the ones who were so high-flown with me, would have been pea green with envy!"

"Your curtsey put the others to shame," he told her. "It was every bit worthy of a Duchess of Sedgwick."

"I am amazed that I did not topple over in that ridiculous gown," she told him. "One had to go sideways through the doors with those huge hoop skirts. It was all I could do not to fall on my bottom when I bowed. And the neckline was cut so fashionably low that my bosom was all but exposed to King George. But he didn't seem to mind. As for the wig I had to wear, it weighed practically as much as a coach and four, Quinton. I thought my neck would crack with its weight."

"I thought the doves flying amid the diamonds a rather nice touch," he remarked, his silvery eyes twinkling.

Allegra laughed. "I vow, sir, if it were possible to use live birds some ambitious mama would do it. I prefer simple clothing."

Like the gown she was wearing tonight, he thought as they danced the final minuet of the evening. Her high-waisted dress was a cream damask silk with an overskirt of shimmering sheer gold silk. Her little gold slippers peeped from beneath the gown, and gold ribbons were entwined amid her dark curls. Her slender neck was encircled with a strand of pearls, and she wore pearl ear-bobs in her ears. The effect was both elegant, rich, and yet simple. Looking really closely at her tonight he realized for the first time how absolutely beautiful Allegra was. Oh, yes, he had seen she was a beauty prior, and God only knows everyone said it. Rich *and* beautiful was all he heard this evening as he was congratulated. But he had not until now truly looked at Allegra.

Her heart-shaped face was perfectly formed. Her nose was straight, and just tilted ever so tightly up at its tip.

Her eyebrows were thick and black, a sign of her Welsh heritage. Her violet-colored eyes, large and luminous, were edged with a heavy fall of black lashes. Her lower lip was fuller than the upper. It was a sensuous and tempting little mouth. He was even now contemplating kissing it. She was tall for a girl, but certainly not too tall for him. She was slender of limb, but her bosom was delightfully round and nicely shaped. He estimated one of her breasts would fit quite perfectly into one of his palms.

It was then he considered the possibility of bedding Allegra. He wasn't certain how he would go about such a thing with a wife. She would, of course, be a virgin. He had never had a virgin. The fact that he didn't love her bothered him not at all. He had never been in love with any of the women he had lain with, but this would, of course, be different. Allegra would be his wife. Could a man love a woman he bedded? Could a wife arouse his desires? Or was passion just a deliciously lustful pastime? And how would an amicably bred girl react to passion? He would have to be tender and gentle with her.

"The dance has ended, Quinton," he suddenly heard Allegra's voice saying. "Please pay attention, my lord, or you will have the gossips chattering about how moonstruck you are. What on earth are you thinking about?"

"Bedding you," he answered her honestly, and was rather pleased to see the blush that came to her cheeks. Innocence was a powerful aphrodisiac he was learning, feeling a distinct tightness in his breeches.

"Ohh," she said, and began to worry her lower lip with her small white teeth. "I had not yet considered that part of our marriage."

*   *   *

After the guests had departed, he led her out onto the terrace that overlooked the garden. He sat her down upon a marble bench, and took her hand in his. "You told me you wanted children, Allegra." His eyes scanned her face for the truth.

"Oh, I do," she answered him quickly.

"Then we must consummate our marriage, my dear. It is the only way we shall obtain children," the duke explained, hoping such frankness would not shock or frighten her.

"I am not a fool, Quinton!" Allegra said sharply. "I know how children are conceived. I would be a complete puddinghead if I didn't. Every girl knows, even if she feigns ignorance."

"But you said . . . ," he began.

"I said I had not *yet* considered that part of our marriage, and I haven't, but I know it must exist between us eventually," Allegra replied. "Do not rush me, sir. I have never even been kissed."

"That is something I can put aright now," he told her. Then he touched her lips with his fingertips even as Allegra's eyes grew wide. Her lips had a texture like rose petals. The duke tilted Allegra's face up to his and kissed her gently, his mouth pressing lightly against hers. Shyly she kissed him back, and the sweetness emanating from her lips overwhelmed him, shocked him, sent his senses reeling.

"That was very nice," Allegra told him. "Are you a good kisser, my lord? You see I shall never know another man's lips, so I am naturally curious as to what your lovers have thought."

He was torn by twin urges. The first was laughter. The second was shock at her candidness. "None of the ladies I have kissed, Allegra, has ever voiced displeasure," he replied.

She sighed. "They probably wouldn't unless you were absolutely awful at it. Women tend to be like that I have observed. We prefer peace."

He felt irritated. "I am quite certain," he said, "that I am an excellent kisser, Allegra. I cannot imagine why you should even ask such a question."

"Oh, dear, I have ruffled your feathers, haven't I, my lord? I am sorry." But the smile upon her pretty lips contradicted her apology.

"Shall I obtain a list of satisfied ladies for you to query?" he demanded, refusing to let the matter rest. It was her first kiss, or so she claimed. She should have been thrilled down to her toes instead of demanding references attesting to his skills as a lover.

Allegra heard the annoyance in his voice, and now it was she who found herself irritated. "I am curious, Quinton," she told him. "I have been taught that curiosity isn't a mortal sin, but rather to be cultivated. As I told you, I have never before been kissed by a gentleman. I am sorry if my interest offended you. If you mean to wed me then you will have to get used to it, I fear."

"I shall also have to get used to your bluntness," he replied, his tone still distinctly annoyed.

Allegra burst out laughing. "Gracious, sir, we are having our first quarrel, and we are not even wed. I will wager that Sirena and Ocky have not quarreled yet."

"They are in love. Cow-eyed, and moonstruck," he answered her, a faint hint of scorn in his voice.

"And we are not in love," Allegra said. She wasn't certain now how she felt about that fact. Then she shook herself inwardly. Love led only to betrayal and unhappiness. Better a couple suit.

"You do not hold a grudge, do you?" the duke said to her, his humor beginning to return.

"Not often," she responded with a small smile.

"Ahh, here you are, my dears." Her aunt came out into the wide terraced balcony. "Your papa was looking for you, Allegra, but I see that you are fine. I shall tell him." She smiled and hurried off again.

"Would you like to see the sunrise?" the duke asked.

"In London? Such a thing isn't possible," Allegra replied.

"We can take my coach and drive outside the city. There is time," he said. "Perhaps Ocky and Sirena would like to come with us."

"If you can manage to live with their constant billing and cooing," Allegra told him, "I suppose I can, too."

He laughed. "Is that your subtle way of saying you want to be alone with me, Allegra?"

"We are to be married in a few months' time, Quinton. I want to know you better," she said. "If you would really like my cousin and her affianced to come, however, I will send a servant for them."

"No," he said softly, and drew her into the circle of his arms. "I want to get to know you better, too, Allegra." He looked down into her small face, a half smile upon his lips.

Her heart hammered suddenly. Damn, he was a handsome man! Those silvery gray eyes were mesmerizing. "Your eyelashes are surely longer than mine," she said breathily.

He smiled openly now. "Are they?"

"Yes!" she said. Then her eyes fastened upon the mouth that had earlier given her her first kiss. It was a big mouth, and yet it had an air of delicacy about it.

"I think, Allegra," the duke said, "that you need to be kissed once more before we go off to see the sunrise."

Then he kissed her again, this time his arms wrapping themselves tightly about her, his mouth pressing harder against her lips.

A shiver raced down her spine. For the briefest moment she felt weak and helpless, then the feeling passed as quickly as it had come. When he drew away she smiled up at him, but this time she uttered not a word. She had learned after their first kiss that gentlemen didn't like to be questioned about their technique. As far as she was concerned his skills pleased her, and wasn't that enough? It was going to have to be, she reasoned to herself.

The duke called for his carriage while Allegra sought out her father to tell him where they were going.

"It was a wonderful ball, Papa," she said, finding him in his library with her aunt. "Thank you so very much." She kissed his cheek.

"And to think you are to be a duchess!" her aunt enthused excitedly. "What a naughty pair you two were keeping such news from me these past few weeks." She wagged a finger at them playfully.

"I wanted Sirena to have her due," Allegra replied. "You know quite well, Aunt Olympia, that had my betrothal been announced when Sirena's was, no one would have paid the least attention to my cousin at all. Part of having a successful season is having the people who thought little, or not at all of you, be astounded by your wonderful success in the husband hunt!" She laughed. "I doubt many thought that the modestly dowered baby sister of the Marquis of Rowley could bag an earl's heir, but Sirena did with her sweetness and her charm. I wanted her to enjoy her triumph, not have to bask in the shadow of mine."

Olympia Abbott's hand flew to her mouth to stifle her cry. Then the hand fell away and she said, "That you love my daughter so dearly, even as if she were your own sister, makes me so happy." Several tears slid down her cheeks with her pleasure.

"Now, now, my dear," Lord Morgan said, and leaning over he wiped the lady's tears from her cheek tenderly. "Of course Allegra loves Sirena like a sister, and have you not been a mother to my dearest child? The mother her own was not?"

"Ohh, Septimius," the good woman murmured, somewhat overcome.

"The duke and I are going to ride out and see the sunrise," Allegra said, wondering as she did if they even heard her. Then she departed the library, leaving her father and her aunt seemingly lost in each other. With a little encouragement he would marry her, Allegra thought, and it was, of course, the right thing to do.

The duke's black coach was wonderfully well sprung and quite comfortable inside. It was drawn by four bay horses with blond manes and tails. The coach took an easterly road leaving the city. Above them the sky was fading from black to a stone gray which eased into a blue that grew lighter and brighter. Atop a hill their vehicle stopped, and they descended into the road.

"Wait for us here," the duke ordered his coachmen, and then taking Allegra's hand they walked forward until ahead of them they could see the first faint ribbons of pink, peach, and lavender decorating the horizon. These colors were followed by a slash of red orange, and at last the sun. Red gold at first as it rose, mellowing as it slipped over the purview of the distant sea.

Allegra sniffed the fresh country air appreciatively. "Ahh, how good that smells," she said. "It seems we have been in town so long that I had almost forgotten what good country air is like. We shall go home after Sirena's wedding, and it cannot be soon enough for me!"

"You do not like London?" he asked.

"Oh, the city is a fine place to visit, but I certainly don't want to live there, Quinton," she told him. "Nor would I want to raise my children in London. Children need the countryside in which to ride, and to run barefoot through the dewy grass of a May morning." She flung out her arms and spun about. "Just a few more weeks, and I shall go home."

"Hunter's Lair will be your home soon," he told her.

"Is it beautiful?" she asked him.

"I think so," he said softly.

"Then I shall love it," Allegra told him.

"I think I had best get you home, Miss Morgan," the duke responded with a smile. "The sun is now up, and you have been dancing all night long." He took her by the hand again. "You danced very well with Prinny. You were every inch a Duchess of Sedgwick, my dear. I was proud."

"Were you?" Her tone indicated that she didn't really care if he was or not. "The prince is very handsome, but I think he is already running to fat. Did you see what he consumed at the supper buffet? I was astounded his waistcoat did not burst open with all the oysters he swallowed down so greedily."

"You will learn not to speak so frankly out of my company, won't you, Allegra?" the duke asked her.

"I am not such a ninny, Quinton, that I would offend the prince," she told him. "But I assume I may be honest with you."

"You must always be honest with me," he said as he helped her back into the coach.

She fell asleep on the ride back into town, her head against his shoulder. What an interesting girl she was, he thought. Mayhap it would not be such a bad match. She might not have a glittering pedigree, but she had manners and was as accomplished as any noble lady. Perhaps even more so. While extremely outspoken, he did not think she was flighty in the least. Her father said she knew how to manage her funds, and God knows that was more than most women knew. Quinton Hunter recalled an ancient aunt from his youth, now long dead. She was always saying he should marry someone of less vaunted family than his own.

"Get some new fresh blood into the line, boy," she would growl at him. "Overbreeding is the ruination of most good families, I tell you. A healthy wench will breed you up more sons than any high-flown miss. Remember what I say, boy!"

Strange that he did remember the old woman's words, but only now that he was betrothed to Miss Allegra Morgan. He turned his head to look down at her. Her dark curls were quite tumbled now. He gently fingered one, and a gentle whiff of her fragrance assailed his nostrils. It was the scent of lilacs, his favorite flowers. How odd, or wonderful, that it should be her perfume. Outside the coach windows the city was coming alive. The vehicle turned into Berkley Square and stopped before Lord Morgan's fine town house. The duke, unable to help himself, bent and kissed Allegra's smooth brow.

"You are home, my dear," he said quietly. "Wake up, now."

"Ummm." The violet eyes opened slowly in confusion and then comprehension, as she realized where she was. "I slept all the way home?" She sounded surprised.

A footman ran from the house to open the carriage door. He helped his young mistress to descend. The duke followed. In the round foyer he gave her a chaste kiss on the lips in farewell.

"I shall call for you at three o'clock this afternoon so we may promenade through the park in my landau.

Now that we are formally engaged it will be expected that we be seen together daily."

"I have a fitting for my bridesmaid gown," Allegra said.

"At three?"

"I don't know when. I just know today," she replied.

"Have a footman bring 'round a note to me when you know," he said. Then he bowed, and turning, departed.

Slowly Allegra ascended the staircase. On the ballroom floor footmen and maidservants were still dismantling the décor. She climbed a second flight to the bedroom floor. Entering her bedchamber she saw that Honor, her maid, was sleeping in a chair beside the fading coals of a once-bright fire. "I'm back, Honor," she said.

The servant's eyes opened, and then seeing her mistress she jumped to her feet. "Ohh, Miss Allegra, what time is it?"

"Almost seven o'clock," Allegra answered glancing at the clock on her mantel.

"*In the morning?*" Honor sounded shocked. "Why Miss Allegra, you've been dancing all night long. Even after all these weeks in the city I'm not used to such hours as you have had to keep."

"We drove out to the countryside and saw the sunrise," Allegra told her maidservant.

"*Who?* Who was with you, and does your papa know?" Honor was seven years older than her mistress, and extremely protective. Like Allegra she had been born and raised at Morgan Court. She counted her young lady almost like family.

"Ohh, Honor! You do not know, and I promised to tell you. I am to marry the Duke of Sedgwick in the autumn. We are going to live in Hereford, not more than a day's journey from Morgan Court."

"That high-flown gentleman who spoiled your first ball? Is that the one you're going to marry? You can't love him, miss. Why you hardly know him," Honor said indignantly.

"That is why our marriage is scheduled for October, and not for June like Sirena's. Shortly after we get home we will go to Hunter's Lair so I may oversee the renovations and the restorations that are needed. I have to marry, Honor. You know that. The duke is, I am assured, an honorable man, but he is poor. I shall be a duchess when I become his wife. He shall be a rich man the moment he weds me. It is an ideal arrangement, and this summer we shall have the opportunity to become acquainted. There will be no surprises when we are married."

"There're always surprises, miss," Honor said dourly as she helped her mistress from her ball gown. "I wish that you could fall in love like Lady Sirena and her nice young gentleman. Your mama married for money, and look what happened there."

"But the duke's family always married for love, and now they are as poor as church mice," Allegra replied. "The duke and I are entering into this marriage with no illusions at all. I believe that I am actually beginning to like him, and I certainly think that he likes me. We shall become great friends, I am certain, and our marriage shall be quite successful, Honor. Now what time does Madame Paul arrive for my fitting?"

"Eleven o'clock, miss," was the response.

"Then I must get some rest before she comes," Allegra said. "Wake me at ten-thirty with a cup of hot chocolate. Madame can measure me here, and then I shall retire back to bed until I must get up and dressed to go out with the duke this afternoon."

"Yes, miss. Where will you be going so I may lay out the proper garments?" Honor asked.

"We are going riding in his landau through the park," Allegra said. "We are expected to be seen together now, and wish to show each other off to the envious ladies and gentlemen of the ten thousand." Allegra chuckled as she climbed into her bed. "Oh lord, Honor, I am so tired," she said, lying back. Her eyes closed, and she was suddenly fast asleep.

"Without even washing her face and hands," Honor said, shaking her head. "Poor lass. She'll be as glad as me to return to the country. This social life with all its running about isn't for us."

Madame Paul arrived promptly at eleven o'clock in the morning. She already knew about Allegra's engagement to the Duke of Sedgwick. "I shall take your measurements for your wedding gown as well, Miss Morgan," she said. "Of course you will want me to do it, won't you?"

"Of course," Allegra agreed, although the truth was she hadn't even considered her wedding gown yet. "I will come up to London in late September for a final fitting."

"Nonsense, I shall come to Morgan Court, miss. It wouldn't be proper for the future Duchess of Sedgwick to come into my shop," Madame Paul replied. "Francine, the bridesmaid's gown, if you please. Let us see what needs to be done."

Allegra was to be Sirena's attendant when she wed on the tenth of June. Her gown was high waisted with lace oversleeves. It was cream-colored silk sprigged with lilac flowers. A purple velvet ribbon ran beneath her breasts, and tied in a small bow at her back. She would wear a large summer straw hat trimmed with feathers and purple ribbons. "It's a lovely gown," Allegra told Madame Paul.

"It suits you," the Frenchwoman said quietly. "Now, Miss Morgan, let us allow you to return to bed. I shall come before you leave London so we may decide upon the material and style of your own wedding gown."

Back in her bed Allegra pondered on her new status. Madame had, of course, always been polite and deferential to her. She was after all the richest girl in England. But there was something different now. Some indefinable thing that had to do with becoming the Duchess of Sedgwick.

When Allegra was awakened next it was past two o'clock in the afternoon. "I want a bath," she said.

"There isn't time," Honor replied. "You won't be ready when the duke comes if you take a bath now."

"Then the duke will wait," Allegra responded. *"I want a bath!"*

"Yer not married yet," Honor grumbled going to the door and telling one of the footmen that "Miss" wanted the bath water brought.

"He'll not cry off because I took a bath," Allegra laughed. "After all, it's all for him, isn't it? Now, what dress have you picked for me to wear on our drive?"

Honor displayed the chosen garment. It was a simple gown of green-sprigged white muslin with a pleated hem, high waist, low neckline, and little puffed sleeves. A bright green ribbon tied about the waistline. The skirt was slightly puffed out in a style called bouffant.

Allegra giggled. "It's so virgin sacrifice," she said almost to herself. Still, she knew it was very appropriate. "It's quite nice, Honor," she told her maid. "No bonnet though. I shall carry a parasol instead. If I keep it open in the carriage I can protect my skin from the sun, but I will be quite visible to everyone. A bonnet would obscure my features. Let there be no mistake today that it is I with the duke, and not some other woman."

Honor shook her head. "I don't know you anymore," she said. "The city ain't good for you, Miss Allegra. I never knew you to be so . . . so deliberate."

"But I am, Honor, if only for a few more days. I think of all those girls who spoke to Sirena, but would deliberately ignore me because my papa was only Lord Morgan, and not an earl, or a duke, or some other high muckety-muck. How they scorned me for being the heiress of the richest man in England. I pretended not to notice those snubs, and even ignored them. But last night after my betrothal to the duke was announced, girls who had never uttered a word to me the entire season were suddenly fawning over me. *Just because I am marrying a duke!* Until we return home I have full intention of swanning about London with my prize catch. When I am the Duchess of Sedgwick, they shall all have to give way to me socially!"

"Miss Allegra!" Honor cried shocked. "I never knew you had such meanness and spite in you. Your papa and your aunt would be very unhappy to hear such words as I have just heard from your mouth."

"Ohh, Honor, I don't mean to be unkind, but you have no idea what it was like for me. If they weren't being snobbish about my lineage, they were jealous of Papa's wealth. In some cases both. I don't know what's wrong with having a fortune. While parents seem to approve of it, other young ladies don't." She laughed. "How ridiculous I must sound, dear Honor." Allegra hugged her servant. "Do not be angry at me. I promise I shall not be obnoxious about becoming a duchess. I shall only preen ever so slightly in public."

"Ohh, miss, I couldn't stay angry with you," Honor

said with a reassuring smile. She was more aware than her young mistress knew of what the girl had had to put up with this season. The servants had a gossip mill that never closed. Still, Honor thought, her young lady was the best of them all no matter her breeding. And she'd have no one say otherwise!

The bath was made ready; the footmen hurrying up the back stairs with their buckets of hot water. Honor poured a bit of oil of lilac into the porcelain tub, and then set a painted screen about it so Allegra, who preferred bathing herself, could have some privacy. Then the maid laid out her mistress's petticoats and stockings. Allegra did not like the pink silk tights that were considered the height of fashion. She preferred stockings and garters.

When she had bathed, Allegra sat while Honor brushed her dark hair. Then she put on her stockings, which were held up with small garters sewn round with tiny rosettes; and two silk petticoats. She stood silent as Honor buttoned up her gown, and then sat while the maid dressed her hair into a mass of ringlets which she decorated with a bright green ribbon. Allegra then slipped her feet into balletlike slippers, and helped herself to a pair of coral earrings and a thin strand of coral beads to wear about her neck. She looked at herself in the mirror and smiled.

"I'll get yer parasol," Honor said as Allegra stood up. The clock on the mantle struck three.

Allegra smiled again. "You see, I shall not be late at all. Perhaps I should keep him waiting just to emphasize that I am not at his beck and call." Her violet eyes twinkled mischievously as a knock sounded upon her bedchamber door.

Honor shook a warning finger at her mistress, and hurried to answer the knock. A footman stood on the other side of the door. The two servants murmured, and then turning, Honor said, "His lordship is downstairs. I have said you will be down immediately. Do you want that nice little lace fichu for your shoulders? I know it's June, but there could be a chill in the park. Won't do to have you catching a sniffle now." Not even waiting for her mistress's answer she fetched the delicate shawl, and hurried downstairs after her young lady.

Honor curtsied to the duke, and put the lace fichu about Allegra's shoulders. He nodded slightly. Oh my, the maid thought. He is handsome, but he don't look easy. Miss Allegra is taking on more than she realizes, I think. She watched as the newly engaged pair made their way from the foyer and down the front steps where the duke helped Allegra into a handsome landau, then joined her. As the vehicle drew away Honor considered they would be the richest couple in all of England; their children would have the bluest blood; and they were certainly the handsomest pair of people she had ever seen.

Chapter Five

"Your gown is charming," the duke told Allegra as the landau pulled away from the house. "Why do you wear no bonnet?"

Allegra opened her parasol, and adjusted it. "Because I wish to be seen, and I assume you wish to be seen with me as well."

"Ahh," he said, immediately understanding, "you are ready to take your revenge." She was proud, and pride was something he well understood. He favored her with a faint smile.

"Do you not wish to take *your* revenge too, my lord? How many mamas of more modest heiresses shooed their daughters out of your path with no regard for your exemplary family, because of your bare purse?"

"I am not certain I am comfortable that you understand me so well, so quickly," the duke said to her candidly.

She blushed at his remark, but replied spiritedly, "If our marriage is to be a successful venture, my lord, I must certainly understand you, and you me."

"How old are you?" he asked her.

"You don't know? I am seventeen. I will be eighteen on the ninth of December. How old did you think I was?" It suddenly occurred to her that they really didn't know anything at all about each other. *Nothing.* Their match had been made for other reasons. She began to worry her lower lip with her teeth.

Quinton Hunter was equally astounded by the reality that he knew naught about this girl except that she was rich. And, of course, there was the gossip about her mother. "Seventeen is a fine age to become a wife," he said slowly. "I was thirty-one this April third past, Allegra. I suppose that seems very old for you."

"You are not as old as my father," she replied frankly. "I think a husband should be older than a wife."

He laughed aloud, and she saw a flash of white teeth. "I suppose I deserved that," he responded.

"You are even more handsome when you laugh," Allegra noted.

"So you think me handsome, do you?" He chuckled. "You are very beautiful, but then, of course, you know that. Beautiful *and* rich were all the congratulations I heard last night."

"The women were confined to: 'A *duke! A duke, my dear!*'" She laughed. "Please tell me we do not have to live in London, my lord. I really do not enjoy this world that is so regulated and rigid. At least in the country we will be accepted as a plain married couple, and not some rule by which all other heiresses and poor, but noble gentlemen are to be judged by in future seasons."

"I thought you wished to take your revenge, Allegra. You must become a famous hostess giving outrageous balls, and other entertainments. You must run up enormous debts in the best gambling halls like the Duchess of Devonshire. You must set the fashion. You cannot do it by living an anonymous existence in the country."

"No, thank you," Allegra said. "I shall have my own back in the next few weeks on the silly chits who have snubbed me. If the kind of lady you describe is the kind of lady you want to wed, then I am not that lady, my lord. I am appalled at the amount of money my papa has expended in just this one season on Sirena and me. Our weddings will cost a fortune. Invested, that money would have yielded a handsome profit. Now it is all gone. As for gambling, I am as opposed to it as are you. Another waste of both time and good coin."

"How do you invest your monies?" he asked her, curious.

"In foreign trade mostly," Allegra told him. "I also own a little spinning mill in Yorkshire that makes thread, and interest in several wagon way routes. I have the controlling interest in one route that is entirely built with cast iron rails."

"It is amazing that a young girl as yourself should find interest in such matters," the duke remarked. "Most girls spend their time at less rigorous pursuits."

"Why?" Allegra demanded. "Women have intellects as well as men. If they are educated, they are capable of almost anything," she told him. "Education is the key to everything. I intend to see that our daughters, as well as our sons, are educated to the utmost."

"You say women are capable of *almost* anything," he replied.

"I don't think I should like to be a member of the local fire brigade," Allegra answered him with a chuckle.

The duke's borrowed landau had now turned into the park where they joined the throng of other carriages parading through the greensward this June afternoon. There were also a number of ladies and gentlemen riding upon beautiful horses. Allegra leaned back and feigned boredom. There was that appalling Lady Hackney and her buck-toothed daughter, Lavinia. She ignored their desperate attempts to catch her eye.

"Nicely done," the duke murmured. He reached for

her little hand, and raising it to his lips, kissed it as another carriage carrying the Countess of Brotherton and her daughter passed by. The Brotherton girl's dowry had been generous, but not showy. Her mama had made a great point of seeing her darling daughter was allowed nowhere near the poverty-stricken Duke of Sedgwick. He had found himself greatly offended even though he knew better. The girl would have to come back next season as she had failed in the husband hunt this year. And her papa would have to increase her dowry, for she wasn't the prettiest of creatures.

"Sedgwick!" A voice familiar to them both pierced the air. "Stop at once! I want to join you!" Lady Bellingham's small carriage drew up next to theirs, and its occupant, with help, transferred herself from it to the duke's landau, giving her coachmen instructions to follow behind.

"Good afternoon, Aunt," Quinton Hunter said. He leaned forward and kissed her cheek.

"Good afternoon, Lady Bellingham," Allegra said. *Aunt?*

"Your fiancé's mama and I were first cousins," Lady Bellingham explained. "Now, when is the wedding to be, my dears?"

"Madame, we have not yet had time to consider a date," Allegra said.

"Why not?" demanded Lady Bellingham.

"This is the first time we have been alone together, Aunt, since last night's festivities and announcement," the duke spoke up.

"Well, you had best proclaim a date within the week, or else the gossips will be saying that one of you has cried off. I shall not have the match of the decade ruined by idle gossip!" Lady Bellingham said.

"It will be sometime in the autumn," Allegra responded. "I plan to spend the summer at Hunter's Lair overseeing the renovations needed. Papa is sending an architect down next week."

"You are not being married before the season ends? You are not being married in London?" Lady Bellingham was shocked.

"There isn't enough time," Allegra explained.

"No," the older woman said thoughtfully. "I suppose there really isn't, for your wedding must be a glorious and most fashionable event, my dears. Still, Allegra, you cannot marry the Duke of Sedgwick in a country church. You *must* come back to London for your wedding. The king and the queen will expect to attend, as will Prinny. Please remember Quinton's bloodline, Allegra. You shall be wed on October fifth at St. George's in Hanover Square," she decided for them. "I shall speak to the rector myself this very day." Lady Bellingham smiled. "*There,* now it is all settled." She waved at her coachman, and said, "Sedgwick, tell your man to pull over. I am disembarking now into my own vehicle."

"October is a beautiful month," Allegra said slowly when Lady Bellingham had left them alone again. "Our little church at Morgan Court is especially lovely then." She sighed. "But your aunt is right, my lord. Your family is of great importance. We should be married in London."

He was touched by her care of him, and found himself saying, "If you truly wish to be married in your own country church, Allegra, then that is where we will wed."

"No, it shall be as Lady Bellingham has decreed, my lord. I will not have it said that Lord Morgan's daughter had no care for her husband's family reputation. We shall marry with pomp, and only the crème de la crème among the ten thousand shall be invited. Papa's secretary, Charles Trent, will decide along with my aunt. Those who are not included will prefer to be out of town that day." She chuckled. "It shall, however, be the last time we are seen in London for quite some while. We have a duty to perform. Our nursery must be filled as promptly as is possible."

"My dear," the duke said with a smile, "you astound me with your practical nature and sensible ways. As you know I do not believe in love, Allegra, but I do think I am going to like you very much."

"And as long as you allow me my own way, my lord, I shall like you in return," she replied pertly, a small smile touching her lips.

Quinton Hunter burst out laughing. He did not understand why such good fortune suddenly smiled upon him, but it certainly had. His bride-to-be was a delight despite her less than noble background. He had dreaded coming to London, certain he would not succeed; certain that if he did he would be saddled with some simpering and brainless girl who would be frightened of him and bore him to tears within six months. Allegra was a refreshing surprise. Oh, she was going to have to learn to not say aloud everything that she was thinking; and her habit of involving herself in business ventures would, of course, have to cease. But she had definite possibilities, and with the proper training would make an excellent Duchess of Sedgwick. Her hand on his sleeve brought him back to reality. His gaze followed her direction, and he bowed from the waist to Prinny and Mr. Brummell as they passed by.

"Thank you," he said to her.

"Just because we are not going to live in London doesn't mean we should give up our social contacts, my lord," Allegra told him. "My papa says you never know when you will need a favor, *or can do one to your own advantage.*"

"Your papa is very wise," the duke answered her.

"Do you like him? Oh, I hope you will like each other," Allegra said, suddenly very much the young girl again. "I love Papa more than anyone else upon this earth, my lord."

"Your papa and I get on very well, and will continue to do so, I promise you, Allegra. Now, did we not agree earlier that you would address me by my Christian name?"

"Yes, Quinton, we did," she responded, "but you are so impressive a gentleman that I sometimes forget I now have that privilege. Ohh, look! Here comes that dreadful Lord Mountiner, and his daughter. Shall we snub them?" Her violet eyes were dancing wickedly, but then she amended, "Or am I being too awful and not a proper duchess?"

He laughed. "You are very fierce, my dear, but I am of a mind to indulge you in this particular piece of naughtiness as I dislike the family heartily. They own the London house that once belonged to my family and have left our coat of arms over the door rather than remove it, which they should have. It seems to please them to be able to brag they possess Sedgwick House."

The landau's horses trotted past the large and rather ornate coach belonging to Lord Mountiner as the duke and Allegra deliberately turned their heads away from the coach's occupants. The two vehicles passed so closely that Lord Mountiner's outrage could be heard even as his daughter said in her high-pitched and nasal voice, "Oh, Papa, they are snubbing us! How embarrassing! Take me home!"

"That was quite successful," Allegra said when they

had left the other carriage in their wake. "Let that be a lesson to all who were unkind to both of us this season."

The rest of their promenade proved uneventful. The landau drove beneath the trees while they bowed and waved to their friends as they passed by. Some were in carriages. Others were riding fine horseflesh. All in all Allegra considered it a most successful outing when they returned to Berkley Square, and the landau drew up before her father's house. A footman hurried to help her out of the vehicle.

"Will you come in and have tea?" she asked the duke.

"Not today, my dear," he told her. "Will I see you tonight?"

"There is no event planned," she said. "I think I shall take the opportunity to go to bed early."

"Will you dream of me?" he teased her.

"I rarely, if ever, dream," Allegra responded, but then she added, "but if I did dream, Quinton, I am certain it would be of you."

He laughed. "Well done, my dear Allegra," he responded. Then he kissed her hand. "I shall call upon you tomorrow."

"Come for luncheon," she replied.

He bowed, and then the landau was gone off down the street and out of the square, the matched bays with the blond tails trotting quite smartly.

Entering the house she found Sirena and Ocky in the garden salon. "Lady Bellingham has set our wedding date for October fifth," she announced to them. "If you are with child by then, Sirena, you must not show it for I will have no one else but you attending me. Imagine the gossip if I postponed my wedding until you were able to attend me."

"Ohh, Allegra, you mustn't do such a thing," Sirena said, sounding genuinely distressed. "It would be too shocking to even consider."

Allegra laughed. "Then be certain you can accommodate me, cousin," she said with a wicked wink at Viscount Pickford.

"We are going to be neighbors," Sirena said happily. "Ocky's home"—she blushed—"his papa's home, I mean, is in Hereford, near Hunter's Lair. It is called Rose Hall. Isn't that a lovely name, Rose Hall?"

"Have you decided where to go for your wedding trip?" Allegra inquired curiously.

"We are going to the sea," the viscount said. "I have cousins with a cottage in Devon. They will be in Kent then at their home, and so they have given us the cottage for as long as we want it. It comes fully staffed. Have you and Quinton discussed your trip, Miss Morgan?"

"We didn't even get around to discussing the wedding date." Allegra chuckled. "Lady Bellingham descended upon us like a storm, and decided it all for us. Perhaps tomorrow when Quinton comes to luncheon we will consider it." Then she patted the viscount upon the arm. "You are marrying my favorite cousin, Ocky. I do think it would be permissible for you to call me by my Christian name." Then with a smile at them, she departed the garden salon, hurrying upstairs.

Honor brought her mistress her supper upon a tray. Allegra wanted nothing more than to recover from the excitement of the last few days. Her father joined her after he and her aunt had dined with Sirena and Ocky.

"Are you all right, my child?" Lord Morgan asked his daughter.

"Just tired, Papa," she responded with a small yawn.

"Are you happy?" he said.

Allegra thought a moment, then answered, "I am not unhappy, Papa. The duke is a pleasant and most agreeable fellow. I am very anxious to see Hunter's Lair." She yawned again.

"It is not as large as Morgan Court, my dear, but its lineage is most impressive. And, of course, it has more lands than the court," her father answered. "I am going to leave my home to your second son, Allegra. I hope you will approve."

"I am not yet wed, Papa," she replied, "and you already have me producing two sons. What of my daughters?"

"The daughters of a duke with Quinton Hunter's bloodline, and the dowries you will be able to give them, will have no difficulties in finding mates. It is the sons who come after the first son who need to find a place in this world. Therefore your second son shall have Morgan Court when I die one day. If there are other boys, we shall manage to provide for them, I promise you, my child."

"What if you remarry, Papa? Would you dispossess your widow?"

"Allegra . . . ," he began, and then stopped.

"You love my aunt, Papa." She took his hand in hers. "She has been widowed for several years now. There is nothing to prevent you from asking her to be your wife. Both Sirena and I fully approve, Papa," Allegra said quietly.

"Do you?" he replied, his look suddenly amused.

"We do, Papa," Allegra told him seriously, releasing the hand.

"And do you think your aunt would accept an offer of marriage from me? We have been good friends for many years. Perhaps that is all she is willing to give of herself. I should dislike to spoil the friendship I have with Olympia."

"You will never know, Papa, unless you ask her," Allegra told him wisely. "I am virtually gone from Morgan Court. Do you really think my aunt would prefer the little dower house at Rowley to being the undisputed mistress of Morgan Court? Sirena and I have often spoken on it. We want you happy together."

"But what if she says *no* to me, my child?" he worried.

"Is *no* such a terrible word, Papa?" Allegra replied.

"As I recall you seemed to think so when you were a little girl," her father teased her. He arose from her bedside where he had been sitting. "Get your rest now, Allegra. Sirena's wedding is but nine days away, and then we shall return home."

"You will ask Aunt Olympia before we leave London?" she queried him.

"I will think on it, Allegra," and bending, he gave her a kiss upon her forehead. Then he left the room.

His daughter's words had made a strong impression upon Septimius Morgan. While he was delighted with his daughter's engagement, and her bright future, the thought of spending the rest of his life alone had been a bleak one. Was Allegra right? Would Olympia accept an offer of marriage from him? Entering his library he found the object of his thoughts sitting by the fire. She looked up and smiled.

"I hope you do not mind my being here, Septimius. Sirena and her beloved are billing and cooing in the salon. I very much felt like a fifth wheel, I fear."

"Shall I pour you a sherry?" he asked her, and when she nodded he filled two glasses upon the tray and brought her one. Then he sat in the tapestried backed chair opposite her. "We shall both soon be alone,

Olympia," he remarked tentatively. "Morgan Court is such a large place for just one man, and the dower house at Rowley is much too small."

"Yes, it is," she replied.

"I should not like to spoil our friendship, Olympia, but perhaps we might take a suggestion that Allegra assures me both she and Sirena approve. Perhaps we should marry."

"To whom?" Lady Abbott asked him, but her heart was fluttering.

"To each other, my dearest Olympia," he said, laughing. Then he slipped from his chair, and knelt beside her. "Will you marry me, Olympia? Will you make me the happiest of men so we may spend our twilight years together? I realize that becoming Lady Morgan is a bit of a step-down from Dowager Marchioness of Rowley, but I hope you will consider it." He looked hopefully up at her.

Her hand had gone to her mouth to stifle her cry at his proposal. Her plump and pretty features were rosy with both her surprise, and her pleasure. Finally, her hand dropped away, and she said, "I could only marry a man who loved me, Septimius."

He stood, and taking her hands in his drew her up so they were facing each other. "But I do love you, Olympia. I believe I always have, though I dared not voice such sentiments while you were yet married to another. You are everything that your sister was not. Kind and wise and gentle. If you do not want to remarry, I will understand. I only beg you not to allow it to spoil our friendship."

Olympia Abbott stood on her toes, and kissed Lord Morgan's lips softly. "Of course I will marry you, Septimius," she said. "I never had any intention of allowing some other woman to snap you up now that Allegra is going to be leaving you."

"We will wed before Allegra's marriage," he said firmly.

"*When?*" she asked him, rather delighted at his eagerness.

"The day after Sirena and young Pickford are wed," he said with a chuckle. "That way both our girls will be able to attend us. Then Sirena and Ocky will depart on their wedding trip. You will come home with Allegra and me. We'll go to Rowley to get your possessions after Allegra is settled at Hunter's Lair. Then, you and I shall have the entire summer to ourselves. Next winter I shall take you to Italy." He gave her a hearty kiss. "Italy is very romantic, Olympia."

Lady Abbott actually blushed. "Ohh, Septimius," she said softly. "I should very much like to see Italy."

"We'll spend the winter in a villa outside of Naples," he promised her, "and then in the spring we shall go to Rome and to Venice."

"I have never been outside of England," she told him, and then her face darkened. "But, Septimius, what if we should meet my sister and her husband? Perhaps we should not go to Italy."

"Mayhap, my dear, we should seek out Pandora and her count," Lord Morgan said.

"Ohh, no!" she cried. "Pandora behaved dreadfully running away and leaving you to deal with the scandal; but I know my sister. It doesn't matter how many years have passed, or that she is happily remarried. She would be furious to learn you took another wife, and that your second wife was her sister!"

"She will know eventually," he said. "Besides, I do not care what Pandora thinks if you do not care, my dearest. I want you to have a wedding trip. France is certainly no place for decent people to go today."

"Well," Lady Abbott considered, "I should like to see Italy."

"Then it is settled," he responded, and gave her another kiss.

They were unable to keep their secret from their daughters, however. One look at Lady Abbott the next morning set the two young women shrieking with glee. They danced about the older woman until she finally ordered them to behave.

"He has asked you, hasn't he?" Allegra said. "Ohh, I am so glad! Sirena and I have wanted it forever!"

"Now we are truly sisters!" Sirena said laughing, and hugging her mother.

"When is the wedding?" Allegra demanded.

"I want to be there," Sirena remarked.

"It must remain a secret from everyone else," Lady Abbott pleaded. "I want you to have your day, Sirena."

"Ohh, Mama, I shall have it no matter," the young girl said. "Now, when is the wedding? Oh, do tell us, Mama!"

"We shall wed quietly the day after your wedding, Sirena," her mother responded. "*And I mean it.* No one else is to know until the day you and Ocky marry. Especially your brother and his wife. Charlotte will, of course, be delighted to be rid of both of us, but I don't want her going about London gossiping. Do you both understand me, girls? *This is a secret.*"

"Yes, Mama. But may I tell Ocky?" Sirena asked.

"Yes, Aunt," Allegra said.

"You may tell your husbands-to-be," Lady Abbott said, "but you must caution them to silence."

"We will!" the two girls chorused.

Sirena's wedding day drew near. She and Viscount Pickford were to marry at St. George's in Hanover Square, the most fashionable church in London. It would not be a large wedding for Sirena did not want a large wedding. Mostly it would be family and several family servants. They would be married at ten o'clock in the morning, for fashionable marriages were celebrated between the hours of eight o'clock in the morning and twelve noon. A wedding breakfast with a bride's cake would be served at Lord Morgan's home after the ceremony. Then Sirena and Ocky would spend the night at Pickford House, several squares over from Berkley Square; the viscount's seasonal guests having removed themselves from the residence earlier.

The Earl of Pickford arrived in London several days before the wedding to meet his prospective daughter-in-law. He was a slender gentleman with a headful of snow-white hair, and bright blue eyes that his eldest son had inherited. He was immediately taken by the sweet and gentle Lady Sirena Abbott. He had known her breeding, of course, for his son had asked his permission of his father before tendering a proposal. But far too often these overbred girls made bad wives. This girl, he quickly saw, loved his son. Not only that, she had character and manners. He was now twice as pleased as he had been earlier.

"After your wedding trip, you'll come home to Pickford?" the earl asked Ocky. "Sirena will want to see what you will inherit one day. She must grow familiar with her new home. You will be a most welcome addition to the family, my dear," he told her.

"Oh, thank you, my lord," Sirena answered him. Then she shyly kissed his cheek.

The season was winding down. Most of the young women who had not found husbands, or who were planning summer weddings, had left London with their families. Sirena's wedding day was upon them. Allegra's childhood friend, Rupert Tanner, had withdrawn several days earlier to return home. The duke had been invited to stay at Lord Morgan's house until he departed London in a few days' time.

They awoke to a perfect June morning. The sky was a vivid blue with not a cloud in it. The sun shone brightly. In Lord Morgan's garden the Damascus roses bloomed in profusion, and perfumed the air. The servants hurried upstairs with trays for the bedchambers, for the dining room was being prepared for the wedding breakfast after the ten o'clock ceremony.

Sirena could scarce contain her excitement. She was a very beautiful bride in an elegantly simple gown of ivory striped silk with a scooped neckline and little puffed sleeves. The gown was tied beneath the waist with a silver ribbon, and there were tiny silver bows on each sleeve as well as at the tips of her shoes. A delicate lace shawl was draped about her shoulders. Her golden blond hair was affixed into a chignon at the nape of her neck, two ringlets falling to her right. Upon her head was another swath of lace that fell to the floor and was affixed with a small wreath of white roses.

"You are the perfect bride," Allegra told her cousin. "I have never seen you look so gorgeous, Sirena."

Lady Abbott began to sniffle softly. "She is right. I cannot believe that my baby is getting married. If only your papa were here to see it, my darling. He would be so proud at how well you have done." Then she turned to her niece. "You are lovely, too, Allegra."

"Thank you, Aunt. Now tell us before we go down to meet the others. When are you going to reveal *your* little secret?" Allegra said.

"Your papa and I shall make our announcement as the wedding breakfast comes to a close," Lady Abbott answered.

"From that moment on I shall refer to you as *Aunt Mama*," Allegra said with a smile.

"You are truly content that I will marry your papa, my dear?" Lady Abbott said. She could still not believe her good fortune.

"Aunt, you have been the mother I never remember having," Allegra said generously. "I welcome you with all my heart!" Then she kissed Lady Abbott on both cheeks, giving her a warm hug as she did so.

There was a knock upon the door, and Lord Morgan popped his head in saying, "My dears, it is time we left for the church. You surely do not want to frighten your bridegroom, Sirena, by being late."

St. George's on Hanover Square wasn't a great distance from Lord Morgan's house on Berkley Square. They rode in an open carriage, meeting Sirena's elder brother at the church. The Marquis of Rowley would give his sister away. His wife was already seated in the first pew as Lord Morgan escorted Lady Abbott into the building. The older woman glared at the younger until she gave way, moving down the pew to allow the bride's mother and Lord Morgan to be seated.

On the other side of the aisle were the groom's father, the widowed Earl of Pickford, with his sister, Lady Carstairs, and her husband. Behind them sat the two younger Carstairs, Ocky's first cousins, the Earl of Aston, Lord Walworth, with their own betrothed wives. In the third pew on the groom's side sat his longtime valet, Wiggins. In the second pew on the bride's side sat Lord and Lady Bellingham with Charles Trent, and behind them the two serving women, Damaris and Honor.

St. George's was the most fashionable church in the city in which to be wed. It was not one of London's ancient churches, having been built between the years 1721 and 1724. Its beautiful and graceful portico with its six soaring pillars was the first ever built for a London church. There were elegant cast iron dogs flanking the main door. The east window of the church contained sixteenth-century stained glass rescued from a church destroyed during the Civil War in England, almost one hundred and fifty years earlier. The altar painting had been fashioned by Sir James Thornhill, and was entitled *The Last Supper*.

To the soft strains of a Bach melody Allegra walked up the church's main aisle, a nosegay of white roses and purple stock in her gloved hands. Behind her she could hear Sirena and her brother coming along. At the altar Viscount Pickford stood with the Duke of Sedgwick, who was to be his witness. The rector of the church smiled perfunctorily as the young couple came before him. He had already performed fourteen weddings this month and had another twenty-five to celebrate before June was out. It was his busiest time in a successful season.

"Dearly beloved," he began.

Allegra looked about her discreetly. It was a beautiful church, but she regretted that she could not be wed in her own church come October. She listened intently to the service. *With my body I thee worship*. A delicate blush suffused her features as she remembered Quinton's kisses the night of her ball. They had not kissed since. How did a man worship you with his body, she wondered? Then she was drawn back from her thoughts as Sirena pushed her own bouquet of white roses, green ivy, and silver ribbons at Allegra to hold while she knelt at the altar rail.

Allegra put her own thoughts aside, and concentrated on the wedding ceremony. When the church's rector pronounced her cousin and Viscount Pickford man and wife she blushed again as the bride and groom kissed most enthusiastically before their guests. Her eyes met those of Quinton Hunter. His demeanor was serious, and to her relief not teasing. Would he kiss her as warmly once they were wed?

Sirena and Ocky hurried from the church. They were both laughing happily, and had eyes only for each other. The duke tucked Allegra's hand into his arm, and escorted her down the steps. The bride and groom were already driving off. The twenty guests followed behind them back to Lord Morgan's house in their own coaches and carriages where the wedding breakfast was awaiting them.

Lord Morgan's French chef had prepared a delicious meal which the servants passed around the dining table. There were eggs, poached in heavy cream, and fine Madeira sherry. There were pink country ham, rashers of bacon, a platter of lamb chops, and one of poached salmon in a dill sauce with carved lemons decorating its silver server. There were freshly baked breads, and little rolls with sesamed tops. There were several cheeses: a wheel of Brie from France, another wheel of sharp English Cheddar, and a nutty flavored cheese imported from Switzerland, which Allegra particularly favored, that had holes in it. There was a bowl filled with fresh fruit: sectioned oranges from Spain, slices of pineapple and yellow banana. There was a crystal bowl of fresh strawberries, and next to it a dish of heavy, clotted cream. A delicate wine was served throughout the meal until the bride's cake with its spun sugar icing and decorations was brought forth. Then the champagne was brought out, and several toasts were drunk to Sirena and Ocky.

The bride shortly afterward slipped from the dining room, followed by her cousin. Upstairs her maid, Damaris, was waiting to help her from her wedding clothes, and into her traveling outfit, although Sirena was traveling no farther than her father-in-law's town house today.

"Mama and Uncle have not yet announced their surprise," Sirena said to her cousin. "You don't think they have changed their minds?"

Allegra shook her head. "Papa said they would make the announcement before you leave."

"I can't wait to see the look on Charlotte's face," Sirena replied with a giggle. "She will be torn between relief and horror that Mama should remarry at *her time of life*, which is how she will put it, I am quite certain."

"How old is Aunt Mama?" Allegra asked her cousin.

"She is surely past forty," Sirena said. "She married Papa at fifteen, and had my brother when she was sixteen. Gussie is twenty-five, I know, so Mama must be past forty."

"She is forty-one," Allegra said with a smile. Sirena had never been particularly good with her sums.

"There, my ladies, you're ready," Damaris said to her mistress. Then she began to weep. "I can't believe yer a married woman," she sniffled, wiping her eyes with her apron. "It just seems like yesterday you come out of the nursery a young lass put in my care."

"Now, Damaris." Sirena hugged her maid. "You'll still be with me, and I've seen the looks you and Ocky's valet have been giving each other. You'll soon be a married lady yourself, and what shall I ever do if you leave me?"

"No man could take me away from you, my lady!" Damaris declared stoutly. "Now, you and Miss Allegra run back downstairs to yer guests. I'll be waiting for you at Pickford House." She curtsied.

Sirena, looking enchanting in a white muslin gown decorated with pink silk ribbons and a charming straw bonnet, also with pink ribbons, set over her blond curls, gave her maid a smile. Then hand in hand with Allegra she descended the stairs of the house into its circular central foyer where her husband and her guests were assembled waiting for her. She went immediately to her mother and her uncle.

Hugging them Sirena whispered, "Tell them now, *please*."

Putting his arm about both Allegra and Sirena, Lord Morgan said in a loud voice, "This has been a most wonderful day for us all. I have seen my dearest niece successfully married off. My beloved daughter will marry her duke on October fifth. Tomorrow, however, shall be an equally happy day, for tomorrow I will marry the woman who has done me the honor of agreeing to become my wife, Lady Olympia Abbott. As you have all wished Sirena and Ocky happy, I hope you will wish us the same as well," Lord Morgan concluded.

"Well, I'll be damned," the Marquess of Rowley said, totally and utterly surprised by his uncle's declaration. Then he reached out, and shook Lord Morgan's hand. "You have my blessing, sir, although you certainly don't need it." Grinning, he kissed his mother heartily. "And you, madame, have my best wishes. Just when I thought you could no longer surprise me, Mama, you have gone and done it."

"Then you do not mind, Gussie?" she said, a trifle nervously.

"No, Mama, I do not mind in the least," he responded, smiling even more broadly.

The other guests crowded about the couple offering their congratulations and good wishes. It was at that very moment in the crush that Sirena and Viscount Pickford chose to make their escape. Hand in hand, they left through the open door of the house, down the marble steps, and into their carriage. When their absence was finally realized, there was much good-natured laughter, and the guests were invited into the main salon of the house to partake of another champagne toast, this one to the next soon-to-be-married pair.

"And another family wedding tomorrow!" Lady Bellingham exclaimed. "My dear Olympia, what a naughty puss you have been keeping such a wonderful secret." She tapped Lady Abbott with her fan, giving her an arch look. "Of course it is the perfect match for you. I imagine your son and daughter-in-law are delighted for you." She turned her gaze to Allegra. "And you, miss, what think you of this turn of events?"

"Sirena and I have been trying to get Papa and Aunt Mama together ever since she came out of mourning," Allegra announced candidly.

"Ha! Ha! Ha! Have you indeed, my gel? Well, good for you!" Lady Bellingham said. "Not a selfish bone in her body, Quinton. You have chosen a fine gel to wife. I shall certainly look forward to returning to London in the autumn for your wedding. Even Bellingham has agreed to give up a few days of his hunting for such an event, haven't you, husband?"

"Indeed, yes, m'dear," Lord Bellingham agreed with a broad wink at the assembled company. "If it pleases you, it pleases me." He took a long sip of his champagne.

"Well I for one am completely astounded that dear Mama would marry again at her time of life," Charlotte said. "Gussie and I have suddenly become quite bereft of family, I fear." She sipped her champagne.

Allegra giggled behind her hand, but when Charlotte glared at her she said bluntly, "Sirena said you would say that, madame. As for being *bereft*, I suspect you are more relieved to have Aunt Mama and my cousin gone

from Rowley. You will have Gussie all to yourself now."
She smiled sweetly at the Marchioness of Rowley.

"Allegra," her cousin the marquess said chidingly, but
his mouth twitched with amusement. "You must behave yourself, and practice more tact now that you are
to become a duchess."

"Oh, Gussie, I fear I shall never become *that* proper,
and poor Quinton knows it. Do you not, my lord?" She
looked to him.

"It will take time, I see, but I believe that eventually I
can persuade Allegra to the advantages of diplomacy,
sir," he said to the Marquess of Rowley.

"That will be a battle worth observing," Lady
Bellingham murmured softly, and her husband chuckled at her words.

The remainder of the guests made their farewells. It
had been a most satisfying and exciting morning to have
been party to, and privy to, they all agreed. The Earl of
Aston and Lord Walworth had both asked the duke to
stand up with them during their upcoming nuptials.
Now both of their fiancées made certain to speak with
Allegra before they left.

"You will come to the wedding with the duke?" both
young ladies asked. "Mama will see you receive an invitation."

"I shall be pleased to accept," Allegra responded as
she waved them both off. How odd to have friends who
were girls, she thought. The only girl who had ever been
her friend was Sirena. What was more, she liked Lady
Eunice Tarleton and Caroline Bellingham. I really am
growing up, she considered to herself.

"We will take the air in the garden," the duke said.
They were now alone. Her father and Lady Abbott had
disappeared.

Allegra slipped her hand through his arm. "The poor

old house feels quite sad," she sagely noted. "Everything is coming to an end. The season is over. Sirena and Ocky are married. Our friends are all gone from London. Nothing will ever be the same again, will it?"

"No," he agreed, "but that is life, Allegra. The world changes about us constantly for good, or for ill."

They moved out into the garden. The afternoon was warm for June. The roses perfumed the air, and there was barely the hint of a breeze.

"Perhaps the world does change with each passing minute," Allegra said, "but I have never before felt it as strongly as I do today." She sighed a long and wistful sigh. "My life has, despite my mother's absence, charted a steady course, and has not deviated. I was raised and educated at Morgan Court. My best, my only friend until a few months ago, was my cousin, Sirena. The years have been a round of passing seasons marked by holidays, family, and schooling. It has always been the same."

"What of your brother?" he asked her. She had never really spoken of her elder sibling.

A look of sorrow passed over Allegra's beautiful face. "Ahh, yes," she said. "My world did change then, didn't it? I had put it from my mind for it is too painful to speak on, Quinton."

"What happened?" he gently probed as he drew her down in the shade of an apple tree to a marble bench. "I only know that he is dead."

"James Lucian—we never for some reason called him anything other than his whole name—died in France. He was affianced to the daughter of the Comte d'Aumont. Because of the political situation it was decided he would marry immediately and bring his bride back to England," Allegra explained. "While he was there the family was arrested, betrayed by someone before

James Lucian could wed his sweetheart. He would not leave Célestine. The authorities, if you can call that rabble in France by such a name, offered my brother his freedom as he stood upon the scaffold with her. She begged him to go, but he would not. James Lucian, it was said, knelt before his affianced, speaking gently to her of their eternal life together even as the guillotine fell. Her head rolled into the basket before him; and he was spattered with her blood. He then arose, and without assistance, knelt for his own execution." Her eyes were bright with unshed tears.

Shocked by her recitation the duke said, "He was a very brave man, your brother." His arm went about her to comfort her.

Allegra shook off the arm. "My brother was a fool!" she cried, and now the tears ran down her face. "He wasted his life for what? *For love!* You say, my lord, that you shall never love me, for you would not commit the mistakes of your antecedents. Well, I shall not love you either, for love brings nothing to anyone but pain. But we shall have a good marriage for it shall be based upon sensible principles. Respect for one another and enough wealth to sustain us. And whatever love either of us can muster we shall lavish upon our children. The love of a parent for its child seems to be the only love that does not hurt."

He wiped her tears away with his own linen handkerchief, but said nothing more. What could he possibly say that would comfort her? It was obvious that she had loved her brother greatly, and his death, three years before, had hurt her terribly. Finally he spoke. "Is the loss of your brother the reason you learned how to manage your own funds?"

"Oh, no," Allegra told him. "I have been interested in Papa's businesses ever since I was a little girl. James Lucian and I used to compete to see who could manage the most successful ventures. We were fairly evenly matched, although I think I probably had the cooler head. My brother always allowed his emotions to carry him away. To his own detriment in the end," she finished.

"When will you come to Hunter's Lair?" he asked, changing the subject lest she begin to cry again.

"When Papa's architect and his builder say my apartments are habitable. From all reports so far, however, I think I will be with you in just a few weeks. Do your friends live far?"

"No," he told her. "Aston's estate is just an hour away, and Dree's home, a charming little holding, less than an hour. It will please me to escort you to both weddings."

"There will be a certain amount of gossip, I fear, when I come to live at Hunter's Lair before our wedding. Will you mind?"

He laughed. "No. Will you?"

"No," she replied, and her violet eyes looked directly at him.

"We are well matched," he replied with a small smile.

"So it would appear," Allegra agreed, and then she boldly leaned over and kissed his cheek. "So it would appear, Quinton."

Chapter Six

The morning after Sirena's wedding dawned as beautiful as had the day before. Lord Morgan's wedding to Lady Abbott would take place in the main salon of his house at nine o'clock in the morning. Then, after a small repast, the family would depart for home although they had originally planned to remain for another day. The duke would come with them most of the way before turning off the main road for Hunter's Lair. Allegra was glad her father had made the decision to leave London immediately. She was anxious to get home, although it would be lonely now without Sirena to keep her company.

There was something different about Sirena this morning. She and Ocky had arrived at quarter to the hour. Her cousin had been radiant with open happiness. She and her new husband kept touching one another with both their looks and their hands. She had little time for anyone other than Ocky. Allegra found it rather disturbing, and not just a little embarrassing. She was also hurt that Sirena had so few words for her.

The minister arrived at five to the hour. Augustus Abbott escorted his mama into the salon. She was wearing a sky blue brocaded gown. Her dark blond hair was piled upon her head and a single curl fell over her left shoulder. There was a tiny pouf of lace netting atop her head. She carried a nosegay of pink roses tied with blue and silver ribbons. Her look was one of complete happiness as she was led up to join Lord Morgan, who was quite elegant in a dark blue coat and breeches. The ceremony began.

Allegra looked about her. The guests were few: Lord and Lady Bellingham, who would sign the marriage register as witnesses, Sirena and Ocky, Lady Charlotte and Gussie, and the duke. Again she thought her cousin looked so very happy. Aunt Mama looked happy, too, as did their gentlemen. They loved one another. Even Charlotte Abbott had a soft smile upon her face, her gloved hand tucked into her husband's, as she watched her mother-in-law taking a second husband. Allegra would have sworn that Lady Bellingham had a tear in her eye, for she kept dabbing at it with her lawn handkerchief. What was the matter with them? Surely they weren't all in love? Love was such a nebulous emotion, and not at all reliable. Certainly Papa of all people knew that.

The ceremony concluded. To Allegra's surprise her father took his new wife into his arms, kissing her soundly. The new Lady Morgan blushed most becomingly as her guests clapped their approval. Allegra quickly stepped up to the newlyweds, and kissed her stepmother first and then her father.

"You know I wish you both happy," she said sincerely.

"Ohh, my dear," Olympia Morgan said, "I have always thought of you as my own child, and now you are!" She kissed Allegra back.

They repaired to the dining room where the chef had set out a lovely wedding breakfast. This morning he offered them pieces of chicken in a wine and cream sauce that he wrapped in very thin rounds of cooked dough he called crepes. There were shirred eggs, a country ham, rashers of bacon, a platter with thin slices of trout sprinkled lavishly with fresh dill and slices of lemon. There were new baby lettuces, raw, which Allegra found most tasty, as well as breads warm from the ovens. When all of this had been cleared away, strawberries with clotted cream brought up from Devon were served along with a small wedding cake iced in sugar and butter and filled with dried fruits. Only champagne was served during the entire breakfast.

After the meal with its toasts to Lord and Lady Morgan, the guests departed—Sirena and Ocky upon their wedding trip, Lord and Lady Bellingham to their country house in Oxford. The Marquess and Marchioness of Rowley left for their estate. Now it was their turn. Allegra chose not to ride in the coach with her father and stepmother.

"They are so embarrassing, very like Sirena and Ocky," she murmured to the duke. "I feel very much the third wheel."

"You are," he told her. "Your father and his wife are in love, as are Sirena and Ocky."

"*Love!*" Allegra scoffed. "I cannot believe such a thing of Papa. Surely my mama cured him of that foolish emotion."

"I think not," Quinton Hunter said.

"Then it is fortunate I am coming to Hunter's Lair shortly," Allegra said. "I do not believe I could bear a summer of their billing and cooing. Neither of them is in the first flush of youth, sir."

He laughed. "Love, I have been told, makes no exceptions for age or infirmity, my dear," the duke answered her. "Your father and his new wife have the best of love, for they were friends first. And then, too, your stepmother is a woman of character. She would never have even considered the path your mama took. *Nor would you,*" he concluded.

"How can you be certain?" she asked him. She had worried silently to herself that something like that might happen to her one day.

"Because, Allegra, you are also a woman of character," the duke told her. "I should not take you for my wife, fortune or no, did I believe otherwise. My family has never in its history had any scandal attached to their name. Nor would I bring shame upon them. Your wealth was the primary factor in my decision to make you my wife; but your reputation was equally important to me. Despite your friendship with young Tanner, I know you to be a virgin of good repute."

They had just left the city behind. Her gelding shied as a cart passed too close, but Allegra held him firm even as she felt her cheeks grow warm. He had made her feel almost like an item to be inspected and bought, which was after all what the duke had done. A tiny curl of resentment brushed at her, but she pushed it away. She had made the perfect alliance, and had departed London in triumph. Hers was the match of the season. The match of the decade, or so Lady Bellingham had crowed to her.

"You are uncomfortable with my blunt speech," he said, noting her expression.

"A bit," she admitted. "Frankness does not disturb me, Quinton, but I have never before found myself the subject of such talk."

He was amused, but held his peace. She was candid, but at the same time she was quite prudish. He had thought he wouldn't care, but now he realized a girl as young and as innocent as Allegra was going to find the conjugal act quite a surprise, possibly even repellent if she were not properly prepared. While their children might not come from a grand passion, he did want Allegra to at least enjoy the sweet lust between a man and his wife. Neither of them could be so detached or indifferent to it if their marriage was to be a success. But how could he explain such things to her? He suddenly saw the wisdom in waiting several months before they married, and his future father-in-law's cunning in sending Allegra to Hunter's Lair to *oversee* its renovations. Lord Morgan obviously hoped that as they came to know each other a loving sentiment might grow between them, thus rendering their marital relations happy ones. It was the best any good father could hope for, the duke realized.

They stopped at midday beside a stream that paralleled the road. A picnic lunch packed by the London staff was now spread upon the grass by the servants, who traveled in their own coach. There was a roasted chicken, ham, bread, cheese, wine, and a large bunch of fat green grapes. They ate, and then the ladies sought privacy to relieve themselves while the gentlemen went in another direction. When they met again by the traveling coach the new Lady Morgan invited Allegra to join them, but the young girl declined.

"Thank you, Aunt Mama, but I dislike coach travel, and avoid it when I can. The day is fair and Quinton most delightful company."

They moved on again.

"You have not told me before that I am delightful company," the duke teased Allegra. "It came as quite a surprise to hear you say it."

"*I will not ride in that vehicle with them,*" Allegra said. "Do you see the looks they gave one another all during our picnic? It was so embarrassing, and is worse now than it was this morning at the house."

He laughed. "Why does it disturb you that your father and your stepmother love each other?"

"It does not *disturb* me," Allegra denied.

"It does," he countered. "And you know why, my dear. You suddenly see your papa as a man with desires and feelings that have nothing to do with you. He is in love again, and is eager to bed his wife."

She blushed scarlet. "How can you say such a thing?" she demanded of him. "They are so old! Why, Sirena told me her mother is forty-one, and I know my papa is well past fifty."

He laughed again. "Both are past the age of indiscretion, my dear, and ready for some fun. There is no crime in it."

"You speak quite knowledgeably," she accused.

"And you prate from your innocence, Allegra," he told her. "Those marital relations between your father and his wife, between any lawfully wed couple, should be pleasant, enjoyable ones even if the marriage has been arranged for other reasons. Passion can be shared, and pleasurable between friends."

"You are no longer speaking about Papa and Aunt Mama, are you, Quinton?" Allegra said softly.

"No, I am not," he admitted. "In a few months' time you and I will share those relations, Allegra. I want such passion between us to be happy for you. I do not want you resenting the children that you will bear me. Can you understand that?"

"You have not kissed me since the night of my ball," she replied. She could feel the heat in her cheeks, and wondered if she looked like a boiled beef at this point.

"Did you like being kissed?" he asked.

"You didn't do it enough for me to form an opinion," she said.

"I thought you quite opinionated on the subject the night of your ball," he reminded her. "As I recall you wanted to know if I was considered expert in such matters, and asked for references."

"I most certainly did not ask for testimonials on the subject," she huffed. "I just asked if you were considered good at kissing. It was a perfectly reasonable question considering I had never before been kissed. I don't understand why you are so put out about it."

"You mean not even the saintly Rupert Tanner kissed you, Allegra? I find that hard to believe," he said.

"Why would Rupert want to kiss me? We are friends, and why do you call him *saintly*?" she countered.

"Because I understand he is taking holy orders, and will have a living from his father's village church when the old vicar there retires," came the reply.

"How do you know that?" she demanded.

"Because he told me. Remember he was at Pickford House with us during the season. He implied that you had an informal understanding," the duke said, and there was just the hint of anger in his voice.

"*What?*" The surprise in Allegra's voice was palpable. "How dare Rupert say such a thing! It most certainly is not true."

"Then he obviously said it in an attempt to drive me off," the duke observed, his good humor restored. "And he must be a saint to have never kissed you, my dear."

Allegra kicked her horse into a canter and rode away from him. She was furious. Yes, she said she wanted to marry Rupert before she had come to London, but only in order to escape a season. Her father had put a firm stop to any such idea. There had been nothing between them at all but a shared childhood. "I shall never speak to Rupert again," she muttered to herself. "How dare he?" He dare, she realized, because they were old friends, and he thought she needed to be saved. How presumptuous of him, especially, as they had grown up together. If anyone should know her it should be Rupert.

The duke let Allegra go. It was obvious she needed to work off her temper. *She had a temper.* That was a discovery. She was a more interesting girl than he had anticipated.

They stopped that night at an excellent inn. Charles Trent had taken an entire wing of the hostelry for his master's party. He was a day ahead of them. They ate their dinner in a private dining room, although Allegra and the duke seemed to be the only ones with an appetite. And when the meal had been cleared away, her father and stepmother were suddenly filled with yawns and deep sighs.

"How can you be so sleepy after riding in a coach all day?" Allegra demanded of them. "Papa, do you not want to play a game of chess? Now that we are to get back to our regular schedule you cannot forget our nightly chess games!" She smiled at him. "Shall I have the board and pieces brought, Papa?"

"I believe, my child, that the excitement of the season has finally caught up with me, and all this good country air is making me sleepy. I think that your stepmother and I shall retire. We will play chess another night, I promise you." He arose, and held out his hand to his bride.

"Come and kiss me goodnight, Allegra," Lady Morgan said. "Did you enjoy your ride today, dearest?"

"Very much," the young girl replied. She dutifully kissed her father and her stepmother. "Good night."

When they had gone she said to the duke, "They want to make love, don't they?"

"Yes," he said, his silvery gray eyes serious.

"I cannot believe anyone that age is still interested in such things, Quinton," Allegra told him.

"Why not? I am sure he had a mistress tucked discreetly away somewhere near Morgan Court."

Allegra was silent, and then she said, "Do you have a mistress tucked away somewhere, Quinton?"

He chuckled. "My dear, do I hear a tiny bit of jealousy in your tone? No, I could not afford a mistress, but so there is no misunderstanding between us, I have also not been celibate either."

"You have visited whores?" She wasn't really shocked, just curious about that part of his life.

"I have not been able to afford whores either." He chuckled again. He brushed an errant lock of dark hair from his forehead. "Allegra, there are always women willing to give themselves for the pure joy of it. I am no satyr, but when I felt the need for passion, there was always someone to satisfy my urges. Does that answer your questions?"

"No," she said, and she arose from the table to come and stand before him. "I have one last question to ask of you, Quinton."

"And that is, my dear?" She was so serious, and so amusing.

"When are you going to kiss me again?" Allegra queried him.

"Why right now, my dear," he answered her, pulling her into his lap. Taking her chin between his thumb and his forefinger his lips met hers in a rather fierce kiss.

She gasped, surprised. His finger caressed her jawline for a brief moment, and then he kissed her again; this time slowly, slowly until she felt as if her bones were melting away. His eyes looked into hers. Allegra felt a wave of heat wash over her and her heart hammered wildly.

"Do you think I kiss well enough for you, my dear?" he asked her wickedly. Actually he had quite enjoyed it himself.

"Quite well enough," she admitted to him. "I will swear that my toes curled, sir."

"You are flattering me, Allegra, and I will quite confess to liking it," he told her. He also liked having her in his lap. She was a delightful armful.

"Kiss me again," she said softly to him, and he complied.

Her pink lips were like two rose petals, soft and yielding. Her breath was just slightly perfumed. He felt her relax against him. He found the softness of her breasts stimulating, and realized with some shock that his innocent wife-to-be was arousing him. Yet he could not stop kissing her, and Allegra in her budding zeal kissed him back with equal enthusiasm. He felt his manhood hardening within his breeches. Quickly he tipped her from his lap lest she sense it. Now was hardly the time for such an introduction.

She looked startled to find herself on her feet. Her sloe eyes and bruised mouth sent the blood pounding in his ears. "Why did you stop?" she demanded of him.

"Kissing," he said, wondering if his voice sounded as hollow to her as it did to him, "leads to other acts of greater intimacy, Allegra. I do not believe, and I must be the judge in such matters, that you are at all ready to meet and taste such delights. Perhaps it is best you retire now, my dear. We have several long days ahead of us." Taking her gently by the shoulders he kissed her upon her forehead. "Good night."

He could see she was slightly bemused as she walked from the little chamber where they had had their meal. He was somewhat confused himself. Going to the sideboard he poured himself a dollop of whiskey, and went to sit down by the fire. What the hell was the matter with him? He had felt lust for Allegra, yes, but there had been something more. They were to marry. He could have seduced her, and what harm would there have been in it? She belonged to him now. Only a few churchly words stood between the legalities of their licit union and the facts. She was innocent, but her girlish kisses told him there was passion in her soul. Treated with tenderness, brought slowly along, she would in time, he suspected, prove to be enjoyable bedsport.

That was it, of course, he decided. He sensed the fire in her that Allegra didn't even know she possessed. Instinctively he realized he had to move carefully with her lest he frighten her off. He wanted to make her bloom with passion, not turn away in fear.

Allegra rode with him each day of their journey. Each night she curled herself in his lap, and, as she quaintly put it, practiced her kissing. "Am I getting better?" she asked him one evening.

"With each passing day," he assured her.

She nodded. "Kissing is very pleasant, but rather repetitive, isn't it?" she said to him.

"There are variations," he told her.

"Show me," she whispered against his mouth.

His tongue slipped between her parted lips, and fervently caressed her. Allegra almost swooned in his arms.

"*Ohhh,*" she gasped. Her heart was hammering erratically, and a frisson of pleasure raced down her backbone. "Oh my, Quinton, that was quite exciting! Are there other forms of kissing? *I must know!*"

"Yes," he said, "but they are much too advanced for you to be taught now. They involve caressing."

"Caressing what?" she asked him innocently.

"You," he answered with a small smile.

"*Me?* What do you mean?" Allegra queried him.

"Your breasts, and other more intimate parts," he told her.

"Do you want to caress me, Quinton?" she asked hesitantly.

"Oh, yes, my dear, I do, but I do not think the time is right for you now. I want you to know me better. I want to know you better before we become closer, Allegra."

"You are considerate of me," she said. "I hope we are not separated for too long," she remarked. "I really am anxious to come to Hunter's Lair. Even if my rooms aren't ready, couldn't we set up a tented pavilion upon your lawns for me? Papa and Aunt Mama are so *involved* with each other. It is as if I do not exist for them, Quinton. I think I shall be quite uncomfortable in my childhood home now. I am beginning to see that I do not belong there any longer. Morgan Court is theirs."

He stroked her dark hair. It was very soft, and fragrant with lilacs. "I expect you will spend little time there, Allegra. I think that your new rooms will be ready for you quickly, and if they are not, I shall see that they are." He suddenly realized he did not like the idea of being parted from her either for he enjoyed her company. How odd, he thought to himself. He could not remember ever before having enjoyed female company. He was not misogynistic in the least, but other than his late grandmother, whom he had admired and respected, and the women who had soothed his carnal desires, Quinton Hunter had little knowledge of women.

They parted the following day. The Duke of Sedgwick rode west into Hereford while Lord Morgan and his family turned off the highway following a smaller, local road to Morgan Court. Reaching home that evening Allegra found herself alone. Honor had begged permission to visit her parents as she had not seen them in several months. As for Lord Morgan and his wife, they had hurried upstairs once the evening meal had been cleared away. It was midsummer, and the twilight was long now. Allegra wandered out to the stables to visit her gelding.

The horse greeted her with a welcoming nicker, obviously pleased to be back home after their journey from London. Allegra saw that the beast had been thoroughly brushed, fed, and watered. She rubbed its velvet muzzle, and then left the stables to walk through her father's garden. The marble summer house by the lake beckoned her. She climbed the three broad, wide steps, and entering the little pavilion, sat down. She already missed the duke. His company had been more than pleasant if she were willing to admit it. She liked being kissed as well.

"I thought I should find you here," a voice said.

"Rupert! How kind of you to come and welcome me home," Allegra replied. "Come, and sit with me. It is such a glorious evening. Do you hear the nightingale singing in the woods? There is no place as beautiful as Morgan Court."

"Then why leave it, Allegra?" he asked her. Rupert Tanner was a pleasant-looking young man with light brown hair and pale blue eyes. "You don't have to marry that duke. Your father is not so cruel as to make you marry a man you don't love."

"But I do want to marry Quinton," Allegra told him.

"Do you love him?" Rupert queried her. "Does he love you?"

"Of course we do not love each other." Allegra laughed. "We haven't known each other long enough to even know if we really like each other, but I think that we do. We get on very well."

"But I love you, Allegra!" Rupert cried. "I have loved you ever since we were children. Even if you did not love me, I should love you. A woman should be loved."

"Rupert, I can never think of you as a husband. You have been my brother, my best friend next to Sirena," Allegra responded. "Now stop being so foolish. My wedding date is set for October fifth in London at St. George's. The king, the queen, and Prinny are coming. Lady Bellingham says it will be the wedding of the year. Madame Paul has already begun making my wedding gown. It is to be white and silver. Quite fashionable, I am told," she finished with a smile.

"You are so young," he replied. "You cannot know what you want. You do not see past the excitement and the glamour of it all. You have never even been kissed!"

"Of course I've been kissed," Allegra snapped, now becoming irritated by this cow-eyed young man. "The duke and I have kissed many times. I quite like it, Rupert."

He suddenly stood, pulling her up with him. Then he kissed her. His mouth mashed against her; his tongue tried to push into her mouth; and he smelled of onions. "Allegra, Allegra, I love you! Marry me, my darling girl. I realize a country churchman's life cannot match the excitement of a duke's, but I adore you. Tell me you will send this duke packing, and be mine."

Allegra struggled from his embrace. She smacked him hard upon his cheek. "How dare you, Rupert Tanner? I was almost ready to forgive you for telling the duke that you and I had an informal agreement; but now I shall not. I am marrying Quinton Hunter because I want to marry him. No one is forcing me to it. It is my duty as my father's daughter to make the best marriage possible. As Papa's heiress a duke is just the right husband for me. Now go away. I do not want to see you again!"

"London has not been good for you, Allegra. You have grown hard," he accused her.

"Oh, Rupert, do not be such a dunderhead," Allegra told him. "My papa loved my mother, and what did love bring him? Scandal, embarrassment, and heartbreak. Quinton's antecedents all married for love. What did it bring them? Poverty, and the loss of much of what his family once had. The betrothal between the Duke of Sedgwick and myself is based upon sound principles. He has the pedigree, and I have the fortune. It is a perfect match. One made in heaven, you might say," she concluded with a small chuckle. "Go home. Find a nice young woman who will make a good clergyman's wife. One who will enjoy teaching the children their Bible stories, and ministering to the sick. I certainly shouldn't. Lord Stoneleigh's daughter, Georgianne, is moonstruck over you. In another year she'll be out of the schoolroom, and ready to marry. You really should ask for her before someone else does. Papa says she has a small, but respectable dowry."

"What has happened to you, Allegra?" he said.

"I have grown up, Rupert, but even before I did, I never said I would marry you, or that I desired to be a clergyman's wife with all the onerous duties it entails. You and I *spoke* about marrying so I might *escape* my London season. It was a childish fantasy, and Papa wisely saw that. I don't care for you except as a brother. I surely never will. In fact I shall never love anyone. Love only brings a host of problems I should rather not deal with, Rupert. Now, please go home. I don't want to see you again. Perhaps after I am married, and come to visit at Morgan Court, I may forgive you your behavior this evening, *but not now.*" She stood stonily as he turned abruptly and departed the pavilion.

Allegra sat back down. Rupert had kissed her, and she

hadn't liked it one bit. *And he had pushed his tongue at her!* Quinton had never done such a thing until she had become used to his kisses. Then she laughed to herself as she remembered asking Quinton if he was good at kissing. Well now she knew. He most certainly was good. *Very good!*

Madame Paul arrived two days later from London ready to fit Allegra's wedding gown. She brought with her a number of fabric samples from which Allegra would choose so Madame could make up a trousseau of gowns for the future duchess. She was full of the latest gossip she had received from France. The little king, Louis XVII, had survived his murdered parents by two years, dying in his prison on the eighth of June, in Paris. "Some say he isn't dead, that the child in the Temple was an imposter," Madame told Allegra, "but those savages would never allow a Bourbon to escape their vigilance. The king is dead, poor child. Did I not hear that your brother was also a victim of the revolution, Miss Morgan? It was when Monsieur Danton took over the royal power in the autumn three years ago. That was when I escaped. It was a bloodbath, I tell you! No mercy was shown. Priests, artisans, people like me who did business with the well-to-do. Who else, I ask you, Miss Morgan, could afford a Madame Paul gown but an aristocrat? And plenty of them died. It was horrible. Little children in their satin gowns and suits guillotined before their parents' eyes. It was terrible! Terrible!"

"Yes," Allegra said tightly. "That was when my brother was murdered." She felt faint, but reaching out she steadied herself, her hand gripping the back of a chair.

"Ahh, Miss Morgan, I have upset you," Madame said, genuinely distressed. "I did not mean to do it. I have tried to put it all behind me, but the news of the young king has brought it all back to me once again." Reaching for her lawn handkerchief she dabbed at her eyes.

"It is all right, Madame Paul," Allegra told the modiste. "You have suffered, too, losing your sister, and having to leave your homeland. We don't even know where my brother's body was interred. There are no niceties in a revolution, are there?"

"No, there are not," the older woman agreed. She did not increase Allegra's sorrow further by explaining to her that the bodies of the slaughtered in Paris, and elsewhere in France, were tossed helter-skelter into open pits. The baskets of heads were dumped atop them, and then lime was poured on the carnage before it was covered with dirt. There were no markers, and by the following year the mass graves were invisible, covered by weeds and wildflowers.

Allegra was measured for her glorious wedding gown. It would, along with Allegra's new wardrobe, be delivered to the Berkley Square house at the appropriate time.

"For you, Miss Morgan, I have turned away at least half a dozen important clients," Madame Paul told Allegra.

"Gracious," the younger woman exclaimed, "why would you do such a foolish thing, madame?"

"My shop is small, and I have but Francine and two seamstresses," came the reply. "I must weigh and balance who I will accept as a client. Your papa is the richest man in England, and your husband-to-be is a duke. Then, too, there is the fact that you pay your bills on time."

Allegra thought for a long moment, and then she said

to the Frenchwoman, "Could you use an investor, madame?"

"An investor?" Madame cocked her head to one side.

"Yes, an investor. Someone who would finance a larger shop, and more staff for you. In return you would render a portion of your profits. It seems a shame that you cannot increase your business when everyone knows you are the finest dressmaker in London. You could still remain exclusive while turning a neat profit," Allegra said.

"Turn a bit for me, Miss Morgan," Madame Paul said. "You could arrange for your papa to invest in my business?"

"Not Papa," was the reply. "Me. My father will tell you I am quite astute at picking my investments."

"And what kind of a return would you expect on such an investment, Miss Morgan?" Madame asked despite the fact her mouth was full of pins.

"I should want thirty percent of your business," Allegra said.

"*Sacrebleu*, mademoiselle! *C'est impossible! C'est fou!*" the Frenchwoman cried. Then her eyes narrowed, and she said, "Fifteen percent, mademoiselle."

"Madame, I will not haggle with you," Allegra answered her. "I am young, but I am no fool. Twenty-five percent, and I will accept nothing less. Think, Madame Paul! A man would not put his monies in a dress shop. Only a woman would, and who among the ladies of the ten thousand would make you such an offer as I. I will not tell you how to run your business, or what clients to take, or what fabrics to purchase. I will be a silent partner, contributing only the monies you need to succeed. In return I will receive twenty-five percent of the profits, and Madame Paul, there will be profits."

"You may step down, Miss Morgan, I have finished," the dressmaker said, and then she added, "you drive a hard bargain, but I agree."

"And Mr. Trent will oversee the books," Allegra added.

"Miss Morgan!" The Frenchwoman looked outraged.

Allegra laughed. "Why should you have to bother with the business of your business, madame? You are an artiste."

Now it was Madame Paul who laughed. "And you are a very clever young lady," she replied.

"Where will you go on your wedding trip?" Madame Paul asked Allegra. "Portugal and Italy are beautiful, I am told."

"We have not discussed it," Allegra said. "I am not even certain we will go away. It seems a waste of good coin to me."

Madame was shocked. "Every young lady of your station should have a wedding trip," she said. "Even if it is only to Scotland."

Allegra laughed. "Then I must certainly ask the duke when we meet again what he has planned. Perhaps he wishes to surprise me."

"You will not have the proper clothing if he does that," Madame Paul said, "but then that is just like a man. Give them two pairs of breeches with matching tailcoats, some neckcloths, and they are content. They do not realize what we women go through for the sake of fashion." She helped Allegra from the gown she was fitting. "Send word to me in London when you know your destination. I will see you have the appropriate garments, Miss Morgan."

When the Frenchwoman had returned to London Allegra found that she actually missed her. She had sent

Rupert away since he could not behave like a gentleman, and Sirena no longer lived nearby. Her father, for the first time since Allegra could remember, was depending entirely upon his secretary, Charles Trent; occupying himself instead with his new wife. They arose late, and sought their apartment early. They rode out over the estate daily, and as each day went by seemed more involved with one another. Allegra had never felt more bereft in her entire life. The knowledge that they were not doing it deliberately was no comfort at all. Several of their neighbors called with good wishes for the newlyweds, but it was Allegra who accepted them, thanking them, and promising that Lord and Lady Morgan would be entertaining quite shortly. Allegra read. She rode her gelding. She wandered about the gardens. And she was growing very bored.

Hunter's Lair was less than a day's ride from Morgan Court. Finally one clear morning in late June, Allegra mounted her gelding and rode off to find the duke. Only Honor knew where she was going, and she had promised not to tell Lord and Lady Morgan until evening came. Allegra wore her riding skirt, but beneath it she had on a pair of her brother's old breeches which allowed her to ride astride, a posture she found far more comfortable than the sidesaddle ladies were supposed to affect. The upper portion of her body was clad in a white shirt, but she had eschewed her jacket as the day was warm. Her dark hair was pulled back and fashioned into a single braid. She wore no hat.

She had never ridden off of her father's lands alone, and found the idea of being on her own very exciting. After two hours she finally reached the high road. She was just able to make out on the worn wooden sign, the word HEREFORD, and the arrow pointing west. The duke's estate was located just over the border that separated the two counties of Worcester and Hereford. Allegra rode past orchards and fields of ripening grain. The road traveled through pastures of sheep and cattle. There was little traffic but for an occasional farm cart to be passed by. When the sun was at the midheaven she stopped to rest her horse, and to eat the picnic she had brought along for herself.

Refreshed, she had traveled onward. Then finally in late afternoon she saw it. A signpost pointing in several different directions, and indicating several destinations, one of which was Sedgwick village. Allegra turned her horse, wondering as she did so how distant Sedgwick was. She had never ridden so far in all of her life, and she was tired. Worse, her bottom ached from the long ride. Coming to the top of the hill she saw it. Stopping, Allegra could only gaze down with pleasure on her new home.

There was the village. Rows of neat thatched-roof cottages with their colorful gardens, all abloom now. There were orchards of pears and apples just as he had described and fields around them with his fine horses grazing peacefully in the summer sunshine. There, just beyond, was Hunter's Lair, set upon a low rise, the sun setting its windows ablaze with the afternoon light. Allegra kicked her horse into a canter, and hurried down the narrow roadway. She slowed her mount as she passed through the village, pleased to see a fieldstone church, and several small shops. And then she was at the road's end, and the gates of Hunter's Lair were before her—open—and to her eyes welcoming.

She was home at last, Allegra thought as she cantered through the gates. She loved this place already, and she fully sympathized with Quinton's passion to keep his seat from the hands of strangers. Then she saw him, and waving, she brought the gelding to a halt, laughing at the surprised look on his face.

"I got tired of waiting for you," she told him as he lifted her down from her horse. "I am bored senseless at Morgan Court. Papa and Aunt Mama see no one but each other. Sirena is no longer there. I had to send Rupert Tanner packing. I could not wait a moment longer to see Hunter's Lair."

"Does your father know where you are?" was his first question.

"I left a note for Honor to give them when they realize I am not there. Perhaps today. Perhaps tomorrow, the way they are carrying on these days. Gracious, Quinton, love makes one foolish, doesn't it?"

"And you rode all the way from Morgan Court unaccompanied?" was his next stern question. He did not look happy, she realized.

"Of course. Who else would I ride with, Quinton? Have I come at an inopportune moment?" She wondered why he was becoming so upset.

"Are you mad?" he began to shout at her. "You have ridden over twenty miles by yourself, Allegra, and it is God's mercy that you were not accosted upon the road!" His heart was hammering. Was she as reckless as he had once been? But his French adventures were over. He had to be sensible now that he was taking a wife. And he was certain that he didn't resent that fact.

"The road was practically empty, sir. There was no danger that I could see," she told him frostily. "And do not raise your voice to me. I do not like it."

She was here. She was safe. He could not help himself. He burst out laughing. "Allegra! Allegra! Are you always this impetuous? What am I to do with you? I cannot get you back home tonight. Pray God your father does not worry himself sick not knowing if you are alive or waylaid along your route. There are highwaymen plying their trade along the roads, my dear. Did you not consider that?"

"Do highwaymen strike in the daylight?" she demanded. "And why would they bother with a girl riding alone with no visible purse or jewelry? Your concern is unwarranted, I think."

"Highwaymen do attack in daylight," he assured her, "and as you are well dressed, alone, and riding a fine beast, a robber would consider you rather excellent prey. And after he had robbed you of your goods and chattels, he might have also sought to rob you of your virtue, Allegra. Did you consider that at all when you set out so capriciously? Even your father's wealth could not have bought you a duke for a husband had you been ruined in such a terrible fashion, my dear," he finished.

"You are horrible!" she cried, but the truth of his words had frightened her. She had not considered any misadventures when she had set out to come to Hunter's Lair. She had only contemplated her own boredom with life at Morgan Court. She flushed nervously.

"Well," the duke said, seeing his words had finally made an impression upon her, "come and see your apartments, Allegra. They are just about finished. You will have to choose your own furnishings from among the house's contents. You may very well want to purchase new items, and of course, you will need fabrics for curtains, drapes, and hangings. Still, my dear, if you wish to move in tonight, I can have a cot bed brought for you. Tomorrow, I will send one of my servants to your father to assure him that despite your willful misbehavior, you are quite safe with me, and to escort Honor back here. I certainly hope our daughters do not have your sense of adventure, Allegra."

"Perhaps we will have no daughters," she said pettishly.

"I hope we have at least one, and that she looks like you, my dear. I just don't want her to be as madcap."

"Where is your brother, George?" she asked, changing the subject. "I am to marry you in three months, and I have not met your closest living relation yet. Why didn't he come to London with you?"

"Because it was all I could do to afford to come to London myself. You will meet George when he comes in from the fields where he is overseeing the laborers. My little brother is a farmer at heart."

"Like the king," she said with a small smile. She was glad he was no longer angry with her.

"Like the king, but without his resources." The duke laughed.

"Perhaps we should buy him a farm," Allegra said seriously.

The duke laughed again. "Don't say such a thing to Georgie, or he will be your slave for life, my dear. He wants his own land more than anything else in this world. I thought that he might prefer a commission in his majesty's armies, or a pulpit in some small church, but he really wants land to farm. That and perhaps Squire Franklyn's youngest daughter, Melinda."

"Then he must have his own farm, for I know no father will give his daughter in marriage to a penniless man—unless, of course, he is a duke," she chuckled mischievously.

He laughed a third time, and this time most heartily. "You are really quite a vixen, my dear," he told her, but his tone was amused, and even perhaps a bit affectionate, Allegra thought. "Ahh," he said, "here is the subject of our discussion even now." He waved, calling, "Come over, George, and meet your about-to-be sister-in-law."

A somewhat younger version of Quinton Hunter rode up, sliding easily off his mount. While his brother's eyes were a silvery gray, George Hunter's were a light blue. He wore no jacket, and his shirt, open at the neck, offered her a view of his damp chest. "This is Miss Morgan?" he asked, smiling warmly at her. "Why, damn me, Quint, she is even prettier than you said, but then you have never been much for words unless it concerned your horses." He bowed to Allegra. "Your servant, Miss Morgan."

Allegra curtsied. "I am pleased to meet you, brother George," she told him. "I am afraid I have shocked your brother by appearing unannounced, but I think he is over his pique now."

"She rode the twenty miles unescorted," Quinton Hunter explained dryly to his younger brother.

"*Did you?* Well, damn me, Quint, she's a game gel. You won't always get your way with her, I can see that," he chuckled.

"Behave, youngster," his elder warned sternly. "Allegra has threatened to purchase a farm for you."

"*She has?*" George Hunter's look was one of astonishment. Then he said, "You are gulling me, Quint, and it isn't fair."

"No, he isn't," Allegra told the young man. "Have you some place in mind, George? What do the owners want for it? Is it good land? Arable, and well watered?"

"Do you mean it? Having my dream come true cannot be this easy, can it?"

"I am not your fairy godmother," Allegra said seriously to the young man. "If you have a farm in mind, George, I will purchase it for you, but you will only own a half interest until you pay me back for the other half. It is business, plain and simple. I provide the capital for this investment, and you provide everything else. Papa's lawyers will write up an agreement for us, if indeed you do agree."

"*Yes!*" he told her without hesitation.

"We shall have the lawyers do the negotiation, lest the price of your heart's desire be inflated when it is learned that the monies come from Lord Morgan's daughter. Now, have you any income other than what you will earn from your lands?"

"One hundred and thirty pounds a year from my grandmother," he said.

"Then, with lands to farm, and your income, you can certainly ask Squire Franklyn for his daughter's hand. It is unlikely, unless she is a great beauty, that she will receive a better offer," Allegra said sensibly. "We shall have two weddings in the family instead of one!" She turned to the duke. "Does that suit you, my lord?"

He was amazed at how she had just taken charge of everything, and rendered all of their lives smooth and trouble free. "I am no longer fearful that you rode here unescorted, Allegra," he said to her. "Any highwayman who accosted you would have found he had met his match, for your wits are far sharper than any weapon a robber could carry." Yet despite his flattering words he could not help but wonder if her no-nonsense ways were suitable behavior for a Duchess of Sedgwick.

Allegra smiled. It was a well-satisfied smile. "Thank you," she answered him simply. She had, she believed, in these past few minutes gained his respect. That respect meant far more to her than any cloying sentiment of love would have meant. Yes, it had been a most successful London season, and it would be a most successful marriage as well.

Part Two

Summer and Autumn 1795
A Most Perfect Couple

Chapter Seven

Quinton Hunter sat alone of an evening in the small room that served him as a personal billet, and from which he conducted the business of his estate. It held an ancient desk and a rather battered tapestried chair. There was a double leaded pane casement window to his right, a paneled door to his left, and a fireplace before him with narrow bookcases built in on either side of the stone hearth. The fire blazed merrily, taking the damp chill off the July evening. The house was quiet now. The workmen had gone for the day. His betrothed wife and her saucy maid were upstairs in the duchess's new apartments. Honor had arrived two days after her mistress, sitting atop a cart that was filled to overflowing with some of Allegra's belongings. The rest, the duke was told, would follow. *And they had.* He had not thought such a young girl could have so many possessions.

The duke's thoughts were troubled. He knew he had to marry. He knew he needed a rich wife. He was committed to marrying Allegra Morgan, and yet now he was questioning the wisdom in that decision. She wasn't at all the sort of girl he felt would make a suitable Duchess of Sedgwick. The women before her had been deferential young ladies, yielding to the wishes of their lords even when those gentlemen were patently wrong.

Allegra, he already knew, was not such a lady. What kind of a duchess would she make him? Perhaps it would have been better to have not married at all. To have allowed his proud line to die with him, and with his younger brother, George.

It was George's situation that had brought about these second thoughts. He had felt so bad for his sibling, and then Allegra had come along, solving George's problems in a trice. Quinton Hunter had to admit to himself that while he was delighted for his brother, he was frankly irritated by Allegra's actions. It had been so easy for her, and damnit, life wasn't that easy. But mayhap it was for the daughter of the richest man in England. And there was the other fact that gnawed at his pride most of all. He had compromised his family's name by making a match based solely on his bride's financial resources. What kind of a man of honor did that? A desperate one, he admitted to himself.

Yet Allegra was a great beauty. She had perfect manners, and a kind heart. But she was also outspoken to the point of rudeness on certain occasions. While patient with her inferiors, she was totally lacking in that virtue where her betters were concerned. She had absolutely no tolerance for fools. And she was so deucedly independent, particularly where monies were concerned.

"I will," she had already informed him, "oversee all the household chits without interference, Quinton. Some servants are apt to become light-fingered when tempted. Best not to tempt them."

"The Crofts have been with this family for centuries," he had haughtily told her.

"I am not speaking of the Crofts," she returned. "I shall have to hire a full staff, Quinton. You cannot expect dear old Croft, and his good wife, to run such an establishment as we shall soon have. I shall, of course, pay the servants myself out of the allowance that Papa has given me. The monies you receive are yours to do with as you please. A wife runs the household; a husband the estate. Or so Aunt Mama had instructed me. Is she wrong then?"

He had grudgingly admitted that the new Lady Morgan was most correct in her assessment of a couple's home duties. But it had irritated him to do so, though he knew not why. And Allegra had blithely gone her way then, tightening her hold upon him and his household by virtue of her wealth. He hated the ostentation of her fortune, yet neither Allegra, nor her exquisite taste could be called flamboyant, or even pretentious. Her father's wealth had saved him and his estates, he well knew, an admission which only seemed to cause him further resentment.

But his home was coming to life as he had never known it. He had to admit to himself that he liked what he was seeing. The exterior of Hunter's Lair was unchanged. It was built in the shape of an H, which had been the fashion in the year 1500 when the first Tudor king; Henry VII reigned, and the house had been reconstructed after a devastating fire. The brick was warm and mellow where it could be viewed beneath the dark green ivy. It had high stone chimneys, and a number of slate gables and roofs. Where the slates had been damaged, or gone entirely, they had been replaced. Every one of the leaded paned windows had been repainted and washed.

His beloved hall, the only part of the original house to have survived the fire of 1498, had been left basically intact as he had requested. But Allegra had put her new band of maidservants and footmen to work cleaning and polishing the stone and paneled walls, scrubbing the stone fireplaces and the window wells enclosing the windows. He entered the hall one day to find footmen on great tall ladders washing those windows. To his amazement he realized there were stained glass designs in each of the windows that he had never even known were there. The tapestries and the silken banners in the hall were taken down and repaired, the dirt and the dust beaten out of them before they were restored to their places. When all was done, the furniture glowed. The highboard as well as the sideboards held bowls of flowers that perfumed the air of the Great Hall in a most pleasing manner.

The once narrow entry of the house with its several small and useless rooms on either side of it had become a spacious and elegant rounded foyer with staircases sweeping down on either side of the room. Six days a week the workmen swarmed about the house. There were buckets of plaster everywhere. A new dining room was being constructed, its walls to be covered in red brocade and hung with fine paintings. Chandeliers had been ordered from Waterford in Ireland, although they would not be ready until early the following year. New furniture had been commissioned from Mr. Chippendale's workshops in London. It would be in place by their wedding day.

The first floor of the house also contained the duke's library, the duchess's morning room, the duke's small office, and a drawing room. The second floor of the house was devoted to the new dining room with its pantry, a magnificent ballroom, and another small drawing room for the family's use. The tiny rabbit warren of rooms that had previously existed had been demolished. They had been of no importance. The third floor of the house held the ducal and guest bedchambers. The fourth floor was given over to the servants' quarters.

Allegra's apartments had been the first rooms finished. They were done in her favorite colors. The private salon had pale green brocaded walls above a gilded
chair rail, and beneath the chair rail the wall was paneled in light wood. The Aubusson carpet had a light
green background with a floral design of deeper green,
gold, and rose. It lay over a wide board oak floor. The
draperies were striped in pale green and gold silk brocade.
The sofa was upholstered in gold brocade sprigged with
a tiny cream dot. The French chairs were done in a gold
and cream brocade. Upon the fireplace mantel stood a
fine gilded clock which chimed not only the hour and
the half hour, but the quarter hour as well. Lord Morgan had personally ordered the furniture for his daughter before they had departed the city. It was made of
mahogany, and its design quite graceful and very elegant. On the delicate side tables were small china bowls
of dried rose petals mixed with gillyflowers. The candelabra and candlesticks were gold gilt over sterling silver.
The lamps were crystal.

The bedchamber was decorated in rose and cream.
The bedstead, which was quite old, was of golden oak,
and hung with rose silk brocade draperies that could be
drawn all about the bed for privacy. Allegra had never
seen such a large bed, but it fit comfortably into the
chamber. It came from the previous century, but Allegra
liked it, and would not allow it to be replaced. There
was a mahogany armoire, a dressing table with its own
carved mirror, a matching chest of drawers, and a small
table by the bed, along with a rose- and cream-colored
tapestried chair by the fireplace. On the wide board oak
floors was another Aubusson carpet of deep rose decorated with a border of cream and lighter pink roses with
deep green leaves. The windows were hung with cream
and rose sprigged silk brocade draperies. There was

also a Chippendale chest with a fine gilt mirror hung over it on the wall that led to the dressing room. On the other side of the dressing room was a pretty windowed chamber for Honor that was comfortably furnished with a bedstead, a drawered coffer, a night table, and a chair. The duke's apartments, now under construction, were next to Allegra's with a connecting door between their bedchambers.

No, he could not complain, even to himself, about the improvements that were being made to the house, Quinton Hunter thought. His bride-to-be's never-ending fortune was a godsend in that respect. The duke had always loved his home, but it was fast becoming the showplace he had always known it could be. That, and his deep sense of honor were what kept him from crying off his match to Miss Allegra Morgan. It was becoming quite obvious to him that once he had sired a proper number of children with her that they would, like so many couples of their day, have to lead separate lives.

And yet his brother was happy. So happy that the duke felt almost guilty in his exasperation. The negotiations were now under way for the purchase of George's farm, some five hundred acres nearby. They would be his by month's end. Squire Franklyn, learning of the quite improved circumstances of his daughter's suitor, was ready to give his blessing to a match between their families. The talk was even being bandied about regarding a late August wedding, which would, of course, be a simple country affair.

The squire, a practical man, had always liked young Lord Hunter, but a man without lands wasn't a fit son-in-law. Now, however, all that had changed. He had even learned that George had a small income in the bargain. His daughter would be Lady Hunter with her own house and an income. Melinda, he proudly told the duke, would have a dowry of one hundred fifty pounds of gold, her own plates, linens, and clothing.

Quinton Hunter smiled in retrospect. Life for his little brother would be happy and uncomplicated. He already envisioned a house full of nieces and nephews. He, himself, faced a different future with a strong-willed girl who would grow into a stronger-willed woman with the birth of each of her children, and the power such births would bring her. Allegra would not follow in her mother's footsteps. Once she became his wife she would remain loyal and devoted to their family for the rest of her life. She had been carefully raised to understand exactly what her duty was, and she would do it.

The duke sighed. Had his antecedents been right when they married for love? Love had brought his family to the abyss of indigence and beggary, but they had been happy in their impoverishment. *Hadn't they?* He sighed again, running his big hand through his dark hair. He had never wanted to be rich, just comfortable. He would have been content to marry a plain girl with a dowry sufficient to restore his home and keep them comfy. Such girls, however, had been looking for richer men. Once his family's name had meant something. He would have been sought after, indeed fought over. No more, he thought sadly. Today it was the rich who prospered even more.

Quinton Hunter shook himself. What the hell was he feeling sorry for, he asked silently? His bride-to-be was a beautiful young girl. Perhaps if he showed her a little more kindness he could cajole her into a more reasonable frame of mind. She was just spoiled. Her father had indulged her. She was barely grown. She would have her outrageous allowance to play with each year, and be as happy as she had obviously always been. Allegra was like a beautiful young mare. She needed to be gentled, and she needed firmness. She was a sensible creature, and in time would come to understand there could be but one rule in their house. *His*.

The days flew by. George's farm was purchased. It had a fine stone house with a good slate roof, a sturdy barn, and a granary. There was an apple orchard, and young Lord Hunter intended turning one of his fallow fields into a second orchard, this one for pears. His fields were currently let to his neighbors, but next year he would grow his own grain. His father-in-law-to-be gifted him with a small flock of black-faced Shropshire sheep. Allegra wrote to her father, and shortly afterward a herd of twelve cows and a bull were driven into one of George's fields.

The betrothal between Miss Melinda Franklyn and Lord George Hunter was announced. The wedding would be celebrated on the last day of August.

Together Allegra and Quinton attended the wedding of the Earl of Aston to Lady Eunice Tarleton on July twentieth. It was held at Astondale, the earl's home village, an hour's carriage ride from Hunter's Lair. It was there that Allegra saw Sirena for the first time since her cousin had gone off on her wedding trip. Sirena was obviously blooming, and very happy.

"Mama says you ran away to Hunter's Lair," Sirena laughed as she hugged her cousin warmly. "You really are a naughty puss, coz."

"I ran away from all their billing and cooing," Allegra told her cousin bluntly. "Really, Sirena, it was quite embarrassing, I assure you. I decided I might as well come sooner to Hunter's Lair, and a good thing, too. The architect needed me. There was far more work to the restoration than anyone had anticipated."

"When may we come and see it?" Sirena begged prettily.

"Ohh, we are not yet ready to receive guests," Allegra said. "The duke's apartment has only just been finished. Ohh, Sirena, you should see my rooms. All my favorite colors, and so beautiful. We will be fortunate to have everything done by the wedding, but I have told Mr. Gardner that it absolutely must be finished in time for my ball on October thirty-first."

"But your wedding is October fifth," Sirena said. "Aren't you taking a wedding trip, Allegra?"

"I have no idea," came the answer, "but if we are it must be a brief one for my ball is most firmly set for the night of the thirty-first of October. It will be my first formal entertainment as the Duchess of Sedgwick, and I want it to be perfect."

"Don't you and the duke *ever* speak together?" Sirena asked.

"When we have something to say to one another."

Sirena shook her head. "If you must marry Quinton Hunter, Allegra, couldn't you at least try to love him a little?" she said.

"Sirena, dearest, we have been over this before," Allegra reminded her cousin. "Quinton and I have a very sensible arrangement. We are both content with it, I assure you."

The cousins met again several weeks later at Lord Walworth's wedding to Caroline Bellingham. Sirena looked rather peaked this time.

"*Breeding,*" Lady Bellingham said archly. "I see it in her eyes."

"*You aren't!*" Allegra squealed excitedly.

"I am," Sirena said, "but I shall still be able to be your attendant, Allegra. I promised you, and I will keep my word."

"Does Aunt Mama know yet?" Allegra wondered.

Sirena shook her head.

"You write her this day, my gel, or I shall," Lady Bellingham said sternly. "Your mama has waited long enough for grandchildren."

"My sisters have children," Sirena protested.

"Why so they do, bless me, so they do!" Lady Bellingham said. "But it is your child that will best please Olympia, I am certain."

"Sirena and Ocky are to become parents," Allegra told the duke as they rode home after the wedding.

"I know," he said. "Are you happy for your cousin?"

"Yes," Allegra said slowly, but without much conviction.

Reaching over he took her hand in his. Their eyes met, and the duke said, "What is it that is troubling you, my dear?"

"Sirena says she will be able to attend me at our wedding, but I do not think she will. She has a delicate constitution, Quinton. A trip to London may be too much for her in her condition." Allegra sighed deeply. "We are more like sisters than cousins. I cannot endanger her, or her child." She bit her lip, but even the sharp pain of the bite could not prevent the tears from slipping down her cheeks.

"If you could choose where we would be wed, my dear, where would it be?" he asked her.

"If I could choose? But I cannot, Quinton. We must be married with all the pomp and dignity due your family's position. Lady Bellingham is right. It must be St.

George's in London. I could not ask anything less of you, my lord."

"Your commitment to my history and my name is to be commended, Allegra, but you still have not answered my question. If you could choose where we would wed, where would it be?" He gave the little hand in his a tiny squeeze of encouragement. "Come, my dear, *where?*"

"The Great Hall at Hunter's Lair," she burst out.

"*Indeed?*" He was very much surprised.

"Yes!" she told him. "I love Hunter's Lair, and the Great Hall is the perfect place for such an event. Especially now that it is clean. And I would have only our family and friends. And we would give everyone on the estate the day off, and set up a feast for them on the lawns. We should come from the hall where our feast was being held, and greet our tenants and workers. It would be wonderful!" Then her face fell. "But I know it cannot be. We must be married at St. George's, and have a proper wedding breakfast afterward with the king and the queen as our guests, and Prinny and Mr. Brummell."

"No," he replied. "We shall be wed in exactly the manner you have said, my dear." Then he kissed her hand, and their eyes met again. He felt as if something had cracked within his chest, and yet he was fine.

"Ohh, Quinton," she said softly, "could we really be married in such a fashion? Then Sirena could come, for her home is not so far away, is it? That would make me so very happy." Her violet eyes were shining with pleasure.

"*Would* it?" he answered her softly, and then he leaned forward, and kissed her lips gently. "I am coming to realize, Allegra," he told her, "that even if you are strong-willed, opinionated, and far too outspoken, that

I am beginning to want to see you happy." Then he added, "There is nothing in our most practical arrangement that precludes our being happy, is there, my dear?" His silver eyes twinkled at her.

"I do not believe so, my lord," she replied, her voice a little breathless. Her heart was hammering rather quickly, and she could feel that her cheeks were flushed.

"Excellent," he said. Then he tucked her hand deeper into his.

"Are you happy with me?" she ventured boldly. "Despite my faults? I do not think I can change, Quinton. I am not certain I want to change. Weak women are always taken advantage of to their detriment."

"I do not believe you shall ever be taken advantage of, my dear Allegra," he assured her with a chuckle. All his doubts, and dark mood of the past few days had vanished suddenly. He wondered, briefly, why he now felt he could conquer the world.

"How far is Pickford?" she asked him. "I should like to go and visit my cousin now that she is home from her wedding trip."

"Just half an hour's drive away, my dear," he told her. *Wedding trip!* Egad! How could he have forgotten to make plans for a wedding trip? "Tell me, Allegra," he began. "Where do you think we should go after our wedding?"

"Must we go anywhere?" she asked.

"Perhaps not right away, if you do not want it, but next spring I should like to take you to Italy. We might go to Rome, or Venice, Allegra, if it would please you, my dear."

"My mother lives in Italy. I should not like to meet her."

"The contessa does not reside in Venice. We shall go to Venice, Allegra, and you shall not meet her. It is a beautiful city, my dear, built on the edge of the sea, and the streets are not paved, but are water, and carriages are not used but rather charming little boats called gondolas ferry people from place to place."

"How interesting," she cried. "Yes. Let us go to Venice next spring. I would like that."

Allegra, despite her little imperfections of character, was going to be an excellent Duchess of Sedgwick. She only needed his guidance, and he was after all fourteen years her senior. He would share his experience with her. Her desire to be married at Hunter's Lair had surprised him, but it had also pleased him very much.

He began to spend more time with her. They rode together in the morning, and then went about their own pursuits, sometimes meeting again at luncheon, and sometimes not until dinner. But he made every effort now to spend the evening with her. They walked in the gardens, and her ability at kissing improved daily. She had proficient skills with the pianoforte, and sang most prettily. One evening he sat next to her on the bench, turning the pages of her music. He found the back of her neck and the two unruly dark curls of her hair, damp with the heat of a summer's night, irresistible. His arms slipped about her narrow waist, and he kissed her nape.

Allegra ceased playing, turning her head to his. His mouth fused itself with hers in a hot kiss. Something had changed, she realized suddenly, as his hand began to caress her breasts. She froze. What was she to do? Was anything required of her but her compliance? Unable to help herself she began to tremble, and a small cry escaped her lips. She found herself slumping against his arm, unable to catch her breath for a moment.

"Damnit, I have forgotten how innocent you truly are, my dear," he apologized to her.

Allegra swallowed hard. "Will this be part of our co-habitation?" she asked in all seriousness. She could, to her acute embarrassment, feel her nipples pushing against the silk fabric of her gown's tight bodice. Her heart was thumping wildly. She hadn't found his touch at all repellent, but rather exciting. And she was filled with questions. Did she get to touch him? And where?

"It is called *love play*, my dear," he told her. "You are so charming, Allegra, I could not help myself. I think it is past time we came to know one another better, don't you? Our wedding is just over a month away now."

"I found it exciting," she said suddenly.

"*What?*"

"When you touched me," she went on. "I found it exciting when you caressed my breasts, Quinton."

"*Did you?*" He was encouraged and a bit shocked by her candidness.

"Am I allowed to touch you?" she asked naively.

"Not yet," he gulped, surprised.

"*When? And where?*" she persisted.

"Eventually, and I shall instruct you," he answered her, and he felt his member tingling. My God, the little witch was arousing him!

"I cannot help but be curious," Allegra told him. "Once I said I had not yet considered the carnal side of our marriage, but you are right. Our wedding day is fast approaching, Quinton. I find my curiosity increasing. We have been so proper when we are together that it makes me giggle when I think what people must imagine has been between us this summer. Not that I care, mind you. My conscience is quite clear. Yours should certainly be as clear, unless, of course, you have some bit of fluff hidden away from me. I have certainly heard no gossip regarding such a matter."

"Nor should you have if I indeed had a mistress, which I do not," he responded stiffly. There was that appalling outspokenness again.

"Oh, dear! I have offended you again," Allegra said.

Quinton Hunter laughed. He couldn't help it. Allegra could be so disingenuous, and at the damndest times. What was he going to do with her? For lack of any other answer he kissed her again. His arms wrapped themselves about her, his lips pressing firmly against her lips until the softness beneath his parted slightly. He ran his tongue along those sweet lips, causing her to gasp softly as her eyes flew open, and she stared at him astounded. "You taste of peaches," he said.

"I . . . I had some at supper," she responded. "Why did you do that? Lick my lips?"

"Because it gave me pleasure to do so, and it will give you pleasure also now that you are no longer surprised," he explained. "There will come a time when we are in our marriage bed that I will want to taste every bit of you. *Even the most secret parts*," he finished.

Heat suffused her body at his words. "Are you attempting to seduce me, Quinton?" she asked honestly.

"Do you want me to?" he countered. His silver eyes were half-closed.

"Perhaps. I am not certain yet if I am brave enough," she answered him. His eyebrows were so black, and so thick.

"Even though we are at home," he replied suddenly, breaking the spell that had been between them, "I do not want our servants gossiping should they find us kissing and alone in the drawing room, Allegra."

Allegra looked up and whispered to him, "I want to be kissed and caressed more, my lord. I quite like it."

"Then you shall be, my dear," he promised her. "I

want you to be happy, Allegra." He was surprised to realize that he meant it.

"I want you to be happy," she said. "I truly do!"

She sat in his lap the following evening in the gardens, sighing as his hands brushed over her small breasts. His kisses were intoxicating now. She wanted more, and more, and more.

He scolded her gently, "You are far too greedy."

"But I adore kissing! And you really are an excellent kisser, Quinton. Rupert Tanner kissed me before I had to send him packing. His embrace was disgusting to me, while I cannot get enough of yours," Allegra admitted quite freely to the duke. Then she changed the subject. "Do you find my gown too constricting? Wouldn't you like to touch my bared breasts?"

"Yes," he groaned. Damn, but she was exciting him!

"Then come to my bedchamber after Honor has gone to her room," Allegra suggested to him. "I want to know what it is like to lie with a man in one's bed. Will we be naked?"

His head was spinning with growing lust. She was a virgin. He knew she was a virgin. Virgins were either shrinking violets, or wildly curious, he had been told. Then he wondered if she had been this curious with Rupert Tanner. Hadn't she just admitted to kissing him?

"Did you let that pious psalm singer touch you?" he growled at her. "Did you invite him into your bed, Allegra?" Jesus! He sounded like a jealous man. Why would he be jealous? Only a man in love would be jealous. He wasn't in love with her. *He wasn't!*

"Do not be absurd, Quinton," she said in a tone that dragged him back into the reality of their situation. "Rupert kissed me once. He was trying to dissuade me from marrying you. As you are aware his sly old papa wanted a match between us—but we were friends, not lovers."

"Were friends?"

"He would not stop pleading his case," Allegra said. "It was quite annoying. I sent him away telling him I should not like to see him again. His behavior was inexcusable, Quinton. I was already betrothed to you, and as I had no objections to the match, why should Rupert Tanner? Perhaps in a few years I shall forgive him, but certainly not now!"

"Of course," he agreed. "He behaved like a perfect cad."

"Poor Rupert," Allegra continued. "It is not easy being a younger son, I fear, but he will find the right girl eventually." Then her violet eyes met his silver ones. "Will you come to my bedchamber later?"

"You are quite shameless, Allegra," he said softly.

"May I not be shameless with my husband?" she asked.

"We are not yet wed, Miss Morgan," he said.

"If you would rather wait until we are I am content to do so," Allegra told him sweetly. "I just thought if we came to know each other better in this manner, then we could consummate our marriage on our wedding night without much ado. It seemed a practical matter to me, but perhaps I am too bold, and do not understand, Quinton. You really must be more forthcoming with me," she concluded.

"Go to your room, Allegra," he ordered her. "When Honor is gone, I shall visit you. You must promise me, however, that you will abide by my decisions in matters that you do not yet understand. Have I your pledge?"

"Yes, Quinton," she replied meekly.

"And wear your night garment," he warned her.

"Yes, Quinton," Allegra answered. Then she turned,

and hurried from the garden. At last she was to learn some of the delights of passion! Sirena had said they were quite wonderful. Of course she loved Ocky, Allegra thought, but even if I don't love Quinton, it should still be quite pleasant. A man's mistress doesn't love him, but she enjoys passion.

Honor was waiting for her mistress. She had Allegra's porcelain high-back tub filled with scented water. "You didn't stay long out in the moonlight with his lordship tonight," she noted.

"There is a chill in the air," Allegra excused herself. "It is August. Lord George's wedding is in just five more days."

"And then comes your wedding," Honor said. "I suppose it will be nice to see old London again." She helped Allegra into her tub, and began putting her clothes away, separating the laundry first.

"The duke and I have decided not to be married in London," Allegra told her servant. "I have already written to Papa about it. Sirena cannot travel to London now that she is breeding. I just can't be married without her by my side. The duke prefers being wed here at Hunter's Lair as do I. Just the family and our friends."

"Well, you won't hear no complaints from me on the matter," Honor admitted. "Where are we going on the wedding trip?"

"We are staying here, but perhaps next spring we shall go to Italy," Allegra told her servant. "Ohh, this water feels so good."

"*Italy?* Lord bless me, miss, I never expected that I would travel," Honor said excitedly.

"The duke says we shall go to a city where the streets are made of water and everybody travels in boats," Allegra continued.

"Go on, miss, you're funning me," Honor said. "Streets made of water? There ain't no such thing!"

"The duke says there are," Allegra replied.

"Since when did what His Grace said mean anything to you?" the saucy maid responded pertly. Then her eyes grew wide. "Ohh, miss! Are you falling in love with him?"

"Of course not," Allegra denied. "What an odd thing for you to say, Honor. Why would I fall in love with him? And how does one fall in love in the first place? Is love a tangible thing? And if it is, where is it that I, or anyone else, could fall into it?" She laughed.

Honor had finished putting away her mistress's garments. Now she took up the large sea sponge and began to wash Allegra's back. "Sometimes, miss," she said, "you say the funniest things. I don't understand half of them, but I love you anyway." She rinsed the soap from the girl's long back. "There, if you've done the other parts, you can get out of your tub." She helped Allegra up, wrapped her in a large warmed towel as her mistress stepped from the tub. When she had dried the girl off she slipped a soft white cotton night garment over her head. "There, miss," she said, satisfied.

Allegra tied the blue ribbons at the neckline into a little bow. Seating herself at her dressing table she loosed her long dark hair, and began to brush it slowly while Honor struggled to fit a painted screen around the tub. Allegra didn't like the tub in her bedchamber. It should really be in the dressing room. She would have it moved there tomorrow.

Her mind was awhirl. The duke was coming to her bedchamber tonight. Had she been too bold with him? It was too late now unless, of course, when he arrived she told him she had changed her mind. Changed her mind about *what*, she asked herself. She simply wanted to know a little bit more about passion before she was committed to consummating her marriage to Quinton Hunter. Girls were supposed to be courted, but the duke had not courted her at all. An *arrangement* had been made. No wonder she knew so little.

As she had once told the duke, girls knew more than they let on about men. She had had an older brother. For a moment her eyes grew teary at the thought of James Lucian. No one could have had a better brother than he, Allegra told herself. His death had been so futile, so damned unnecessary, and she hated the French for it. They had wantonly murdered her beautiful sibling because he had refused to leave the girl he loved. He had died with her rather than be parted from her. *Love!* Faaagh! It was a ridiculous emotion that drove sensible people to madness. Her darling brother. Her mother, who had deserted her children and husband for love. And now her father was behaving like a cow-eyed fool over his new wife. If she hadn't loved her aunt mama it would have all been too unbearable, Allegra considered.

"Ready for bed, miss?" Honor came into her view.

"Are you?" Allegra teased. "I have noticed the looks that the duke's valet, Hawkins, has been giving you, Honor."

Honor colored becomingly. "Ohh, miss!" was all she said.

"Do not allow him to take advantage of you, Honor," her mistress warned. Then Allegra smiled. "Run along. I shall not need you until the morning. I am perfectly capable of getting into bed by myself."

Honor hurried off through the dressing room to her own chamber, shutting the door behind her as she went. Allegra walked across the room to the windows and looked out. The moon was quite full tonight, and silvered the landscape. She could see the dark shadows of the horses in the pasture beyond the lawns. She had known from the first moment that she laid eyes on Hunter's Lair that she was going to be happy here.

She did not turn, but her heart beat a bit faster as she heard the door that connected her bedchamber and the duke's click open. He walked across the floor to stand behind her. "You came," she said softly.

"Am I still welcome, and are you still eager to learn more about what transpires between a man and a woman?" he asked her. His arm slipped about her slim waist, drawing her back against him.

"*Yes,*" she whispered breathlessly, feeling him nuzzle her head.

"Good," he replied. Then his fingers skillfully undid the blue ribbon that held the twin halves of her night garment together. His hand slid beneath the fabric to cup a small perfect breast in his palm. "Exquisite," he said softly.

His breath was hot in her ear, and she felt suddenly weak, as if her legs would not continue to hold her up. "I never . . . ," she began, but she could not continue.

"*I know,*" he said. Then his lips touched the skin where her neck and her shoulder met. The hand holding her breast tightened ever so slightly upon the tender flesh.

"*Ohhh,*" she murmured. My God, this was heaven! She had never imagined that anything could be quite this exciting.

The hand released her, and he turned her about to face him, pushing her nightgown off her shoulders so that it fell first to her waist, and then to the floor below where it puddled about her feet. Allegra was momentarily stunned. She had not expected quite so bold a move.

He stepped back, and his eyes swept over her. Quinton Hunter was utterly bedazzled. She was absolute perfection. Her skin was flawless with not a mark upon its surface to mar it. She was tall for her sex, but her height was in her torso not her legs. Her bosom was in perfect proportion with the rest of her body. "My God!" were all the words he could muster.

Allegra was silent. She had absolutely no idea what she should say in such a situation as this. She had, after all, never stood stark naked before a man.

The duke swallowed hard, at last able to find his voice. "No one should be as beautiful as you are," he told her. "And you have no idea, you wickedly audacious little virgin, of the power you will wield over me one day." He shook his dark head in wonderment, then taking her hand led her to her bed. "Get in," he ordered her.

She complied, and finding her own voice said softly, "I like it when you touch me, Quinton. Do it again."

"No," he said. "This was not a sage idea, Allegra. I had no idea how lovely you were without your clothing. So often a pretty face disappoints. You, my dear, do not. Indeed the whole surpasses the sum of your parts. I am a weak man, and if I remain, you will, I promise you, be well fucked by morning's light. Your virtue is the most precious gift you bring me, Allegra. We will accept it on our wedding night, and not a moment before. And afterward I shall teach you the delights and the joys of lust. Tempt me no further, my dear. Now, go to sleep. You have, to my embarrassment, discovered that like all mortal men, I have an appetite for sweet flesh. The tiny taste you have given me has revealed my fault." He took her hand up, and kissed it. Then he left her alone in the moonlit darkness.

Safe within the precincts of his own bedchamber

Quinton Hunter groaned. His member was rock hard, and it ached, unsatisfied. He cursed softly under his breath. What the hell was the matter with him that he had considered such a sortie even if she had asked him? She was spoiled and impetuous. *And far too curious.* Curiosity wasn't a good trait for a duchess, especially for a Duchess of Sedgwick to have in abundance. And once he opened her to the delights of carnality, could he keep her satisfied, or would her curiosity lead her to take lovers like so many women of their class did once they had provided their husbands with heirs? He groaned again. He would kill any man who looked with interested jaded eyes, or disrespect, upon Allegra. *She was his! His, damnit!*

And then Quinton Hunter knew in a burst of clarity that he had fallen victim to his family's curse. *He was in love.* In love with a willful and uninhibited wench who was going to wrap him about her finger even if she didn't know it yet. But know it she would if he showed her the slightest bit of weakness. She was rich and she was stunningly beautiful, but she didn't love him. It was unlikely she ever would. Allegra did not understand love. He knew instinctively that she was afraid of it. She could not know how he felt about her lest she flee him, and he could not bear it if he lost her. He laughed softly to himself. He was in love, but at least unlike his romantic antecedents he had fallen in love with an heiress. Even so, he seemed to have no predilection for gambling as of yet. He laughed again. Perhaps he did, for he was taking the greatest gamble of his life by marrying Allegra Morgan.

Chapter Eight

"You should have asked the duchess to be your bridesmaid," Squire Franklyn's wife scolded her daughter on her wedding day. "She is going to be your sister-in-law."

"She isn't the duchess yet," Melinda pertly answered her mother. "And besides, we have only met two or three times. It would have been most presumptuous of me, Mama, to solicit such a favor."

"She might have asked you to serve her in such a capacity," Mistress Franklyn replied.

"No, her cousin, Viscountess Pickford is to be her matron of honor," Melinda said. Thank heavens George had come up to scratch, not that she had ever doubted he would. She could hardly wait to be in her own house tonight, to be quit of her mother. Melinda Franklyn was her parents' youngest child, and at almost nineteen had been in danger of being left on the shelf had not George Hunter's good fortune saved her. She didn't quite know how he had come into possession of his farm, but she really didn't care. They were to be wed this morning, and that was all she wanted to know. By noon she would be Lady Hunter.

The squire's wife had now hurried away to make certain her servants were not slacking off in the wedding breakfast preparations. Tables had been set up outside the house, for the dining room was not large enough. Melinda, foolish girl, had wanted a small intimate family wedding, but Squire Franklyn and his wife would not hear of it. Their youngest girl was marrying very well, and they wanted everyone in the county to know about it. And with the duke and his betrothed to sit at the bridal table, no one had cried off. Squire Franklyn's wife smiled smugly. It would be a triumph, she was quite certain.

At the church George Hunter peeped from the sacristy, and gulped nervously. "They have invited the whole damned world," he complained to his older brother.

The duke laughed. "You cannot blame them, George. You are, after all, a prize catch for pretty Melinda."

"Laugh while you may, my brother, it will be your turn soon enough," George Hunter threatened.

"Ahh, but as Allegra and I have decided not to be married in London, we shall have the wedding we want. The family, and our friends, Georgie, in the Great Hall of the house, and afterward . . ." He smiled.

"What has happened to you, Quinton?" his brother asked. "These past few days you have seemed different."

"Nothing has happened," the duke quickly replied.

"Quinton, we are brothers. Don't try to outfox me, sir," George Hunter said. "I know you too well. What is it?"

"You are letting your imagination run away with you, youngling. It must be your nerves playing tricks on you as your doom approaches," the duke teased.

"No," George persisted, and then his face grew a look of surprise. *"My God! You're in love with Allegra!"*

The duke hit his brother a blow that took the wind

from him. "If you dare to spout such nonsense, George, Melinda will be a widow before she is a bride. Do you understand me?" He glowered at his younger.

"Uuumph!" George Hunter doubled over briefly, but then he straightened up again. "What the hell is the matter with love?" he wanted to know. "Love is wonderful, Quint."

"Allegra and I have made a sensible and practical marriage of convenience, George, as befits our station. Love has nothing to do with it. If you must know, the mere thought of love is repellent to Allegra, and to me as well, given the examples we have had of it."

"All your friends are in love with their wives, and I absolutely adore Melinda," George Hunter admitted.

"But I am not in love, nor is Allegra, and we are quite content with our situation as it is. Now, stop spouting nonsense. If it were not for Allegra's kindness, love would have gained you nothing. Your beefy father-in-law-to-be was not about to give you his youngest child just because you are Lord George Hunter and in love. He wisely saw his daughter provided with a husband, a home, and a modest income."

" 'Tis time, my lords," the vicar of St. Cuthbert's said as he hurried into the little room. "If you will follow me, please."

George Hunter had never before thought of Squire Franklyn as beefy, but as her father led Melinda down the aisle of the church, the young Lord Hunter hid a smile, concentrating instead upon his Melinda—a pleasingly plump young lady with chestnut brown curls, and dancing brown eyes. She smiled tremulously at him as he took her hand.

And afterward at the wedding breakfast he could scarcely take his eyes off his new wife. If Quinton wasn't in love he had no idea what he was missing,

George decided as he stole another kiss from his bride. And Quinton was a fool not to love Allegra. By day's end his sister-in-law-to-be had the entire district wrapped about her little finger. She was charming and gay, dancing the country dances with verve, refusing no partner. At one point he saw his older brother watching his fiancée. A sly smile touched Lord George Hunter's lips. Whatever he might say, Quint was in love with his betrothed. How the mighty have fallen, he thought, amused. Love was indeed a great leveler. Then he felt sorry for his brother, for it was obvious that Allegra was not in love with Quinton.

"When can we leave?" Melinda whispered to him finally.

"Are you anxious to depart our celebration, Lady Hunter?" He smiled wickedly at her, and she blushed, but shook her head in the affirmative. He took her hand. "I will call for the carriage, sweeting."

After they had gone with much tah-rah, the howls of Mistress Franklyn still echoing as she bid her *baby* good-bye, the duke turned to Allegra suggesting that they, too, depart, to which she readily agreed.

On the carriage ride home they spoke of how pleasant George and Melinda's wedding had been, although Mistress Franklyn had invited far more people than would be coming to their own wedding.

"She considered my brother quite the catch," the duke remarked.

"Not until he had his own farm and house," Allegra said pithily.

"Are you a cynic then, my dear?" he teased gently.

"No, Quinton, I am a realist," she replied seriously.

"George and Melinda love each other," he said.

"How fortunate for them, but it would have made no

difference, indeed it did make no difference to
Melinda's parents until George had his own holding.
Love has nothing to do with the success of a marriage."

"Your father loves his wife," the duke persisted.

"At their age they are allowed the luxury of love," Allegra answered. "And they began as friends. Each
knows the other, and there will be no surprises. Surrounded by lovers I wonder if you are having second
thoughts, Quinton. Are you?"

"No," he told her quietly. "Ours is a most practical
arrangement, my dear Allegra, and we shall be a most
perfect couple."

"Yes," she agreed, and then her eyes strayed to
Hunter's Lair which lay ahead of them in the late afternoon sunlight. It was even more beautiful now than
when she had first seen it. The lawns were manicured by
the great staff of gardeners now in their employ. The
gardens had been restored to their former glory, and a
delightful little marble summer house had been installed
only two weeks ago by the lake. As she exited their vehicle Allegra's gaze swept over the wonderful new entry
foyer with its pale yellow walls, decorative plaster
moldings, and black-and-white marble floors. It was all
so wonderful.

"Is it not perfect?" she said to him, looking around.

"Yes, it is, thanks to you," he told her.

"Honor and I should return to Morgan Court until a
few days before the wedding," Allegra said.

"Why?" he asked. He didn't want her to go. He had
grown quite used to having her about.

"The house is finished. The workmen will be gone in
a week's time. The architect leaves tomorrow. I have no
reason to remain," she told him.

"When has the appearance of propriety meant anything to you?" he asked her. "Soon you will be my wife."

"I have matters to resolve at Morgan Court," Allegra responded.

"Is Rupert Tanner one of those matters?" he demanded, suddenly angry, and openly jealous.

"*Rupert?* What does he have to do with anything?" Allegra said, genuinely puzzled. "I must look over the wedding gifts that are being sent to us, and arrange to have them transported here. Madame Paul will be coming from London to do the final fitting on my wedding gown and on Sirena's gown. She will be visiting her mama while I am there. We spoke on it at Lord Walworth's wedding. I have little gifts to buy for the servants who have looked after me my entire life. I want to bid them all a proper farewell. And then Papa's secretary and I must list the gifts sent to us, and send thank you notes. I have a great deal to do, Quinton, and I can only do it at Morgan Court. When I have finished, I shall return here before our wedding." She smiled at him. "I should think you would be glad to be rid of me for a few weeks, Quinton. There will be no one to boss you about and complain because the painters could not get the color quite right. You shall have peace and quiet. *But only until I return,*" she finished with a twinkle, and she smiled up at him.

"I shall miss you," he admitted. "I have become used to your presence. I have even grown to like your company."

"Have you? How nice," Allegra replied.

He wanted to strangle her where she stood. Could she not see that he was in love with her? Did she see him at all except as the Duke of Sedgwick? Had she no emotions? No feelings? My God, he thought, I am behaving like my brother, or Ocky. But at least their wives reciprocated their affections. Allegra is as cold as a marble statue. No. When I touched her body she melted like ice in the summer's sun. I can make her love me in spite of herself. If I have fallen in love, then surely she can fall in love, too.

"I shall look forward to your return with much anticipation, my dear," he told her. "And I shall look forward to our wedding day . . . and night even more."

She had the grace to blush, then said, "Honor and I will depart tomorrow, sir, the sooner to return."

*H*ome at Morgan Court again Allegra was horrified at the number of wedding gifts that had already arrived. "But the wedding is to be held at Hunter's Lair and will be most private," she said to her father's secretary, Charles Trent. "Must we keep them? Or can they be returned, Charles?"

"I fear you must keep them, Miss Allegra, even the ones in questionable taste. Remember that the duke's family is an ancient and revered one. Now that he is to have the power and prestige that being wealthy again will bring him, there are those who will want to keep, or gain his favor. I have listed everything that has arrived so far, along with the names of the donors. The thank you notes are written. You have but to sign your name to each one."

"It is astounding," Allegra said, shaking her head. "Neither the duke nor I intend joining London society. We are both agreed that we prefer the country life. We can be of little influence for anyone."

"Ahh, but who is to know that, Miss Allegra?" Charles Trent said with a small smile. "I'm certain Hunter's Lair has storage rooms where much of this may be put away from the light of day."

"Gracious! What are these?" she demanded, pointing.

Mr. Trent chuckled. "They are from a gentleman nabob who does business with your papa. I believe the elephant with his trunk upraised is a symbol of good fortune, Miss Allegra. The pair are a third life-size, overlaid with gold leaf, and decorated with semiprecious gemstones. Their tusks are genuine ivory. Perhaps if the duke would consider it, they could be installed outside his library doors."

"*Never!*" Allegra said emphatically. "Our home is both classic and elegant, but certainly not gaudy. What could this man have been thinking?"

"Most likely of impressing your papa with his generosity. It is a most expensive gift," Mr. Trent said dryly. "These nabobs, Miss Allegra, have great wealth, but many are self-made men of little or no background."

Sirena came shortly after Allegra had arrived home. The cousins greeted each other happily. Octavian Baird saluted his wife's relation warmly.

"How did you leave Quint?" he asked her.

"Strangely not happy to be left alone, although I thought he should enjoy a bit of peace and quiet after the uproar of the last few months. The house is finished at last."

"I shall pay him a visit then while Sirena stays with you," Viscount Pickford said.

"Not fair," Sirena cried. "Then you shall get to see the improvements to Hunter's Lair before I do."

"As you have never been to Hunter's Lair, it should make no difference at all," her husband said sensibly. "Enjoy your visit with Allegra and your parents, my darling."

The two young women had been placed back in their girlhood bedchamber. Allegra suddenly found the room old-fashioned after her beautiful and spacious apartment at Hunter's Lair, but she and Sirena were soon gossiping away as if they had never been parted.

"I see what you mean about Mama and Steppapa," Sirena told her cousin. "They are behaving quite like April and May."

"More like September and October," Allegra replied. "I had hoped that after a few months away they would have become more dignified again, but they are worse than ever."

"They are in love," Sirena said softly. "Is it not wonderful that your papa and my mama were able to find love again at their time of life? I am so happy for them."

"You sound like Charlotte," Allegra teased Sirena.

"Ohh, speaking of my sister-in-law," Sirena said, "she is at last with child! Gussie is over the moon and nothing is too good for his darling girl. About time she produced for the line. Why Ocky and I were married in June, and I shall have my baby in March. Charlotte and Gussie have been married forever."

"Tell me about *it*," Allegra begged her cousin. "What is it like when your husband . . . makes love to you?"

"Haven't you and the duke . . . ," Sirena began. "Well, I thought with your being at Hunter's Lair all summer you might have . . ." Her voice trailed off. "Didn't you even consider it? *Not even once?* Lord, Allegra, you must be a saint. He is so handsome!"

"Do you think so?" Allegra asked.

"*Don't you?*" Sirena responded.

"We do kiss," Allegra said.

"*And?*" Sirena demanded.

"I have let him touch my breasts," Allegra admitted.

"*Nothing more?*" Sirena was disappointed. "You really are a backward child, I fear, cousin. Why before I met Ocky I had been kissed and cuddled by half a dozen young men." She sighed. "You do know what a manhood looks like, don't you?"

"Of course!" Allegra said. "They are long and thin appendages that dangle between a man's legs, though for the life of me I do not understand how they can enter a woman's belly."

Sirena giggled. "Women have an opening in the secret place," she explained. "That's where they put it."

"How can that be, Sirena? That floppy thing?" Allegra was most disbelieving.

"It doesn't stay floppy, or thin," Sirena told her cousin. "They get hard and thick. It hurts the first time and you'll bleed, but after that . . ." Sirena's eyes grew dreamy.

"After what?" Allegra demanded impatiently.

"After the first time, it's just wonderful! Sometimes I even think I'm flying among the stars," Sirena admitted. "Of course now with the baby coming we must be very careful, and eventually Ocky and I will not be able to do it, but until then, it's wonderful. Marvelous!"

"But how do you do it?" Allegra wanted to know.

"Oh, the duke will tell you," Sirena said.

"No! You will tell me, Sirena. You cannot leave me in abject ignorance. I need to know what to expect," Allegra said.

"Mama will kill me if she learns I have told you," Sirena fretted.

"I will kill you if you don't. Besides, Aunt Mama will not tell me what I need to know. She will make some pronouncement about yielding myself, despite my delicate sensibilities, to my husband's wishes."

Sirena giggled. "Yes," she agreed, "that is exactly the kind of twaddle she will utter despite the fact that she and your papa have been fucking like rabbits ever since they were wed. . . ."

"Sirena!" Allegra half shrieked.

"Well they have, and you know it," Sirena said. "Why do you think you have been so uncomfortable around them. It is horrifying to think of one's parents behaving with such abandon, although now that I know what fun it is, I cannot say that I blame them."

"Tell me what I have to do," Allegra said.

"You'll be on your back," Sirena said. "The duke will lie atop you. He will want you to open your legs. Wait until he asks else you look like a wanton. Then he will put his manhood into your entry. That's all there is to it."

"There must be more," Allegra determined.

"There is," her cousin agreed, "but that is the part you must find out for yourself because, Ocky says, it is different with each partner. You will be in excellent hands. Ocky says the duke is considered an excellent lover. Men know about these things, as they certainly should."

"Well," Allegra said, "I suppose I must content myself with what you have told me. I hope I do not prove a perfect fool on my wedding night, Sirena. You know how I dislike being ignorant."

"You are a virgin, Allegra," Sirena said, suddenly sounding very wise. "Virgins are supposed to be unschooled and backward. Men like it that way. Ocky never knew, nor will he ever know of the boys I kissed and cuddled with before I came to London." She giggled. "He thinks he was my very first kiss. I hope he never runs into Jeremy Carstairs."

"Best to hope Jeremy Carstairs remains a gentleman," Allegra laughed. "You make yourself sound so worldly-wise, Sirena, but you were as big a virgin then as I am now."

Sirena nodded. "Of course I was," she agreed with a smile. "I love Ocky so much that I could not deceive him that way, and I didn't."

"What is it like to be *in love?*" Allegra asked her cousin.

"Are you in love with the duke?" came the question.

"I don't know," Allegra said. "I like him except when he becomes pompous; and I actually find that I miss him now that I am back at Morgan's Court. I have never thought I should fall in love, whatever that may be, but I should like to know what it is like. It would seem to me that the emotion called love isn't very practicable, or particularly sensible. I shall not expound my views as you have heard them often enough, but I am still curious."

"Love," Sirena said slowly, "is caring for someone even more than you care for yourself. It is wanting that person happy. It is the ability to give of yourself totally without losing yourself. I don't know if that makes any sense to you, Allegra, but it is the best explanation I can give you."

"I understand, or I think I do, and yet I don't," came the reply. "Perhaps it is better that I remain in ignorance. The duke feels as I do, and does not love me, nor will he ever love me."

"And yet you will marry him," Sirena said sadly.

"He is handsome and charming," Allegra said. "He respects me, and will make an excellent mate, Sirena."

"And you can give yourself body and soul to him without love?" It seemed so cold, and yet she well knew that most marriages among those of their class were made for reasons other than love. She loved Allegra.

She wanted her to have the happiness that she now possessed.

"Oh, Sirena," Allegra comforted her cousin. "I am content with everything. Quinton is kind. Hunter's Lair is beautiful. What more is there to life than that?"

"I suppose you are right, Allegra, even if it troubles me," Sirena said, and she gave her cousin a little smile.

"You were ever the romantic, Sirena dearest," Allegra teased.

"And you were ever the sensible one," Sirena replied.

"Madame Paul will be here tomorrow," Allegra said. "Your gown is to be pale blue to match your eyes, and my wedding dress will be white and silver lace. I can hardly wait to see it!"

"You always loved new clothes," Sirena laughed. "I vow you will leave instructions about what to bury yourself in one day."

"I certainly will!" Allegra agreed, and then she laughed, too. "Can you imagine us as old ladies, Sirena? You will still be the romantic, I suspect, and I shall be quite crotchety, waving my cane about."

"What cane?"

"The one with the silver dragon's head I intend having when I am a dowager. It will be polished black ebony with its silver dragon. Perhaps I shall have a whole dragon, and not just its head. Its silver body and tail could curl about my walking stick. I shall wave it at everyone who displeases me."

Sirena laughed harder. "Ohh, Allegra," she said, "you can be so amusing when you choose to be."

"I am quite serious, cousin," came the answer.

"You wouldn't wave that cane at the duke, would you?" she asked, her blue eyes twinkling mischievously.

"Particularly at the duke," Allegra said. "He can be

very aggravating at times. But on the whole he has been quite nice to me."

"All husbands can be difficult on occasion," Sirena said.

"You speak with such authority," Allegra teased her.

"Well I have been married almost four months," Sirena replied.

It was as if they had never been apart. The next few weeks sped by. Madame Paul arrived with her assistant, Mademoiselle Francine, to do the final fittings for the wedding. She clucked with disapproval when she found Allegra had lost almost a full inch in her waistline. She purred with pleasure that Sirena, despite her delicate condition, fit perfectly into her gown.

"Another month, however, *chérie,*" she told Viscountess Pickford, "and it would be another story, I fear."

Three days before the wedding Viscount Pickford arrived with the duke to escort the bride and her family back to Hunter's Lair. Allegra found her heart beating a bit faster at just the sight of Quinton Hunter. Still, they greeted each other with restraint; she curtseying, he bowing and kissing her hand.

"What is the matter with them?" Sirena whispered to her husband.

Octavian Baird smiled mysteriously. "Can't you tell?" he asked her, and when Sirena shook her blond head, puzzled, he continued. "They are in love with each other, but neither will tell the other, or admit to it, my adorable angel."

"Why on earth not?" Sirena squealed, excited.

"Because each fears the other will reject such overtures. Neither has any reason to believe in love, given their family history, but love, as you know, my darling, makes no allowances for such things. Quinton is horrified to find that he actually cares for Allegra. He feels it would be off-putting to tell her of his emotions toward her. He believes she will never reciprocate such feelings, and if there is one thing Quinton Hunter is, it is overproud. To be spurned or dismissed by the girl he loves would be an insult he could never forgive. So he will remain silent, and so, my darling girl, must you."

Sirena nodded. "Yes, I will," she told her husband. "I believe that Allegra likes the duke very much, but I do not think she is in love with him despite what you think. *Not yet.*"

"Do you actually believe she will admit to loving him one day?" her husband asked hopefully. "God, how happy Quint would be if that occurred! He cannot believe what has happened to him, or the delicious turmoil this duchess-to-be of his has caused with his heart."

"She seems to get on with him, and as I have said, she likes him. They have become friends, and friendship is the best basis for a lasting love, Ocky," Sirena said wisely. "Ohh, how I would like it if my cousin really fell in love, and was as happy with her duke as I am with you!" The knowledge that the duke loved her cousin reassured Sirena. Now she was not as fearful of the marriage as she previously had been.

Hunter's Lair welcomed back its mistress. To Allegra's delight everything she had ordered done in her absence had been completed. Her father was well pleased with the renovations to the house, and her stepmother admired the décor, pronouncing it "exquisite." Sirena was delighted with its homey quality.

"I was so afraid it would be one of those huge grand houses that can never quite be a home," she said, "but this is wonderful!"

Lord Morgan took the duke aside. "Mr. Trent has

seen to it that a deposit has been made to your account, sir. He will make those deposits quarterly, both for you, and for Allegra."

"Thank you, sir," the duke replied.

"And the architect and workmen have been settled with so you need have no worry on that account," Lord Morgan continued.

"You have been more than generous, my lord," the duke said.

Lord Morgan smiled dryly. "Treat her well, Quinton. I am not a man to marry off his daughter and then be done with her. She is my flesh, and I love her."

"Allegra is a delight, sir," the duke answered. Then he smiled a wry smile. "As well as being willful and stubborn, but I believe that we suit despite it all."

"Yes," Lord Morgan said, "I think this bargain that we have made will turn out quite well for all of us. Give me grandchildren as soon as you can, Quinton. Nothing settles a woman quite like a family of her own to care for and worry over."

The guests began arriving the next day. Lady Bellingham, her good husband in tow, came first. Her jaw fell as she entered the house. "God bless me, I have never seen Hunter's Lair look so fine!" she pronounced. "Have my bags taken up. I must have a tour this moment!" Lord and Lady Walworth came shortly afterward, followed by the Earl and Countess of Aston. The Marquess of Rowley came, but without his wife. Lady Charlotte would not travel in her delicate condition, but Gussie refused to miss his favorite cousin's wedding. Allegra had also asked her father's secretary, Charles Trent, to be their guest.

That evening Allegra received her first inkling of what it was going to be like being the Duchess of Sedgwick as she presided over her twelve guests at the dinner table. It was the first time the new dining room had been used. Its great black marble fireplace blazed with enormous logs that had been set across the silver andirons. The table was set with pristine Irish linen. The silver candelabra glittered with the reflected light of the candles. To Allegra's delight the chandeliers from Waterford had arrived earlier than expected. Two of them now hung over the table, the crystal sparkling with their many candles. Blue and white bowls of flowers from the greenhouse decorated the table. The servants were resplendent in their hunter's green with silver braid livery. Footmen stood behind each guest's chair as the lavish meal was served. Still in all it was a happy gathering of friends, and not quite as formal as it would have been in London.

Afterward when the dessert had been cleared away, the ladies retired to the drawing room next to the ballroom to gossip while the gentlemen were left to their port. The gentlemen would join them shortly, and they would play cards among themselves.

"I am so glad you decided to have your wedding here rather than return to London," Lady Walworth said.

"They should have been wed with pomp and circumstance," her aunt, Lady Bellingham, replied.

"Now, dearest Lady B.," Allegra responded, "Quinton and I love Hunter's Lair. We can think of no more perfect place in which to be married than the Great Hall of this house. Besides, if we had returned to London, Sirena couldn't have been my matron of honor. The trip would have been too much for her. Here she is but an easy drive from her home. All our guests are."

"The king and queen would have come," Lady Bellingham said regretfully.

"They have sent us a beautiful gift," Allegra told her.

"Four silver and gilt saltcellars. Would you like to see them? Our gifts have been laid out in the ballroom with their cards. Perkins!" Allegra signaled a footman. "Take Lady Bellingham to the ballroom so she may view the display set up there. You are all welcome to go."

"The rest of you may look another time," Lady Bellingham said. "Stay with Allegra. The gentlemen will be coming soon enough, but if he's in the mood for cards, Bellingham won't notice if I am here or not," she concluded with a chuckle. Then she let the young footman escort her from the little salon.

"She won't be back for an hour at least," Lady Caroline said. "She'll examine each gift, and its card, and have an opinion on it all when she finally returns to us."

"Your aunt terrifies me," Sirena said.

"Oh, you must not be afraid of her. She is really quite softhearted, although she would roast me for saying so," Lady Caroline answered.

"It was she who introduced me to Marcus," Lady Eunice said. "I shall never be able to repay her for that particular kindness."

At that moment the door to the drawing room opened, and the gentlemen came in, greeting their ladies as they did. Three tables of four were already set up for Whist, and two were quickly filled by the guests. The duke did not gamble, as everyone knew, but he did not mind his guests indulging themselves as long as the play did not get too deep. Lady Caroline and Lady Eunice were still more interested in seeing the wedding gifts. Allegra sent them along in the company of a footman.

"If you are comfortable," she said to her guests, "I beg to be excused for a moment. I must make certain that the preparations in the Great Hall are going along well." She curtsied, and hurried from the room. In the Great Hall the servants were busily hanging the green garlands entwined with white silk roses that would decorate the room for the festivities on the morrow. The highboard was set up as it had been in olden times. She looked about, and saw that the chairs had been placed in the Minstrel's Gallery for the musicians.

"The staff is working very hard, Miss Allegra," Mr. Crofts said to her as he came to stand by her side. "It will all look quite fine when 'tis done."

"It does look lovely, doesn't it, Crofts," Allegra said. "Please thank the staff. They have worked very hard. Those who serve at the table tomorrow will receive a silver shilling each so they may celebrate on their next day off. Do not tell them though until afterward."

"Very good, miss," the old butler said with a small smile. The duke was very fortunate in his choice of a wife. They were all very fortunate, he thought to himself.

Allegra returned to the salon. Lady Bellingham, Caroline, and Eunice had returned from the ballroom where the gifts were displayed. They were most admiring of the generosity offered to the duke and Allegra. They could, however, speak of nothing else but the two elephants with their ivory tusks and bejeweled coverings.

"I am going to build a glass conservatory off this salon," Allegra said. "It will be filled with plants, and I believe I can hide the elephants among the foliage. That way I do not insult Papa's nabob. I suppose he thought it was a wonderful gift, but gracious!"

Her companions laughed, and then Sirena said, "I believe the four of us are going to be very good friends. Allegra has said she will hold the duke's annual hunting parties, and so we shall see one another often."

"Do you hunt?" Lady Caroline asked.

"I do not," Allegra said. "I have already told Quinton that I will entertain and feed his parties, but I shall not careen about the countryside with my leg slung over a pommel. When I ride I wear breeches. Besides, I like deer and foxes."

"Thank heavens," Lady Caroline said. "Now I shall have the perfect excuse. I thought I was the only one who hated hunting."

"I don't like it either," Lady Eunice admitted with a delicate shudder.

"Nor I," said Sirena.

"My dearest." Lady Morgan had come up to put an arm about her stepdaughter's waist. "You are being married at nine o'clock tomorrow morning. I think it is time for you to retire."

"But should I leave my guests, Aunt Mama?" Allegra wondered.

"They will understand, *and,* my dearest, we must talk," Lady Morgan said seriously.

Sirena caught Allegra's eye, and she struggled not to laugh. Her friends were endeavoring not to giggle, their pretty mouths twitching. Newly married, they had all had to endure *the talk* on the night before their weddings. They bid their hostess good night, and watched as she was escorted from the drawing room by her stepmother.

Honor was waiting for her mistress with a hot tub already drawn, but Lady Morgan put up a restraining hand and dismissed the servant for a few moments while she spoke with Allegra.

"My dear," she began, "there are certain duties a wife must perform for her husband. I find them most pleasant, although some women claim not to find them so. Just remember that if it is done with kindness, and possibly love, all will be well."

"Aunt Mama," Allegra said quietly, "let me relieve you of what must surely be an embarrassing moment. I have spoken with my three friends to ascertain the nature of my wifely *duties*. They have kindly been most forth-coming, and enlightened me. You need go no further, I assure you. I understand what is expected of me, and the notion is not at all unpleasant. Indeed, I am very cu-rious to experience these *duties* myself," Allegra con-cluded, her look mischievous.

Lady Morgan gave a gusty sigh of relief. "Bless you, Allegra, for being a sensible girl. I do not care how close a mother and her daughter are, it is a delicate and often awkward moment between them. No girl wants to con-sider her mother possesses such knowledge, and no mother wants to imagine her child under such circum-stances." She laughed, and Allegra laughed with her. "I hardly gave poor Sirena any instructions at all, and would have felt most guilty did I not know how much she and Octavian loved each other. She kept looking at me with those wonderful big blue eyes of hers, and frankly I was most discomfited. I kept seeing her as that adorable little girl with the lovely long curls who played with you at Morgan Court."

Allegra walked over to the sideboard in her salon, and lifting the crystal stopper from a decanter poured two small glasses of sherry. Turning, she handed one of the glasses to her stepmother. "I salute you, madame. You are the best mother any girl could have had even if you are my aunt." She raised her little goblet and drank.

"Ohh, my dear," Lady Morgan said, "and I salute you. My foolish sister lost a wonderful child in you, but I gained another daughter to love and to cherish." She raised her goblet and drank.

Their glasses emptied, the two hugged each other, and then Lady Morgan kissed Allegra on both cheeks. "Good night, my darling girl. Sleep well. I shall see you in the morning." Then she turned, and hurried from the room, but not before Allegra had seen the tears of happiness welling up in her blue eyes.

Thank heavens that was over and done with, Allegra thought to herself. Heaven only knows what Aunt Mama would have told her if she had not weaseled the information out of Sirena. And she had taken any blame from Sirena's shoulders by claiming that all three of her friends had spoken with her on the subject. "Honor," she called as she began to loosen her gown. "She is gone."

Honor hurried from the dressing room. "You could have asked me *anything*, miss," she told her mistress.

"*Anything?*" Allegra raised a dark eyebrow.

"Girls in my position grow up faster, miss," the servant replied.

"Honor, you haven't!" Allegra wasn't certain she should be shocked by such a revelation.

"No, I most certainly haven't," Honor quickly answered. "I wouldn't be fit to work in a decent household if I was that kind of loose baggage. I just said we grow up faster when we're servants. We see things. We hear things. We talk among one another, and are far easier among ourselves than the gentry are. We are not bound up by all your manners and rules of polite society, Miss Allegra."

"*Oh.*"

Honor took her mistress's lovely silk gown, and laid it aside. "Now let's get you bathed for you'll not have time in the morning," she said, and then she pinned Allegra's dark curls atop her head.

The bath, smelling of lilacs, was wonderful, and Allegra did not want to hurry, but she knew Honor would be awakening her early. She washed quickly. Her hair had been washed earlier in the day, and so she did not have to bother going to bed with a wet head and risking a chill. She exited her tub into a warmed towel held by her servant. "I shall be a married lady this time tomorrow," she said aloud.

"You're sure you are happy about it?" Honor asked boldly.

"Yes, I am content," Allegra replied softly. "He is a kind man, and he seems reasonable."

"Are you softening toward him then?" Honor queried. Although she was not a great deal older than her mistress, she had been with her since Allegra had left the nursery at age six. At twenty-four she felt eons older than her mistress. Their relationship allowed for such questions occasionally.

"I like him." Allegra took out her pins, and sitting at her dressing table began to brush her hair free of its tangles.

"Ummm," Honor observed, and said no more.

"And what does *that* mean?" Allegra demanded.

"You can sometimes be slow in coming to a decision, miss," was the answer.

"What decision can I not make?" Allegra demanded.

"Whether you love him or not."

"*Love him?* Honor, do not be ridiculous! I have told you before I do not love him."

"If you say so, miss," the servant replied. "Now let's get you into bed so you can get some sleep." She tucked the down comforter about her mistress. "Good night, Miss Allegra. It's the last night I'll say that. From tomorrow on it will be *Your Grace*." Then with a quick smile, Honor left Allegra for the night, closing the dressing room door behind her as she went.

Allegra stared at the canopy above her. *Your Grace.* Good Lord! The time had come for her to become the Duchess of Sedgwick. It was autumn. Spring and summer had long flown, and tomorrow she was to marry the duke. What an odd thing for Honor to have said. That she couldn't make up her mind if she loved Quinton Hunter, or not. Of course she didn't love him, and he most certainly didn't love her. And even if her feelings toward him were to change, she would certainly not embarrass him by gushing romantic twaddle.

This summer past they had become friends. They both loved Hunter's Lair. They both wanted a simple life with family and children. They were highly fortunate, they both knew, in having no financial worries. But that was all there was to it. Allegra's eyes felt heavy. There really was nothing more to their relationship. Why on earth had Honor said what she had said? Why does she persist so? Did she know something her mistress didn't? Allegra yawned, and her eyes closed. "He doesn't love me, and I don't love him," she said softly. And then she fell asleep.

Chapter Nine

Allegra's wedding day did not dawn brightly. The autumn rain fell in sheets outside the house, knocking against the windows. The hall, however, was warm and bright with the light of many candles and the twin fireplaces which blazed, crackling with sparks of golden light as the red flames danced in the downdraft from the wind outdoors. The vicar from St. Luke's, the village church, had come early, riding through the stormy weather to reach Hunter's Lair a full hour before the nine o'clock ceremony was scheduled. His wet clothing was taken from him to be dried while he changed into his cassock and white and gold chasuble. The clergyman was pleased to have been asked to marry the duke and his bride. His stipend for the service would be generous, he had not a doubt, and the duke could have sent for the local bishop instead. The vicar graciously accepted the goblet of wine offered him, and looked about.

Heavy carved gold candlesticks and a jeweled gold crucifix had been placed atop a white linen runner on the highboard to serve as an altar. There were vases of flowers upon stands set around the temporary altar. The air was sweet with the scent of late pink roses, pink and white lilies, and lavender.

At the appointed hour the small group of guests were seated upon narrow backless oak benches that were a part of the hall's original furnishings. The rest of the hall was filled with the servants, and as many of the duke's tenants as could crowd in. They arrived silently, wiping their muddy boots under Mr. Crofts's stern eye before they were allowed into their master's house.

Sirena looked lovely in a simple pale blue silk gown with its puffed sleeves and high waist. Her gown was tied with a narrow pink ribbon sash. She carried a small nosegay of pink roses and lavender. There were pink roses in her short curly coiffure, which was now cut in the latest style. Sirena could not keep herself from smiling. She had so wanted to share this day with her beloved cousin, and Allegra, generous of heart, had made it so.

The bride was pale, and to her surprise, nervous. Her voice was soft. It almost trembled as she spoke her vows. She was very embarrassed, and wondered if anyone, particularly the duke, had noticed. It was childish of her to feel any anxiety. While her blood might be nowhere as blue as the duke's, she was fully confident that she would make Quinton Hunter a perfect duchess. This was what she had wanted, and she knew that she looked absolutely beautiful this morning.

Madame Paul had outdone herself. The wedding gown was an exquisite creation of pure white silk into which had been woven tiny silver stars. High waisted, it had a delicate bouffant overskirt of the sheerest silver net. The bodice had a rounded neckline. The little puffed sleeves were decorated with diminutive silver bows. The duke had given his bride a necklace of large pearls from which dangled a blue-white diamond heart and a pair of diamond and pearl earbobs, which Allegra now wore.

Her thick, long, dark hair was fashioned into a smooth, elegant chignon, atop which had been placed a wreath of white roses holding a long filmy veil of silver netting. Allegra stared hard at the heavy band of Irish red-gold and diamonds that the duke had placed upon her finger. The reality of her situation suddenly slammed into her, even as the vicar spoke the final words of the ceremony.

"I now pronounce you husband and wife. Those whom God has joined together, let no man rend asunder." The cleric paused, then said, "You may kiss the bride, Your Grace."

The duke's hands cupped Allegra's face as her startled gaze met his. He kissed her, and for a brief moment Allegra soared. But then he released her, smiling into the confusion in her eyes, saying, "Shall we see to our guests, Your Grace?"

They turned to receive the good wishes of their family, their friends, and all the others in the hall. The musicians in the Minstrel's Gallery began to play a sprightly tune. The servants hurried forth with the wedding breakfast and the wine as the hall emptied of all but the chosen few. The new Duchess of Sedgwick invited them to take their seats, indicating where each should sit. She and the duke sat in the king and queen's chairs in the center of the highboard facing out into the hall.

Allegra stole a look at her new husband. She had always thought him handsome, but today he seemed even more so in his white brocaded satin suit embroidered with gold. His brother, who had been Quinton's witness, had chosen to wear a sky blue satin suit that matched Sirena's gown. Lord George Hunter now arose from the table to make a toast.

"To my brother, Quinton, who had the good sense to marry the most beautiful, and certainly the most generous girl in all of England. May he and Allegra have many happy years together. God bless!"

"Here! Here!" the other guests agreed, raising their crystal goblets of wine and drinking.

Now the duke arose, and raising his glass, looked directly at his new wife, who blushed. "To Allegra, who has brought happiness to my family and given a new life to Hunter's Lair. I thank her for marrying me." Quinton Hunter drank a sip of wine. Then placing his goblet upon the table he took Allegra's hand up and kissed it.

More toasts were offered during the long meal while poached eggs in a cream and Marsala sauce were presented, along with a small pink country ham that was thinly sliced, and rashers of bacon. There were fresh, warm, and dainty rolls; breads, sweet butter, and plum conserves. There were bowls of oatmeal mixed with heavy cream, cooked apples, and cinnamon sugar. There was beefsteak, tiny lamb chops upon a silver platter, creamed cod, sliced salmon that had been poached in white wine and dill and served upon a bed of watercress and sliced lemons. There was a dish of baked apples with clotted cream, and another dish of stewed pears with nutmeg and sherry. Finally there was a wedding cake with its tiny white spun sugar decorations covering the golden fruited confection. It was early afternoon by the time the entire meal had been concluded.

Outside the rain continued to fall. The servants and the estate workers had their own feast moved from the outdoors to the barns. The wedding party and their guests took the opportunity to visit them during a brief respite in the storm. There the bride and groom were toasted again in honest English ale and cider. They danced several country dances with their humbler guests before returning to the house, where Allegra saw the carriages of her guests already drawn up before the

front door of Hunter's Lair. She realized that her friends
and family would be leaving shortly as they all wanted
to reach their various homes before sunset. Even in the
country the roads could be dangerous after dark.

"It was a most beautiful wedding," Sirena said. "Do
try to be happy, Allegra."

"I am," the bride insisted.

"You know what I mean," Sirena replied meaningfully.

"We shall leave you alone for a week," the young
Countess of Aston said, "but after that you will come
and visit us." She kissed Allegra on both cheeks.
"Good-bye, darling!" Then Eunice and her husband
were gone out the door.

"You *must* come to London this winter," Lady
Bellingham insisted, giving the bride a warm hug. "It
has been a most delightful time, dear girl." There were
more kisses. Then Lady Bellingham and her quiet husband departed.

"We will see you at Eunice's," Caroline, Lady Walworth, said before she left with her husband in tow.

"George said you were the most beautiful and generous girl in all of England," Melinda Hunter said shyly.
Then she grew bolder, continuing, "and I know why,
Allegra." Lady Hunter kissed her sister-in-law. "Thank
you. Without your kindness and generosity I should not
be so happy. I wish you the same joy with the duke as I
have had with his brother."

Allegra flushed. "Families are supposed to help one
another," she said in reply.

"I echo my wife's thanks," George Hunter said quietly. Then he kissed his brother's bride, and Lord and
Lady Hunter were gone.

"What did you do?" Sirena wanted to know.

"Another time, dear heart," Allegra told her softly.

Sirena nodded. "Very well, I shall contain my curiosity." Then with a wave, she and her husband were off.

"Well, my dear," Lord Morgan said, "I shall bid you farewell for now. Be a good wife to your husband." He kissed her on the forehead.

"Yes, Papa," Allegra responded dutifully.

"God bless you, my darling child," Lady Morgan said. Then she departed with her husband. There was nothing left she needed to say to her stepdaughter. It had all, thank goodness, been said.

They stood alone in the round foyer. Allegra wasn't certain what was to happen next. It was much too early to retire, she thought, as the tall clock struck half after two o'clock. The servants were bustling back and forth clearing away the remnants of the wedding feast.

"Would you like to ride?" the duke suddenly asked her.

"In the rain?" Allegra thought her voice sounded rather hollow.

"It is only drizzling right now," he answered.

"Perhaps a game of chess," she suggested.

"Ahh," he agreed. "The very thing."

"I shall have it set up in the family salon," Allegra said. "Perkins," she called to the passing footman. "Set up the game table in the family drawing room, and bring the chess pieces, please."

As the footman hurried off, the duke said to his new wife, "You looked . . . look," he corrected himself, "very beautiful today, my dear. Every inch a Duchess of Sedgwick, if I may say so."

"You may," she replied, "and if I may return the compliment, sir, you are most handsome in that satin suit."

He actually flushed with her praise, then took her by

the hand. "Come along, Allegra. We have not played chess in some weeks, and I am anxious to see if you have improved."

"You are anxious to see if I have gotten any worse," she mocked him with a smile. "Prepare yourself for a drubbing, my lord. I have been playing with Papa these last few days, and he is a brilliant player."

Their family drawing room was decorated in pale blue, buff, and cream color. It held a mixture of old oak furniture and new maple pieces from London. Perkins set up the game table between the two wing chairs by the fireplace. When Allegra had seated herself he handed her the ebony and ivory box banded in silver that held the playing pieces.

She opened the box. "With your permission, sir, I shall take the white pieces, and give you the ebony."

He nodded in agreement, and set up the board so they might begin their play. For several hours the duke and his new duchess vied with each other over the chessboard. They played several games, and were, Quinton Hunter had to admit to himself, equally matched. He won two games and she won two. Outside the storm continued to rage about them. A footman came into the room to make certain the fire was still burning. He trimmed the lamp and candlewicks, even as a fifth game ended in a draw. It had grown dark outside.

"I have set up a supper in the dining room, my lord," Crofts said as he entered the drawing room. The clock on the mantel struck six o'clock.

"Gracious!" Allegra exclaimed. "How the time has flown."

There was capon, ham, and a venison pie on the sideboard in the dining room along with a bowl of green beans, fresh bread, butter, and cheese. When they had eaten all they could, Crofts appeared with a dish of fresh pineapple from the greenhouse and some sugar wafers. Allegra loved the tart-sweet fruit and was almost childlike in her greediness for it.

The duke could not help but smile, but when she had finished he said quietly, "You will want to go upstairs now, my dear. I shall join you in an hour or so." He raised his wine glass and sipped slowly at the fragrant wine.

Allegra paled for a brief moment, but then she arose, curtsied, and without a word walked sedately from the dining room. Her heart had begun to beat furiously. *Soon!* Soon she was going to know what all the fuss was about. Did she really want to know? Did she have a choice? She was Quinton Hunter's wife, and subject to his will by English law, and by God. She ran lightly up the staircase to her apartment where she found Honor awaiting her with a scented tub.

"Good evening, Your Grace," her servant said with a small smile, and a quick curtsey. "Let me take your things, and get you ready for bed." Honor was behaving as if it were any other night. Swiftly and efficiently, she helped her mistress undress herself, and then helped her into the tub. Allegra had already pinned her hair up as she always did. Then Honor bustled about the apartment putting garments away, or setting them aside to take to the laundress as Allegra washed herself. Finally she helped the new duchess from her tub.

Allegra sat down upon her dressing table bench as Honor dried between each of her toes. "Do you remember," she said, "when I was a little girl how you told me my toes would fall off if I didn't dry between them? I cannot tell you how long I believed you."

"No proper lady would have wet toes," Honor said.

"At least that's what me ma always said." She paused a moment then told her young mistress, "I'm leaving a basin of warm water and some cloths by the fire."

"What on earth for?" Allegra asked her maid.

"You'll understand later," Honor said, getting up quickly. "Now, come and get into your night garb, m'lady." She held out a white silk garment that she slipped over Allegra's head, carefully tying a single white ribbon at the neckline. "There, now into bed with you."

Allegra climbed into the large bed, sniffing delightedly at the lavender scent coming from the sheets. Even the large pillows propped up behind her were scented.

Honor curtsied. "Good night, Your Grace," she said, and hurriedly left the bedchamber, closing the door firmly behind her. She had not, Allegra noted, gone to her own room.

The Duchess of Sedgwick lay in her bed watching the play of the firelight on the walls. Outside her heavily draped windows she could hear the roar of the storm with its howling winds and beating rains. It had been a wonderful day, but now she had to face reality, except she wasn't really certain what that reality was. All her guests had been so happy today. Happy for her, for Quinton, especially happy with one another. Sirena loved her Ocky. Caroline and Adrian Walworth seemed radiant. As for Eunice and Marcus, they had scarcely been able to take their eyes off each other. Her father and Aunt Mama four months after their union were still acting like April and May. Why even Lady Bellingham and her husband seemed to evince tart affection for each other.

"But I don't believe in love," Allegra muttered to herself. "These are but aberrations." Neither a man nor a woman can be faithful to their mate except in rare circumstances. And for the one who loves, the pain of betrayal must be horrific. Papa and Aunt Mama, as well as the Bellinghams, are old. Perhaps when one is old, love, true love, enters his life. As for Sirena, Caroline, and Eunice, we will see what happens to them five years from now, she thought to herself. It was better that she and the duke had a more sensible arrangement.

The door connecting their two bedchambers opened, and the duke stepped through. He was wearing a white linen nightshirt which he immediately removed. Then he climbed into bed with her.

"*Oh, my!*" Allegra gasped.

"Let me take that charming garment off, my dear," he told her, and before she could protest, he swiftly whisked it over her head, and deposited the nightgown by the side of the bed. "There, now we are equals."

Allegra leapt from the bed, snatching up the discarded garment to clutch before her. "I do not think I can do this," she said nervously.

"Do what?" he asked, lying back amid the pillows. Damnation, she was utterly adorable. He had to be patient even though his male member was already evincing interest in her delectable form.

"Con . . . con . . . oh, damnit, Quinton, you know what I mean," Allegra almost shouted at him.

"*Consummate?*" he inquired helpfully.

"Yes! Consummate! I can't do it." Now she *was* shouting.

"Get back into bed, Allegra. No one is going to do anything to harm you," he told her calmly. "It is natural that a virgin would be frightened of her first experience, but I promise you it will be all right. Come," he held out his hand to her, "you are going to catch an ague."

She was cold. What on earth had made her behave in such a childish manner? "Do we have to . . . right away?" she asked him.

"Not right away, my dear," he assured her, "but I promise that you will soon want to do it, Allegra." The duke smiled. He knew he loved her. It was unlikely she would ever love him, but that didn't matter right now.

She dropped the nightgown she had been holding, and slowly climbed into the bed with him. Almost at once he enfolded her in his arms. To her mortification she trembled. She couldn't meet his gaze.

The silken softness of her flesh sent a fierce bolt of desire through him. He forced it back. She needed to be taken gently, not with brute force. He ran his fingers across her lips. "You are most kissable, my dear," he told her, and his mouth met hers.

Ohh, God! She could feel the hardness of his masculine body. It was deliciously exciting. His mouth was warm and enticing against hers. She felt herself melting in his embrace. I have the heart of a whore just like my mother, she thought to herself with shock, but she couldn't stop herself from kissing him back. He was her husband, she reasoned. They were supposed to cohabit like this.

Their lips parted. "Look at me, Allegra," he said to her.

"I can't," she whispered back. "I feel shy. I have never before found myself in bed with a naked man."

He laughed softly. "No, I expect you haven't, my dear, but here we are. Husband and wife. *And it is our wedding night.*"

Her violet eyes finally looked into his silvery gray ones. There was something there she didn't understand at all. A look that totally confused her. But at least he was not slavering over her body like some fierce bestial animal.

"Would you like to see what I look like?" he asked her, and before she might refuse he threw back the down coverlet. Then he lay back.

Her curiosity overwhelmed her, and Allegra stared unabashedly at his long lean body. His shoulders and chest were broad, but she had known that, for even clothed she could see he was a big man. He was lightly furred upon his chest. Her eyes followed the delicate line of dark fur as it ran down his flat belly to a thick tangle of dark black curls between his muscled thighs. Allegra swallowed hard, but she was unable to turn away from her first sight of his manhood. "My brother was not so big," she remarked frankly. "I used to spy when he and his friends compared themselves."

"Ahh," he said, his unspoken question answered.

"Your feet are big," she noted.

"Yes," he answered her.

"But not wide. And your arms and legs are hairy. James Lucian was not hairy at all as I remember it," Allegra told her husband.

"Each man has slight differences," he advised her, "even as women do."

"I suppose you would like to see me," Allegra responded, and threw back the coverlet on her side of the bed. "I hope I compare favorably with the other women you have known, Quinton."

"Very favorably," he assured her. Then he bent down, and licked at her nipple.

"Oh my!" she said again. His touch was thrilling. His dark head against her milky flesh intoxicating. Unable to help herself she reached out with a hand and touched his head, threading her fingers lightly through the black hair. *"Ohhhh!"* His mouth had closed over the nipple, and he suckled upon her.

"Ohhhh good, or ohhhh bad?" he asked amused, raising his head, and piercing her with his silvery gaze.

"Good," she whispered, blushing, barely able to look at him.

"You are being very brave, Allegra," he told her with a chuckle.

"You are being very kind, I think," she replied.

"You have lovely breasts, my dear. They are like small round peaches, summer-ripe and bursting with sweetness. I will want to continue to adore them, Allegra. Will you let me?"

"Yes," she said. "I like your touch."

"There will come a moment when I become overwhelmed with your loveliness, and shall not ask your permission further, my dear. You must not be fearful, however, for I shall not harm you," the duke told her.

"Will you put your manhood inside of me?" she asked him.

"Yes."

"Will it hurt? Sirena said it hurts the first time," Allegra confided in him, although her cheeks were now fiery hot.

"Yes," he answered her. "It will hurt the first time, but how much depends on how tightly your virginity is lodged, my dear. I will be as gentle as I can be, I promise."

Allegra swallowed hard. "Very well then, sir, let us soldier on now. I should be rid of this troublesome virginity so you may have your pleasure of me. I am told men enjoy this fucking very much."

Now it was Quinton Hunter who swallowed hard. Actually he wanted to laugh. Most young women, he assumed, would have been reticent to speak, would have been shyly reluctant, and maybe even frightened on their wedding night. Allegra had passed through those stages quite quickly. He didn't think he had ever heard a proper lady use the term *fucking*. Nor mention in an offhanded manner that she had heard men enjoyed it. "They do," he agreed, "but women also enjoy fucking as well, my dear. They can be as enthusiastic as any gentleman," the duke assured his new wife.

"Indeed?" Allegra remarked. "Well, sir, then let us get to it, shall we. Is your manhood serviceable?"

Now he could not help himself, and he did burst out laughing. "Allegra, Allegra! Your innocence is charming, but passion is not something one can force to one's will. We began nicely, but your questions have turned the mood between us. Can you, my dear, be quiet now, and let me lead you down Eros's path to pleasure? I find that I most surely do want to make love to you." He tipped her face up, and kissed her cherry lips, gently at first, and then with a little more passion, as he pushed her back against their pillows. "You are a most talkative little puss, my dear, but the time for talking has now come to an end. Would you agree with me on that?" He kissed the tip of her nose softly.

"But . . . but," she protested faintly, "I have questions, sir."

"Which shall all be answered, my dear, in due time, I promise you," Quinton Hunter told his wife. He kissed her ear, licking at it very provocatively, and then blowing softly into it. "I love the taste of your skin, Allegra," he told her, his lips wandering down her neck, and across her shoulder.

"But what should I do?" she pleaded.

"Nothing, my dear, but be quiet and still, follow your own instincts, and let me make love to you. No one has ever touched you before tonight, Allegra. I know that. No man shall ever have you but me." His voice had suddenly become very harsh. *"You are mine, my dear!"*

His words sent a shiver of excitement through her. She shuddered as his tongue licked at the straining column of her throat. He scattered kisses across her breasts. She could feel her bosom. It was tight, and the nipples were beginning to ache, but it was not a hurtful sensation. It actually felt good. He was restraining one of her hands by her side with his own, but her other hand began to caress his lean form in return. She stroked him slowly, reaching farther and farther until she was fondling the curve of his buttock and hip. Allegra hadn't known she could be so bold. She pulled her hand back to trail her fingers across the nape of his neck.

Her exploration, shy as it was, aroused him. Slowly, slowly, he drew her beneath him. Now he lay atop her, and he began once again to kiss her with slow, fiery kisses. Her body was soft, yet firm with her youth. He drew both of her hands up now, positioning them over her dark head. His tongue pushed itself into her mouth, stroking, fencing with hers. His excitement was rising with each passing moment. His manhood was now rock hard, pressing with urgency against her thigh.

"Open your legs for me, Allegra," he murmured softly in her ear. "I want you, my dear. I want you very, very much."

She trembled at his passionate words. The time had come for her to be initiated into the mysteries of Venus and Eros. Slowly, slowly she spread herself beneath him. Her heart was hammering, and she was unable at last to speak. She trembled again as he knelt between her thighs. His hand reached out to cup her entire Venus mont within his big palm, squeezing. Allegra drew a sharp breath at his touch *there*. She didn't dare to look at what he was doing.

He watched her and smiled to himself as he released her plump mont. She awaited her deflowering with a certain amount of trepidation, he realized, but he needed a moment more. Slowly he pulled her nether lips open, gazing upon her lovebud, all coral and wet with her excitement. She was almost perfect, he thought, and he very much wanted to love her in that special way, but tonight was not the time for such an introduction, he decided. Holding her open with a thumb and a forefinger he touched her lovebud with the tip of his finger, and rubbed it suggestively. Allegra murmured a little cry, and shivered. Her love juices were beginning to pearl against her flesh. He groaned low. "You are so beautiful, Allegra," he murmured to her, smiling again as even with her eyes closed she blushed furiously.

Leaning forward he kissed her, positioning himself for the tender onslaught he was about to make on her innocence. She felt the tip of his lance pressing against her most intimate place. It pushed through her slowly yielding flesh until it was just lodged within her body. He kissed her again, slowly, tenderly, then his mouth fused against hers in a fierce kiss as he thrust hard and deep within her.

Pain radiated throughout her lower extremities. Her legs felt wooden; her belly as though a hot poker had been jammed into it. She tore her head from his, and cried out, tears beginning to flow from her eyes. She couldn't speak. She couldn't breathe. And then as suddenly and as violently as the hurt had come, it faded away to a dull ache that eased more and more with each strong stroke of his manhood.

He released her hands, whispering, "Put your arms about me, Allegra."

She drew him close. Something was happening to her. The pain was now entirely gone. A delicious euphoria was beginning to fill her body. She moaned softly, her hips instinctively pushing back at him with each downward stroke. "Ohhh yes!" she cried, unable to remain silent any longer. "Ohhhh!"

He smiled down at her although with her eyes still

closed she didn't see him. The little minx was enjoying herself! She had easily discovered the delightful pleasure of shared lust. He thrust farther, and deeper into her. Of course a virgin was unlikely to reach passion's peak her first time, but she had not been repelled by their consummation. He was near his own nirvana when to his surprise her body stiffened, and he felt the quivers of complete fulfillment radiating throughout her body. Unable to control his own desires any further he exploded into her eager young body.

Allegra was suddenly soaring. She had never known such pleasure as was now racing through her. It was uncontrollable. It was wonderful. Golden stars burst like fireworks behind her eyes, and drifted into her conscious. Did this happen to everyone? She was going to have to ask Quinton, because if this happened to everybody, no wonder Papa and Aunt Mama were now so happy. "Oh! Oh! *Ohhhhhh!*" she gasped, and then she felt herself falling into a warm and gentle darkness.

As she slowly came to herself again Allegra felt the duke stroking her long hair. "There, my dear," he said softly, "the worst is over, and I do believe you have obtained a certain pleasure from me as I have obtained it from you." He dropped a kiss upon her head.

Opening her eyes she turned to look into his face. "Oh, yes, Quinton," she agreed. "I have had my pleasure of you indeed. Why do women not speak on such wonders?"

"Did your cousin not say anything of the delights of passion to you?" he asked her quietly.

"She said that making love was wonderful, but when I pressed her further she then told me I should have to find out for myself, and I surely have, Quinton." She snuggled against him. "Is it done more than once each night?"

"It can be," he said, struggling against laughter again.

"Will we?" Her tone was distinctly hopeful.

"Not tonight," he replied, and kissed her pretty lips.

"Why not?" she demanded, her violet eyes growing stormy. "I liked it, Quinton. I liked fucking very much!"

"I could certainly see that, Allegra," he told her, "but it was your first experience with the sport, and you will be tender. I promise you that we will most definitely make love again tomorrow, and tomorrow, and the tomorrow after that. You are quite delectable, and I believe I have gained quite a bargain in you."

"Ohhh, you are a beast," she cried, and punched at his shoulder with her small fist. "Am I a purchase to you then?"

He laughed. "You are my beautiful and delicious young wife, Allegra," he said as he slid from his place in her bed. Picking up his nightshirt he drew it over his dark head. Then bending he kissed her once more, tweaking her right nipple playfully as he did. "Good night, my dear. I will see you in the morning."

"*Quinton!* Would you leave me then?" she cried.

"I sleep in my own bed, Allegra," he told her. Then he was gone through the connecting door that separated their bedchambers.

If he loved me, or I loved him, she thought, he would have remained with me. I'll bet Ocky doesn't leave Sirena's side at night. Still her solitude gave Allegra time to ponder on what had just happened between them. He had been so gentle and thoughtful of her. If I believed in love, she considered—but of course, I don't—I believe I could love this man. I think I am, however, gaining a small affection for him. I really should if we are going to have children together. His seed is in me now. Perhaps I am already with child. I am, one day, going to be the mother of the next Duke of Sedgwick. My son. *My son, the duke.* And then she fell asleep.

Next door the duke lay in his cold bed. It had been so difficult to leave her, but couples slept apart. It was expected. Of course having grown up with no memory of a mother in the household Allegra wouldn't know that. But he hadn't wanted to leave her. She had been so warm and passionate. *After she had been so sensible and practical.* What would she say if she knew he loved her? Would she be horrified? He dared not tell her until he could be certain that she would return his love, or at least not mock it. He slept at last.

Honor brought her mistress her breakfast in bed, noting the unused basin by the fire. She would, the maid-servant decided, tell her ladyship about its use later. She also noted that Allegra was naked in her bed, her night garment thrown carelessly aside. And her mistress was sleepy yet, poor thing. All the excitement leading up to the wedding, and then last night to contend with, Honor thought. Still, her ladyship didn't look unhappy. "Good morning, Your Grace," she said.

"I'm going to remain in bed this morning," Allegra announced, slipping into her nightgown.

"Very good, your ladyship," Honor answered. Then she hurried to the new mahogany chest, and took out a delicate lace shawl which she draped about her young mistress's shoulders.

"Is the duke up yet?" Allegra asked as she bit into a piece of toasted bread. She was still tired, but she was also hungry.

"Up and out riding. Crofts said he was whistling

when he went out the door," Honor giggled. "Crofts said he seemed a happy man."

"*Oh,*" was the only reply the maidservant received.

In midmorning Crofts opened the door to Hunter's Lair to be faced with elegantly attired gentlemen. "Good day, sirs," he said, and bowed slightly from the waist.

"We have come to see the duke," the taller of the two gentlemen said. "Tell him Prinny and Brummell are here."

Crofts gaped openly. He looked at the two gentlemen again, and then he recognized the blond, blue-eyed gentleman with the rosy complexion from a drawing he had seen in the London paper. He bowed again. This time lower as he looked at the prince. Carefully he addressed the royal gentleman. "His lordship is out riding, but I shall send for him immediately. If you will come into the drawing room I shall see you are served wine."

"Much rather have a good breakfast," the prince said peevishly. "Damned inn we overnighted in was a pigsty. Was frightened to death to touch a morsel lest it kill me."

The taller Brummell smiled amused. "His Highness is quite hungry, having not eaten since luncheon yesterday," he explained calmly to Crofts.

"Perkins!" Crofts almost shouted to the footman. "Go to the kitchens, and tell cook a *full* breakfast for His Highness, Prince George, and his guest. *Immediately!*" Then he turned back to Prinny and his companion. "Let me show you to the dining room, gentlemen."

In the kitchens Perkins had created an uproar with his request from Mr. Crofts.

"*Prince George?*" the cook said. "Our prince? What in the name of all that is holy is the prince doing here?"

"The gentry don't tell me their business, cook, but I heard the other fellow say the prince ain't eaten since yesterday noon."

The cook blanched, but then she recovered, and began to issue orders. In an amazingly short time the servants were hurrying into the dining room with platters of lamb chops, beefsteak, fresh bread, cheese, butter, poached eggs in heavy cream and dill, a platter with slices of pink salmon and lemon wedges, and a small ham. The cook was pleased to learn the prince smiled broadly and had dug into her hastily arranged feast with gusto.

When Crofts was certain that the royal guest and his companion were well taken care of, he sent another footman for the duke. Then he hurried upstairs to inform his mistress of the unexpected arrival. He knocked on the duchess's apartment door, to be admitted by Honor.

"Yes, Mr. Crofts, what is it?" the maidservant asked.

"Unexpected guests, Honor. *Very important guests.* I must see her ladyship."

"I'll have to awaken her," Honor said. "Please wait." She disappeared into Allegra's bedchamber, reappearing a few moments later. "Come in, Mr. Crofts," she beckoned the majordomo.

Slowly the elderly man entered the duchess's private chamber. She was seated in her bed, looking rather sleepy. He bowed.

"What is it, Mr. Crofts?" she asked him.

"The prince, Your Grace. *Prince George,* and a Mr. Brummell are here. Downstairs. In the dining room. Having breakfast," Crofts managed to get out. "I have sent for the duke."

"Good lord!" Allegra said, astounded. What was she to do?

"If your ladyship could come down," Crofts suggested. "I don't know how long it will take the duke to return to the house."

"To arrive so unexpectedly and without warning," Allegra said almost to herself.

"They should be well occupied for the next hour with cook's breakfast," Crofts offered.

Allegra nodded. "I will be down shortly," she said. She flung back the coverlet, and jumped from the bed. "Honor! What am I to wear?" Then she saw the elderly majordomo averting his eyes as he backed from her bedchamber. Allegra chuckled. "Gracious, Crofts, you are older than my papa, and have surely seen your good wife in her night attire many times." She padded hurriedly across the room, unconcerned.

"Indeed, Your Grace, I have," Crofts said as he scuttled from the room, his withered cheeks flushed, closing the door behind him.

"You must gain more dignity, your ladyship," Honor scolded her mistress.

"What on earth can Prinny and Brummell be doing here?" Allegra wondered aloud, ignoring Honor's suggestion. "Neither of them paid a great deal of attention to me in London except when I once danced with the prince. Brummell never, I will vow it, spoke a word to me when we passed. He did nod though. What am I to wear?"

"Simple, day-after-the-wedding-like," Honor said, and drew out a rosebud sprigged white silk gown with a round, scooped neckline, and puffed sleeves. "This should do it."

"I need to bathe," Allegra protested.

"A birdbath will do, your ladyship," Honor said. "I've reheated the basin I left for you by the fire last night."

"Oh, I forgot all about it," Allegra said. "What was it for?"

"A lady should always wash her private parts after making love with her husband," Honor said bluntly. "Now, go and give yourself a quick sponge while I get your stockings and slippers."

There was blood on her thighs! She stared, horrified, and then she recalled that Sirena had said there would be. *And on the bed linens as well.* She blushed. Such an intimate fact, and it would be known soon enough by the whole household. Well, Allegra thought, at least her virtue would never be in doubt. She carefully washed herself, noting as she did that she was indeed tender. And Quinton had been so considerate.

As she dressed she wondered why on earth the prince and his friend would come to Hunter's Lair the day after their wedding. It was indelicate to say the least, but then princes did what they wanted, and devil take the hindmost. She sat quietly in her petticoat while Honor dressed her hair in its chignon. She selected her wedding necklace and earbobs to wear, and put on her dress. Slipping her feet into her slippers she said, "I am ready, Honor." Then she left her apartment, going down the stairs and into her dining room where the prince was just finishing his repast. Allegra curtsied. "Welcome to Hunter's Lair, Your Highness," she said.

Chapter Ten

"My dear Miss Morgan," Prinny said as he arose from the table, smiling. Then he kissed her hand. "We have come for the wedding," he announced.

"*The wedding?*" Allegra was somewhat taken aback, but there was no help for it. "The wedding, Your Highness, was yesterday," she replied truthfully.

"*Yesterday?*" The prince looked quite astounded and then aggrieved.

George Brummell's face looked as if he was struggling to hold back his laughter.

"*Yesterday*, Your Highness," Allegra confirmed. "If you had but informed us you were coming . . ." Her voice trailed off helplessly.

"When word came that you had decided to marry here and not in London," the prince began, sitting heavily in his chair, "I thought that young Brummell and I would come to surprise you with our presence. I did not think that you would be wed so early in October." There was a faintly reproachful tone to his voice, as if she had done something wrong.

"I am sure that Her Grace did not mean to disappoint," George Brummell quickly interjected. He was a slender gentleman with an elegant nose, beautifully coifed dark hair, and blue eyes that were always alert.

"No, no, of course not," Allegra said quickly. "If you had but sent us notice, Your Highness, we would have waited. What a great honor it would have been for us all to have you at our wedding."

Prinny, however, looked very disappointed. As if he were a child who had expected some wonderful treat that had failed to materialize.

"But I am so delighted, Your Highness," Allegra continued, "that you have honored us with a visit. You will remain, of course. My husband has a hunting party each October. The other guests will be arriving in a few days. They will be thrilled to learn Your Highness and his companion, Mr. Brummell, are here."

"But if you were wed yesterday, won't you be going on a wedding trip, Your Grace?" the prince asked.

"Gracious, no, Your Highness. We plan a trip next spring, perhaps to Italy. Quinton has spoken to me of a city called Venice." She smiled at the prince. "Can you imagine a city where the streets are water?" She laughed. "I must see it to believe it."

"Well, it will not be soon, Your Grace," the prince told her. "That rascal Corsican, name of Napoleon, is on the march in Italy, and believe me, Venice is threatened. The whole damned Venetian empire is."

"Oh dear," Allegra said, disappointed.

"You'll have to take an old-fashioned wedding trip to Devon, or to the lakes," Prinny said with a sympathetic smile.

Brummell saw the look of disappointment on Allegra's face. "Do not be sad, Your Grace," he told her, "that Froggie rogue will soon be marched to Madame la Guillotine. His own peers can't abide him, and when the Bourbon king is restored, he'll have no friends at all at that court."

"And then may I see the city of water?" Allegra said.

"Indeed, madame, you surely will," Brummell agreed.

"*Your Highness!*" Quinton Hunter strode into the room. "Welcome to Hunter's Lair. You honor us." He swept the prince a bow, nodding at George Brummell in greeting.

"We came for the wedding," the prince repeated, "only to learn from your charming bride that it was celebrated yesterday. Should have been here but for the wretched weather. Roads were so muddy and foul we had to stop our journey. Stayed at a dreadful place called The Royal George, and by Jove, I'll have the name of the place changed, I will! Food wasn't fit for pigs, and the beds were flea-bitten."

"I have asked the prince to remain for your hunting party," Allegra told her startled husband. "It seemed the hospitable thing to do, my lord, with our guests arriving in just a few days' time."

George Brummell saw the surprised look that appeared, and was as quickly gone from the duke's face. Why there is no hunting party planned at all, he thought, amused at the clever temerity of the young Duchess of Sedgwick. *But there would be.* And in very short order, too, he expected. Brummell restrained a chuckle. He hadn't paid a great deal of attention to Allegra Morgan last season, but now he realized his mistake. The young woman was no foolish creature. She was intelligent; she was quick; and he admired her audacity. Their visit was going to prove very amusing.

"Who is included in this hunting party, Your Grace?" he asked wickedly, his blue eyes dancing mischievously.

Allegra easily saw that he was on to her, but certainly the prince wasn't. His Highness was as dense as pudding. "It's a small party, just my husband and his three closest friends. They have hunted together for years at this time every autumn, Mr. Brummell. Lord Walworth, the Earl of Aston, and Viscount Pickford. It is very intimate, you understand, and now that these four gentlemen are wed, the party shall be even merrier," Allegra said sweetly. Then she turned to the prince. "I hope that Your Highness will not be bored. Now that you are here, I shall invite the widowed Lady Perry and her sister, Lady Johnstone. That way we shall be even at dinner." She smiled brightly at them.

"Excellent! Excellent!" the prince agreed.

"Now, if you gentlemen will excuse me, I will go and have two of our guest chambers readied for you and Mr. Brummell, Your Highness," Allegra said. She curtsied, and moved serenely from the dining room.

"By Jove, Quinton," the prince pronounced, "that's a fine girl you've married! Going to make you an excellent duchess, even if she ain't of the first order blood-wise. It don't hurt to improve the stock with something less than a thoroughbred young mare now and again."

"Thank you, Your Highness," the duke replied, bowing, and feeling just the faintest prick of irritation over the prince's remarks. I am so damned proud of Allegra, he thought. What instincts she had! She had greeted their unexpected royal guest, fed him, and turned his disappointment into pleasure. And he had not a doubt that this hunting party was going to come off without a hitch.

Crofts was awaiting his mistress outside of the dining room doors. "I have had the Lake Suite prepared for His Highness and the Blue Bedroom for Mr. Brummell, your ladyship."

"Excellent," Allegra replied. "In one hour, Crofts, I shall want a footman to take my letters to the stables. Send one groom, mounted, for each letter, and they are to await the reply. We are having a hunting party in two days. As far as the prince and his companion are concerned, this event has been planned for some time."

"Very good, your ladyship," Crofts said, hiding a smile. He had served two previous Duchesses of Sedgwick, and this third was more than their equal.

"I will be in my drawing room. Send Honor to me with my writing case," she further instructed him.

"At once, your ladyship," he replied, bowing, and hurried away.

As soon as she had her lap desk, Allegra hastily penned notes to Sirena, Eunice, and Caroline explaining that the prince had arrived without warning, and she had invited him to remain for a hunting party. They must come in two days' time. She then wrote a note to Lady Perry apologizing for her last minute invitation, and requesting that the lovely widow and her sister join them. Sealing her missives with red wax and impressing her seal ring in the wax, she rang for the footman.

"Has Crofts given you your instructions?" she asked the footman.

"One groom for each letter, and await the reply," Perkins said. "Is that correct, your ladyship?"

"Go along then," Allegra said nodding.

The next two days were spent in preparations, but those arrangements were made with the utmost discretion so as not to arouse the suspicions of their guests. The prince and the duke spent the day out-of-doors riding and hunting waterfowl. Mr. Brummell, however, begged off. They ate great breakfasts and suppers. The evenings were spent playing Whist for no stakes as Prinny well understood the duke's aversion to gambling, although he was unable to refrain from one small complaint.

"Seems to me a man so plump in the pockets shouldn't be so stingy, Sedgwick," he grumbled. "Especially when he's winning."

"But if we were playing for real stakes, Your Highness," Allegra remarked, "you should owe my husband both Devon and Cornwall by now. Quinton is but saving your kingdom for you."

Brummell burst out laughing. "A clever sally, your ladyship," he said. "I hope you will come to London this winter."

"It is unlikely, Mr. Brummell. We are country folk, and happy to be so," Allegra said to him.

"Nonsense!" Prinny answered her. "I command you to come, Duchess. Can't ever have enough beautiful young women about me, I fear. You will be a triumph, I vow."

"How flattering you are, Your Highness, but remember I have a duty to fill my husband's nursery even as your wife is now doing. I must attend to that before I come back to London," Allegra told him.

"Prettily put, Duchess, but unless you are breeding, I will expect to see you dancing at Almack's," Prinny replied. "God bless me! I believe I have won this hand, gentlemen."

Quinton had not come to Allegra's bed the second night of their marriage, but she had been far too busy with all her preparations to notice his absence. Now on the third night she lay quietly, unable to sleep, and wondering why he was not by her side, when the door to their rooms opened and the duke entered the bedchamber, climbing into the bed next to her.

"My lord, I had begun to believe you had forgotten you had a wife," Allegra said frostily. But secretly she was delighted to see him. "Our guests will be arriving tomorrow. We will have no time for each other, I fear."

He pulled her into his arms, giving her a long, slow kiss that set her pulses racing and her toes tingling.

"I could hardly forget you, Allegra," he told her when he had thoroughly kissed her, leaving her breathless and slightly dizzy. "And this is not my idea of a perfect first week of marriage. Damn me, my dear, if we shouldn't have taken a wedding trip after all."

"It would have been fine," Allegra replied, "if Prinny hadn't got it into his head to come to Hunter's Lair for our wedding, and then arrived after the fact. Why isn't he at home with his wife? She is expecting a baby after all."

"He despises Princess Caroline. If the truth be known the princess is gauche, rough-spoken, and not given to bathing as frequently as she might. You know how fastidious Prinny is, my dear. I went to the wedding in April. The prince was drunk to the point of collapse. The king had to run after him when he wandered away from the altar during the ceremony."

"How sad for his wife," Allegra said softly.

"Why sad?" the duke probed. "Their marriage, like ours, was a sensible and practical matter, Allegra."

"They might not be in love, Quinton, even as we are not in love, but you are kind to me. I do not believe if I were carrying your child that you would leave me to wander about visiting your friends and acquaintances," she responded. "You would not desert me."

"No, my dear, I would not," he agreed softly. He lay her back against her pillows, smiling. "Dare I hope that you missed me last night here in your bed? I know that I missed being with you."

"Did you, sir? Then, pray, what kept you from me?" she demanded.

"Our guest and his passion for Whist, I fear," was his answer. "It was quite late when Prinny decided he would go to bed. Mr. Brummell is far more sensitive to our newly married state despite his youth and bachelor status. He attempted several times to coax Prinny from the card table, but to no avail."

"You are here now," she said in a tone he would have sworn was seductive.

"Madame, are you flirting with me?" he teased, and chuckled when she blushed. There was still so much innocence about her. He reached out, and pulled the ribbons of her night garment open. A single finger flicked each side apart. "Are you suggesting, madame, that I make love to you?" He looked directly at her.

"Yes," she replied eagerly, taking his breath away when she drew his head down, and brushed her lips across his mouth.

He needed no further encouragement. Burying his face between her two little breasts he began to kiss her most passionately. "You are delicious, Allegra! I want to devour you, my dear. *I shall devour you.*" His mouth fastened over a pert nipple, and he suckled upon her flesh. His head was spinning. His heart was hammering with his excitement. How could he have been so blind about love?

Allegra sighed happily as his mouth and his hands began to roam over her warm flesh. What was happening to her? *You are falling in love,* the little voice whispered in her head. *"No!"* she cried aloud.

"What is it, my darling?" the duke said, raising his head from her breasts. "Are you all right? Do you want me to cease?"

"No, no," she said. "Don't stop, Quinton." *Why had he called her darling?* "Oh, yess!" she murmured as his lips moved down her shapely torso. "Ohh, that is nice, husband," she told him as he licked at her belly. "Ohh, I want to do it!"

"Do what?" He had stopped in his worship of her body.

"I want to make love to you. Wives can do it, can't they?" she asked. "I don't want to be some passive lump of dough. I want to learn to make love, too, Quinton. Can I? Will you show me how?"

Sitting up, the duke yanked his nightshirt off and threw it by the bed. "You have but to do what I do to you. And yes, wives can make love to their husbands in return, Allegra. I am flattered that you want to make love to me."

"You give me pleasure, my lord. We are friends now, and I would give you pleasure in return."

He lay back. "Then do so, madame," he told her.

Matching him, Allegra pulled off her own nightgarb. Then she sat cross-legged at his side studying him for several long and silent moments. Finally she reached out with her hand and touched the hair upon his broad chest. "It's soft," she noted aloud, her fingers ruffling across it. Then she traced the narrow line down his flat belly curiously. She wanted a better view of him, and so to his surprise Allegra climbed atop him, plunking her bottom upon his thighs. Reaching out she ran the palms of her hands over his long hard torso. Her fingers teased at his male nipples. Leaning forward she brushed them with her own nipples.

He drew his breath in sharply, unable to help himself, amazed by her boldness.

"Did you like that?" she asked curiously.

"Your touch is arousing," he admitted honestly.

"You have a beautiful body, Quinton," she told him. "I saw pictures of ancient statues in books in Papa's library. That is how I may make my comparison."

"I would not have thought otherwise, my dear," he responded gallantly. His male member was absolutely throbbing, imprisoned between his thighs beneath her round buttocks. He wanted to roll her over and plunge himself into her sweetness.

"What is the matter?" she asked him, seeing the look in his silvery gray eyes that she didn't understand.

"Climb off me, you little bluestocking, and I will show you," he said, half laughing.

Allegra obeyed. Then she gasped at the sight of his risen manhood, which thrust from between his muscular thighs. It was the first really good look she had had of it, and Allegra could scarce take her eyes off of it. Tall, blue-veined, and hard, it bobbed before her eyes. She was mesmerized by the sight.

Quinton Hunter lay his bride back amid her pillows once again. Mounting her, he pushed gently into her love sheath with a single smooth motion. She was very wet and hot. "Do you understand the power you can exert over me, Allegra?" he asked her softly as he bent and kissed her lips lightly. Then he began to move upon her, slowly at first, and finally with quick, hard strokes of his lance that sent her senses reeling with mindless pleasure. Allegra cried out, unable to restrain herself.

"Ohhh, it is so wonderful! Do not stop, Quinton! *Do not stop!*" Then with some silent, ancient instinct guiding her she wrapped her legs about him allowing him even deeper passage within her eager body.

Her unexpected action rendered him hot with new lust, and he drove himself deeper and deeper into her until he could hear his heart thundering in his ears. Her body was shuddering with their fulfillment, which once again, as on that first night, they shared together.

"Ahh, Allegra, I cannot help myself, but I adore you!" he cried out. "Do not hate me for it, my darling! I want you to love me even as I love you." He caught her face between his hands, and began to kiss her with a desperate passion.

She hadn't heard him say he loved her. *Had she?* She was so fuzzy and replete with her satisfaction. "We don't believe in love," she murmured almost to herself. "Love hurts."

"It doesn't have to, my darling," the duke said. "Ohh, Allegra, open your eyes and look at me."

Slowly the heavy, thick, dark lashes lifted themselves from her pale cheeks. Her violet eyes stared directly into his.

"I love you," he said quietly. "I know we meant this marriage to be a logical and judicious match without the encumbrance of foolish emotions, but I find I am, alas, like my romantic antecedents. I have fallen in love. Can you forgive me? Can I one day teach you to love me, my darling Allegra?"

"Oh, Quinton," she said weakly. "I do not know what to say to you. If I am honest with you, and I must be, I have to admit to feeling some emotion I cannot comprehend with regard to you. But is it love? I do not know. I have never been in love, and the love I feel for Papa, Aunt Mama, and Sirena is, I know, an altogether different thing. *You really love me?* Why?"

Rolling onto his back the Duke of Sedgwick thought a moment. "I really don't understand it myself, Allegra," he admitted. "But I know that I love you. Those few weeks you were away from me I could not bear your absence. Ask Ocky. I was a perfect fool, waiting for and anticipating your return. At one point I convinced myself you might not rejoin me. It was agony."

"Why on earth did you think I wouldn't come back to marry you, Quinton?" she asked him. This was a proud man, and his sudden revelations were most startling to say the least.

"What have I to offer you but a title? Having come to know you this past summer, Allegra, I knew that my title wasn't reason enough, for you are too honest to be awed by such things."

"But I gave my word to the match," she replied. "You surely didn't think I would break my word?"

"Logic and reason, I have discovered, play no part in love," he said quietly.

"I see," she said. "But do you trust me?"

"With my life, my darling," he swore.

Allegra laughed. She couldn't help it. A starburst of happiness was beginning to fill her. "You love me? You *really* love me?"

"*Yes!*" He pulled her into his arms, and kissed her hungrily.

"Oh, my." She laughed again. "Dearest Quinton, this is going to change everything," she told him.

"I know," he admitted, and kissed her again, his big hands beginning to wander over her body.

Allegra purred with open contentment. He loved her. She had never before believed in love, but suddenly his devotion was very important to her. "It is most unfashionable for a husband and his wife to be in love," she said, then murmured happily as his kisses covered her torso, to be followed by his warm bathing tongue. "Ohh, Quinton, that is nice," Allegra said softly. "Ahhh, yes," she agreed as he suckled upon her breasts until she thought they would burst from the sheer pleasure. When he began to lick her ear she imitated his action, whispering to him, "Do you want to fuck me again, Quinton?"

"*I am going to fuck you again, Allegra,*" he replied as he pushed slowly into her, teasing her by withdrawing and entering again several times until she began to protest.

She wrapped herself about him, silently demanding his full attention and homage. "I want to feel the *soaring* again!" she finally told him. *"Don't stop! Don't stop!"* Her nails dug into his shoulders, and then raked down his back sharply.

The light pain honed his appetite for her. He drove deeply into the hot marsh of her sex making her whimper. The body beneath his strained and writhed as he forced her fiercely to passion's peak. His own desire for her was enormous. "You are mine, Allegra. *You are mine!*" he groaned, unable to withhold his own passions any longer.

"Oh! Oh! *Ohhhh!*" she cried in return. What was happening to her? It had been wonderful before, but this time she didn't think she was going to survive their shared lust. She was dying. Ohh, God, she was dying! *And it was incredible!*

When Allegra came to herself again it was within her husband's arms. Her cheek was pressed against his chest, and she could hear his heart thumping beneath her ear. His hand was gently stroking her dark hair which had come undone from its proper nighttime plait.

"You are revived," he said softly.

"Am I still alive?" she wondered aloud.

He laughed. "You have an incredible capacity for passion, my darling young wife," he told her, and she felt him kiss the top of her head. "You leave me breathless, Allegra."

She was silent for several minutes, and then she said, "Will you leave me tonight, Quinton?"

"No, my dear," he answered her. "It is unlikely I shall ever leave your bed again, no matter the gossip involved."

She smiled then closed her eyes, feeling more at peace

with herself and with her life than she had ever felt before.

Quinton Hunter sensed his wife relax, but he was not yet ready to sleep. He had no idea what had made him admit his love for Allegra, but at least she hadn't been repulsed by her new knowledge. She had even said she harbored some sort of feeling for him, but she had not said she loved him. That would surely come in time, he decided. For the first time in his life he understood his father's drinking himself to death after his mother's death. To be without the one you love was surely a hell on earth.

Allegra awoke early. Quinton still lay by her side, curled onto his side, sleeping peacefully. She studied him closely for the first time. He was handsome, but it was not his beauty of either face or form that attracted her. Looking into his face she saw something else. She saw strength and honesty. *But I don't believe in love,* she thought once more. *You don't?* the little voice in her head mocked. *Then why do you care that his demeanor is one of strength and honesty?*

Quinton Hunter opened his eyes, and looked into Allegra's beautiful face. Her gaze was suddenly startled by what she saw.

"You do love me," she said wonderingly. "I can tell. It is the look in your eyes, Quinton. Oh dear! Oh dear!" God almighty! She sounded like a perfect ninny, but his words last night while surprising were nothing compared to the emotion she saw now in those silvery depths.

"You think too much, my darling," he told her. "Get up, madame. We have a houseful of guests arriving today, and a future King of England in the Lake bedchamber even as we speak."

Allegra couldn't help it. She giggled. "I never expected to be so rudely tossed into my duchessdom this quickly, my lord," she told him. "We should have been gone when Prinny and young Mister Brummell arrived. They say we will not go to Italy next spring as some French general is harrying the Venetians."

"I will make it up to you when the French stop harrying the Venetians," he promised her. "Besides, I am longing to make love to you in a gondola, my darling Allegra. Mad, passionate love beneath the moon as we glide by the Piazza San Marco on a warm summer's night."

"Sir, I think you quite mad," Allegra told him, arising. "Ohh!" She whirled about, rubbing her bottom which he had just lovingly smacked.

"I could not resist," he told her with a grin.

She laughed, then told him, "Go back to your own bedchamber now, my lord. I wish to dress, and so must you. His Highness will want to hunt, I have not a doubt."

The duke had no sooner finished his morning ablutions and descended the stairs to his dining room when he heard Prinny and his traveling companion coming down behind him. A swift glance about the room told him that breakfast was more than ready.

"Good morning, my lord," Crofts said calmly.

The Duke of Sedgwick nodded his greeting, delighted and amazed at the same time that his household was running so smoothly. Allegra was truly a wonder, he thought to himself.

"Good morning, Your Highness," Crofts said pointedly.

The duke turned quickly, and welcomed his guests. The footmen seated the gentlemen and began bringing about the silver dishes and covered platters that held the breakfast. The prince almost purred as he helped himself to a rare and juicy beefsteak, and allowed the footman to ladle a sauce of cream, braised onions, and peppercorns over it. He murmured his approval of the eggs poached in heavy cream and Marsala wine and dusted with nutmeg. He hummed with delight as the various platters were presented to him. Then he ate, and he ate, and he ate, washing down his meal with a goblet of wine that never seemed to empty itself. His companions ate more sparingly.

When he had finished he leaned back in his chair, sipping his wine. "We are in the mood to hunt," he announced.

"Of course, Your Highness," the Duke of Sedgwick said, rising. "Will you be hunting with us today, Brummell?"

"Brummell doesn't hunt," Prinny chuckled. "Such raucous activity would disturb the perfect cut of his neckcloth, eh, Brummell?"

"Indeed, Your Highness, it would," Brummell answered without rancor. "Not to mention getting mud all over my excellent boots. My man spends at least an hour a day on each of my boots. It would send him to Bedlam if I dirtied my boots before noon."

"I have not asked after Princess Caroline's health, Your Highness," the duke said politely as they left the dining room.

"Fat, breeding, and dirtier than ever," Prinny said with a shudder. "If she whelps me a son she will have done her duty, and I can be done with her. I only married the bitch to get an increase in my allowance. The renovations for Carleton House have beggared me."

"It is to be hoped then that Your Highness will get his wish," the Duke of Sedgwick said. He found he was appalled by the prince's attitude towards his wife. Caroline Amelia Elizabeth, Princess of Brunswick, was her husband's cousin. She was ill educated, having been raised in her parents' unsophisticated court. Her mother was the eldest sister of King George III. She was the worst possible choice for a wife for the future George IV, but her mother had prevailed upon her brother, and so the match was made.

Caroline was not stupid, but she was uncultured. She was clever and witty, but willful and filled with high spirits. Her sharp tongue could be cruel and thoughtless. She had grown up with a rather dull mother who knitted stockings and netted embroidery at her homey palace outside of Brunswick. Caroline's father lived happily apart from his wife and family in his capital with his mistress, Frau Hertzfeldt.

The princess had been brought up without religion so that she might adapt to whatever faith her husband espoused. She could barely read, wrote poorly, and had scant knowledge of the world outside of her mother's palace. She had no musical abilities, could not paint watercolors, and did not dance well at all. She disliked fashion and had no sense of either style or color. Everything about Caroline was diametrically opposed to her husband. Consequently they had nothing at all in common.

She was not a male heir and so virtually no attention had been paid to Caroline of Brunswick, yet attention was what she desperately sought. Her personal hygiene left much to be desired. She cared little for her appearance, and could not be guided by those who knew that how a princess presented herself to the world made a great deal of difference to those by whom she must be accepted.

Her eldest sister had been a Duchess of Württemberg and had disappeared under rather odd circumstances while in Russia with her husband. It was rumored she was unfaithful to her husband with the Grand Duke Paul. The Duke of Württemberg had returned home with his children. The Russian tsarina, Catherine the Great, imprisoned the duchess in the castle of Lode on the Baltic. Two years later the news of her death was announced, although how she had died and when she had died was never revealed. And her younger sister, it would seem, also had an eye for the gentlemen. It was even possible she was not a virgin on her wedding night for there had been rumors of an affair.

Meeting his bride-to-be for the first time Prinny was horrified by the sloppily garbed girl whose body odor was quite discernible to his fastidious nostrils. "Harris, I am not well; pray get me a glass of brandy," he cried to the Earl of Malmesbury, who had brought the princess to England. Then the prince left the room, not hearing Caroline say to the earl, "Mon Dieu! Is the prince always like that? I find him very fat, and nothing as handsome as his portrait." Nonetheless the wedding took place three days later in the Chapel Royal in St. James Palace.

The Duke of Sedgwick had been there. He remembered how drunk Prinny had been, wandering about the chapel singing nursery songs to himself, having to be led back to the altar by his furious father. He managed to consummate his marriage, but then spent the rest of the night drunk, lying in the fireplace grate as his bride was happy to relate to any who would listen. From that one coupling, however, came the princess's current pregnancy, for Prinny never slept with her again. He would not even live with her, but went about his life as if his marriage had not occurred at all.

Quinton Hunter had married Allegra for her fortune. There had been no polite deception about it, but many couples wed for wealth and status. How a gentleman treated his wife, however, was a different matter altogether. Had he not fallen in love with Allegra, Quinton

Hunter would have still treated her with respect and courtesy. He pitied Prinny's wife. Even Henry VIII had come to a comfortable arrangement with Anne of Cleves. There was no excuse for such discourtesy, or unkindness.

"The horses are ready, Your Grace," Crofts said, coming to his side. He gestured towards the open door.

"Excellent! Excellent!" the prince said with a smile. He turned to Brummell. "Find the library, Georgie. We'll be back in time for a hearty luncheon."

Crofts nodded imperceptibly to his master.

Allegra ate a petit déjeuner in her own apartments. Then she dressed, preparing to meet her guests when they arrived. Downstairs Crofts informed her that the duke and the prince had gone out riding. Mr. Brummell was in the library, and luncheon would be served at one o'clock.

"Do we have enough supplies for the kitchens?" Allegra asked. "This prince eats enough for three men, I fear."

"Cook gave the list to Perkins, and he departed for town early this morning, my lady. He should be back shortly with the cart."

"Crofts, this house could not run without you," Allegra complimented the elderly majordomo. "Thank you."

"Shall I tell Mr. Brummell that you are up and about, your ladyship?"

"Not yet. I wish to write a letter to Aunt Mama before I must be entertaining. I shall be in the family drawing room."

The duke and the prince returned home with several brace of rabbits to show for their morning's ride. Allegra was in the drawing room with Mr. Brummell when they arrived. Brummell shuddered delicately at the sight of the rabbits hanging from a footman's hand, but the prince was delighted with his morning's venture. Luncheon was served, and the prince ate as if he hadn't eaten in a month's time. Allegra wondered how long he would remain their guest as she watched him consume a platter of salmon, a dozen lamb chops, a beefsteak, and a small chicken by himself. He then fell asleep in the drawing room, watched over by Mr. Brummell.

The guests began to arrive. Sirena and Ocky first. Allegra saw that her cousin looked worried as she alighted from her open carriage. While the duke and Ocky greeted each other, the cousins linked arms, and walked into the house.

"What has happened?" Sirena demanded.

"What on earth do you mean?" Allegra responded.

"You are married less than a week, and you give a house party with Prinny as your guest of honor! You said nothing of this several days ago when you were wed. Are you all right? Has the duke been cruel?"

"Ohh, dearest Sirena, what a worrywart you are," Allegra laughed softly. "Everything is wonderful. Prinny, however, arrived the morning after the wedding expecting to come to the wedding. He was mightily disappointed that it was over and done with, and so I invited him to a hunting party. I claimed it was an annual event for Quinton and his three closest friends. That is why I hurriedly sent you and Ocky invitations. I couldn't allow Prinny to know it was all a Banbury tale so his feelings would not be injured."

Sirena heaved a gusty sigh of relief. "Thank heavens! I was imagining all sorts of terrible things."

"Why on earth would you?" Now Allegra was puzzled.

"Well, yours is a marriage of convenience, cousin. I was afraid that you and the duke had had a falling out," Sirena admitted. "He is a very proud man."

"I had noticed," Allegra said mischievously, "but you may cease your worrying, darling. He claims to be in love with me, and I believe it to be so."

"Thank heavens!" Sirena cried.

"But I am not yet positive of my feelings for him," Allegra continued. "I am still not certain I understand this emotion called *love*. Until I do, I can make no admissions of my own. And, Sirena, darling, you must say nothing to anyone but Ocky."

"Oh, Allegra, I am so happy for you!" Sirena's blue eyes were teary.

"Why on earth are you happy for her?" The Countess of Aston and Lady Walworth entered the foyer.

"The duke is in love with Allegra!" Sirena exclaimed, and then she clapped her hand over her mouth, her eyes wide.

"She promised not to tell," Allegra said dryly.

"Well, of course he's in love with her. You mean you didn't know, Allegra?" Eunice, Countess of Aston was surprised.

"I thought everyone knew he was in love with Allegra," Lady Caroline Walworth said. "Gracious, he told both Bain and Dree; and Ocky was, of course, the first to know."

"But I didn't know," Allegra said. "I thought my marriage was one of convenience. That is what I wanted. That is what I expected."

"To be loved is far better," Eunice remarked with a shy smile.

"Are you in love with him?" Caroline demanded, very much to the point, and like her formidable aunt.

"I don't know," Allegra admitted.

"A woman can't help but love a man who loves her. He's handsome and amusing. The love is sure to come," Caroline said firmly. "Now, why on earth are we here but four days after your wedding? You and the duke should be off somewhere billing and cooing, darling."

Allegra laughed, and once again explained the situation to her friends. She finished by saying, "I have also invited Lady Perry and Lady Johnstone. Both are widows, and are very lively, I am told."

"I wonder which one Prinny will take to bed," Caroline said mischievously.

"Probably both," Eunice said drolly. "Or possibly he will share with young Mr. Brummell."

"Brummell wouldn't take such a healthy woman to his bed," Caroline riposted. "She might muss his hair, or his garments. Do you think he is as elegant in his nightgarb as he is said to be in his clothing?"

"Is it true he wears black to dinner?" Eunice wondered aloud.

"He does," Allegra said, "and frankly I think it extremely elegant. Far more so than suits of peach or sky blue silk. You will find him most charming as I have."

"He barely acknowledged us in London last season," Caroline recalled. "Aunt thinks he is too high-flown."

"I asked him about it," Allegra said. "He told me he finds debutantes tiresome and boring for the most part. Marriage, he says, makes a woman far more interesting."

"Lord, how superior the man is. I vow I am terrified to meet him," Eunice said, and they all laughed.

Crofts came, and offered to escort the ladies to their bedchambers. "Lady Perry and her sister are arriving, your ladyship," he told Allegra. The others hurried off,

and Allegra went out to greet the last of her guests to
arrive.

They stepped from their carriage. Lady Perry was a
petite blonde in her late twenties, and her sister a bit
older and plumper.

"Duchess, how kind of you to invite us," Georgianna
Perry said in an elegant, well-modulated voice.

"I am in your debt, both of you," Allegra responded
charmingly. "The prince arrived unexpectedly," and
then she went on to explain the situation to the two attractive widows.

"We shall, of course, keep your secret," Margot, Lady
Johnstone said. "How sensitive of you to protect the
prince's feelings."

"I am seating you on either side of him at dinner," Allegra told them.

"Of course," Lady Perry replied, understanding the
situation immediately. "My sister and I shall endeavor
to keep Prinny amused."

"Do you hunt?" Allegra asked them. "The gentlemen
go out at dawn."

"*Do you?*" was the response.

"No," Allegra admitted.

"Then we shall be more than glad to follow your lead,
Duchess," Lady Perry told her hostess. "Amusing
Prinny in the evening is one thing, but I believe we are
wiser to leave the gentlemen to their blood sports while
we get our beauty sleep. Don't you agree?"

"Oh, yes!" Allegra said with a broad smile, and then
she escorted her guests into the house.

*C*hapter Eleven

*T*he dining room at Hunter's Lair was filled with laughter and clever banter. The mahogany table was covered with a beautiful white damask cloth from Ireland, edged in lace. A large silver bowl filled with late yellow roses and greenery was centered, and flanked on either side by magnificent silver candelabra burning pure white beeswax candles that were scented with rose oil. There were twelve at the table tonight, and each place was set with a beautiful silver service and fine china from Dr. Wall's Royal Worcester pottery. Behind each chair stood a footman in green and silver livery, while other servants passed around the dishes being offered this evening.

The fish course consisted of fresh raw oysters served from a large bowl, steamed mussels, fat prawns with a mustard sauce, and sliced salmon and trout, both of which had been poached in wine and were placed on silver platters amid a bed of fresh cress. Next came the meats, poultry, and game. There was a side of beef that had been packed in salt and roasted over a slow fire. There was venison, partridges cooked to a golden turn, rabbit pies oozing brown gravy, a turkey stuffed with bread, apples, and chestnuts, and two large hams covered with cloves and brown sugar, as well as several silver plates of lamb chops, the prince's favorite.

There were bowls of green beans with slivered almonds, small onions in a cream sauce with black peppercorns, tiny whole carrots glazed with honey and sprinkled with nutmeg, and a bowl holding a large cauliflower dripping with melted cheese. There were potatoes in a Hollandaise sauce, and another bowl containing tiny potato puffs. There were several platters of lettuce and cucumbers in a piquant sauce, flavored with vinegar. And there was wine poured continuously into goblets that were never allowed to be empty.

Finally, came the sweets. There were several kinds of cheese cakes, spongy Genovese cake filled with a coffee cream, tarts of both lemon and raspberry, two soufflés—chocolate and orange—pineapple creams, and caramel custards, as well as bananas, grapes, and oranges. Small wheels of cheese were set upon the table: one of cheddar, one of Stilton. There were delicate little sugar wafers, and of course, champagne.

"Madame," Prinny said, unbuttoning his waistcoat two buttons, "a most delicious meal. I do so enjoy simple country cooking. My compliments to the kitchen, Crofts."

"Thank you, Your Highness," the majordomo said, bowing.

"Now," Prinny said, "perhaps some cards before we retire for the night. We are doing some serious hunting in the morning, Duke, aren't we?"

"Indeed, Your Highness, we are. There is, I have been told, a rather rowdy old boar in my forest who has been troubling my tenants' gardens. The gamekeeper says he should make good sport for he's a wily beast; but we must begin early. At first light."

"Excellent!" the prince approved, arising from the table, and offering his arm to Lady Johnstone. "Do you gamble, m'dear?" he asked her.

"I adore it, Your Highness, but alas, I am a widow, in modest circumstances," she replied. She was a striking woman with dark red hair, very white skin, a lush form, and warm amber eyes.

"Allow me to stake you, m'dear," the prince said, smiling broadly.

"But how shall I ever pay you back, Your Highness?" she replied.

"Not to worry, m'dear. We shall come to some little arrangement, I am certain," Prinny purred, letting his blue eyes wander to her deep cleavage. He led her off to the drawing room where the tables had been set up.

"Come, Lady Perry," young Mr. Brummell said, offering that lady his arm. "You, too, I am certain, will eventually find favor with his highness."

"Do you really think so?" Georgianna said ingenuously.

"Oh, yes," Mr. Brummell predicted, and led her off after the prince.

"If you continue to entertain like this you will never get rid of him," Caroline teased Allegra when Brummell was out of their hearing.

"You certainly picked him the right partner for his evening's entertainment," Eunice told her hostess mischievously. " 'Oh, how shall I ever pay you back, sir?' " she mimicked Lady Johnstone.

"I would die if he looked at me *that* way," Sirena said, shuddering.

"Allegra chose just the perfect guests," the duke said quietly. "Both Lady Perry and her sister are women of the world, and experienced. They will keep Prinny amused in the evenings. Then perhaps he will not remain up all night playing cards, and we can go to bed with our beautiful wives."

The other gentlemen laughed, as the ladies blushed prettily.

"Poor Quint has been forced to make a fourth at Whist before we arrived, but refused to play for stakes," Ocky said. "Prinny wasn't very happy."

"They played for English counties instead. Quinton was given Worcester, Hereford, and Wales to start; but he would have been king of England in just another night the way Prinny plays," Allegra said frankly. "I am not certain he fully understands the game at all. He wants to win, but he is too rash."

"We had best join our guests," the duke told them, smiling at his wife's little sally.

The prince, Brummell, and their two ladies were already deep into a game when the others entered the drawing room. There was another table set up. Lord Walworth, the earl, and Ocky, along with Lady Walworth, sat down to cards. Allegra went to the piano and began to play while the duke turned the pages for her. The other women sat talking and listening.

"You are amazing," Quinton Hunter said softly to his wife. "We have been married less than a week, and you are entertaining as if you had been my duchess your whole life, Allegra. The prince has already told me half a dozen times how much he is enjoying himself." He dropped a kiss atop her dark head.

"I am happy you are pleased, my lord," she answered, her heart racing just a bit faster as she felt his lips. Then she looked up at him and smiled mischievously. "Please do not think that I shall allow such lavish meals to be served when we are alone. I do not want you looking like Prinny. I have noted that you have an appetite for sweets, for you ate two slices of Genovese cake, not to mention a lemon tart and some chocolate soufflé tonight."

"They were delicious," he replied with a chuckle. "I was not aware cook knew the recipe for Genovese cake."

"She didn't. I gave her Aunt Mama's recipe book. My stepmother had copies made for both Sirena and for me," Allegra told him. "Once the guests are gone, sir, it will be a simple life, and simple meals for us."

"If the truth be known, Allegra, and I think it no secret to our friends, you are the only sweet I truly desire," the duke told her.

She stopped playing, and looked up at him. "Will you always say such lovely things to me, Quinton?"

"Yes, Allegra, I will," he vowed. "Believe me, no one is more surprised than I to find myself in this particular situation. I can only hope that someday you may come to love me as I love you."

"I will try, Quinton," she promised him. "I truly will."

The prince, having won several hundred pounds for a change this night, went off to bed before midnight. It was no secret that Lady Johnstone joined him shortly afterward to pay her debt. The following morning found the heir to Britain's throne in an excellent mood and ready for the hunt at the hour of six o'clock. Before leaving, the gentlemen consumed an early breakfast of eggs, bacon, oat stirabout, freshly baked breads, butter, and cheese, not to mention creamed cod and a platter of salmon.

The ladies, however, remained abed the entire morning, but for Allegra, who was downstairs by ten o'clock to go over the menus with the cook and consult with Crofts regarding the pantry, for she was still worried that there should not be enough food. The majordomo reassured his mistress that Perkins had brought back more than enough supplies the day before.

So the next few days slipped by with the gentlemen hunting in the morning and early afternoon, while the ladies enjoyed one another's company. In the evenings a sumptuous meal was served followed by cards until the prince deigned it was time for bed. The pesky boar was killed as were two fine deer and a number of waterfowl. Prinny was pleased, but then he began to grow bored with country life, and announced he would be returning to London the following day. The next morning the four young couples waved him and Mr. Brummell off, but only after Prinny had consumed a huge breakfast, and a large picnic hamper was stored in his coach.

"Delightful time," he assured his host and hostess. "Can't remember when I've had such fun." He bowed to them all, and kissed the ladies' hands.

Lady Johnstone and Lady Perry were not there to bid His Highness a farewell. The prince had invited them both into his bed the evening before. They were frankly exhausted, for he was a tireless lover. He had casually invited them to London. They had promised to visit—*eventually*. It was not until midafternoon that their carriage collected the two ladies, who thanked the duke and duchess for including them in their little party and departed. They were the last of the guests to go for the others had left shortly after Prinny, promising to return for Allegra's first ball at the end of the month.

The autumn deepened. The trees were turning wonderful colors on the estate, and in the hills around them. The duke was pleased to learn that four of his mares were breeding, and would foal in the spring. Although he wanted to take Allegra away to some wonderfully romantic place, he was glad they would be here then.

The French general, Napoleon, was making difficulties in Italy, and the duke didn't think they would be able to travel there in the spring after all. Still, he would take her to London this winter so she might enjoy her status as his wife. The country was a dull and quiet place in winter, and there could be no harm in spending a few weeks in town after the new year had begun.

The ball given by the new Duchess of Sedgwick in late autumn was to be a great success. Allegra had decided it would be a costume ball, and had invited all the families of note in the county. No invitation was refused, for there were many people curious to meet the new duchess, whose blood was hardly blue, but whose purse was overflowing. As Hunter's Lair was not a large house, many of the guests were staying with friends and relations who lived close by. The ball was to begin at ten o'clock in the evening. A buffet would be served at midnight when everyone would unmask; and then dancing and gambling would continue until the dawn when a breakfast would be presented to those remaining guests.

"I do not like costumes," Quinton Hunter told his wife.

"You will make a marvelous Caesar," Allegra said sweetly.

"And what are you to be? Caesar's wife?" he demanded.

"Cleopatra," she replied. "Mistresses are far more interesting than wives, or so I have been told," she finished mischievously.

"*Cleopatra?* Cleopatra was a . . ."

"*Queen,*" Allegra finished for him.

"I will not have my wife parading about in scanty draperies," the duke said firmly. "Everyone in the damned county is coming, and there has never been any unseemly gossip about a Duchess of Sedgwick."

"How unfortunate for you that your female antecedents have been so dull," Allegra replied tersely. "And do not tell me what I will or won't wear, sir. When did you become an arbiter of fashion?"

"*Allegra!*" he shouted. "You are my wife, and you will obey me, damnit."

"How dare you assume that I am so birdbrained as to flaunt myself before the county in, what was it you called it? *Scanty draperies.* My costume is rich and elegant, but there will be no one who can call it improper, unseemly, or unsuitable," she shouted back at him. "Ohh, you are the most irritating man!"

"And you are the most impossible woman!" he responded before sweeping her into his arms and kissing her soundly.

"You shall not get around me that easily," Allegra cried, pounding on his chest with her two little fists.

"Ohh, but I shall," he mocked her fury, and then he kissed her again until her knees were jelly, and she was furious at herself for the weakness of character she was exhibiting by yielding to him, but she just couldn't seem to help herself.

"*Stop, stop,*" she said desperately.

"Why?" he demanded.

"Because I cannot think clearly when you kiss me, damn you."

"Gracious, you have now taken to swearing," he teased, releasing her from his embrace. "You are not at all the proper girl I married, madame. You have turned into a naughty wench who swears and is deliciously wanton in our bed. I find that I like it, as long as the image you present to the public is one of decorous and cool behavior as befits a Duchess of Sedgwick."

"Damn the Duchess of Sedgwick," Allegra muttered at him. What the hell was the matter with her these days? He was right. She did enjoy their time together in their bed. In fact she was enjoying it more each time they came together which was practically every night. His passion for her was great, and she was astounded at how well he could engage her lust. But it wasn't love, *was it?*

On the night of their ball he saw her costume for the very first time. It was exactly as she had said, rich and elegant. She wore a white linen gown, a long straight pleated skirt, and a simple sleeveless bodice with a high rounded neck over which she wore a magnificent collar of turquoise, gold, and black beads that lay flat upon her chest.

"My God," he swore softly on seeing the necklace. "They look most authentic." He bent to examine it more closely.

"It is," she said. "One of Papa's clients bought it for me in Egypt several years ago. That is why I wanted to be Cleopatra, so I might wear it at long last. I never have before. Can you imagine my appearing in London last season in such a splendid necklace? Do you like the earbobs that go with it?" She shook her head slightly so they would jiggle.

The Duke of Sedgwick was amazed that she could be so casual wearing such a valuable antique. "You are most beautiful, Allegra," he finally said. He liked the full-length cloth of gold cape that she wore with her plain white gown. On her bare feet were golden sandals, and she wore an ornate black and gold wig, topped with a gold circlet from which sprang a golden snake with ruby eyes.

"And you are very handsome as a young Caesar," she returned the compliment. "I am, however, regretting my decision to let you show your knees, sir, for they are most tempting. Perhaps I should have had you outfitted in a long gown worn by the elderly senators of that ancient time. Try not to flaunt yourself too greatly, Quinton. No Duke of Sedgwick has ever done such a thing, and we certainly don't want you to start now."

"I believe the law allows me to beat you, madame, provided the stick is no thicker than my thumb," he growled at her.

"I'd rather you spank me, Quinton," she murmured teasingly to him, kissing his earlobe. "I believe I can be very naughty if you spank me, my lord."

"I am going to forbid Eunice and Caroline in this house," he told her. "They are suggesting wicked notions to you," he said, pretending to be very shocked, but he grinned at her. He damn well knew such proposals came from them, for Sirena and Ocky were too in love to entertain such vagaries of passion.

"We had best go down to dinner. Our houseguests will be waiting for us," Allegra said sweetly, as if nothing at all had occurred between them. She smoothed her skirt.

Viscount Pickford, the Earl of Aston, and Lord Walworth along with their wives were the duke and duchess's houseguests. The earl was dressed as one of his Elizabethan ancestors, in black velvet with a starched white neckruff, and Eunice was a lady of the same period in a black and gold gown. She wore marvelous diamond jewelry. Lord Walworth was an Indian prince in scarlet silk and cloth of gold with a gold turban sporting a large black pearl and several ostrich feathers. But Caroline had chosen to dress herself as a medieval jester in a bright tunic costume of red, blue, and yellow. There were bells on her shoes, and her cap. Her legs were sheathed in red and yellow striped tights, and appeared most shapely. Viscount Pickford made them all laugh in his brown monk's costume, for he said he felt like a monk right now. Sirena blushed as she laughed, teasing him that one could not make a cake without breaking eggs and baking it in the oven. She was garbed in the full blue and silver brocade of a medieval lady, which nicely concealed her delicate condition.

They had barely finished dinner when the guests began arriving. The duke and the duchess hurried to the ballroom to greet them. Most had never been inside Hunter's Lair, and those few who had marveled at its transformation.

"What wonders have been accomplished," a plump gentleman said.

"Money can buy anything," sniffed his wife, her beady eyes darting about.

"Except good taste," drawled another lady, "but it would appear that the duchess has a great deal of that. Everything is exquisite."

The musicians played a minuet as the Duke and Duchess of Sedgwick opened the ball. Familiar country dances followed. Those guests not interested in dancing found the drawing room set up for cards, and the play began in earnest.

Allegra kept a sharp eye out that the candles in the candelabras and sconces did not smoke, but she need not have for Crofts was carefully watching, too. He had been in service in this house for sixty years, but never had he seen a party such as the one being held tonight. He felt his chest swelling with pride. This was the way the Dukes of Sedgwick should have always entertained.

At midnight the masks came off, although everybody had already known who was beneath them. The dining room doors were opened, and the guests trooped into the beautiful room to enjoy the buffet. Long tables covered in fine Irish linen, and filled to overflowing, greeted them. There were two whole sides of beef being carved expertly. There was venison, salmon, trout, raw oysters, and roast geese. There were several turkeys, quail, partridge pies, and rabbit pasties. There were bowls of macaroni and cheddar cheese, potato puffs, potatoes with Hollandaise sauce, green peas, onions in milk and butter with black pepper, baked carrots and apples, green beans, and braised lettuce in white wine. There were six large hams that had been baked with honey, brown sugar, and cloves. There were platters of lobsters and mussels steamed until their shells opened. There were prawns served with a mustard and mayonnaise sauce. The guests didn't know where to begin.

The dessert table was equally resplendent with a dozen Genovese cakes; tarts of lemon, raspberry, and mince; apple, pear, and apricot fritters; several different cheese cakes; both pear and apple tarts; six large caramel custards; tiny pots au chocolat; and at the last moment the servants brought out soufflés of lemon and chocolate. There were also delicate sugar wafers, and decanters of sweet port wine on the dessert table.

"Never seen such an elegant spread hereabouts," Lady Bealle said approvingly. "Most generous. Most hospitable." Lady Bessie Bealle was the local dowager with the most influence in the county. Her favor was eagerly sought by all the hostesses.

"She is surprisingly mannerly, and well-spoken for a young woman of lesser family," the Countess of Whitley noted.

"But of course Sedgwick married her for her money," said Lady Margaret Dursley. "The Hunters are overproud, and have always taken only the best girls for wives."

"The best gels with the smallest, or nonexistent fortunes," Lady Bessie Bealle reminded them. "Poor Sedgwick was down to living in one room if the gossip be true. He could hardly take a respectable wife under such circumstances. And, my dears, he may have married her for her money, but have you noticed how truly attentive he is to his beautiful wife? It's a love match if I ever saw one!"

Her companions grudgingly agreed, as about them the other guests ate and drank and gossiped.

Sirena left the ballroom shortly after one o'clock in the morning. "I am constantly exhausted these days," she explained to her cousin. "It has gotten a bit better of late, but I must seek my bed. Do be sure that Ocky behaves himself and doesn't drink too much."

"I will, darling," Allegra said, kissing her cousin on both of her cheeks. "Sweet dreams."

The festivities went on, and while she had to admit that even she was getting tired, Allegra remained the perfect hostess. The musicians played endlessly. The guests danced and gossiped and gambled. By dawn when breakfast was served in the large dining room, over fifty people remained. The duchess, however, bid each and every one of her departing guests a personal farewell, thanking them for coming. She had gained Lady Bealle's approval fully, and that was good enough for the other hostesses in the county. The Duchess of Sedgwick's family might not have been at the top of the tree, but they had raised her to take her place there; and such a position as she now held suited her perfectly.

Finally the last of their guests were waved off on a gray and chilly November first morning. The houseguests had already hurried off to their rooms as the duke escorted his wife upstairs to her apartments. Closing the door behind him he took her in his arms, and kissed her slowly and very sweetly.

"I could not have chosen a better duchess," he told her honestly.

"It did go well," she agreed with a small smile. "The servants must be given their due in all of this, Quinton. They performed their duties admirably." She sighed, and put her head against his chest. "I am exhausted, my lord."

"Honor will help you, my dear," he said, and then kissing her hand he left her to go to his own apartments next door.

"It was grand, your ladyship," Honor said enthusiastically. "I watched from the stairs for a time last night as they came into the house. I have never in all my life seen such beautiful clothes as were worn by your guests. It was a sight out of the stories my old granny used to tell." She took the cloth of gold cape off Allegra's shoulders, laying it aside.

"Some of the costumes were fantastic," Allegra agreed with a smile. "Well, Honor, I have had my baptism of fire as the Duchess of Sedgwick, and I have survived. Old Lady Bealle fully approves of me."

"And well she should," Honor replied loyally as she helped her mistress from the heavy wig, and the rest of her clothing. Then she said, "I know it's late, or rather early, m'lady, but I drew a small bath for you in your dressing room. Will you be taking it?"

Allegra nodded, and walked naked across the bedchamber into her dressing room where her porcelain tub was set up now. Stepping into the lukewarm scented water she sank down and sighed. "Oh, this is wonderful, Honor. You are a clever girl." She did not linger long, however, just long enough to quickly wash. Honor dried her with a large towel, which was a great deal warmer than her tub had been, and slid a soft white cotton night garment over her mistress. Then Allegra climbed gratefully into bed, and was asleep almost instantly. She did not hear her husband come into the room shortly after Honor had left. And she certainly never felt him climb into bed next to her.

When she awoke in midafternoon he was lying next to her, snoring lightly. She rolled onto her side and studied him. They hadn't even been married a full month yet, but there had been no time to really study Quinton Hunter. Yes, he was handsome with his black hair and thick eyelashes that now fanned across his high cheekbones. Those eyelashes were every bit as thick as hers, Allegra thought. His eyebrows were heavy and bushy. He had a long, and what was referred to as an aquiline nose. *And his mouth.* She sighed softly. It was big, and gave her the most delicious kisses. She considered his chin. It was square, and there was a dimple directly in the center. It was really quite outrageous.

Then suddenly his silvery eyes were staring into her violet ones. Allegra gasped, startled. "You are awake," she said, wondering how long he had been aware of her scrutiny.

He smiled lazily at her. "May I assume that you approve of what you see, madame?" he said.

"What on earth do you mean, Quinton?"

"You were studying me quite closely, madame." He rolled her suddenly onto her back, his hands restraining hers quite effectively. "Admit it, duchess." He gave her a quick kiss.

"Never." She laughed, and then she shrieked. "Sir, you are a randy fellow. Why your manhood is hard as a rock against my leg."

"I have to pee," he announced, releasing her, and then getting up to find the chamber pot. "But when I am finished, Duchess, you have my permission to make me randy," he told her with a wicked grin. Then turning his back he pissed into the flowered china chamber pot, sighing with relief as he pushed it back beneath their bed. He turned about, and advanced upon her once again.

"*Quinton*. We have guests," Allegra cried.

"Who, if they are awake, my dear duchess, are probably doing exactly what you and I are about to do," he told her, grinning again.

"It is daylight," she protested as he climbed back next to her. "Can you do it in the daylight?"

Quinton Hunter burst out laughing. "My darling duchess," he said, "you can do it any time and almost anywhere, I assure you."

"How interesting," she purred, her voice suddenly very seductive. "*On the rug?*" Her look was questioning.

"Yes."

"*In the garden?*"

"Absolutely."

"*In my bath?*"

"A charming idea," he agreed.

"*Any time?*"

"*And almost any place,*" he repeated softly, kissing her ear.

"But what if I were dressed?" she demanded.

"I should take great pleasure, Duchess, in lifting your skirts in order to have my way with you," he murmured wickedly, blowing into her ear now.

"Oh la, sir, you are very naughty," Allegra accused him, but her heart was beating wildly. He was half atop her, their legs entwining in a sensuous embrace. His lips were employed in kissing her lips, her throat, her face, and every part of her body that he could reach. Her round little breasts were crushed against his hard chest, his soft fur irritating her nipples which suddenly seemed extraordinarily sensitive.

Her perfumed skin was utterly intoxicating, he

thought. Unable to help himself, he began to mouth her with his lips. Was it possible to eat her up? He certainly wanted to devour her for she was to his thinking most delicious. His lips moved across her belly. He could feel a pulse fluttering beneath his mouth. She was making little noises that seemed to come from the back of her throat. She was writhing beneath him, and he held her fast so he might continue kissing her. His manhood was beginning to hurt, throbbing with desire, eager to plunge within her fragrant warmth. Finally Quinton Hunter could wait no longer. Covering her lush body with his, he pressed forward.

"Ahhhh," Allegra cried as he entered her. "Ohh, Quinton! *Oh, darling, yes!*" Her slim arms clutched at him. Her long legs wrapped themselves about his lean torso. "Yes! Yes! Yes!" The words were almost a prayer.

He was lost within her. His thoughts disappeared. There was only sensation, and the wonder of the pleasure they were giving and sharing with each other. His hips drove relentlessly against her hips. His hands tangled themselves into the dark mass of her hair, holding her head tightly as their kisses fired volley after volley of hot desire that coursed through their veins until they could kiss no more. They were breathless with the hunger they seemed to engender within each other. They were so finely attuned to each other that once again they exploded together, then collapsed into each other's embrace.

For several long minutes the sounds of their breathing, at first ragged, and finally less harried, filled the room.

"You are magnificent," the duke finally said to his wife, kissing her softly as he rolled away from her. Propping himself upon an elbow he looked down into her beautiful face.

"You called me *darling*," he said.

"*I didn't,*" she quickly denied.

He laughed softly. "You did, Allegra. Could it be that you are beginning to harbor a *tendre* for me, Duchess?"

"I hardly know you, sir," she said, struggling to keep herself from falling headlong into his silvery gaze.

"You have known me since April," he said, chuckling, "and you have lived at Hunter's Lair with me since mid-June *and* you have been my wife for four weeks."

"Is it four weeks?" she said innocently.

"Say you love me," he coaxed her. "You know that I love you," Quinton Hunter said softly.

"You lust after me," she said. "Is that love, my lord?"

"Lusting after you is part of my love for you," he explained to her. "But the thought of being without you—*ever*—drives me to darkest despair, Allegra. *I love you.* And I think you love me."

"I don't understand love," Allegra persisted.

"Do not be evasive, Allegra," he gently scolded her. "Answer yourself this question. Would you rather be with me, or without me?"

"With you," she cried without hesitation.

"You love me," he said quietly.

And the reality slammed into her. *She did love him!* She didn't understand anything about love, or why she felt the way she did toward him, but she did. "*I love you,*" she said wonderingly. "Oh, Quinton, I do."

"I know," he replied, enfolding her into his arms. "Despite our careful resolve, my darling duchess. Despite the plain facts that would caution us against such folly, we have nonetheless fallen in love with each other." He kissed the top of her head. "I do not understand it either, Allegra, but there it is."

"I suppose it isn't a bad thing," she grudgingly considered.

"No," he agreed, "it seems to be quite a pleasant thing."

"I shall never betray you like my mother did my father," she promised him. "Mama, they say, was always emotional and indiscreet. I am my father's daughter, Quinton, I swear it."

"I know you are, my dearest Allegra. Despite your great fortune I should have never married you had I believed for one moment that you would betray me or bring embarrassment upon my family's name."

"What do we do now?" she asked him.

"We live happily ever after, I believe," he answered her with a broad smile. "We make love and have little heirs and heiresses, and live happily ever after, Allegra."

"It seems simple enough, but life, I have found, is rarely that simple, Quinton," she replied. "It ought to be, but it isn't."

"It will be for us, my darling," he promised her.

The clock on the mantel struck four o'clock.

"Good lord!" Allegra cried, leaping up in their bed. "We have guests in the house to attend to, my lord. This is their last night with us. Our friends go home tomorrow, and I don't know when we will see each other again." She squirmed from his embrace, and jumped from their bed. "Oh, lord, I hope no one has come downstairs and asked for us yet. Oh, Quinton! Get up! Get up now, my lord!" She yanked the bell pull for Honor. "I have to get dressed. I have to see that the dinner menu is correct."

"Crofts will attend to the dinner menu, Duchess," her husband said calmly. "You have a most adorable bottom, madame."

"Ohh!" Allegra flushed bright pink. She was completely naked. She had come from her bed unawares, so great was her concern for their friends. Then she laughed. There was no use grabbing for something to cover herself now. "Get up, Quinton," she repeated sternly.

He grinned lazily at her, and slid from the bed, as naked as she. "I had best retire to my own quarters before I shock poor Honor," he said with a chuckle. Then he blew her a kiss from his fingertips, and was gone through the connecting door.

At that same moment Honor entered her mistress's bedchamber. "Good afternoon, my lady," she said calmly, avoiding looking at Allegra directly as she was unclothed. "Shall I bring you something to eat?"

"Our guests?" Allegra almost squawked.

Honor calmly went to the wardrobe and took out a silk chamber robe which she draped over her mistress. "Only just beginning to stir, my lady. Mr. Crofts has everything under control."

"I must get downstairs as quickly as possible," Allegra said. "It will not do to have the guests without their hostess."

"Yes, my lady," Honor replied. "I'll send an undermaid for your tea right away."

*W*hen Allegra descended the stairs an hour later she found the house still quiet. She peeped into the ballroom as she came, and discovered it neat and empty. The beautiful wooden floors were swept clean. The chairs and the settees lining the walls were neatly covered. The great chandeliers had been done up again in dust cloths until the next ball. The tall pedestals were bare of their flowers, and the heavy gold satin draperies were drawn, allowing only slivers of afternoon sunlight to creep between their panels and streak across the floor. Entering the family drawing room she found Sirena sitting, sewing upon a tiny garment.

"You are awake. Crofts said you had not got to bed until after seven o'clock," Sirena said. "You must be exhausted. It was a wonderful ball, cousin. I hope to come to others in this house when I am less encumbered by my belly." She smiled at Allegra.

"*I love him,*" Allegra answered. She simply could not keep such news from her beloved Sirena.

"I know," Sirena replied, looking up and smiling.

"How could you know when even I did not?" her cousin demanded. "Do not be smug, Sirena, or I shall be very cross with you."

Sirena laughed. "Ocky and I both knew the day you married Quinton that you were in love with him. It was simply a matter of you coming to terms with it, facing the truth, and admitting it to yourself. Love is neither practical nor sensible, Allegra, but when it touches you, you are forever changed. We saw that change even before you could face it yourself. I am not being smug. I am relieved, *and* I am happy for you both. Now I know that everything will be all right."

"I shall not change because I am in love with my husband," Allegra protested.

"I do not care how you justify it, cousin," Sirena said quietly. She held up a tiny gown she was working on. "Isn't it sweet? It is so amazing to realize that in late March or early April I shall be putting this wee gown on my baby." She set her sewing aside, and placed her hands upon her belly. "I thought I felt something very much like a butterfly within me this morning, Allegra."

Now Allegra smiled. "Wouldn't it be wonderful if one day my daughter married your son? We must arrange the match one day."

"Are we dressing for dinner?" Caroline Walworth entered the room now in the company of Eunice Bainbridge.

"No," Allegra said. "I shall ask Crofts to set up the highboard in the Great Hall tonight. We can amuse ourselves afterward, but since you are all leaving in the morning, I imagine you will want to make an early night of it." She sighed. "I shall miss you when you are gone."

"Bain says we are going to spend part of the winter in London," Eunice said.

"So are we," Caroline squealed. "I know that you don't like the city, Allegra, but the country is so dull in the winter months. You must come, and we shall all be together."

"I can't come," Sirena said sadly.

"No, you can't," Caroline replied in a practical tone, "but you were the first wed, and so it is only natural that you are the first of us to have a baby, Sirena. There will be another time for you, dearest, but if the rest of us aren't with child, or at least admitting to it, then we should go. If it snows this winter none of us shall be able to leave home. The snow does not seem to bother anyone in London."

"Are we keeping city hours, madame?" Quinton Hunter demanded of his wife as he entered the drawing room with the other gentlemen. "Where is the dinner, Duchess? We are all ravenous for a good supper."

"Patience, prithee, I pray you, Duke," Allegra said to him. "I must ask Crofts to set the table in the Great Hall, but the food, I will wager, is ready, although when you slugabeds were going to join us was a mystery." Then she curtsied to them all, and hurried from the room to find Crofts.

The dinner was served shortly thereafter, and the hall was filled with merry laughter as the eight friends ate and talked. Lady Caroline presented her plan that they should all meet in London in mid-January. The plan was heartily approved by all present except the viscount and his wife.

"I suppose you could go if you wanted to," Sirena said forlornly, but they could all see she really didn't mean it.

"You wouldn't mind?" Ocky said hopefully, but then he looked about at the others, and noted their looks of disapproval. "Of course you wouldn't mind for you are an angel, my darling," Ocky quickly recovered himself, "but I shall not leave you at Pickford with our heir so close to being born. What if there was a storm, and I couldn't return to be by your side? No, Sirena, we shall winter at Pickford together."

"Ohh, Ocky, that is so sweet," Sirena murmured happily.

After their meal the men decided to play at dice. The ladies insisted on being shown how to play.

"I am not certain that is a good idea," the Earl of Aston said.

"Afraid of losing to a lady, Marcus?" his wife murmured.

"Damnit, Eunice, there are some things a lady doesn't do," was the swift answer.

"Ladies play at gambling all the time," Allegra responded. "We play at cards, but this game you call Hazard looks like more fun."

"I thought you didn't like to gamble," Lord Walworth said.

"She doesn't, except among friends," his wife replied. "What is the harm, Adrian, in teaching us your little game?"

"Caroline!"

"Teach them," the duke said.

"*What?*" the earl cried. "You are encouraging this, Quint? *You* of all people?"

"I do not gamble for real stakes, and neither does my wife. I trust Allegra's good sense not to gamble with strangers, or for any real wager. I must assume that you trust your wives as well," the duke said.

"Bravo!" Caroline cried, and her female companions clapped.

The Earl of Aston laughed, and held up his hands. "I surrender, ladies. Very well, here is how you play the game. Hazard uses two dice. The caster who controls the dice throws until he, *or she,* scores five, six, seven, eight, or nine. Your first throw is called the *main.* Your second, which must equal the first cast, is called the *chance.* If your second throw equals your first then you have *knicked* it. If you throw crabs, which is a two, three, eleven, or twelve, you have thrown out, and lost. You must continue your play until you win or lose. It is simple enough."

Soon the Great Hall of Hunter's Lair was filled with noisy laughter as they all played Hazard. They made wagers such as a kiss, or a sip of port, or a sugar wafer. When Allegra suddenly realized that the tall clock in the hall had struck ten she called a halt to their game, reminding them of the time.

"What a wonderful evening," Caroline said enthusiastically. "We shall have such a grand time in London this winter. We really don't need any other friends but one another. And on our way home in March we shall all come to Pickford to pay our respects to the new heir, Sirena."

"And you will tell me of your adventures, and I shall be most envious. Ocky, we must not have another baby for at least two years."

They laughed, and hand in hand the four couples ascended the stairs once again to their bedchambers.

Chapter Twelve

Allegra celebrated her eighteenth birthday on December ninth with her husband, her father, and her stepmother, as well as Sirena, Ocky, George, and his wife, Melinda. Melinda chose the occasion to smugly announce that she was expecting a baby in midwinter.

"The gel might have picked another time for her little proclamation," murmured Lady Morgan to her husband. "I believe the wench has delusions of grandeur. I heard her say it was to be the next Sedgwick heir. The nerve of her! Allegra had best put a stop to that nonsense! The gel's mother has obviously been filling her head with all matter of silliness. I should not have thought Squire Franklyn's daughter such a bold baggage."

"Allegra will mother the next duke, my dear," Lord Morgan said quietly. "Are you not the mother of a fine family?"

Lady Morgan blushed prettily. "I am," she agreed.

"Then we shall not worry," Lord Morgan said.

The duke gave his wife a pretty cart, painted green and silver, along with a fat black and white pony to draw it. "You may not always want to ride about," he told her. "And if the weather is inclement, and you wish to go over to Pickford, the cart will do nicely."

"I shall have to go to Pickford now that Sirena is limited in her travels," Allegra said, putting an arm about her cousin. "Thank you for coming today, darling. You have suddenly popped and are showing your belly, Sirena. It is most becoming."

"Your godson is thriving," Sirena laughed. "Ohh, Allegra, I shall miss you this winter when you are in London."

"I'd be just as happy to remain here," Allegra said. "I don't really like the city, but Eunice and Caroline insist we come. We shall only remain a few weeks, I promise."

"Where will you stay?" Sirena asked.

"At Papa's house," Allegra answered. "It is foolish of us to purchase another house as Papa's will belong to us one day. Besides we like Berkley Square, and it is quite conveniently located."

Sirena laughed. "I wish I could go," she said. "You will have so much more fun than when we were debutantes, Allegra. We had to be so prim and proper then lest we spoil our chances for husbands. There is the theatre, Vauxhall Gardens, fetes, costume balls, opera, and the races! I will think of you when you are gone, cousin."

The Season always began in March or April, but ended by mid-June, when everybody who was anybody returned to their country estates and homes. A Little Season began in September, but by November the town was deserted again by the well-to-do. In January when Parliament began, many of the fashionables returned to town and the country was deadly dull. The duke and his three friends, who usually did not involve themselves in politics, had decided to attend the government session while they were in London. The Earl of Aston and Lord Walworth would be renting the old Earl of

Pickford's house during their stay as he was not coming to Parliament this year in anticipation of his grandchild's birth. He wanted to be there when his next heir made his debut.

Allegra and the duke traveled to London in a large, comfortable traveling coach drawn by six horses. The interior of the vehicle was well padded, and it was well sprung. The seats were upholstered in a soft beige leather. Beneath each seat was a metal box for hot coals so that the coach might be heated. The heat escaped through a brass latticework at the bottom of each of the two benches. There were small crystal oil lamps, banded in silver, for light. The windows were glass, and could be raised or lowered depending upon the weather. The windows had cream-colored velvet curtains that could be drawn for privacy. The back of the seat facing the rear of the coach could be drawn down. It held its passengers' food and wine. The coachmen's box held two men. There was a bench behind the coach for two footmen. The top of the vehicle was deep enough and wide enough for a goodly supply of luggage.

The weather was so cold that even the duke would not ride outside, but remained within the coach with his wife. His vehicle was followed by a second carriage in which Honor, and the duke's valet, Hawkins, rode with the rest of the luggage. This auxiliary vehicle had but one driver, the second undercoachman. It would be his duty in London to oversee the stables and ducal transport while they were there.

While cold, the weather held, though it was gray and cloudy. They stopped for luncheon, and then for dinner and lodging at inns that were expecting them. They did not have to change horses because the animals were well cared for, and well rested each night. Allegra was very grateful for the hooded beaver-lined velvet cape her husband had given her for Christmas. She unashamedly wore several flannel petticoats beneath her skirt. This was no time to be fashionable, and besides, who was to know, she thought, as she snuggled into the dark green velvet of the fur-lined and -trimmed cape.

It took them several days to reach London, but when they did, the servants hurried from Morgan House to help them out of their coach and escort them into the house. Marker, the family butler, came forward, bowing, a smile upon his face.

"Welcome home, Your Grace," he said. "Your father is here, and will see you and His Grace in the library when you are settled."

"Papa! Ohh, let us go now," Allegra said, unfastening her voluminous cape and handing it off to a footman.

"Very well, my dear," the duke agreed. He hadn't thought his father-in-law would be here, but then why wouldn't he? It was his house, and he certainly always had business in London.

Septimius Morgan arose from his chair by the fire to greet his only child and her husband. "I shall not be with you long," he reassured them with a smile. "I am anxious to return home as soon as possible. Your stepmother hasn't felt well of late."

"What is the matter?" Allegra cried, a worried expression crossing her beautiful face.

"Nothing more, my child, than a winter ague," her father assured her with a smile. "How it pleases me that you love Olympia as I do." He indicated a settee opposite his chair, and the couple both sat. "How long do you plan to remain in town?" Lord Morgan inquired as he seated himself.

"Only a few weeks," the duke replied. "Our friends, Aston and Walworth, are also here with their wives. We plan to make a time of it, Septimius. We shall visit the opera, the theatre, perhaps even Vauxhall if there is something of note to see. I should also like to go to Tattersall's. While I have an excellent stud, I could use some good blooded mares to improve my stock. We will certainly be gone before *The Season* begins."

"Do you intend to take your place in the house, Quinton?" his father-in-law asked him.

"Yes, I think I should like to see what is going on right now," the duke answered.

"I have never asked you this," Lord Morgan said, "but are you a Tory, or a Whig?"

"I think I am a little of each, sir, which is why I do not visit Parliament too often," the duke responded with a small smile. "Nothing in this life is only black or white, Septimius. I cannot become enthusiastic over a political party and cleave only to it. Politics are made up of men, and men, I have learned, are quite fallible."

Now it was Lord Morgan's turn to smile. "You have married a wise man, my child," he told Allegra.

"And you, sir," the duke said. "Are you fish, or fowl?"

"Like you, Quinton, neither. A man in trade such as myself, even with a *Lord* before his name, cannot afford to take sides. I leave that to cleverer heads than mine, and those whose passions run higher."

The duke chuckled, and turned to his wife. "You have a devious and clever father, my darling."

"As long as the country is well run," Lord Morgan said, "I am content." He looked closely at his daughter, and what he saw pleased him greatly. Sirena had written that Allegra had fallen in love with her husband, who was already in love with her, but now that he saw it with his own eyes, he was happier. They had only been at

Hunter's Lair overnight for his daughter's birthday, and he had had no real chance to observe the pair. Olympia would be delighted, for it was really she who had engineered the match with Lady Bellingham's aid.

"When will you leave us, Papa?" Allegra asked him.

"In two or three days, my child, but I am leaving Charles Trent behind to oversee my business. He will be a shadow, of course, but should you entertain, he will be an excellent extra gentleman for the table. He has offered to tuck in at my offices, but I said you would not hear of it."

"No, no," Allegra agreed. "He must remain here in his own rooms."

The next morning while her father and husband had gone off to the House of Lords, Allegra sat down with Charles Trent. "It will be expected that I give an *at home*," she said. "How long will it take to arrange the invitations? I assume you know to whom my cards should be sent? We do not intend to remain in London long, but I know that as the Duchess of Sedgwick I cannot come and not have an *at home*."

"The invitations are already engraved, Your Grace," Mr. Trent answered her. "It only remains for you to choose the day. Might I suggest the last day of February?"

"We intend leaving shortly afterward," Allegra said thoughtfully. "How ridiculous that we must give people a month's notice. Sirena and I went to several *at homes* last season. What a silly custom. You push into a huge crush of people, remain only fifteen minutes, and then leave. There is no food, no drink, no entertainment at all. And your levee is not considered a success at all unless at least one woman faints dead away, and the crowds are overwhelming. I do not see the point of it all. Still, it is the fashionable thing to do, and so I must. I would not want the gossips saying I was not worthy of my husband's name and title."

"I am inclined to agree with Your Grace on both counts," Mr. Trent said with a small smile. "It is ridiculous, but the gossips will indeed cry you are ill-bred if you do not do it. Shall we say the last day of February?"

"No, make it the twentieth, if it is not a Sunday," Allegra said. "Then at least we will have a pleasant final week in town."

"Very good, Your Grace," Mr. Trent answered.

"How odd to hear you call me that instead of Miss Allegra," she replied. "I am still not used to such grandeur, although here in London I suppose I must play the role to the hilt."

"Indeed you must," he advised her. "Wealth and position mean a great deal to most of the people with whom you will have to associate while you are in town, *Your Grace.* In one short season you have climbed from the bottom of the tree to the top of the tree. There will be many who still resent it, completely overlooking the fact that it is your wealth, and the duke's family, that have made you such a perfect match. You do, however, have an excellent friend in Lady Bellingham."

"Is she in town yet, Mr. Trent?"

"I believe she arrived with her husband several days ago."

"Please send her an invitation to tea tomorrow," Allegra instructed her father's personal secretary.

"Of course, Your Grace," Mr. Trent replied.

The duke and Lord Morgan returned from Parliament's opening late in the afternoon. Allegra had tea served in the smaller green drawing room. Marker set the large silver tray on a table before the young duchess, and then stepped back politely. Allegra poured the fragrant India tea into French Sèvres cups for her husband and her father, while a footman passed around the crystal plates holding bread and butter, and small cakes filled with fruit that had been iced with a white sugar icing.

"Was it interesting?" she asked the two men.

"There is a small visitors' gallery," her father said. "Any day that you and your friends would like to visit, I shall arrange it. Depending on what they choose to argue about makes it interesting, or else deadly dull. Today the king opened the session, and while colorful, it is usually quite boring. I must say the day lived up to its promise, eh, Quinton?" he finished, his eyes twinkling as he looked at his son-in-law.

"Indeed," the duke replied. "The Whigs are out of power right now, and seem to become more radical with each passing day. All they can talk about is reform, reform, reform. That usually involves taking from those who work hard, and giving it to those who do not. Since many of the more prominent Whigs are wealthy men, you can be certain they will not penalize themselves."

"But there is much poverty, especially here in the city," Allegra said. "I have seen it myself."

"You can be sure the government will do only what they are forced into to care for the poor," her father said dryly.

"But what about the Tories?" Allegra asked.

"They are more conservative," the duke replied. "They have, since their inception in the sixteen hundreds, favored the Stuarts, and opposed any attempts to deny our Roman Catholic citizens their rights. When King James II was overthrown in what the historians like to call *the Glorious Revolution*, and his daughter Mary came to England to rule with her Dutch husband, the Tories favored the Jacobite cause. But they were not averse to the Hanoverian succession after Queen Anne died. The Whigs, however, used the Tories' former Jacobite leanings against them. Tories were very neatly excluded from government by the first two Georges. The current Prime Minister, Mr. Pitt the younger, has changed all of that," the duke said.

"How?" Allegra asked her husband.

"Now, my pretty darling," the duke responded patting her cheek, "certainly you don't want to fill your pretty head with such stuff as politics."

Lord Morgan watched amused as he saw his daughter stiffen her spine, an irritated look crossing her pretty face, her eyes becoming hard with her annoyance.

"Quinton," she said in a soft, well-modulated voice, "if you do not answer my question, I shall smack you. If I were not interested, I should not have asked. Surely you know better by now than to classify me with those silly creatures who flutter about our world giggling, and fluttering their eyelashes and swooning at the drop of a hat."

At first startled by his wife's suggestion of violence, the duke then recovered and said, "Mr. Pitt has done many good things for England, Allegra. He managed to place the East India Company under government control, which is much better for trade. He has tried to ease the problems in the Canadian colony, which as you certainly know is peopled by both English and French colonists. He did this by dividing it into Lower Canada, which is predominantly peopled by the French, and Upper Canada, which is English speaking. He has reduced customs duties which has undoubtedly been of great help to your papa's business ventures. He has established a *sinking fund*, which takes a percentage of the government's revenues, and uses it to pay off the government's debts. Not all of it, of course, but some. Of course the trick is to keep the politicians from using the sinking funds for other purposes instead of the ones that they're intended to cover.

"Mr. Pitt the younger was quite committed to parliamentary reform, but he has put it aside in the wake of what is happening in France. He has also, due to the difficulties in France, suspended the writ of Habeas Corpus, but you wouldn't know what that was, Allegra, would you?"

"It is a law requiring anyone detaining another individual to produce that person in a court of law within a specified period of time, and to furnish reasons for the detention then. I believe the law was first written in the sixteenth century. It has been revised somewhat over the years, but it is basically the same now as it was then, except that originally it was only used for criminal charges, and now it is used for civil charges as well. Habeas Corpus was suspended during the Jacobite uprisings at the beginning and middle of this century. Is that the Habeas Corpus you are referring to, my lord husband?" Allegra smiled sweetly.

"Did you let her study the law, Septimius?" the surprised duke asked his father-in-law, but then he began to laugh. "What other surprises have you in store for me, my darling?" he asked.

"Now, that, sir, would spoil all my fun," Allegra responded pertly, and she laughed, too.

Lady Bellingham came to tea two days later, and was delighted to find her niece and the young Countess of Aston had been invited as well. "What, Caroline, you are in town, and did not call upon me?" she demanded of Lady Walworth.

"We have not even settled in yet, Aunt," was the quick reply.

"Where are you staying? Has Walworth rented a place, for I know he has no house of his own," came the next question.

"Adrian and Marcus Bainbridge have rented the old Earl of Pickford's house, Aunt. Sirena is breeding, and could not travel, so they have no use for the house in London this winter."

"An excellent address," Lady Bellingham responded. "Well, what is it that you three intend to do in London?"

"We mean to sightsee," Allegra said, "and visit all the places like Vauxhall, that a proper debutante could not go to without fear of ruining her reputation, Lady Bellingham."

"Be careful you don't ruin your reputations *now*, my gels," Lady Bellingham said sharply. "Marriage is not a blanket license to run wild. You don't want to follow in the Duchess of Devonshire's footsteps. Why the gossip about her is outrageous, but true, I fear. She is in debt up to her pretty ears, I am told. Loses thousands each night at cards and in the gambling halls where ladies are not supposed to go. Most shocking!"

"I certainly do not gamble," Allegra replied. "Oh do try some of the salmon, Lady Bellingham."

"Salmon? Why, m'dear, 'tis an especial favorite of mine," Lady Bellingham said, helping herself to a small rectangle of buttered bread with an equally small sliver of pink salmon upon it. "Delicious!" she pronounced. "But I am too clever an old fox to be wheedled off the subject, Allegra. What is it exactly that you young women intend doing?"

"We really have come to sightsee, Aunt," Caroline, Lady Walworth assured her elder. "And there is the theatre, and the opera since Allegra and Quinton don't gamble, and as neither Walworth nor Bainbridge have the ready for such high stakes as here in London."

"You are wise, my gels, for the gambling is entirely out of hand thanks to Prinny and his friends. Fortunes are made and lost in a single night. Many lives have been ruined. Prinny and his friends may mock the king, but he is a good man who has set a good Christian example for us all. What a pity his son cannot follow it, especially now that he is a father himself. I would not come to London at all nowadays but that Bellingham must attend Parliament. How he loves his politics, and, of course, Mr. Pitt is such a fine man."

"You would not prefer to remain in the country, and let my uncle come up alone?" Caroline asked mischievously.

"Gracious, child," her aunt exclaimed. "One should never allow a husband to come up to London alone. Much too much temptation for a gentleman, even the best of them. There are women, not the kind we would associate with, I assure you, just looking for unaccompanied gentlemen like my poor gullible Freddie, to take advantage of, and fleece. No! No! As long as Frederick Bellingham wants to come up to Parliament, I shall be at his side, I can assure you." She helped herself to another bit of salmon.

"*Poor uncle*," Caroline murmured softly to her friends who struggled not to giggle. They all knew that old Lord Bellingham, a rather charming gentleman, was under the firm control of his forceful wife whom he simply adored.

The cards had been sent out for the Duchess of Sedgwick's *at home*, and the responses were pouring in each day. No one was going to miss the opportunity to see how the duke and his bride were getting on after three months of marriage. They all thought it rather odd that their society wedding planned for St. George's in Hanover Square had been changed to the family chapel, or wherever it had been, at Hunter's Lair. Why on earth had they done *that*? Was the duchess enceinte? But then she couldn't be if they were in London. It was a most aggravating mystery.

Prinny, of course, had arrived at Hunter's Lair with young Mr. Brummell. Usually Brummell had something caustic to say about everyone, but he had nothing but praise for the duchess's exquisite taste, the wonderful house, and the obviously contented couple. It was all just too annoying, but now they should see the truth of it. After all, blue-blooded Sedgwick had only wed the Morgan chit for her fortune. They all knew it, and he even admitted to it last season. It was a marriage of convenience, nothing more, whatever Brummell saw.

Allegra was fascinated by the London she now saw. Last spring her whole time had been spent on seeking and finding a husband. Her movements were carefully monitored and watched. She could only come or go in a prescribed manner. Now, however, she and her two friends were able to go about town in one another's company while their husbands visited the Parliament and their clubs. Each evening they all met for dinner, or some form of entertainment. They played Whist together; sang accompanying each other on the piano; enacted out charades, the ladies against the gentlemen.

Allegra, Caroline, and Eunice, in the company of Lady Bellingham, visited Westminster Abbey one morning. It was a great Gothic structure of French design with wonderful stained glass windows and gray stone buttresses. The interior was made up of chapels, naves, tombs, and monuments. King William the Norman had been crowned here. The Coronation Chair which had been made for King Edward I was brought into the abbey in the year 1272. It had been used at all the coronations that had followed. The tombs were legion, and very impressive. There was the one belonging to St. Edward the Confessor, as well as Edward III and young Edward VI. There was the tomb of Henry III and the first Tudor king, Henry VII. Richard II had his tomb in the abbey, as did Mary, Queen of Scots, her son, James I, and his grandson, Charles II. The second Hanover king, George II, was buried in the enormous church. And there were famous women as well: Eleanor of Castile, Anne of Cleves, Queen Mary II, and her sister, Queen Anne.

The marble and the stonework were extremely impressive. The colorful stained glass windows almost brought tears to Allegra's eyes. It was early afternoon before they realized it, and left reluctantly, having gained a new sense of their country's history and its importance in the world in which they lived.

On another day, bundled up in their furs, they visited the Tower of London with its colorful Beefeater Guards in their red, black, and gold uniforms. The royal menagerie was located here, but it was not particularly impressive right now, consisting only of a moth-eaten ancient tiger, a toothless grizzly bear, an Indian elephant, and several peacocks. Allegra was more interested in the Tower Green where two of Henry VIII's wives had been beheaded.

"What a horrid fate!" Caroline said.

"I heard they betrayed the king," Eunice replied. "They deserved it if that was the case."

"In Anne Boleyn's case the charges were probably trumped up as the king had an eye out for his next wife, Queen Jane, who mothered his son. Poor Anne miscarried two sons and only produced her daughter, Elizabeth, who, of course, went on to become England's greatest queen."

"What about the other wife?" Eunice asked.

"Catherine Howard was Anne Boleyn's cousin. She wasn't very smart, and was, so I have read, a trollop who was no better than she ought to be. The king adored her, which made her betrayal of him with a lover all the worse to stomach. In fact, he didn't."

"You are quite learned," Caroline said. "How is it you are so well educated when most of us are not?"

"I studied with my brother and his tutor," Allegra explained. "Then when James Lucian went off to school, Papa allowed the tutor to remain to teach me even more."

"Wasn't it rather dull?" Eunice inquired.

"Not at all," Allegra assured her. "I liked it. A woman should really know more than how to paint pretty watercolors and play the piano while she sings. If I had not married Quinton I should have been quite capable of carrying on my own life without a husband."

"You are very brave," Caroline said. "Far braver than I am, I will admit it honestly. I am so glad that Dree and I suit. I should not like to be without a husband."

"Nor I," Eunice noted. "I adore my Marcus, and it is quite a great deal of fun to be the Countess of Aston. Don't you like being the Duchess of Sedgwick, Allegra?"

"I like it quite well," Allegra said, "but if Quinton and I had not made a match of it, I should not weep and wail." A gust of icy wind off the river blew her fur-trimmed hood back, and Allegra shivered. "Let us go home, and have tea," she suggested. "We are going to the theatre tonight."

"I wish it were warm enough to visit Vauxhall," Caroline said as they hurried from the Tower of London to their waiting coach.

"Probably next month before we go," Eunice remarked.

"Where did the gentlemen go today?" Caroline asked.

"The cockfights," Eunice remarked. "Disgusting!"

The other two nodded their heads in agreement.

"Last week Dree asked me if I wanted to go to Newgate with him to see a hanging," Caroline said, shuddering. "He brought me back a printed leaflet, a biography of the criminal hanged. There was a line drawing of the fellow. He was very young, but he was a highwayman."

"Quinton says he would like me to come to Tattersall's when he purchases the new mares," Allegra told them.

"Ohh, that would be fun," Caroline replied. "May we come, too? I could use a new mare, and my birthday is coming up," she finished with a wicked smile.

"You speak to Adrian then," Allegra said, "and let him ask Quinton. It will be a question of two men buying horses then, and not an entertainment for us. Quinton is very serious about these purchases, and I can certainly understand his point. His stud is a magnificent beast, and has already sired several fine racers on less than distinguished stock. With really fine mares what will he do? We shall have the most sought after racers in all of England," Allegra said proudly, and her friends smiled.

It had begun to rain—an icy rain—when Allegra arrived home. Her two friends had decided to return to Pickford House rather than stop for tea. The big house was quiet. Mr. Trent was nowhere in evidence. He really was the epitome of discretion. Her father, of course, had already returned to Morgan Court.

"Good afternoon, Your Grace," Marker said, coming forward to take her cape.

"Has his lordship come home?" Allegra asked the butler.

"He is in his rooms, Your Grace. Hawkins says he has caught a bit of a chill at the cockfights."

"Have tea brought up to my apartments," Allegra instructed Marker, and then she hurried up the stairs. She found her husband soaking in her tub, and smiled. "Boys will be boys," she greeted him. "You did not wear a hat this morning, did you, my lord?"

"Do not scold, my darling," he replied, and then he sneezed.

"What are you doing in my tub?" she demanded.

"I was chilled to the bone, Allegra," he answered, and sneezed again. "Damned cock ring was out of the city, and in the open."

"Hawkins, get your master out of the tub," Allegra instructed the valet. "Dry him thoroughly, and we'll tuck him into bed. *My bed.* Honor, there is tea being brought up. Get a warming pan, and warm the sheets, and I'll want another down coverlet. Really, Quinton, and we were to go to the theatre tonight. I'll send around a footman to tell Dree and Marcus we shall not be coming this time."

"You can go," he told her. "There can be no gossip if you are in the company of friends," he told her.

"Do not be ridiculous," Allegra said sharply. "I am not the Duchess of Devonshire to appear socially in public without my husband at my side. Hawkins, where is the duke's nightshirt?" Then seeing it, Allegra snatched it up herself, and dropped it over his head. "Get into bed, Quinton, before you are really sick. With luck we shall have you cured by the morrow."

Honor had gotten the brass warming pan and was taking the chill from the sheets so that the duke might get into bed. When she had finished she said, "You'll want the supper upstairs tonight." It wasn't a question.

"Yes," Allegra said shortly. "Nothing heavy, tell cook." She helped her husband into their bed, and put a nightcap upon his dark head. "We'll try and undo what you have done, Quinton."

"You are harder than my old nurse," the duke said. "I did not know you could be such a scold, madame."

"After dinner, sir, I shall punish you properly," Allegra murmured softly.

"Will you keep me warm, then, madame?" he murmured back, his eyes dancing with amusement.

"*Very warm,*" she promised him, and then she kissed his lips. "Now," she straightened up, "I must go and send a note around to Pickford House to tell the others we are not coming. Drink some tea. It will help to warm you up."

He caught her hand for a moment. "I do not mind that we are to have an evening alone, my darling," the duke told her. Then, turning the hand over, he kissed its palm ardently.

Allegra colored, then smiled. "Neither do I, Quinton. Next winter we need not come up to London. By the time we go home to Hunter's Lair we will have tasted all its pleasures, and not need to come back at all until our daughters come for their seasons."

"We have no daughters," he reminded her.

"We will . . . eventually," she promised him. "Now let me go so I can send my note off to Pickford House."

"I don't think I can ever let you go, Allegra," her husband told her.

"To be loved as you love me is sometimes overpowering," she answered him, and then taking her hand back, hurried off.

Quinton Hunter lay back against the lavender-scented pillows. Her words rang in his head. *To be loved as you love me is sometimes overpowering.* And she loved him back. Passionately in his arms, but with words Allegra was more reserved. He hoped one day she would not be. It was his own personal weakness, although he would never admit to it, that he needed to hear her voicing her love for him. He closed his eyes. It had been a long time since he had been ill. He was going to enjoy being taken care of by his beautiful wife.

Allegra had left her bedchamber where her husband lay. She passed through her salon, and hurried downstairs to the small family drawing room. "Fetch Hawkins to me," she told an attending footman, and when the duke's valet came she said, "Was the duke wearing flannel drawers today, Hawkins?"

"No, Your Grace," the valet replied. He could see that the duchess was in a fine fettle.

"In future you will see that His Grace is dressed properly for the winter weather, Hawkins, which means his hat as well. If he complains at you you will say that I have given you your orders. Is that understood?" She looked hard at the valet.

"Yes, Your Grace," he replied.

"You are dismissed," Allegra told the valet.

Hawkins departed the room, and as he did he ran into Marker. "Her's got a good temper on her, eh, Marker. You must have been given the back of her tongue many times, her growing up in this house."

"Her Grace is generous of heart, and sweet-natured most of the time," Marker replied stiffly. He thought the valet presumptuous to say the least. "If she has chastised you then it is because you deserved it. I understand the duke has returned home with a chill. Obviously he was not warmly enough dressed by you this morning. You had best watch your place, Hawkins. There are those who would be eager to serve His Grace if you cannot."

"Tough old bird, ain't he?" Hawkins heard behind him, and turned about to see Honor standing there.

"I've had two dressings-down in a very short time," Hawkins said sourly. "For a lass with no background so to speak, your mistress is a proper Tartar, Honor."

"You watch your mouth, Hawkins," Honor said, suddenly angry. "I'll hear naught against my lady. You didn't do your duty."

"He don't like flannel drawers," Hawkins said stubbornly, "and I can't make him wear a hat if he don't want to. I'm his valet, not his ma."

"You have your orders from Her Grace," Honor warned him. "The duke will obey if you tell him she says it. He loves her something fierce."

"I'd like to love you," Hawkins said slyly to Honor.

"When you do your duty better," Honor said, "we'll see if I let you walk out with me."

"Didn't say nothing about *walking out*," Hawkins replied.

"Then you'll not be *loving* me. I'm a proper girl, Hawkins, and best you understand that right now," Honor answered him. Then with a flounce of her skirts she was off.

In the little drawing room Allegra wrote her note to Caroline and Eunice. She dispatched it with a footman, and returned upstairs to where her husband lay. Supper was brought. Cook had followed the duchess's instructions. There was a thick, rich soup which Allegra fed to her husband, sitting on the side of the bed as she spooned it into his mouth. Then she coaxed him to eat a bit of capon with some bread and butter. And finally the cook had provided a silken egg custard that the duke very much enjoyed. And when her husband had been fed, Allegra sat down at a small table and ate her own supper as Quinton watched, slowly sipping a glass of ruby port as he did so.

A footman came, and cleared the dishes away. Then Honor helped her mistress to prepare for her bed. When she was washed and in her nightgown and cap, Allegra dismissed her maidservant for the night. Wrapping a lacy shawl about herself she sat down by the fire.

"Come to bed," the duke said softly.

"Shortly," she replied.

"Why do you sit by the fire?" he asked her.

"So I may have the privacy to say my prayers," Allegra responded. "I pray each morning and each evening, Quinton."

"Who taught you to do that?" he wondered aloud. "You had no mother."

"Papa taught me. He said that one day I would have children of my own, and it would be my duty to teach them to pray to our creator. Didn't your mama teach you and George to pray before she died?"

"I think I remember her with me, but George was too young," he replied.

For several minutes the room was silent but for the crackle of the fire. Finally Allegra arose, and snuffing out all the candles in her bedchamber climbed into bed next to her husband. "There," she told him, snuggling into his arms.

"What do you pray for?" he asked her, curious.

"For us. For you. For our family. *For children*," she said. "We must strive harder, Quinton, for our children."

"Madame, I am more than willing to answer your prayers," he said with mock seriousness.

She giggled. "Do not be sacrilegious," she tried to
scold, but she suddenly found herself being kissed as he
cradled her beneath him. *"Ohh, Quinton!"* She sighed,
and kissed him back fervently.

Lilacs. She always smelled of lilacs, and it intoxicated
him. His hand caressed her heart-shaped face. "Whatever made me believe I would not fall in love with you,
Allegra? How could I not love you, my darling?" His
silvery-gray eyes devoured her. "I have learned that I
could not live without you, Allegra. You have become
the very reason for my existence." His lips descended
upon hers again, and he felt her melting into his arms.
His fingers undid the ribbons on her nightgown's neck,
loosening it, and his hand slipped between the fabric
and her skin as he moved to cup one of her small breasts
in his palm. He fondled her, and felt her heart beat more
quickly.

She loved him, Allegra thought as his hand aroused
her passions. Oh yes, she loved him, but when she tried
to tell him she could not quite manage the words. Oh,
she had said it to him once, but she wanted to tell him
more, except her tongue became tangled. He could not
live without her? *She could not live without him.* She
could not even imagine her life without Quinton
Hunter. Allegra pushed her thoughts aside, and concentrated on the wonderful feelings that he could kindle
within her. She sighed, and moved against him, letting
him know that she loved everything that he was doing
to her, and that she wanted more. For a moment she
struggled from his embrace, and pulled off her nightgown and cap. Then she lay back against their pillows,
her look inviting.

He responded in kind, drawing his own nightshirt off,
then leaned forward to kiss her adorable breasts. One
hand kneaded her while his mouth attached itself over

the other nipple and he suckled. She writhed and murmured beneath him, stoking his passions until he knew exactly what he wanted from her tonight. Something he had never dared to do with her, but he needed to initiate her completely into this passion. Raising his dark head from her milky white breasts he said, "I don't want you to be afraid, Allegra." Then his head dropped again and he began to kiss her body.

His lips moved slowly, slowly over her torso. Sometimes his tongue snaked out to lick at her warm flesh. She murmured with pleasure. The dark head moved lower and lower down her lush young body. He cupped her dark mont in his palm. The thick dark curls were soft against his palm. Releasing her from the intimate grip he fingered her nether lips, teasing, and playing with her until she began to squirm slightly and grow moist beneath his touch. The ball of his forefinger found the tiny bud of her sex. He caressed it until she was moaning aloud. He slid his large body down until he was firmly between her open thighs.

"*Quinton?*" Her voice registered fear.

"Don't be afraid, Allegra," he pleaded, and then leaning forward he began to tongue that quivering little nub of flesh.

Her body arced up in shock, but he held her tightly so she could not escape him. She was at first scandalized by what he was doing. She had never in her wildest imaginings conceived that *this* . . . this was part of passion. And yet she very quickly decided that she liked it. Oh yes! She liked it very much. Her body quivered. That tiny part of her that she hadn't really known existed tingled and tingled until it seemed to burst into a blanket of deliciousness that covered her and left her weak and breathless. "*Oh, please,*" she murmured helplessly.

He pulled himself up, covering her trembling form,

and slowly pushed himself into her love sheath. "God, Allegra," he groaned. "I want you so desperately!"

He was so hard, she thought. She could feel each stroke of his manhood with every fiber of her being. She felt herself tightening about his lance, trying to keep him from leaving her. *"Don't stop!"* she begged him. "Ohh, Quinton, I want you so very much!" Her nails dug into his muscled shoulders, and she pushed her tongue into his ear. Her legs wrapped themselves tightly about his straining form. *"Ohhh, sweet! Sweet!"* she cried as they together approached nirvana.

"Ahh, you precious witch, you have unmanned me!" he told her as his boiling tribute poured forth, and they collapsed together in a tangle of arms and legs. They lay still entwined for several long minutes amid the wreckage of their bedclothes, their breathing finally slowing and calming. And then the duke sneezed.

"Oh, lord." Allegra scrambled from their bed, and grabbed up his nightshirt. "Put this on, Quinton, else I kill you with my love." She caught up her own night garment and quickly pulled it over herself.

He began to laugh as he complied with her order.

"What is so funny?" she demanded, climbing back into the bed, and pulling the covers up over them.

"I am so damned happy," Quinton Hunter told her. "A year ago when the four of us decided we must find wives and finally settle down, my darling Allegra, I never imagined, no, I never even dared to hope that I should be this happy. I have never been happier in my whole life, and it is all due to you, my darling. It is all due to you."

"You are a fool, Quinton," she told him, but her own heart was soaring with happiness.

"I love you," he said. "And you love me."

"I suppose I do," she grudgingly admitted.

He laughed again. "Say it, you adorable witch! Say you love me, and you will never love anyone else but me."

"I do, and I won't," she teased him mischievously.

"Say it, damnit." He rolled over to face her, his look fierce.

Her heart melted then and there. "I love you, Quinton Hunter, and I always will," she said softly. "I expected a comfortable arrangement and a mutual respect. I never expected to know this phenomenon that is called love. I still don't understand it, but I seem to love you dearly, Quinton. Now are you satisfied, and will you go to sleep before you become truly sick?"

"Yes, Duchess," he said, and then taking her hand in his, he finally fell asleep.

Part Three

Winter and Spring 1796
A Dangerous Game

Chapter Thirteen

The day had arrived for Allegra's *at home* reception. Not one of the two thousand invitations that had been sent out had been refused. Allegra was relieved that it was midwinter, for if it had been the height of the season, she might have had double or triple the acceptances. People were expected to come, remain for fifteen minutes, no more, and leave their cards if they could not personally manage to greet the duke and the duchess, which most would not. Since no refreshments or music would be required, there would be little preparation except for the tall footed columns with their urns of flowers scattered about the gracious foyer and public rooms. Roses and sweetstock, lilies, tulips, narcissus, iris, and daffodils, all brought up from Lord Morgan's greenhouses in the country. The arrangements were lush and colorful.

The Earl and Countess of Aston, in the company of Lord and Lady Walworth, had arrived early. Quinton Hunter was recovered from his chill, which had required several days of intense nursing on his wife's part to resolve. And during that time they had remained in the house, keeping to themselves while their meals were brought to them.

"Will you be well enough for the theatre this evening?" Marcus Bainbridge, the Earl of Aston, asked his old friend.

"We were beginning to be seriously worried," Adrian, Lord Walworth said. "I've never in all the years of our friendship known you to be sick more than overnight, Quint."

"Allegra took wonderful care of me," the duke said with a smile in his wife's direction, and a wink to his friends.

"Why you devil," the earl chuckled. "Just how sick were you?"

"Not very," Quinton Hunter said, "but Allegra was so enjoying nursing me, I hated to spoil her fun."

"Or your own," Lord Walworth replied with a grin.

Allegra had taken a great deal of care with her gown today. She knew her appearance and the house would be the focus of the gossip that would follow her reception. Her gown was relatively simple as this was an afternoon gathering, but rather than the usual white, Allegra had decided to be both bold and original. The bodice of her dress was gathered, and of pale lilac silk brocade. Its neckline was most fashionably low, and edged with a teasing lace ruffle. The silk sleeves had pale lace oversleeves dyed to match the bodice. The bouffant skirt was of lilac and cream striped silk. Its hemline was just off the ground. The waist of the gown was short, and tied with a deep violet velvet sash. Her low-sided violet silk slippers had small jeweled bows on each toe. Her hair, which had been piled upon her head, was a mass of mahogany ringlets decorated with bejeweled cream-colored bows. She wore pearls in her ears, and her wedding pearls with its diamond heart lying upon her chest, its tip pointing to her décolletage.

The duke wore gray pantaloons to the knee with snow-white stockings. His shoes were black and had silver buckles. His coat was dove gray, his shirt and stock white. His black hair was cut short. A quizzing glass hung from a narrow gold chain about his neck.

Allegra had hoped that the guests would arrive slowly, but everyone was so anxious to meet the Duchess of Sedgwick that it would seem they all came exactly at the hour of three o'clock. Berkley Square was filled with carriages that circled about it dropping off their passengers, and then continuing to circle until they could be picked up again. This made it difficult for more carriages to get into the square, and some of the guests exited their vehicles and walked, only to have to wait in line to get into the house.

The duke and duchess, seated in the main drawing room of the house, greeted those guests who could reach them. Mr. Brummell casually pushed his way past the line of guests snaking up the wide staircase of Morgan House, and entered the salon.

"Duke," he said, greeting Quinton Hunter, and then he turned to Allegra. "My dear duchess, you are a succès fou once again. You know how much I both admire and appreciate originality. Your gown is a triumph! I am pleased to see you make your own fashion rather than stooping to the bad taste of others." He bowed to her, and kissed her hand.

"As do you, Mr. Brummell. You have a new haircut, I see. It is deliciously becoming. What is it called?" Allegra asked him.

"À la Brummell," he replied dryly. "Do you really like it? It isn't too short?"

"For someone else, perhaps, but not for you. You have such an elegant head, Mr. Brummell," Allegra told him.

"And here in England it will remain upon my shoulders," he chortled. "Good day, Duchess." He bowed again, and then moved off.

"He has such exquisite manners," Allegra murmured to her husband.

"He is a fop," Quinton growled back. "And I didn't like his hairdo. I will admit, however, black evening clothes are damned smart."

"We won't have to worry once we are back in the country," she reminded him with a small smile.

It was well past six o'clock in the evening when the doors to Morgan House were closed to visitors.

"Let us not go to the theatre tonight," Allegra pleaded with her friends. "We can go tomorrow night. Besides, the curtain has already risen anyway. I hate to miss the opening."

"Only if you agree to give us a decent tea," the Countess of Aston said, and she sat back upon a silk settee, kicking her slippers off.

"Marker," Allegra called. "Tea."

"At once, Your Grace," the butler answered as he hurried off.

"Did the Duchess of Devonshire come?" Eunice asked.

"She never made it up the stairs, but here is her card," Allegra said gleefully. "I'm amazed she came at all. She is up until dawn gambling. One wonders when she sleeps."

"I saw Mr. Pitt the younger," Caroline said excitedly. "He did manage to get into your drawing room."

"He is very nice," Allegra recalled. "But, Caro, where was your aunt? Lady Bellingham accepted my invitation, and it isn't like her not to come to such a levee. I know she wouldn't have missed it for the world. All of society is in town now, and the gossip to be had is quite marvelous."

"No," Caroline admitted. "It isn't like Aunt to miss such a gathering. I cannot imagine what has happened to her."

"Perhaps I should send a footman around to make certain that she is all right," Allegra suggested, and then she did just that.

Marker brought the tea. He was followed into the room by several young footmen carrying large silver trays. Upon one were the tea sandwiches. Salmon with a sharp *moutarde* dressing, thinly sliced cucumber, roast beef, cheese, delicate breast of capon, and precisely cut slices of bread and butter. A second tray contained freshly baked scones, bowls of clotted Devonshire cream, and strawberry conserves. A third silver tray held the desserts. There were thinly sliced pieces of fruitcake, dark, rich, and filled with raisins. There were tarts of lemon, raspberry, and apricot; a caramel custard; and the duke's favorite, Genovese cake with its coffee cream filling.

Allegra poured the tea from a large silver pot into dainty Sèvres cups while the footmen passed about plates of sandwiches, scones, and desserts. They gossiped about this afternoon's *at home*, and what people had worn, and who came. Even the gentlemen joined in enthusiastically. They were almost sated with tea when the footman returned from the Bellingham house.

"You have no message for me?" Allegra demanded, seeing that he carried nothing in his gloved hand.

"I was told to tell Your Grace," the footman began, "that his lordship received a letter from foreign parts this morning that has quite upset both him and her ladyship. They send their be-be-belated," he declared triumphantly, "apologies." Then the footman bowed to the duchess.

"Thank you," Allegra said. "There was nothing more?"

"Nothing, Your Grace."

"You are dismissed," Allegra told the footman. She turned to Caroline Walworth. "Who lives abroad that might send a letter that would distress your aunt and uncle so greatly?"

Caroline thought for several long moments, and then she said, "Uncle Freddie had a younger brother who married a French lady, but other than that I know nothing."

"Then we must go at once to Lady Bellingham and learn how we may help her," Allegra said. "She has been so kind, and good to all of us. How can we not at least try to repay that goodness?"

Everyone agreed, and so capes and cloaks were brought, as the carriages were advised to stand ready before the house. The six young people hurried out, entering their vehicles which set off through the dark London streets. The traffic was light as it was that time between the theatre and any formal dinners or parties to be held. Lord and Lady Bellingham lived but two squares over on Traleigh Square. The butler opening the door to their house looked quite surprised, for he had not been told that there were to be guests tonight. Then he saw Lady Caroline Walworth, his mistress's niece.

"Tell my aunt we have come to learn how we may help," Caroline instructed the butler as the single footman on duty struggled to take all of their outdoor garments.

"At once, m'lady," the butler replied as he showed them into the main drawing room.

They sat and waited in silence until the door opened

and Lady Bellingham came into the drawing room. They were all shocked by the good woman's appearance, for she was drawn and pale. It was obvious she had been crying most of the day as her eyes were puffy and red. She was dressed in a housegown, and her hair disheveled. It was as if she had not prepared for her day at all. "Ohh, my dears, how good of you to come," Lady Bellingham said, and then she burst into fresh tears.

"Aunt, what is the matter?" Caroline cried, going to her relation, and putting her arms about her.

"It is your cousin, the Comtesse d'Aumont," Lady Bellingham managed to say before she wept again.

"I have a cousin who is a French countess?" Caroline said, bemused.

"Come, dear Lady Bellingham, and sit down." Allegra began taking charge of the situation as it was obvious no one else was going to do so. "Quinton, a sherry for the poor woman." She drew the older lady to a settee and sat down next to her. "Here, drink this. You must calm yourself, Lady Bellingham," Allegra continued. "Whatever the problem is, you will not solve it by weeping. If we are to help then we must know what is troubling you."

"Ohh, my child, I do not think anyone can help us," Lady Bellingham said, but she nonetheless sipped her sherry until she felt a bit more at peace with herself, and able to speak.

The others sat down about her, and waited patiently. Finally the distraught lady was able to begin. "My husband," she began, "has two younger brothers. Caroline's father as you know is the rector of St. Anne's Church down at Bellinghamton. It is a modest living, but one that allowed him and his family to be comfortable. The youngest brother, Robert Bellingham, had the good fortune to marry a Frenchwoman. She was the only daughter of the Comte de Montroi, and he doted upon her. Consequently her dowry portion was very generous on the provision she and her husband remain in France. With nothing in England for him, Robert Bellingham saw no reason not to remain in his bride's homeland. So they were married. I remember going to France for the wedding. It was thirty-five years ago. We never even got to Paris, for Robert's wife, Marie-Claire, lived in Normandy." ·She stopped a moment to sip the remainder of her sherry, and then held out her little glass to the duke for more. He complied silently.

"A year after the marriage they had a little girl who was baptized Anne-Marie. Sadly there were no more children. Anne-Marie was married when she was eighteen to the Comte d'Aumont, a neighbor. She is some years your senior, Caroline, which is why you have never met. Robert and his family were quite content to be country folk as were Anne-Marie and her husband. They have never been to England, and Robert never returned after he married.

"When Anne-Marie was twenty her parents were killed in a carriage accident. The shock caused her to miscarry a child, but the following year she bore her husband a daughter, whom she named after her mama; and then two years later, a son, Jean, after her husband, and Robert, after her papa." Lady Bellingham swallowed down some more sherry, then continued.

"They lived happily for some years, but then fifteen months ago the Comte d'Aumont was caught up in the Reign of Terror, and guillotined. It was a terrible accident of fate that it ever happened. He was in Paris. An old friend had been detained by the Committee for Public Safety. Jean-Claude had gone to his aid. The comte was, you see, a Republican himself. He believed in the

Revolution, but when he visited his friend in prison to see how he might help he, too, was arrested. It was so naive of him to have gone, but he truly trusted in reform, although how he could after the murders of King Louis and his wife I do not understand. He was a kind man, I am told." She sniffled into her handkerchief.

"Anne-Marie and her husband were very much like our own country people despite their aristocratic backgrounds. They were kind to their tenants, and when the harvest was bad they never demanded their rent, but rather helped to feed their people. They are loved in their village of St. Jean Baptiste. After her husband was killed we begged our niece to come to England where she and her children would be safe until this horror is over, however it ends; but Anne-Marie is all French despite her English father. Her little son Jean-Robert is now the Comte d'Aumont. His lands are all he has. Anne-Marie is afraid if she leaves those lands, they will be taken away from the family. So she has stayed, and now this!" Lady Bellingham broke into fulsome sobs again.

"*What?*" Allegra asked her gently. "What has happened?"

"Our niece is under house arrest. The local revolutionary authorities are threatening to take her children away from her!" wailed Lady Bellingham.

Now the Duke of Sedgwick found himself drawn into this tale of woe. He knelt before the distraught woman and said quietly, "How is it that you know this, Lady Bellingham? How has the information come to your attention and that of your husband?"

"My niece lives near the coast," Lady Bellingham explained. "One of her servants took Anne-Marie's letter to a cousin who is a fisherman. The fisherman brought it across the water, and gave it to a fish merchant he knows who was coming up to London, with instructions that the fishmonger would be rewarded if he delivered the letter to us immediately. Freddie gave him a whole guinea!"

"How long did it take for this letter to reach you?" the duke said. "Did your niece date her missive?"

"She wrote but five days ago," Lady Bellingham said. Then she turned her tearstained face to the duke. "Ohh, Quinton, you must help us! You must go and fetch Anne-Marie and her children from the dreadful people in France!"

"You said she would not come," Allegra reminded the older lady. "You said she didn't want her son to lose his inheritance."

"She will come now, child, I am certain of it. She sees the futility of trying to hold on to her son's estate. Whoever has sought to have her placed under house arrest and steal her children away means to destroy the d'Aumonts, and have what is theirs. Anne-Marie is helpless before such an enemy. She is a country wife and has no influence with the authorities." She burst into fulsome tears once again, her shoulders shaking with her grief.

Caroline rushed now to comfort her aunt while Allegra and her husband stepped aside.

"Why," Allegra asked her husband, "did she ask you to rescue her niece and her children, Quinton?"

"Three years ago when the terror began, Ocky, Dree, Marcus, and I rescued a friend in Paris. It began as a lark. We knew Harry was in Paris visiting distant cousins. Then came word he had been arrested with those cousins. He had managed to get word out of prison because he was English, and had the ready to pay bribes. His family was all atwitter, and didn't know how to proceed. His father kept blustering that the Froggies had no right to arrest an English citizen, but there was poor Harry incarcerated, and a tumbrel's ride away from Madame la Guillotine. So we sailed Marcus's yacht across the channel, rented horses, and rode up to Paris.

"There, with supreme arrogance so common to us English, we went to the prison and demanded to see the governor of the facility. Marcus and Dree had brought a little money, and Ocky had just gotten his allowance from his father for the term. We threw money around as if we actually possessed it, but for me. My French is said to be peerless, and so I did the talking when the governor of the prison appeared. I explained that Lord Harry Carew was a wayward but beloved cousin of the English king who had sent us to request his return. And all the while I talked I kept jiggling this velvet bag in my hand. It jingled quite convincingly. As we anticipated, the governor was greedy.

"He could," he said, "release the unimportant Anglais to us for a small price. No, said I. We wanted the Englishman and his relations unless, of course, they were criminals. The governor considered. Harry's relations, it turned out, were two elderly ladies. So the governor decided he would be generous if we were generous. The exchange was made. We promised to take the ladies home to collect their belongings and leave Paris before nightfall. The governor agreed, especially as we got the ladies to sign over their house near Notre Dame to him."

"So much for revolutionary ideals," Allegra noted dryly.

The duke laughed. "You can only imagine our surprise when we got to the old ladies' home and discovered that the Marquis and Marquise de Valency, along with their children, had been hiding in the cellars all that time! When Harry and his old cousins were arrested, the real prize was completely overlooked. Not knowing what else to do they had remained hidden in the house. We had passports for ourselves, Harry, and the old ladies, but how were we to get the de Valency family out of Paris with us?"

"And how did you?" Allegra inquired. She was fascinated by this tale, and would have never expected such heroism or derring-do from Quinton, although she did not think him a coward. How she wished he had been there to help her brother.

"The old ladies had a small coach, nothing however that you could hide anything in, and so we decided to take a baggage cart as well. We hid the marquise and her two youngest children in a small space beneath the cart bottom, and then we piled the luggage atop it. The marquis and his son we dressed as Parisian peasants. Their clothing was ragged and filthy. Only the marquis had wooden clogs on his feet. His son was barefooted. We made certain they were dirtied. Because they had been on the run for several months, they were not plump with good living any longer. Indeed they were quite thin and gaunt, which was fortunate for the deception.

"We took the chance that we could squeak the marquis and his son, who were driving the vehicles, by the authorities. When we got to the gates of Paris we showed our passports to the guards there. Then we explained that the drivers would be returning in a few days' time to Paris with the carriage and the cart. That because the old sisters, and their English relation, had to be out of Paris by nightfall there was no opportunity to get the proper papers for the drivers. They would remain if the authorities wanted them to do so, and we would drive, but then how would the carriage and the cart get back to Paris? We said the two ancient mademoiselles were giving the transport to their drivers as well as paying them in good French livres. This would mean the two citizens could earn a living when they returned to Paris.

"The guards at the gate hemmed and hawed for a few moments, and then having been slipped some silver coins, waved us through. It took us several days to reach the coast. A bit longer than if we had gone a direct route, but we traveled the back roads so we did not have to hide the marquise and her children beneath the boards of the baggage cart. Like the others, they were garbed poorly in case anyone saw us. We bought our food along the way and slept rough. We reached Marcus's yacht without delay, sold the carriage, the cart, and the horses to an innkeeper, and set sail for England." He paused, and then continued. "The four of us had such fun on that adventure that we returned to France several times after that to help friends, or relations of friends. That is why Lady Bellingham thinks I can save her niece, but I am not certain we can. She may have waited too long to ask for help, and the four of us have responsibilities now that we did not have then."

"We must try, however," Allegra told her husband. "First, let us find out where the Comtesse d'Aumont lives. How near it is to the sea, and where exactly it is located. Then we can make our plans."

"*Our plans?*" the duke repeated.

"Of course," Allegra said quietly. "You don't think I am going to let you go to France and have all the fun, do you?"

"If any attempt is made to rescue the Comtesse d'Aumont and her children, Allegra," the duke said sternly to his wife, "it will be a very dangerous undertaking, not a pleasure trip, my darling girl, but I love you for your bravery in wanting to go."

"Quinton, when will you learn not to treat me as if I

am some delicate creature whose frail sensibilities must not be distressed? You were damnably lucky in Paris three years ago when you rescued your friend. This is a whole different matter and must be approached as such. I will need to think on it, but we must act quickly."

"*Allegra!*" He sounded exasperated.

"Quinton, listen to me," she said quietly. "My brother was murdered in that damned revolution. Many other innocent people have been. More honest simple people than the aristocrats the revolution claims to hate. Women are far more devious than men, my darling. Who sit beneath the guillotine grimly as heads fall? Who incite their men to revenge? Women! You are going to need me if you have any chance of rescuing the Comtesse d'Aumont. I have to do this for James Lucian's sake. It is the only way I have of avenging his death. *You must let me come.*" Her fingers dug urgently into his arm, and she looked directly at him.

"It is madness," he murmured, but he understood.

"I can help you," she promised him.

"I will think on it," he finally agreed.

"We will go together," she said with a smile, indicating that the matter was closed.

"We will all go," Eunice, the Countess of Aston said brightly.

"*What?*" her husband exclaimed.

"Yes," Caroline, Lady Walworth agreed, looking up from her place at Lady Bellingham's side. "I have to help the comtesse, too. She is my cousin, even if I didn't know it until today."

"Ohh, my dears," Lady Bellingham said, looking at them all with misty eyes. "How can I thank you?" Then she wept some more.

"Where is your husband?" the duke asked Lady Bellingham.

"Poor Freddie has taken to his bed," she replied. "He feels responsible that he did not go to France himself when the Comte d'Aumont was killed and bring Anne-Marie and her children back. He will be so happy to learn you dear young people are going to rescue his niece and her family." She arose from her place on the settee. "I must go and tell him at once," she exclaimed, and hurried from the room.

"God damnit, what a muddle!" the duke exclaimed.

"We'll have to go now," the Earl of Aston said.

"Of course we will," Lord Walworth agreed. "Poor old girl is so distressed. Repay her for her kindness to us all, eh?"

"How soon can we leave?" the earl asked.

"Two or three days at the most," the duke answered. "We'll need to learn from Lord Bellingham where his niece lives. We'll take your yacht again, Marcus. She's fast and she's tight."

"Decide what we need to take," Lord Walworth said, "and I will see we are well supplied."

"Listen to them," Allegra said to her two friends. "Making plans without us, and not having any real idea of what they are going to do at all. Men can be so irritating."

"Are we really going to go?" Caroline said.

"Of course we are," Allegra responded. "She is your cousin, and she needs our help. How do you think the comtesse is going to react to three English gentlemen barging into her home, if they can even get near her home, and announcing they've come to take her and her children back to England? She won't know if she can trust them, if they really are who they say they are, or if they are part of the plot to steal her son's inheritance. A woman, however, could convince the lady that all is well, and that she need not fear."

"You realize that they plan to leave us behind," Eunice said softly.

"We won't let them," Allegra said with a twinkle. "Ohh, I am so sorry that Sirena can't join us in this adventure."

"Do you have a plan?" Caroline inquired.

"How good is your French?" Allegra asked in return, looking at both of her friends.

"Excellent," Eunice replied.

"Very good," Caroline responded.

Allegra smiled. "Unfortunately my husband tells me that he is the only one among his friends to speak adequate French. The gentlemen will have no choice but to allow us to help them."

"But do you have a plan?" Caroline persisted.

"I think so," Allegra responded, "but give me a day to convince Quinton that it is the right plan, ladies."

Lady Bellingham returned to her drawing room as the three couples prepared to leave. They promised to visit her the following day, at which time they would learn exactly where the village of St. Jean Baptiste was located, and prepare to leave for France.

"Freddie is so relieved," Lady Bellingham told them, "and so am I. Oh, my dear Quinton, what would we do without friends like you to help us? I am so glad I was able to have a tiny part in you and Allegra finding happiness. Now an heir to complete the matters, and everything will be perfect."

"Everything will be perfect, dear Lady Clarice, only when we have brought your niece and her children safely to England," the duke said gallantly, kissing the lady's hand. He bowed smartly. "We shall see you at eleven tomorrow morning."

They bid their friends farewell out on the street before

the Bellingham house. Once inside their coach Allegra snuggled against her husband and murmured contentedly, "How wonderful," she said, "that we can help dear Lady Bellingham."

The duke sighed. "My darling," he said, "you cannot really mean to go. It is much too dangerous, and as for Caroline and Eunice, they are charming featherheads. We would all be killed if caught, I fear. Leave this to the men, Allegra. We will rescue the comtesse and her family, I guarantee you."

"*How?*" Allegra asked him innocently.

"How?" he repeated, puzzled.

"Yes, my darling, *how*? Just what clever plan have you formulated to rescue this lady and her children? I cannot rest easy until I know, Quinton, because as you have so thoughtfully pointed out to me, it is a very dangerous task that must be completed. So, how will you do it?"

Some men might not have recognized Allegra's tone, but Quinton Hunter did. And the truth was he was totally stumped as to how to gain safe custody of Lady Bellingham's niece. "I suppose we will bribe those guarding the comtesse and her family," he said slowly, his mind grasping futilely for more detail, but he could not think of a thing.

"I see," Allegra said, nothing more.

There was that tone again, he thought nervously. He remained silent for a moment, but then unable to help himself he said, "How would you rescue the lady and her children?"

"You have said yourself," Allegra began, "that you are the only one among your friends who speaks passable French. That the language as spoken by Marcus, Dree, and Ocky is execrable. But Caroline, Eunice, and I speak excellent French. What if we, along with you three gentlemen, arrived at the comtesse's home dressed as peasant women. Only the four of us would speak. Marcus and Dree could murmur the occasional *'Oui,'* but other than that leave the talking to the rest of us. Don't you think we could convince whoever is guarding the comtesse that we had come to get her and her children? That they had an appointment with Madame la Guillotine for tea. If we are as forceful as those horrible hags who knit beneath that instrument of execution are, or so I have heard it said, we can get Lady Bellingham's niece and her family from the house. If there are not too many guards, and I suspect there are not, for those trying to steal the d'Aumont property won't consider anyone would come rescue this country aristocrat. And whoever is attempting the nefarious act probably is doing it because there is no one to tell them they can't do it. Once we have the comtesse and her family, we'll bind the guards. That way they cannot go into the village, and learn of our deception."

The Duke of Sedgwick was speechless for several long moments. Part of him knew that his wife was an intelligent young woman, but another part of him relegated her to the same status all women of his class held. Beautiful. Charming. An ornament. But Allegra was not a toy to be displayed and then put away. She was clever and quick-witted. "It is a perfect plan," he finally said to her, "but not without its element of danger."

"I know," she replied. "We must be very careful, and we must know everything we need to know before we attempt a rescue. For instance, who is doing this to the poor lady? *And why?* That is why we must set sail for France in two days' time, no more. We will need a few days once we are there to learn what we must know. Then we should act swiftly, and without any hesitation."

"Agreed," he replied, realizing even as the words

came from her mouth that he was indeed agreeing to her whole plan.

"Then you understand why Caroline, Eunice, and I must come?" she queried him.

"I do, although it will be a difficult thing to explain to their husbands, my darling," he responded.

"If you are willing to allow me to be in danger, how can they do anything else?" Allegra said quietly.

"Do you think your friends are brave enough to carry this off, or will they panic at the first sign of danger?" the duke said.

"I believe we are all brave enough, Quinton, but who among us can say for certain how brave we will be until we directly face danger? Besides, if we do this thing properly, there should be little danger to any of us. I believe that we can outsmart a couple of lackwit peasants. After all, we are English," she concluded.

He laughed. "God bless me, my darling, you suddenly sound most patriotic and grand. Very well, I shall speak to Dree and Marcus first thing in the morning. Then we shall go to the Bellinghams, and tell them only that a rescue attempt will be made. I will not tell them that you ladies are to be involved, for it would distress them, and send them both to their beds with the vapors. While I am dealing with my friends, you must explain to yours what we plan to do, and Allegra, you must give both Eunice and Caroline the opportunity to cry off if they wish to do so. And they may upon reflection. If they do, you cannot be angry. Do you promise me that?"

"They will not cry off," Allegra said with certainty. "Do you know how dull London has been for us? Parties. Museums. The Tower Zoo. Never again! At least this will afford us a little excitement before we return home to the country to do our duties, and fill our nurseries with those babies that you gentlemen seem to want." She smiled at him, and kissed him softly. "We must work very hard to have those babies, Quinton. *Very hard.*"

He tipped her face up to his, and kissed her. "You will gain no argument from me, madame, on that point," he told her, and his hand slid beneath her fur-lined cloak to fondle her breasts.

"Ummm," she sighed contentedly, melting into his embrace. But then their carriage came to a definite stop.

"We're home," he noted, a tone of regret in his voice.

"We can continue this upstairs, if my lord wishes," she replied playfully, her little tongue licking at her lips provocatively.

"I must pen notes off to Dree and Marcus, but I will join you shortly, mon coeur," the duke whispered against her lips.

A footman opened the coach door and offered a hand to the duchess who descended and hurried into the house, going directly up the staircase to her apartments. She entered to catch Honor and the duke's valet, Hawkins, in a torrid embrace. They broke apart guiltily and red-faced, as she stepped through the doors.

"M'lady!" Honor squeaked. Her bodice was quite awry.

"If you seduce my maid and put her in the family way, Hawkins," Allegra said, "you must be prepared to make an honest woman of her."

"Yes, my lady," the valet said nervously.

"And you are prepared to do so? No wife, or dear friend tucked away in another place here in London, or down at Hunter's Lair?" Allegra persisted. "Honor, for goodness' sake, straighten your bodice."

"No wife, or friend, my lady," the valet said, shuffling his feet.

"Very good, Hawkins," the Duchess of Sedgwick told her husband's valet. "You are dismissed. Go and be ready to help your master to bed. He will be up shortly." Allegra turned to Honor, who was lacing her gown front. "And I am ready for my bed, Honor. Come and help me." She turned and moved from her salon into her bedchamber.

"Whew!" Hawkins breathed softly as Allegra disappeared into the other room. "She's a proper cool one."

"Haven't I taught you better yet about speaking rude against my lady?" Honor scolded him.

"Guess I need more lessons," the valet said with a wink, and then he was gone out the door, and to his master's room.

With a smile Honor hurried to her mistress's aid. "You ain't mad at me, are you?" she asked.

"Just be careful," Allegra said quietly. "I'm not certain that I trust Hawkins where you are concerned, Honor. I love you too dearly to allow him to harm you in any way."

"He's more bark than bite, my lady," Honor answered her mistress, "and he surely ain't as smart as I am," she chuckled. "If he means to find himself by my side in bed, he'll have visited the parson with me first. A kiss and a cuddle don't make babies. Of that much I'm certain."

Allegra laughed. "I shouldn't have worried," she replied.

"I'm glad you do," her maid responded. She knelt, and pulled her mistress's little slippers off. "Lord, my lady, your poor wee feet are as cold as ice. These little slippers may be fashionable, but they ain't meant for the cold streets of London."

"Honor, I need your help," Allegra said quietly. "I

know I don't have the right to ask this of you. You are free to tell me so, and I shall still love you. Do you remember when I was a little girl and you would sit with me when James Lucian and I had lessons? And how one day when we were doing a French exercise you corrected us and we were so surprised? It was then we discovered that you had learned the language right along with us and could speak it beautifully."

"I remember, my lady," Honor said.

"Do you think you could speak it again? I mean, given a bit of practice?" Allegra wondered.

"I wouldn't know until I tried it, my lady," Honor said honestly.

"*Comment vous appelez-vous,* mademoiselle?" Allegra responded.

"*Je m'appelle* Mademoiselle *Honneur,*" the maid replied.

"*Quel âge avez-vous?*"

"*J'ai vingt-quatre ans,* madame," was the answer.

"You do remember!" Allegra cried.

"Guess I do," Honor said, sounding surprised.

"Then let me tell you what we are going to do," Allegra said, and she explained the situation with the Bellinghams' niece, the Comtesse d'Aumont, and how they were going to France to rescue her. "If you are willing to come with us it would help tremendously," Allegra said. "I need it to look as if the local committee of safety sent a leader and enough citizens to bring the countess and her children to justice. And you speak French well."

"Can the other ladies?" Honor asked.

Allegra nodded.

"I'll go," the maidservant told her mistress. "It's an adventure, and one day if I have grandchildren, I'll tell

'em how their old gran helped save three innocent
lives."

"Bless you, Honor," Allegra said wholeheartedly. And
then she added, "but let me tell his lordship. I have only
just convinced him that this is the right thing to do."

"Men don't have a whole lot of common sense,
m'lady," Honor replied. "I think that's why God created us womenfolk. Men surely need someone to tell
'em what's right, and what ain't."

Allegra giggled. "Oh, yes, Honor," she said. "How
absolutely correct you are!"

Chapter Fourteen

*J*rederick Bellingham looked at the three young men standing before him. "Are you certain you want to do this?" he asked for at least the third time. "It is dangerous, but she is my brother's daughter. I must get her safely to England. Yet do I have the right to put you three in danger?" Past sixty, Lord Bellingham looked weary with his worry.

"We have discussed it carefully, my lord, and we are willing to help you. The plan is formulated, but I shall not burden you with the details. You, however, must tell me where your niece and her children live. How far from the coast are they?"

"The village of St. Jean Baptiste is located but eight miles from the town of Harfleur, which as you know is directly on the sea," Lord Bellingham told them. "My niece's home is nothing more than a large gray stone house. The family's small wealth comes from their flocks of sheep and their apple orchards. It's a most modest establishment."

"A perfect little estate for someone now in a position of power to confiscate for himself," the Earl of Aston remarked. "A helpless young widow and her children. The fellow, whoever he is, is a proper villain, I fear."

"And you are certain your niece is willing to give up

her home under the circumstances?" the duke asked. "Her missive to you has said so? She will come to England?"

"She writes that she has been foolish, and should have put her son's estate with a trusted friend, and then come to England until order is restored in France. She never expected that anyone would bother them, for they are neither rich nor powerful. They are just simple country folk," Lord Bellingham said, sighing again. "What kind of a monster would prey on a woman and her children? The Comte d'Aumont was a good man. A hero of reform!"

"More ordinary folk have died in this revolution," Lord Walworth noted. "That dressmaker who does for our wives, Madame Paul. She lost family to the guillotine. What harm could a dressmaker's family have possibly caused to have required such a sentence as death?"

"I will give you a letter to carry to Anne-Marie," Lord Bellingham said to the duke. "That way she will not be afraid."

"Does she speak English?" the duke asked the older man.

"I have no idea," he replied. "We always spoke French to her on the rare occasions that we saw one another. She writes to us in French," he noted.

"Probably don't speak the king's *langue*," the earl remarked. "You'll have to do all the talking, Quint."

The duke nodded, and then he said to Lord Bellingham, "We will go tomorrow, sir. We will inform you when we return."

The two men shook hands.

"God bless you all, whatever happens," Lord Bellingham said.

"Ah yes, God bless you, my boys," Lady Bellingham said. Silent until then, she wept.

*   *   *

*O*utside they entered the duke's coach which took them directly to Boodle's. Settled in the club's dining room they ordered their luncheons. Boodle's was noted for its excellent food, and was a particular favorite with country gentlemen come up to town.

"You said we're going tomorrow?" the earl remarked.

"I assume your yacht is anchored at Brighton as usual," the duke returned. "The coach will carry the ladies, and we will ride."

"You can't be serious about taking our wives," Marcus Bainbridge, the Earl of Aston said. "You know it ain't no pleasure jaunt we're off on, Quint. Too dangerous for the ladies. Much too dangerous."

"Nonetheless they are going," the duke replied.

"Tell me why I am going to allow Caroline to put herself in such jeopardy," Lord Walworth said quietly.

Quinton Hunter explained, and when he had finished he said, "Well, is my wife not clever?"

"Damn me!" the earl replied. "If that ain't cunning. What's more, I think it will work, Quint."

"Allegra has spoken with Madame Paul this very morning. She will have the clothing our ladies need ready by the time we leave tomorrow. The old lady wanted to come with us," the duke chuckled, "but my wife convinced her otherwise."

Lord Walworth sighed. "If I don't let Caroline go she'll never forgive me. All she's done is natter on about this cousin she ain't never even met, and how she must help her. I suppose we'll be obliged to take 'em in when we get 'em here."

"Maybe they won't want to live down in the country," the earl said helpfully.

"They live in the country now, Marcus, you dolt," Adrian, Lord Walworth grumbled. "Well, as she's a

widow, maybe we'll be able to match her up with some
lonely gentleman and marry her off quickly."

Their luncheon was brought. The three gentlemen
tucked into the beefsteaks and potato soufflés. The attentive staff made certain their goblets were kept filled
with good red wine. Afterward the duke left his two
friends off at the house they were sharing, and returned
to his own house on Berkley Square.

"Where is Her Grace?" he asked Marker as he entered the foyer.

"The duchess is upstairs napping, my lord," the butler replied.

The duke hurried up the staircase to his wife's apartments. Entering her salon he found it empty. He moved
through the room into her bedchamber. Allegra lay,
wrapped in a muslin chamber robe, asleep on her bed.
Her dark hair was loose and lay all tumbled across the
lavender-scented pillows. Quinton Hunter smiled to
himself. If he lived to be a hundred years old, he would
never understand how he had been so fortunate as to
have found a wife like Allegra. This time last year he
hadn't even known she existed. And in his pride he had
believed there was no woman in all of England fit to be
his duchess. What a fool he had been. Yet his angel had
guided him safely. Reaching out, he fingered one of her
soft curls.

Allegra opened her eyes, and seeing her husband
standing over her opened her arms to him. "You're
back," she murmured sleepily.

He pulled off his cloak, and lay next to her. "It is all
settled, my darling. We leave early tomorrow morning
for Brighton. We'll be there by noon, then off with the
tide."

"And we sail for France," she replied. "Where is the
countess?"

"About eight miles from Harfleur," the duke said.

"We'll probably have to walk it to avoid suspicion," Allegra responded thoughtfully.

"*Walk?* Eight miles? Do you think that you can?" the duke wondered. "Surely we can find a cart."

"We probably should," Allegra considered upon reflection. "We will need to get away from the countess's home as quickly as possible, but as for walking, my darling, we are all country lasses, even if we are fancy ladies. We must not, however, draw attention to ourselves, Quinton. I shall have to think carefully upon it."

"Do not think now," he said, kissing her brow, his hand slipping beneath her robe to cup a breast. His thumb brushed lightly over the nipple as he bent to find her lips.

Her senses reeled. They always did when he touched her breasts which they had both discovered were very sensitive. "Mmmmmm," she murmured against his mouth, and then she pulled away. "Get out of your clothes, my lord. I do not want your dirty boots mucking my coverlet." She gave him a gentle shove.

With a chuckle he arose, and began to draw off his garments. Boots first. Then his shirt and neckcloth. His stockings, his breeches and his drawers. Allegra watched him. He had wonderfully firm buttocks. Her fingers itched to touch him. He turned about to reenter the bed, and she sighed with pleasure at the sight of his manhood, which stood at half-mast amid the tangle of his dark bush.

"Why you shameless wench," he teased her, noting the direction her eyes had taken.

"It's like an ivory pillar," she told him. "All blue-veined, and beautiful."

"If the French ever get out of Italy," he said, "I shall take you there one day to view the art, Allegra. The ancients sculpted a great many nudes of men and of women. I can see you have an appreciation of such things." He lay next to her, fingering her curls.

"There are statues of naked people?" she asked him, surprised.

"Oh, indeed there are," he said, unfastening the sash of her chamber robe, and pushing back fabric. "But none, my darling, are as fair as you are." He bent his head to kiss her breast.

"And these statues are displayed in public?" she continued.

"They are." His mouth closed over a nipple, and he began to suckle upon her.

"Oooo," she released her breath with an audible sigh. His mouth was warm, and the tugging upon her flesh was very exciting. Allegra knew she had more questions to ask him, but somehow they all fled from her mind as he filled her with pleasure. Her fingers found the nape of his neck, and she began to knead it with one hand. He had imprisoned her other hand with his as he feasted upon her breast.

She excited him. God in His heaven, she excited him! He could never get enough of her, but he was certainly going to try. He began to explore her body with his lips and his tongue. She made little noises indicating her pleasure as he caressed, and kissed, and licked at her. Her skin was petal soft, and just faintly fragrant with the scent of lilac. There seemed to be pulses wherever he touched her. It roused his senses even further.

"*Do it!*" her voice suddenly pleaded urgently, squirming against him in a suggestive and provocative manner. "*Please!*"

"Do what?" he teased her, almost cruelly. He was fairly certain of what it was she wanted.

"With your tongue. *Please!*" she cried to him.

"*Where?*" he taunted. Now he was positive of her need.

"*There!*" she almost screamed. She was going to kill him if he didn't put his tongue on her, and make her mindless.

"*Here?*" he questioned, his tongue probing her navel.

"I hate you!" she half sobbed.

"Or perhaps," he paused, positioning his big frame properly. "*Here!*" His tongue made contact with her little love button, and he heard her shriek softly. Slowly, slowly, he licked it, tasting the salt and the musk of her, watching as it grew swollen with her desire. Then the duke did something he had not done before. His palms lifted Allegra's bottom up, and he pushed his face against her hot sex, his tongue seeking, and then finding, her passage to push as deep as he could within, using it as he would his manhood.

It was then she screamed, feeling that digit thrusting inside her in an incredibly intimate and secret act. "Ohh, God!" she sobbed. "Ohh, I didn't know!" She dug her fingers into his shoulders. Her nails pressed deep. She clawed at him desperately. "*Make it happen!*" she begged him. She was so close, and yet she could not reach her heaven. His tongue continued to tease and torture her until she thought she would explode with her longing.

His manhood was hard. It was raging to plunder her sweet depths. He couldn't continue until he had ravaged her completely. His head lifted from the hot and marshy depths. He covered her body with his, his rod thrusting into her. Her cry of utter pleasure almost cost him his own. He leaned forward and kissed her hard, his hips pressing against hers in a rhythmic cadence of ancient lust that she met eagerly. He groaned, his head awash with his passion for her. For his beautiful and desirable wife. *For Allegra!*

Her own senses were reeling with her longing and the hot sweet delight that he offered her. She soared. She flew higher, and higher until her cravings all seemed to come together, and burst in a fiery balloon of lustful triumphant joy. And then she was falling, falling, falling, down into a dark and warm abyss where the pleasure slowly, slowly drained away. Then all was nothingness.

When her senses finally began to return she discovered that he was sprawled across her, still panting. Their bodies were wet with their efforts. "You . . . are . . . wonderful," she managed to say to him, and she caressed his dark hair.

He pulled himself off of her, and rolled onto his back. "You," he told her sincerely, "are incredible, my darling duchess."

"I love you," she replied, drawing the coverlet up over them.

"And I love you, Allegra," he responded, reaching for her hand. "Oh, my darling girl, how I love you!"

*W*hen the morning came they discovered that Madame Paul had already delivered the costumes that they would wear on their mission to rescue the Comtesse d'Aumont and her children. She had come herself, knocking on the door in the darkness of the predawn. Allegra opened the box, and was astounded by what she found. There were four ragged and grubby skirts, and an equal number of dirty tricolor sashes. Four patched white blouses, four pairs of wooden shoes, and four limp dingy mobcaps. In a second box were three grimy men's shirts, three pairs of baggy pantaloons, three short carmagnole peasant jackets, and three red felt Phrygian caps ornamented with the tri-color cockade. There were also wooden shoes for the gentlemen.

"It's wonderful," Allegra said. "Dressed up in this lot we will look just as we should."

"Why are there four sets of women's costumes?" the duke asked his wife quietly.

"Because Honor is going with us," Allegra said as quietly. "She speaks excellent French, Quinton, and she has very good common sense in matters of which we may not be familiar."

"How is it your maid speaks *excellent* French?" the duke demanded, curious.

"Because she sat with me in the schoolroom for years, my darling. One day when James Lucian and I were having difficulty conjugating a verb, Honor chimed right in with the correct conjugation, and in a rather good accent, according to our tutor. She had, it seems, been learning right along with my brother and me. She will be very helpful, Quinton. You will see."

He laughed. It would, he knew, be useless to argue with Allegra. Worse, she was probably perfectly correct. And it was rather amusing to boot. His wife's country girl of a servant spoke, to quote Allegra, "excellent French." "If you believe Honor can aid us, and if she is willing to risk the danger involved," the duke told his wife, "then I can have no objection, my darling duchess."

Allegra threw her arms about her husband, and kissed him. "Oh, thank you for not disagreeing with me, Quinton. I am so relieved that you trust my judgment in this matter."

He smiled down into her wonderful violet-colored eyes, and then gave her a quick kiss. What choice did he actually have, he wondered silently to himself.

"We should not be seen in these clothes until we reach France," Allegra said. "I will have Honor stuff them into a little bag we are to bring aboard Marcus's yacht. They can be no worse for the wear for such treatment than they already are," she concluded with a chuckle.

"What I want to know," the duke said, "is how she came into possession of such garments? It is most curious that she had them."

"Perhaps," Allegra said thoughtfully, "they belonged to some of the émigrés from France. Or, mayhap there are others who do what we are going to do to help out their family and friends. I have heard a rumor while we have been in London about some fellow who is known as the Scarlet Pimpernel. He is supposed to go into France to rescue innocents."

"It is comforting to know that there are others as foolish as we are," the duke replied dryly.

"It is our English sense of fair play," Allegra said. "One simply does not execute a king, although I seem to recall that we English did so once ourselves. But we did not conduct a reign of terror then against everyone who disagreed with us."

"No," the duke remarked, "we just went to war against one another. Innocents were killed in that conflict as well."

"But that was almost two hundred years ago, Quinton," Allegra noted. "These are modern times. People should not be so savage today."

"But they are, and so we will go to France, and attempt to bring back the Bellinghams' niece and her little family," Quinton Hunter said.

Honor and Hawkins had packed their master and mistress's trunks. While it might be considered a bit odd to visit Brighton in early March, it was the best excuse that they could think of for their absence from London. Charles Trent had been told of their mission, and while he did not approve, there was little he could do but to see that the duke and duchess had the funds that they would need for their journey. He even included a bag of French coins.

"You may need to resort to bribery," he said. His disapproval was most obvious. "What am I going to tell your father?" he demanded of Allegra.

"Tell him nothing," she said quietly. "We will be back in England as quickly as we can, and I do not choose to fret him. Aunt Mama has not been well this winter, and he is worried enough."

"Tell me your plan," her father's secretary asked.

She quickly explained.

He nodded. "It should work, but you cannot linger. Go in, get the lay of the land, retrieve the Bellinghams' kin, and get out as quickly as you can. There will be less danger for you that way. Do you understand, Your Grace? These charades you are playing at are terribly, terribly dangerous."

"I know, Charles," she said, using his Christian name, which she rarely did. "But I believe we can do this, and the Bellinghams have been so good to us all."

"I understand your reasoning, Your Grace, but if anything happened to *any* of you, it would put a terrible burden of guilt on the Bellinghams. They are not young, and this situation with their niece has distressed them greatly. Remember, your first duty is to your husband and his family. If the choice is between your safety, and the d'Aumont family, you must think of yourself first."

"You worry far too much, Charles," Allegra replied, and then standing on her tiptoes she kissed his cheek, causing him to blush a bright beet red. "We will be back before you realize we have been gone at all," she promised him. Then Allegra went out the door to join her husband in their traveling coach.

The sun was just coming up as they cleared the city and took the road to Brighton. They would meet up with their friends at an inn there known as The King's Arms. The trip, along what was called the New Road, was the most direct to Brighton, and in the best condition. Mr. Trent had arranged for four changes of horses along their route. Consequently their trip took only five hours.

The King's Arms was located on the harbor. It was a large comfortable establishment, popular with travelers, although the difficulties in France had taken away some of their business. Mr. Trent had arranged for a suite of rooms for the duke, and large bedrooms for the earl and Lord Walworth. All were located next to one another in a separate wing of the inn. It had been decided that Hawkins would remain behind to watch over the luggage. The rooms had been paid for in advance. It was more than likely that they would need immediate shelter upon their return for the Comtesse d'Aumont and her children. They would also not want to cause any disturbance upon their arrival that would draw attention to themselves. Brighton had its share of spies, or so they had been told.

The landlord hurried forward to greet them personally. "Welcome, Your Grace," he said bowing to the duke. "Your friends have only just arrived. Come in! Come in! Your rooms are ready for you."

"You have been told," Quinton Hunter said in his most superior and ducal voice, "that we will retain our rooms while we cruise on the Earl of Aston's yacht? My man, Hawkins, will remain behind. You'll see that he's fed? Hawkins don't like the sea, do you Hawkins?"

"No, Yer Grace, I don't," the valet said as he had been told, nodding vehemently.

"He may have ale with his supper, but don't go allowing him to get drunk," the duke instructed the innkeeper. "Hawkins does like his ale, don't you, Hawkins?"

"I do, Yer Grace," the valet said enthusiastically with a grin.

"Of course, Your Grace. Everything will be just as you require, Your Grace. You needn't worry." The innkeeper bowed again, then led them to their suite.

There they found their friends awaiting them.

"Ohh, this is so exciting!" Caroline said.

"Do you have the costumes?" Eunice inquired.

"Yes," Allegra answered her, "and when you see them, you will not believe it. Everything is so real. Honor is coming with us."

"Your maid?" Eunice and Caroline spoke in unison.

"Honor speaks quite good French," Allegra explained, "and as a servant, will know more about the common folk than we do."

"How amusing that your Honor should speak another tongue," Caroline said. "Why it is almost like having one's own French maid," she giggled. "Even if she does come from Worcester."

"Can we see our costumes?" Eunice asked.

"Honor, get the little bag with our special clothing, and let us show Lady Walworth and Lady Bainbridge," Allegra instructed her maid.

The bag was brought, opened, and Honor pulled out a skirt, a sash, and one of the mobcaps. Caroline snatched the headpiece, and pulled it over her curls. Eunice wrapped the sash about her narrow waist. They stared at each other and burst out laughing.

"This is not a jest," Allegra scolded them. "If we are caught we could all face the guillotine. These revolutionaries are not respecters of nationality. Being English will not protect us. Are you two certain that you want to go? As Quinton keeps reminding me, this is a dangerous game that we are playing at. We must travel eight miles from the coast to arrive at the d'Aumont estate. Then we must gain custody of the countess and her children from whoever has them. And finally we have to travel back to the coast without being caught, reach the yacht, and sail back to England without attracting the suspicions of anyone. I will not think badly of either of you if you have changed your minds."

"No," Caroline said. "She is my cousin."

"No," said Eunice. "I will admit we are both nervous about this undertaking, but not once has either of us considered crying off, Allegra."

"But how are we going to get to the countess?" Caroline asked.

"We shall be bloodthirsty peasant ladies from Harfleur who have come to bring the countess and her children before the revolutionary tribunal for justice. The Committee for Public Safety in the town has sent us to fetch the woman, Citizeness d'Aumont, and her brats. If the people holding the countess and her children attempt to stop us, we shall become very aggressive and threatening toward them. France is ruled by fear. The mere threat that her captors are not concurring with the local authorities will bring about their immediate cooperation, I am certain," Allegra told her friends. "Remember, despite their revolutionary talk, these people are used to obeying their superiors. We shall have to be very convincing, however."

While the women continued to speak among themselves, the gentlemen were also making their plans.

"When do we sail?" the duke asked the Earl of Aston.

"Captain Grant suggests we leave on the evening's

tide. It is just before midnight. The weather is good, the winds fresh. If it all holds, we should reach France the day after tomorrow."

"Is he familiar with the territory into which we are venturing?" Quinton Hunter asked his friend.

Marcus Bainbridge smiled. "He knows a hidden cove right near the town of Harfleur. We will anchor there."

"And just how is he aware of such an ideal anchorage?" Lord Walworth wondered aloud.

"Damn me, Adrian, where do you think that fine French wine you like so much comes from?" the earl chuckled. "You surely don't think the damned French can cut off an Englishman's supply of good wine? When I don't need the yacht, and frankly nowadays, I don't use it a lot, I allow Grant to make little trips for his own amusement. If he brings me back some wine, so much the better."

"In other words, Marcus, your captain is smuggling," Lord Walworth said. "This situation becomes more dangerous by the moment. If your yacht is recognized by the authorities, could we not all be in terrible peril? I do not like it at all."

"Grant has only done a wee bit of smuggling, Dree, and he has never been caught. Not even pursued. The Froggies are too busy killing each other and destroying their society to worry about an English captain out for a bit of wine. It is perfectly safe."

"If this were not Caroline's relation," Lord Walworth said, "I should not allow it."

"You are free to remain here," the duke told his friend.

"No. I value my marriage too much, Quint. Caroline would never forgive me, I fear," Lord Walworth said, resigned.

"You'll feel better after a good supper," the earl told his friend. "I always feel better after a good supper."

"You'll become as stout as Prinny one day," the duke teased his friend.

"I need my food, Quint. Eunice may look like a cool and elegant little countess, but she's a wildcat in our marriage bed. I need my strength to keep up with her."

"What we need is heirs," Lord Walworth said. "After this little adventure, if the almighty God allows us to return to England unscathed, we had best settle down to getting 'em. I want a son I can take up on my horse with me. I want several for that matter. One for the title, one for the church, one for the army, and one for the navy."

"What does Caroline say?" the duke asked dryly.

"Why, she agrees with me, of course," Lord Walworth said. "Why wouldn't she? Damn me, Quint, only a year ago we were discussing finding ourselves wives, and look at us now. Old married men, by God!"

His friends chuckled, and then the duke said seriously, "I hope we live to be old married men, lads. If it were not for the Bellinghams I should not be here in Brighton today, but rather on our way home to Hunter's Lair. I'm sorry Ocky can't be with us, but Sirena will whelp her young 'un any day now."

"He's going to be mighty jealous when we tell him what we did," chortled the earl. "Ocky has always liked a good adventure, and this one, gentlemen, is likely to be our last."

"I think," Lord Walworth replied, "that from now on I can do without adventure. I'll be happy to settle down to a comfortable and dull existence at the hall with Caroline and our children."

"Agreed," the earl and the duke said in unison.

The sea breezes of Sussex's coast had drawn the fashionable crowds to Brighton since the mid-1780s when Prinny arrived to spend a summer. Three years later he had purchased a simple farmhouse on the west side of the Steyne. Of course, unable to restrain himself, he had hired an architect and remodeled his dwelling into what became known as The Royal Pavilion. For the next thirty years Prinny continued to remodel, expand, and renovate his Pavilion. Fashionable London followed him to the seaside each year. The height of the season was always on August twelfth, the prince's birthday.

Early March was not a time when fashionable people visited Brighton. Most of the houses on the Steyne were shut up tight. The two chief hotels, Old Ship and Castle Inn, were open, but barely. The theatre on the New Road with its large gallery and two tiers of boxes was closed for the season. The race track was deserted. Very few fashionables were in residence except those too poor to keep a London house, or those who claimed they preferred living at the seaside for their health. The King's Arms was not a watering place for the ton, but their brief stay there would not attract the attention of any who by chance might know or recognize the three couples, and wonder why on earth they were here in Brighton at this gloomy time of year.

Hawkins pulled Honor aside just before they left. "Now, listen, old girl," he said to her, "don't go taking any chances for some foreign lady you don't even know. I want you coming back safe and sound."

"And just why is that, Peter Hawkins?" Honor demanded of him.

"You know why," he muttered, shuffling his feet.

"No, I don't," she replied.

"Don't we have an understanding, Honor Cooper?" he asked her.

"If we do, you didn't tell me," she shot back.

"Well, we do, damnit, and I don't want you getting

yourself killed by those Froggies," Hawkins said fiercely, and then he kissed her hard upon her lips.

Honor grew pink with pleasure, but then she said, "Now, don't you go confusing me, Hawkins. I haven't said we have an arrangement, but then I won't say we don't. I'll be back." She gave him a kiss in return, and hurried out of the inn after the others.

The earl's sailing yacht was anchored at the end of a long stone quay. It was not a large vessel, but neither was it small. It stretched seventy feet from bow to stern, was twenty-three feet in width, and one hundred eighty tons. Although it was a pleasure craft, it carried several small cannons. Its sails were ketch-rigged. There was a sumptuous day cabin beneath the poop deck where they would shelter from the elements.

"Welcome aboard, your lordship, Your Grace, my lord," Captain Grant greeted them. "Bobby will show you to the cabin. We'll be under way shortly." He bowed to the gentlemen and to the ladies.

"I keep a small crew aboard," the earl said. "This is Bobby, the cabin boy. He's a good lad, aren't you, Bobby?"

"Yes, my lord, I try to be," came the earnest reply. The boy, about twelve years of age, hurried ahead of them, opening the door to the day cabin where they would be staying. "There's wine, and fresh biscuits, my lord." He ushered them inside. Then with a tug on his cap, he hurried back out again.

"Where are we going to sleep, Marcus?" the Countess of Aston demanded of her husband. "It's all very beautiful, but hardly cozy."

"It isn't meant to be, my darling. I used to race *Seagull* before we married. Quint, Dree, and Ocky have all been aboard before. You will sleep here, in these bunks hidden behind the elegant paneling." Pressing a hidden button with his hand, the earl smiled at their astonishment as the paneling slid back to reveal two tiers of narrow bunks.

"They are not very big," Eunice noted.

"You'll be able to stretch out and rest, my dear wife," the earl assured her.

"There are seven of us, and only six of those narrow little berths," the countess noted.

"I shall get my rest on the settee," the earl told her.

"Very well," Eunice agreed. "I suppose we should all go to bed now. There seems to be nothing else to do."

Wrapping themselves in their capes and cloaks, they settled themselves down for the night. Allegra awoke at one point to feel the roll of the sea beneath the vessel. It was very quiet. She could hear the wind outside just faintly. She had never been on the sea, and she wasn't certain if she was frightened or not, but everyone else seemed quite peaceful, except for some snoring. So she fell back asleep.

The next day dawned gray and damp. A light rain fell, but the winds were steady, and the seas relatively calm. The *Seagull* seemed to skip along the waves easily. Bobby brought them a platter of eggs, ham, and buttered brown bread. They ate gingerly, waiting to see if their food settled, but it did. They spent the day playing cards for imaginary stakes, except for Honor and the duke. Allegra's maid went over each garment Madame Paul had supplied, making certain every piece was ready to don come the morning. The duke walked the deck of the yacht as he considered what they were attempting to do for the hundredth time. It was madness, he knew, and yet friendship demanded that they help the countess and her children.

Captain Grant joined him at one point, saying, "If the

winds keep up, Your Grace, we should anchor some time tonight, late."

"How far is it into the town?" Quinton Hunter asked.

"Only a mile and a bit, Your Grace."

"You know the town?"

"Aye," the captain nodded.

"We'll need a horse and a cart," the duke told him.

"I know a man," the captain offered, "but it will cost, and you must pay in French coin, not English."

"Agreed. You will go with us?"

"Nay," the captain said. "It is better that you not be seen in Harfleur, Your Grace. These days everyone watches, and strangers are easily and quickly ferreted out."

"You are known then," the duke noted.

"I am. I will fetch the horse and cart. My friend will think it is to meet the man who helps me smuggle certain items. I always leave the horse and cart at a set location afterward so I am not seen. Let me make the arrangements, Your Grace. The cove where we will anchor is just below the road you must take to reach the Countess d'Aumont. The d'Aumonts are well known in the region for their charity. The people were devastated when the count was executed in Paris. It would not have happened here. The man with the horse and cart has a sister who labors on the d'Aumont farm. When the earl told me who you were attempting to rescue, I was glad that I could be of help to you."

"Thank you, Captain Grant," the duke replied.

"I will ask my friend what he knows regarding the countess's arrest," Captain Grant said.

"No, do not," the duke advised. "This man is willing to deal with you because it puts money in his pocket in particularly hard times, but he is a loyal Frenchman first. If you attempt to compromise his loyalties he may turn on you. Let him, as you have earlier suggested, believe you are merely here to smuggle wine and other goods as you usually do. Do not arouse his suspicions by even mentioning the Comtesse d'Aumont."

"You are absolutely right, my lord," Captain Grant said.

Just before sunset, although the entire day had been gray, they could just make out the outline of the French coast in the hazy distance. The duke explained to his companions that the captain would fetch them a horse and a cart for their journey. They would leave as soon after the dawn as they possibly could. They ate ham, bread, and cheese for their evening meal, drinking a rather good wine which warmed them and eased them all into sleep.

𝐵obby, the cabin boy, awoke the duke as soon as the captain departed the ship to row himself ashore. Awakened, the women stepped out onto the deck of the yacht into a chill and dank darkness, allowing the gentlemen to change into their costumes. They did not speak. The three men exiting the cabin some minutes later did not look at all like three English milords. The women returned to the cabin to change into their own garments. When they were dressed but for their mobcaps, Honor loosened their hair, tangling it, and rubbing dirt from a jar she had carried with her into their tresses. Then she passed the jar around, suggesting they dirty themselves on their faces and about the neck where their collars rested.

"Plain folk don't bathe as much as your fine ladies do," she told them in her perfect French.

"She truly can speak French," Caroline squealed.

"And you had better, lady, from now on," Honor advised. "Sound carries over the water, and we don't know who is listening."

As the maidservant's words died they all looked at one another, realizing the game, this dangerous game, was now truly on, and a careless slip of the tongue could destroy them all.

Eunice, Countess of Aston, swallowed visibly, suddenly shaken, but seeing Allegra's look of alarm, said calmly in her rather good French, "It is all right, Allegra. I am afraid, but ready to do my part."

"We cannot call ourselves by our own Christian names," Allegra said softly. "We will need simple French names. I will be Marie. Honor, you are the only one who can keep her name. Honneur. Eunice, you are now Jeanne, and Caroline, Prunelle. We must tell the men, and rechristen them as well." She pulled her mobcap over her long snarled black hair. *"Allons, mes amies!"* The four women exited the cabin.

The name change explained to them, the gentlemen became Joseph, the duke; Pierre, the earl; and Michel, Lord Walworth. Then they waited. When the captain returned they exchanged places with him in the rowboat.

"Gawd, your lordships, I wouldn't have recognized you, but that I know it is you," he exclaimed softly. "You will find the cart and the horse at the top of the path. How long should I wait?"

"Until we return, Captain Grant, unless you find yourself and my yacht in danger," the earl said. "I do not know how long it will take us to retrieve the comtesse and her family. With luck we shall be back by nightfall."

"I'll keep a single light burning at the stern of the vessel, my lord," Captain Grant said. "God bless you all, and bring you safely back to us quickly, and madame countess with you."

The duke rowed their little boat to the shore. Getting out, they pulled it up upon the beach, the sand crunching beneath their wooden shoes, then began the climb up the hillside. They were in France. *The game was indeed on!*

Chapter Fifteen

The Comtesse d'Aumont stared disbelieving at the man before her. He was stocky and of medium height. There was enough of her late husband in his face to make his words unreal. She could not believe what he was saying.

"You were his brother," she finally managed to say. "You are a d'Aumont."

"Half brother," he corrected her. "I was our father's bastard."

"You were raised with him. You were with him your whole life," Anne-Marie d'Aumont cried. "He loved and respected you."

"We were five years apart in age," the man replied. "I was raised to be his servant. I was the older, and yet he was the heir, only for an accident of birth. Now I shall have what rightfully belongs to me."

"This estate belongs to my son, the Comte d'Aumont," Anne-Marie said, her voice shaking. "Jean-Robert is the heir to Le Verger."

"Did I ever tell you how I was conceived, madame? My mother came into this house as a servant at the age of twelve. My father raped her when she was thirteen. I was born when she was fourteen. She died shortly thereafter, and I was raised by my *grandmère*."

"Do not think to shock me, Reynaud," the comtesse said. "I know how you came into being, but your father was drunk when he attacked your mother. That does not excuse his crime. It was bestial, but he never touched her again. And he paid your *grandmère* to care for you. She wanted to put you out on a hillside for the wild animals. Did you know that? He would not permit it, for you were his very flesh. He paid her very generously to look after you, although she used precious little of his coin for your care. That is why when you were four he brought you into the house to be raised by his wife, along with the baby she was carrying. Rachelle d'Aumont was good to you, Reynaud. And your father tried to make up for what he had done to your mother as best he could. *And* my husband, your brother, treated you as an equal all his life."

"Yes," Reynaud said. "Jean-Claude was a good brother, I will admit. That is what made it so hard for me to betray him. But alas, I had no choice."

"What are you saying?" she gasped, going pale, her heart beating violently against her chest. My God! My God! It could not be.

"Once we were in Paris it was very easy for me to put a note in one of those boxes the Committee for Public Safety scattered about the city to give anonymity to those wishing to expose traitors to the new regime. They are very efficient in Paris. Jean-Claude was quickly arrested. I, of course, was fortunate to escape the authorities, and I knew my dear little brother would not expose me as his companion. I went to see him beheaded, and even walked alongside the tumbrel as it took him to the guillotine. He begged me to see to your safety, and that of his children. He had absolutely no idea that it was I who had betrayed him." Reynaud smiled, and the smile was so like her husband's that Anne-Marie cried out as if in pain.

"Monster!" she accused.

"Then I returned here, and joined our local Committee for Public Safety. I became so invaluable, so skilled in hunting out the enemies of the people, that the authorities in Harfleur gave me total authority over the committee in St. Jean Baptiste. I am the one responsible for your arrest, Citizeness d'Aumont. Your fate is in my hands entirely." He laughed aloud.

"God will punish you, Reynaud," she told him. "You cannot hide from God."

"I am arranging," he continued as if she had not spoken, "for your son to be sent to the army."

"*He is ten years old!*" she shrieked at him. Then she began to tremble as the realization of how helpless she was penetrated her consciousness.

"Old enough to carry water, or ammunition, or if he pleases the men in his unit with his elegant behavior, he might even become a little drummer boy for his regiment. You need not worry, Citizeness, my nephew is a pretty little fellow. He will find friends to protect him."

His meaning was very obvious, and the Comtesse d'Aumont was unable to suppress a shudder of revulsion. "No," she cried weakly.

"And as for your daughter, I have arranged for her to be apprenticed to a glovemaker in Paris. She will learn to be useful, Citizeness, and not grow up to be a worthless little aristo. The glovemaker told me that he likes young girls." He smiled again. "He will take good care of my niece, I am certain." He chuckled knowingly.

"*Please,*" the comtesse pleaded, "*please, I beg you!* Do what you will with me, but leave my children alone. We will leave Le Verger. It is yours. I have family in England that I can go to for shelter and aid. I will do whatever you want. Just do not harm my babies!" She fell to her knees before him, and clutched at his jacket. *"Please!"* The tears were streaming down her pretty face.

He looked on her dispassionately, his brown eyes cold, cruel. *"Anything, Citizeness?"* he said softly. Loosening his breeches he pulled out his flaccid manhood. *"Anything?"* he repeated.

"Anything," she sobbed brokenly. She would do what she must to save her children.

"Very well then, open your mouth, Citizeness, and entertain my rod. If you please me we will speak further on these matters. Now, suck, you aristocratic bitch. *Suck!"* His fingers cruelly dug into her head, threading themselves into her thick brown hair.

Anne-Marie d'Aumont closed her eyes and obeyed as she prayed that God would forgive her; her dead husband and their parents would forgive her; that she would one day forgive herself. But she had no other choice. *She had to save the children!* Why, oh why, had she not taken her English uncle up on his offer to shelter them when he had first made it? She knew now that she could not trust Reynaud d'Aumont, but she had to hope his desire for Le Verger was greater than his need to punish the legitimate branch of the d'Aumont family for their existence. That if she let him have his way with her, he would let them all go. She felt his flesh growing thicker in her mouth, and sucked harder on him.

"Ahh, yes, you little bitch," he groaned, his eyes closing with the pleasure she was giving him. "You are skillful indeed. That's it. *That's it!* Ah! Ah! *Ahhhhh!"* His fingers loosened their grip on her tresses, and he sighed with his release.

She continued to kneel before him, her head drooping

with her shame. She had swallowed every bit of his juices, struggling not to vomit them back at his feet. That, she knew, would not please him, and she had to please him if she was to save the children from his power.

Reynaud rebuttoned his breeches. "You have hidden talents, Citizeness."

She looked up at him. "My children?"

"I may reconsider my decision, Citizeness. Leave your bedchamber door open tonight, and we shall converse further on the matter," he told her. "Now get up, and see to the dinner. I wish to go over my brother's accounts."

Anne-Marie d'Aumont stumbled from the library where they had been speaking. The house was quiet.

Only two of the servants had remained after her arrest. They hadn't wanted to go, but she had sent them away, fearful for their safety under the circumstances. She had paid their year's wages so they would not starve. The old cook had remained, and her maid who was now with the children. She hurried to the kitchen. "Thérèse," she said in what she hoped passed for a normal voice, "do we have anything for supper? Monsieur Reynaud is remaining."

"That one!" Thérèse spat. "What does he want, madame?"

"Le Verger," the comtesse answered softly.

"Oh, the wicked devil," the old cook cried. "If the monsignor were alive he would not dare. He cannot take Le Verger from the petit monsieur Jean-Robert, madame."

"He can, and he means to do it. He wants to send my son to the army, and my daughter to a glovemaker in Paris, Thérèse. I am trying to reason with him. We must please him. Help me, I beg you!"

"Finely ground glass in his soup, madame," the cook muttered balefully. "Or," she made a slicing motion across her throat.

"We cannot kill him, Thérèse. He is the head of the Committee for Public Safety in St. Jean Baptiste. He is well known in Harfleur. If he disappeared we would all face Madame la Guillotine, I fear."

"I can make a rabbit pie, and I have a chicken I can roast," the cook said grudgingly. "I will do what I can to help, madame, but it will not please me to see Reynaud *le bâtard* sitting in monsignor's place at the head of the table tonight."

"Nor will it please me, Thérèse, but the times have changed. It is no longer the world we knew. If I can persuade Monsieur Reynaud to simply take Le Verger, I intend to make my way to my uncle in London with the children. I will see you have your wages, and a bit more I can spare."

"Madame! Madame!" The old woman threw her apron over her face, and began to sob. "If you go, take me with you. My granddaughter, Céline, and I have no one but the *famille* d'Aumont. We will not serve Reynaud *le bâtard*. Take us with you."

"Are you sure Céline does not want to remain here? What of that young man she was walking out with, Thérèse?" the comtesse asked.

"He was taken to serve in General Bonaparte's army, madame, and has not been heard of since," Thérèse said.

Anne-Marie sighed softly. "If Monsieur Reynaud does not object, Thérèse, then you and Céline may come with us, but I do not know how we shall survive in England. I have little money, I fear."

"Money." The cook spat scornfully. "We will go with you, madame, for no money at all. Our family has served the d'Aumonts for centuries. A revolution will not change that for Céline and for me."

The comtesse hugged the old cook, her blue eyes filling with tears. "*Merci*, Thérèse. *Merci*. We will all survive . . . somehow."

"*Oui*, madame, we will, and we will be together," the cook declared, as she hugged her mistress back.

"Feed the children here in the kitchens, Thérèse. I do not want *him* near them. And tell Céline to remain with them tonight. They are to sleep in the nursery as they did when they were younger," the comtesse instructed the cook. "I will go now, and set the table."

"*Très bien*, madame," the old cook said, understanding more than her mistress would have believed she did.

To Anne-Marie's amazement Thérèse managed to present a wonderful dinner. The countess had set the table in her *salle à manger*, and then changed her gown for something cleaner. She dressed her hair herself, twisting it into a neat chignon. She needed to give Reynaud the idea that she was not entirely helpless, or afraid, and was ready to bargain with him for her children's safety. And Thérèse certainly did her part.

They began with a wonderful soup of onions and red wine. Next Thérèse brought forth trout, broiled in butter. There followed the rabbit pie with its thick brown gravy, *petites carottes*, and little shallots; a roasted chicken with an apple and bread stuffing, *petits pois*, bread, and sweet butter.

Reynaud d'Aumont ate heartily, smacking his lips, mopping up every bit of the winy gravy with bread. "The old lady hasn't lost her touch," he said, "but I have a younger woman to take her place."

"Then you will not mind if she comes to England with me," Anne-Marie said softly.

He grinned. "We have yet to come to a final arrangement, Citizeness," he told her.

"You may have whatever you want of me, Reynaud," she said. "You may have Le Verger, and everything in it. Just let me go with my children. We will take nothing but the clothing on our backs. Just let us go. Surely you must have some feeling for the brother you betrayed. Marie-Claire and Jean-Robert are his children. They have loved you. Does your need for vengeance really demand the destruction of innocents? Have mercy, I beg you!"

"Go up to your bedchamber and wait for me," he said. "We will see how well you can bargain for your children, Citizeness."

She arose from the table, and curtseying to him left the room. Upstairs there was not a sound to be heard. Céline and Thérèse had obviously fed the children, and they were now in bed, sleeping, she prayed. Her bed, the bed she had shared with Jean-Claude, was turned back. She undressed without any help, leaving only her chemise on for a night garment. These days with no one to do the laundry, many of her garments did double duty, and were only washed when absolutely necessary. Undoing her hair she brushed it out, starting as the door to her bedchamber opened, and Reynaud came into the room.

Wordless at first, he removed his own clothing and boots. Finally clad only in his shirt he turned about and said to her, "Take off your chemise. I want to see what it is you have to offer me, Citizeness."

She quickly obeyed, and stood naked before him. He walked around her, stopping behind to press himself against her, his big hands moving to cup her breasts.

"Very nice," he murmured his approval, "especially considering your age, and the fact you have whelped two brats." He squeezed her breasts hard, smiling when she winced. He was surprised to find that the mere thought of fucking this aristo was very exciting. He rubbed himself against her, his manhood sliding against the split between her bottom. "Did Jean-Claude ever give it to you there, Citizeness?" he whispered into her ear, "or will I be the first to taste that pleasure?"

She couldn't answer him. Her heart was beating so fast, and she could feel the bitter fear rising in her throat.

He laughed nastily. "First things first, however, Citizeness. On your knees again, and suck. I will tell you when to stop, and you had best be as skillful tonight as you were earlier today. Ahh, yes, bitch, that is good. Very good!" He closed his eyes, and when he was hard, but not yet ready to loose his juices, he said, "Now, my pretty little citizeness, on your back, and open your legs. Then I want you to tell me how much you want to be fucked by me. How long has my brother been dead now?" He pushed her back onto the bed. "He was a virile man, Jean-Claude, and you're not so old yet that you didn't enjoy his husbandly attentions, are you?" He fell atop her. "Now tell me, Citizeness, how much you want me to do it to you!"

"Reynaud! In the name of *le bon Dieu*," she pleaded.

"Tell me, you aristocratic bitch, or our discussions are over, and your children are gone on the morrow!" he snarled, slapping her.

"Please," she begged him, and realizing that wasn't enough, she continued, "please fuck me, Reynaud. Oh, do it to me. I want it. I need it. Fuck me! Fuck me! Fuck me! *Ahhhhhh!*" she shrieked as he rammed himself into her cruelly. His mouth mashed down upon her lips, kissing her hungrily, his tongue stabbing at her tongue as she struggled not to gag. She realized almost immediately that if she didn't exhibit a measure of enthusiasm he was not going to be satisfied. She groaned beneath him, her nails raking down the broad back beneath his shirt. She wrapped his torso about with her legs. "Oh, yes," she murmured into his ear. "Oh, yes, Reynaud! Do it to me hard!" And he did.

He grunted, and sweated over her body. The walls of her love sheath seemed to grasp him tightly, and he howled with his lust. He could feel her full breasts beneath his chest, their nipples hard as little iron points. Then his excited desires burst, and he was angry for a moment until he realized that he had an entire night ahead of him. He was going to suckle and bite those breasts until she screamed with both pain and pleasure. He was going to make her suck him to another stand, and then he was going to put himself into her rosette. That was something he knew his brother had never done, but he would do it. And she would love it, he was quite certain. He had always wanted Anne-Marie. Now she was his slave for as long as he desired her. He did not think he would grow tired of her too quickly. But when he was, he would sell her to a madame he knew in Harfleur, and dispose of her children exactly as he had planned to do. The boy would go first to the army, and the girl would serve her apprenticeship in Paris. But not, perhaps, before he violated her as his father had once violated his mother. Now that would be true revolutionary justice! He laughed aloud with his silent thoughts, and the woman beneath him trembled at the evil sound.

That she had lived through what was undoubtedly the worst night of her life amazed Anne-Marie d'Aumont when she awoke the following morning. Reynaud d'Aumont lay snoring like a pig next to her. He had violated and degraded her in ways she had never imagined.

She crept from the bed, aching and sore all over. Finding a pitcher of water in the warm coals of the fireplace, she attempted to wash his filth from her flesh. She doubted that she could ever erase the memories, but if it would save her children she would do it all over again. As clean as she could be she dressed swiftly, and escaped from the room, hurrying down the stairs to the kitchen where her children were waiting to see her.

"*Maman!*" they cried.

Then Marie-Claire, aged twelve said, "What is the matter, *Maman?* Why did Papa's valet eat with you last night, and then remain?"

"Monsieur Reynaud is now the new owner of Le Verger," she began slowly.

"Le Verger is mine," Jean-Robert cried indignantly. "My uncle is the bastard. I am the true heir."

"*Non, mon bébé.* Le Verger is now Monsieur Reynaud's. So the revolution has ruled. We are going to England soon, to my uncle's home in London. Ohh, you will like London, *mes enfants.* And Thérèse and Céline will come with us, Jean-Robert. Won't that be nice?"

"The English are our enemies," the boy said stonily.

"Grandpapa was English, Jean-Robert. You are named for him," she reminded her son gently.

"Stupid boy," his sister said. "Monsieur Reynaud has stolen Le Verger, and there is nothing we can do about it."

"I will go to the king," the boy responded hotly.

"There is no king, Jean-Robert," his sister reminded him. "*Not anymore.* They cut off his head just the way they did to Papa."

Jean-Robert began to sniffle.

"Marie-Claire," her mother scolded her, but she knew her daughter was being practical.

"When are we going?" the girl asked.

"Soon," her mother promised her. Then she turned to her maid, Céline. "Take the children to *Père André* for their lessons," she instructed the younger woman. "Do not come back for a while."

"*Oui*, madame," Céline said, understanding. "*Allons, mes enfants.*" She led the two children from the kitchens.

"I have hot water," Thérèse said. "I have filled the little oak tub in the pantry. Go and bathe, madame. Get the stink of that beast off of you now, or you will never get it out of your nostrils."

The comtesse flushed. "*You know?*"

"I know that dog, Reynaud, madame. You did what you had to do to protect the children, but do not trust him."

"I do not. Ahh, Thérèse, I am so ashamed." And she began to weep softly.

"It is he who should be ashamed," Thérèse said fiercely. "I would kill him if I thought I could keep us all safe, but nowadays one does not know who one's friends are, madame. Go and bathe now."

The Comtesse d'Aumont washed herself thoroughly, and when she had finished she felt much better. She sat down and ate the boiled egg and the fresh bread that Thérèse had prepared for her, sipping at a cup of watered wine. She had no sooner arisen from the table when there came a pounding upon the front door of the house. "I will get it," she said to the cook whose hands were all floury, and she hurried upstairs to answer the ferocious pounding. Opening the door the Comtesse d'Aumont found herself facing a group of peasants.

"We have come for the Comtesse d'Aumont and her brats," said the obvious leader of the group, a woman who wore an eye patch over her left eye.

"I am the Comtesse d'Aumont," Anne-Marie quavered, her heart beginning to pound furiously.

"We have been sent to take you to Harfleur, Citizeness. Your children, too," the woman said. "Where are the men who are supposed to be guarding you? Heads will roll for this infraction of the rules!"

"The guards went back to St. Jean Baptiste yesterday when Monsieur Reynaud, the head of the Committee for Public Safety arrived. He is here now, but he is still sleeping," she told them.

"*Where?*" demanded the woman.

"Upstairs," the comtesse said. "Will you not come in?"

"Madame," the leader said softly, "do not be afraid. We have come to rescue you. We carry a letter from your uncle, Lord Bellingham. This is but a charade." Honor handed the comtesse the small message. She opened it, and the relief upon her face was palpable.

"This is a miracle," she whispered.

"Who are these ruffians, madame?" Thérèse had come up from the kitchen, a large carving knife in her hand.

"There is not time to explain, Thérèse. Whatever happens, do not be afraid. It is all right, and I will tell you as soon as I can," Anne-Marie d'Aumont said in low tones. "They have come to rescue us."

"What the hell is going on down here?" Reynaud d'Aumont stood at the top of the staircase. He was halfdressed. He stomped down to face them. "Who the devil are you?"

"You are Monsieur Reynaud of the Committee for Public Safety in St. Jean Baptiste?" the woman with the eye patch demanded authoritatively.

"I am," he replied.

"I am Citizeness Honneur Dupont. These citizens and I have been sent from Harfleur to take Citizeness d'Aumont and her offspring into custody. We have been given our authority by the Committee for Public Safety in Harfleur. Charges have been made against this woman."

"What charges?" demanded Reynaud.

"I do not know," Honor replied surlily. "I am not made privy to such things. It is my duty to collect those people the committee wishes to see. Was this woman not already under arrest?"

"Yes," he said slowly.

"Then why are you standing there arguing with me, Citizen Reynaud? If you have any questions or complaints to make, I suggest you come to Harfleur with us. If, however, you defy the wishes of the Harfleur Committee for Public Safety, I can only imagine what your fate will be." She made a chopping motion with her hand. "This citizeness and her children have been asked to tea by Madame la Guillotine. I am certain you do not object to enemies of France being exterminated." She glared at him, hands upon her hips. *"Well, Citizen?"* she growled.

"No. No," Reynaud said. Then he thought, what a fortunate coincidence that Anne-Marie and her children should be taken away now. While he would have enjoyed having her about to torture for a while longer, it did not matter really. Le Verger would now be his without any questions. "Where are the children?" he asked Anne-Marie.

"With Père André," she said low. "They are your blood, Reynaud. Do not let them be killed! Keep them here with you. I beg you!" She fell to her knees before him, and he thought of when she had done the same thing yesterday. The memory of it made his rod tingle.

"Get on your feet, Citizeness," he snapped at her roughly, yanking her up. "The committee in Harfleur outranks me. You will go with these citizens." He turned to Thérèse. "Go and fetch the brats, old woman."

She glared up at him.

He stepped forward and shouted down into her face. "Did you not hear me, you old bitch? Or are you too stupid to understand?"

"I understand very well, Citizen Reynaud," Thérèse said softly, and then she plunged her carving knife directly into his heart. "I understand everything, but you will not have Le Verger. It belongs to the true heir, and not some bastard. Do you hear me? Or are you too stupid to understand?" Thérèse stepped back from him as he collapsed to the floor. Then drawing the knife from her victim's chest she wiped it off on her skirt.

"Good God," the Earl of Aston exclaimed in English.

"Be silent, Citizen Pierre," Honor said in a hard voice.

"I will go to fetch Céline and the children now, *Madame la Comtesse*," Thérèse said quietly. Turning, she walked from the house.

"Who was he?" the Duke of Sedgwick asked the stunned Anne-Marie.

"My husband's half brother," she replied. "He was his father's bastard, and was raised to be my husband's servant. Jean-Claude loved him as he would any brother. I always thought they were friends, but then yesterday I learned that it was Reynaud who had betrayed my husband when they were in Paris last year."

"Is that why the old woman killed him?" the duke continued to query. "It was, if I may say so, quite nicely, and neatly done."

Anne-Marie d'Aumont crossed herself, but said nothing.

"My lord," Allegra murmured softly to her husband, "it is obvious the old woman killed the villain because he has abused the comtesse. It is unlikely she will want to speak about it, for it will have been a terrible and shameful experience for such a virtuous and gentle woman. Let it be, and let us concentrate on leaving here as quickly as possible." She turned to the countess. "Madame, gather any jewelry or monies that you have secreted away, and hide them well on your person and those of your children. We can allow you to take nothing else. Remember, we are supposed to be bringing you to Harfleur to face revolutionary justice. If we are stopped on the road that is the story we will tell, and that is what must be believed."

"Who are you?" the Comtesse d'Aumont asked softly.

"I am madame la Duchesse de Sedgwick. This gentleman is my husband, *monsieur le duc,* and these are our friends. The woman with the eye patch is my maid, Honneur."

"*Why?*" the comtesse asked.

"Your uncle has been very distressed, as has your aunt, when you did not come to England immediately after your husband was killed. My brother, too, died in Paris, refusing to leave his affianced, although he was offered his freedom because he was English. This is our way of avenging him, and helping our friends, the Bellinghams."

"So you have come to rescue me and my children in his memory, eh, madame? You are mad, but then all the English are mad my papa used to say. How can I ever thank you?"

"We are not safe yet," Allegra reminded her. "Now go, and fetch your valuables."

"One thing," the comtesse said. She looked to the duke. "I cannot leave my two servants behind. They will come with me."

The duke laughed ruefully. "In for a penny, in for a pound," he remarked. "It won't make any difference if we are caught helping three people or five to escape France. Yes, madame, of course your servants may come. I do not think I should attempt to argue with that fierce old woman who killed Monsieur Reynaud."

The countess bit her lip, and then she laughed softly, too.

Thérèse returned with her granddaughter, Céline, and the two children in tow. Their mother, coming back down the stairs to the foyer, explained all to them. Then she secreted her valuables among the five of them, explaining that it was all they would have to live on once they arrived in England.

"Oh, no, madame," Caroline burst out. "I am your cousin. You will come and live with my husband and me."

"You are my kin?" the comtesse said, and then she began to weep. "Ahh, to think that the little family I have left in England would care for me and for my children, that they would endanger themselves to come and rescue us." She embraced Caroline. *"Merci! Merci!"*

"It is time we were going," the duke said to them.

"What is to be done with *that*?" Allegra asked, pushing at the body of Reynaud d'Aumont with her wooden shoe.

"It will be taken care of, madame," Thérèse said grimly. "I have told the priest, and he will see to it. Reynaud *le bâtard* was not well loved among us. His body will be buried deep in the woods where it is unlikely anyone will ever find it."

"It will take us longer to return to the coast than it took us to get here," Allegra noted. "We shall have to walk most of the way back, I fear. The comtesse must ride in the cart with her servants and children. Two of us at a time will ride with her. The rest of us walk."

"Forgive us, madame," the duke spoke, "but we must march you from the house should anyone be watching. It should look as if you are being taken away."

"I understand," Anne-Marie said.

The duke and his party led the comtesse and her little family from their home, pushing them into the cart. Eunice and Caroline joined them, Caroline sitting next to her newly found cousin so they might speak. The duke and Lord Walworth climbed up upon the wagon seat, and chucking the reins, moved the horse into motion. The others walked next to the cart as it rumbled along. Here and there they passed peasants in the fields, preparing the soil for the new growing season.

"*Vive la révolution!*" they shouted, and the peasants in the fields responded in kind, "*Vive la révolution!*" but then they looked away, recognizing the Comtesse d'Aumont and her children, realizing what surely was happening to them, and feeling guilty at their own helplessness.

They traveled slowly over the rutted dirt road. The day which had begun gray turned grayer. A cold rain began to fall, turning the dusty track into a muddy trail. They had brought some bread and cheese from the yacht, and finally they stopped in the shelter of a hillside to rest the poor horse and feed the children who were chilled, and despite their mother's explanation, not just a little frightened. In the first hour of their travel Caroline explained the relationship between them to the countess.

"I knew my father had two brothers," Anne-Marie said, "but other than that, I knew little. Only my Uncle Frederick wrote regularly."

"Do you speak English at all?" Caroline asked her cousin.

"I fear not," came the reply.

"You will learn, and the children, too," Caroline said. "I do not know about your rather fierce Thérèse though."

"Her family has been with the d'Aumonts for centuries," the countess said. "When the revolution began her daughter ran off with a soldier, but her granddaughter, Céline, remained."

In late afternoon as they neared the coast they met a small troop of soldiers who came cantering toward them.

"Sing!" Allegra said to her companions. "*Allons, enfants de la patrie, le jour de gloire est arrivé!*" She waved merrily to the horsemen. "*Vive la révolution,* citizens!"

The cavalrymen waved back, continuing on their way. The road ahead of them was empty. No one wanted to be out unless they had to be on such an afternoon. A wind began to blow, and they could smell the sea as they drew near to it. Finally they reached the place where Captain Grant said they must leave the horse and cart. It was about a half a mile from the beach. The passengers were helped from the cart, the horse unharnessed and tied beneath a shed roof.

"We walk from here," the duke told them, and they followed. As they reached a crossroad they heard the sounds of hooves in the distance. "Into the ditch," the duke said urgently, and they tumbled into the dirt, ducking down so they could not been seen.

A party of cloaked men galloped by, taking the road

to Harfleur. As soon as they were out of sight the duke signaled with his hand that they could be on their way again. They climbed, wet and shivering from the ditch, and hurried off toward the beach. Gaining the hilltop they struggled down the bluff, the sandy path giving way beneath their feet so that they half fell as they climbed down. Below they could see their boat, but the tide was coming in, and while it had been on the sand this morning, it was now beginning to bob gently in the incoming tide.

The Earl of Aston practically threw himself down the rest of the hill, and picking himself up, ran across the beach to catch at the boat and prevent it from floating away. His companions hurried after him. They helped the countess, her children, and her servants into the boat. Caroline and Eunice squeezed in along with the earl who would row. Lord Walworth, the duke, Honor, and Allegra pushed the boat out into the sea, watching as it made its way through the waves to where the *Seagull* lay at anchor in the rain and haze.

"We have done it!" Allegra said triumphantly to her husband.

"Wait until we are back aboard our ship to gloat," he said to her. "I will not feel at ease until I see England again, my darling."

"We were fortunate that we had no guards to beard. I thought Honor quite wonderful with her eye patch facing down that Reynaud man." She turned to Honor. "The eye patch was a stroke of genius."

Honor chuckled. "I always thought an eye patch intimidating, my lady. It wasn't hard talking down to that fellow who was at the house. I recognized his type. He was a bully, and bullies can usually be bullied."

They turned back to the sea and saw the little boat

had reached *Seagull*. They could just make out figures climbing up, and then down the rope ladder that hung over the side of the vessel. Then the boat began to make its way back to the shore. When it arrived they found Captain Grant rowing. They hurried to climb into their transport, and head back to the ship. On board again they were eager to change from their revolutionary garb into their own clothing, which was much dryer. Bobby took the clothing from their French passengers to dry in the galley. Allegra and the others wrapped the countess, her children, and her two servants in their warm cloaks until their garments were dried again.

Captain Grant entered the cabin. "We'll weigh anchor immediately, my lords, and set a course for England. It may be a bit choppy returning. The wind has begun to come 'round from the north, but 'tis no bad storm." He bowed to them, and was gone.

Bobby brought chicken, bread, and cheese for them to eat. The two children were put to bed in two of the narrow bunks. The clothing was returned, not quite dry, but serviceable. The countess retired to one of the bunks along with Eunice and Caroline, who were both exhausted from their exciting day. The men sat together in a corner talking in low tones while Céline and Honor chattered, the French maid delighted to find the English maid spoke her tongue so well. Now she felt less afraid of their future.

Allegra sat quietly, old Thérèse next to her. "The man, Reynaud," she began. "Did he harm the comtesse, Thérèse? Should she be seen by a physician when we reach England?"

"*Oui*, he hurt her," the old woman said. "Though I didn't ask, and she did not say, I know he violated her. He always coveted his brother's wife, the cowardly *cochon.* But I will take care of her, madame. As long as my mistress has Céline and me by her side she needs no one else."

"I understand," Allegra said. "We will not breach her privacy, Thérèse."

"You are brave, you Englishwomen. You could have been caught," Thérèse remarked. "If you had come two days ago I do not believe you would have been so successful, but perhaps you would have. That *Honneur* has courage. She is resourceful. She is your servant?"

"Since my childhood," Allegra replied. "She was born upon my father's estate."

Thérèse nodded. "Tradition is a good thing, madame. These revolutionaries would destroy our way of life. That was not what Monsieur le Comte wanted from the revolution. He wanted justice and equality, but he did not want to see tradition pulled down the way it has been. They did not have to kill the king and his family, poor souls." She crossed herself with a sigh.

"Change can sometimes be cruel," Allegra agreed.

"Ahh," Thérèse said, "you have suffered from this revolution too. Madame la comtesse told me." She patted Allegra's hand in a kindly fashion. "Yet despite it all you risked your life for ours. You are obviously very much like your brother, Madame la Duchesse."

Allegra's hand went to her mouth to stifle her cry. How she had raged to all who would listen when her brother had given up his life for love. Yet she had been willing today to risk her life for the friendship she had for Lord and Lady Bellingham. Jamie, she thought, I learned more from you than I realized. A tear slipped down her cheek, but she said nothing, and Thérèse, understanding, closed her eyes and leaned back against her chair to sleep.

It took them two full days with the winds to reach England once again, but finally they sailed into Brighton and disembarked from *Seagull*. Ensconced in The King's Arms they dispatched messages to London to Lord and Lady Bellingham, and to Charles Trent. Then they settled down to a hot meal and a warm bed.

Chapter Sixteen

The Comtesse d'Aumont awoke to a knocking upon her bedchamber door. Céline struggled up, bleary-eyed from the trundle where she had been sleeping. She hurried across the cold floor, and slowly opened the chamber door. She was immediately pushed aside by a fashionably dressed older lady who entered the room and burst into tears.

"Ohh, Anne-Marie, it is really you," the lady cried. "Thank God you are safe! Where are the children? The duke sent a message up to London last night, and nothing would do but that your uncle and I set out before the dawn this very morning to see for ourselves that you were safe." She bent, and hugged the startled young Frenchwoman, who also began to cry.

"*Tante! Tante!*" she sobbed. "How can I thank you? What can I say that you will understand how your intervention has saved us all from a horrible fate?" She clung to Lady Bellingham, weeping.

"*Maman! Maman!*" Marie-Claire and Jean-Robert ran into their mother's room. "Is everything all right?" the elder of the two asked.

Lady Bellingham straightened herself up, and addressed the two children. "*Mes enfants,* I am your *grand-tante*, Lady Clarice Bellingham. Welcome to England, my darlings. Welcome!"

Immediately Marie-Claire curtsied, and young Jean-Robert made a most elegant bow. "*Merci, grand-tante,*" the young girl said.

"*Merci, grand-tante,*" Jean-Robert echoed his sister.

"Lady Bellingham." Allegra entered the bedchamber.

"Allegra, my dear gel, what are you doing here?" the older woman said, surprised to see the Duchess of Sedgwick.

"Aunt, it was the duchess, her friends, her maid, Honor, and their husbands who rescued us. They came to the house dressed as those horrible creatures who always sit below the guillotine, knitting. Honor was wonderful. She boldly faced down the head of St. Jean Baptiste's Committee for Public Safety, suggesting that if he did not cooperate he would face a dire fate."

"We can speak of this over breakfast," Allegra said. "Come, dear Lady Bellingham, and sit down to eat with us."

Lady Bellingham had gone white with her niece's brief explanation. "You, Honor, and who else?" she gasped. "Not Eunice and Caroline?"

"Good morning, Aunt." Lady Walworth popped around the door.

"Ohh," Lady Bellingham cried, and sat down heavily upon the bed. "I cannot believe what I am being told. You might have all been killed!"

"But we weren't," Allegra said airily. "In the end it was all quite simple." She took the good woman by her arm, and drew her up. "Come, and join us. We have a private dining room, and if we do not come now, the gentlemen will have eaten everything." She laughed.

They repaired to the dining room where Lord Bellingham was being regaled by the duke and his friends regarding their adventures of the last few days. The old gentleman was most impressed, and quite delighted by their success. When his niece, in her dressing gown, entered the room, he greeted her with great affection, welcoming her and her little family to England.

"You must stay with us, of course," he told her.

"Only for a short time," the comtesse said softly. "We cannot impose upon you. I have jewelry, and a cache of gold coins I brought out with me. I must find my own home so I may look after myself, the children, and my two servants who have come with us. Without Thérèse and Céline, my children and I would not have survived."

"We will speak on it after you are well rested, m'dear," Lord Bellingham said in kindly tones, and he patted her shoulder lovingly.

"*Frederick!* What have you to say to these foolish gels?" Lady Bellingham demanded.

Lord Bellingham turned, gallantly saluting Allegra, Caroline, and Eunice. "My dears," he told them, "I stand in awe of the three of you. What courage. What clever planning. Allegra, I understand it was your maid, Honor, who carried the day."

"It was, my lord," Allegra admitted.

"*Frederick!* They could have all been killed!" Lady Bellingham said.

"But they weren't. Now, wife, I am hungry, for you rousted me from my bed at an early hour to make the trip down here to Brighton. I can wait no longer for a beefsteak, and some of those delicious-looking eggs."

Everyone laughed, including the comtesse who had not understood her uncle's words, but his tone was very telling.

* * *

They departed for London at noon, and arrived back in town shortly after dark. Reaching Morgan House on Berkley Square they discovered Lord Morgan awaiting them. Marker took their outdoor garments.

"I am relieved to see you both," Lord Morgan said as they went into the small family salon where a warm fire was burning. A young footman hurried in with the tea tray and set it down.

"Tea, Papa?" Allegra asked her parent. "I must admit to being surprised to see you up in town today."

"How was Brighton?" Lord Morgan said. "Or perhaps I should say France."

"I asked Charles not to tell you," Allegra said, calmly handing a cup of tea to her husband, and then another to her father.

"He had no choice, Allegra. I arrived in London yesterday. Had I come today he might have been able to keep your folly from me, but when you did not return by late last night he had no choice but to tell me. Only Quinton's message saved me undue worry." He turned to his son-in-law. "And you, sir? Could you not prevent your wife from playing this dangerous game?"

"Sir," the duke returned, "when you were her guardian, could you prevent her from her headstrong ways?"

Lord Morgan sighed. "I had hoped her fondness for you would have made her change. I see now that it has not."

"Oh, Papa," Allegra wheedled him, "do not fuss. We have been, and gone. The Bellinghams are delighted that we were able to rescue Anne-Marie and her children. We even brought two of the countess's servants with us. The old cook, Thérèse, killed the head of the Committee for Public Safety so we might escape. And remember when you thought it amusing that Honor learned to speak French? Well, Papa, it was Honor who was our greatest heroine. She pretended to be our leader, and knew just how to speak to this dreadful man. She had him quite intimidated, Papa. I don't know what we would have done without her."

Lord Morgan sighed. "It is over now, thank goodness, but Allegra, I hope that you and Quinton will never do such a foolish thing again."

"No, Papa, we are going home to Hunter's Lair in a few days," Allegra told her father. "We have had enough excitement, and enough of London now to last a lifetime."

"I want you to stop down at Morgan Court before you go home," he told her. "Your stepmother has not been well at all, and wishes to see you both."

"Papa! What is the matter?" Allegra looked truly worried.

"Nothing dire, daughter, but Olympia wants to see you. That is why I came up to London. I shall return tomorrow. Then you and Quinton will follow in a few days' time when you have made all your good-byes."

"Aunt Mama has not been well for several months," Allegra told her husband later that evening as they cuddled together in their bed. "I wonder what the matter can be. She and Papa love each other very much. I should not like to see him hurt. You don't think she is going to die, Quinton, do you?" Her violet eyes were troubled.

"Your father said it was nothing dire. I believe we should take him at his word, my darling," the duke replied. "Now, I seem to recall that before we left for France, you made me a rather earnest speech about our need for heirs." His look was mischievous. "I believe we should now begin attempting to remedy our lack, Duchess, eh?"

To his surprise she pushed him away. "Forgive me, Quinton, but I am too worried about Aunt Mama to involve myself wholeheartedly in passion. Do not be angry with me, please." She kissed him lightly.

He was admittedly surprised, but he actually understood. "I love you, Allegra, and nothing can change that," he told her.

"You are so good to me, my darling," she responded.

They set off for Morgan Court two days later. It was a journey of several days from London, and then their own home was another few days farther. The inns in which they stayed were comfortable, but Allegra found herself more worried about her stepmother as each mile passed. Olympia had virtually raised her, and Allegra loved her. She had been so happy to marry Lord Morgan, and he had certainly been happy to have a wife after all his years of enforced bachelorhood. What could have gone wrong?

They reached Morgan Court at teatime. A footman hurried from the house to open the coach door. He lowered the steps of the vehicle, and helped the Duchess of Sedgwick dismount her carriage. Her dark green velvet cloak with its beaver-trimmed hood clutched about her, Allegra went straight into the house, flinging her cloak to a footman, her husband following behind. Her father came forth to greet her.

"My dear child. Come, Olympia is waiting for you both," he said, and led them into a small salon where his wife awaited their visitors.

Lady Morgan arose from her settee, and came forward, her hands outstretched in greeting. "Allegra. Quinton," she said, greeting them.

Allegra gave a little shriek of surprise. "Aunt Mama! What has happened to you?" she cried, quite distressed.

Her stepmother's body was swollen and misshapen. "What is this terrible and abnormal growth that has taken ahold of your body? Do not tell me, I pray you, that you are going to die. I could not bear it!"

Olympia Morgan laughed softly. "Thank you, my darling, for loving me, but no, I do not expect to die. Sit down, Allegra. Your father and I have news to share with you. We would have told you sooner, but we could not believe it ourselves, and for several months ignored the signs. I am expecting a child, Allegra. Come May, you and Sirena will have a new baby brother, or sister. Both your father and I assumed we were past such things as infants, but it would appear that we are not. I have not told Sirena yet for her time is too near, and I would not shock her as I have obviously shocked you," Lady Morgan concluded.

Allegra's gaze went from her stepmother to her father. *They were having a baby. Together.* They were old. *Old!* Yet they were having a baby. She had been wed over five months, and she was not with child, and she was young. Quinton was young. Her father and Aunt Mama were old, but there her stepmother sat, fat and burgeoning with new life. She did not know if she could tolerate it. It was simply too awful!

"We shall, my lord, have to discuss the terms of Allegra's marriage portion," Lord Morgan said to the duke, "and renegotiate it under the circumstances, as I will now have another heir to consider."

"Of course," Quinton Hunter agreed. "I perfectly understand, sir."

Allegra stood up. "I want to go home," she said, and walked from the salon without so much as a farewell to her father and stepmother.

"It is late, the horses are tired," the duke called after her.

"We will take fresh horses from the stables," Allegra said in a stony voice. *"I want to go home!"*

"There," Lady Morgan said to her husband. "Did I not tell you we should have told her sooner, Septimius? Now Allegra is upset, and heaven only knows how Sirena will respond when we finally speak to her."

"I will fetch her back," the duke told them. "She has gone out without her cloak."

"No," Lady Morgan said. "I know Allegra better than you, sir, and believe me, this has come as a terrible shock to her. Take her home, and let her digest all of our news. Until she can come to terms with herself she will be unhappy. And, Septimius, there will be no renegotiations regarding Allegra's status until *after* our child is born. Is that understood?"

"Yes, m'dear," Lord Morgan said. Then he turned to his son-in-law. "Go along, Quinton. We will talk again eventually."

The duke found his wife huddled in their coach shivering. He wrapped her fur-lined cape around her, having retrieved it from a footman. "Where are we going?" he asked, his voice laced with humor.

She glared up at him. "How can you jest, sir, in light of this revolting development? There is an inn about two hours away on the road home. It is respectable enough though not grand." Then clutching her cloak about her she turned away from him, and remained silent for the next few hours until they had reached their destination.

Although they had never stayed at the Ducks and Drake, the innkeeper recognized them at once. Bowing, he ushered them into his establishment, apologizing that it was small, and he could but offer them his largest bedroom.

"We are grateful you are able to accommodate us at all," the duke told him graciously. "We will want supper. Do you have a private room where we may dine, sir?"

"Indeed, my lord, I do," the innkeeper assured him, bowing again. "And I have smaller rooms for your servants, too."

"Excellent," the duke said heartily. "Now if you will show us to our private room, we are ready for our supper. It has been a long day, and it is still quite chilly even if it is spring."

"I have some rather good sherry, Your Grace," the innkeeper said. "Shall I bring it?"

The duke nodded with a smile, and then escorted his wife to the little dining room the innkeeper offered them.

Allegra managed to hold her peace as the innkeeper and a maidservant bustled about them, taking her outdoor garment, bringing the sherry, pouring it into small glasses. However, when the door closed behind those offering them service, she burst out, "I cannot believe it! How could they do such a thing? It is so embarrassing that two people their age should have an infant. I realized what they were doing behind those closed doors before we were married, but I never expected that their excesses should lead to a *baby*!"

"Why not?" her husband asked.

"*Why not?*" Her voice was close to a shriek. "My father is over fifty. And Aunt Mama is over forty. That is why not. People that age do not have babies, Quinton. My stepmother's last baby was my cousin, Sirena. Heaven only knows what poor Sirena will think when she learns about this. Her own baby's aunt, or uncle, will be younger than her own child. It is obscene!"

"I think it rather romantic," the duke told his wife.

"How you have changed," she said scornfully. "There was a time when you were a practical man, Quinton. Now you consider it romantic that your aged father-in-law and his wife are about to be new parents when we are not. My father does not need an heir. *He has one.*"

"So, that is what troubles you, Allegra," her husband said quietly. "You will have to share your father's wealth with a new sibling."

"Did you not match the bluest blood in England with the richest girl in England, sir? I shall no longer be the richest girl in England, Quinton. If my father has another son, we shall be poorer by a considerable amount. You had best pray Aunt Mama whelps another girl. At least then we shall retain half of what we have."

"It doesn't matter," he told her, taking her hands in his. "A year ago I would not have said such a thing to you, nor believed it if anyone had said it to me. I went to London to seek a rich wife. I found her. I did not, however, plan on falling in love with her, yet I did. Hunter's Lair has been restored. Nay, it is better than it ever was, Allegra, and that is thanks to you and your father's generosity. Your father negotiated a fabulous yearly sum upon you and upon me. Neither of us has spent a great deal of those monies for we are both frugal by nature. We could live comfortably for the rest of our lives on what your father has given us this year alone. And what of your investments, my darling duchess? Unless one of us takes to gambling, we shall never be poor, Allegra. Whatever your father decides he wants to give us after this child is born will be suitable. Septimius Morgan is a fair man." Quinton Hunter put his arms about his wife. "I am content with just you, my darling."

"It is not only the wealth involved," she said to him.

"Do you know how embarrassing it is to be barren at my age, especially when both my cousins and my step-mother are about to have a child? My wealth is going to be taken away from me, and I cannot even give you an heir, Quinton. It appears to me that you have gotten a bad bargain in me."

"Do you love me?" he asked looking down into her distraught face. "Do you love me, my darling duchess?"

"*I do!*" she cried. "How can you ever doubt it?"

"Then why do you doubt me, Allegra? I love you, and all your wealth means nothing to me as long as you love me back," he told her. Then he kissed her passionately.

She clung to him, her eyes welling with tears. He was a good man, but she knew he could not possibly really mean what he was saying. He had not yet had time to consider the situation. But, oh, she wanted to believe! They would return to Hunter's Lair, and he would soon see his wife with her pittance as a very bad bargain. Especially if she could not at least keep her end of their marriage bargain and produce a son for him.

He sensed her distress. How was he to make her believe that he loved her no matter what happened? He sighed, and held her close, his lips brushing the top of her hair.

Their dinner came, but Allegra ate little. She had lost her appetite, and nothing tasted good to her. The duke on the other hand ate heartily of roast beef, Yorkshire pudding, salmon broiled with dill sauce, green beans, bread, butter, cheese, and a caramel custard. The innkeeper had a surprisingly good supply of good French Bordeaux, and Quinton Hunter drank three goblets down with his meal.

The next morning they departed early after a hearty country breakfast that Allegra picked at while her husband ate, as she put it, "like a field hand." The inn-keeper provided them with a basket for luncheon. They stopped to rest the horses at noon, and by two o'clock were on the road again. At four as they were about to pass by a rather prosperous-looking inn a man ran out and flagged them down.

"Duke of Sedgwick?" he asked.

"I am the Duke of Sedgwick," Quinton Hunter said, sticking his head from the carriage.

"Lord Morgan has sent ahead, Your Grace. We have your accommodations and your own prime cattle wait-ing in the stables. Lord Morgan asks that his men be al-lowed to return his horses tomorrow. If you'll turn in, and come this way, my lord." The man swung about, and taking the harnesses of the lead horses escorted the duke's coach into the innyard.

"How thoughtful," Allegra said sourly.

"She's in a right evil mood," Honor murmured softly to Hawkins as they descended the carriage. "I've never seen her this way, and I've been with her since she was a child."

"Spoilt rotten she is," Hawkins pronounced.

"You keep on like that, and I'll not wed you," Honor snapped.

"You have to now that I've put that baby in yer belly," Hawkins grinned wickedly. "As soon as we gets back to Hunter's Lair, my girl!"

"Shut yer gob, Peter Hawkins! That's all she needs to know, that I'm having a baby and she ain't! You say one word, and I swear, I'll kill you!"

"Don't know how long you can keep it a secret, lass," he said.

"Long enough if I have to," Honor replied.

"She don't deserve you, lass," the valet said softly.

*   *   *

Another day's travel, and they finally reached
Hunter's Lair. They had been gone for two months, having left in the dead of winter to go up to London. Now,
however, spring was here. The hillsides about them
were green, and awash with golden daffodils. The trees
in the orchards were beginning to look alive, their buds
swelling. Several of the duke's mares had foaled, and the
youngsters were already turned out into the fields during the day with their dams. The house looked wonderful in the late afternoon light, the sun turning the
windows facing west a luscious red and gold like
molten fire.

Allegra felt herself actually cheering up at the sight of
her home. She smiled to herself, and the duke was heart-
ened when he saw that small smile, and the pleasure in
her eyes. Reaching out, he took her gloved hand in his
and gave it a little squeeze. Her eyes met his, and she
smiled again.

"I never want to leave here," she told her husband.

"Neither do I," he said. "We shall be as snug as two
bugs in a rug forever, my darling duchess."

Crofts came forth from the house to greet them.
"Welcome home, Your Graces," he said warmly. "I
have a message for you that came this morning from
Viscount Pickford. The footman who brought it says
Lady Sirena has had her baby." He handed Allegra the
sealed packet.

Allegra took it, and quickly broke open the seal. Her
eyes flew over the page, her smile widening. Then she
looked up at Quinton. "It's a boy!" she told him.
"George Octavius William, and we are his godparents.
Is the footman still here?" she asked Crofts.

"No, Your Grace, I sent him back. We did not know
when to expect you," Crofts told his mistress.

Her face fell, but then she brightened. "I need time to write to Sirena. I shall send one of our people over in the morning. Perhaps we shall go ourselves, Quinton. A little boy! How happy they must be," Allegra said almost wistfully.

"You must rest for several days," the duke told her. "A winter in London, followed by our recent adventures, and all this travel make it very necessary for you to take your ease for a short while. I do not want you getting sick, Allegra." He took her hand up and kissed it tenderly. "Remember, Duchess, we have work to do yet if we are to catch up with Sirena and Ocky."

Allegra smiled sadly, pulling her hand away from him. "I shall go, and write to Sirena now so that it may go off first thing in the morning."

They ate their dinner in silence. Allegra had to admit that she was tired. They climbed into bed together, and he cuddled her in his arms, kissing the top of her head, but he knew instinctively that she was not in the mood to make love. Allegra, the duke understood, needed, as her stepmother had said, to come to terms with what was happening. He slept soundly in his bed, awakening to find the sun streaming into the chamber, and Allegra gone from their bed. He called to her, but received no answer. He pulled on the bell cord.

"Good morning, Your Grace!" Hawkins answered his summons almost immediately.

"Has the duchess gone down to breakfast?" he asked his valet.

"No, my lord. Her Grace ran off at first light. I believe Honor said she was going to visit the viscountess and the new baby."

"Damnation!" The word slipped out before he could prevent it, and he saw Hawkins hide a smile. He turned the subject. "When are you and Honor getting married?"

"Three weeks, Your Grace," the valet answered. "The banns have got to be read. And it won't be a moment too soon, if you gets my drift, my lord." He winked at his master.

"Good lord!" the duke exclaimed as his valet's words sunk into his sleep-befogged brain.

"Honor says we can't tell Her Grace, my lord, but I thought you ought to know," Hawkins said.

"Yes," the duke agreed, "but Her Grace will know eventually, won't she, Hawkins?"

"Aye, sir, but 'tis to be hoped that Her Grace will, by then, be in the family way herself," came the reply. Then Hawkins actually blushed. "Begging your pardon, my lord."

Quinton Hunter waved his hand. " 'Tis all right, Hawkins. Are my clothes and shaving gear laid out in the dressing room?"

"Aye, sir."

"Then see that there is something for me to eat, and then go to the stables and have my stallion saddled. I'll have to ride over to the Earl of Pickford's estate after my breakfast," the duke told his valet. He climbed from his bed, lifting his nightshirt to pee in the chamber pot that Hawkins held out for him.

He dressed, and after a hearty breakfast, rode out. He didn't know whether to be angry at Allegra or not. She was exhausted, he knew. Their adventure in France, for all the ease with which they had accomplished their mission to rescue the Comtesse d'Aumont, had been harrowing. She was distressed by her father and stepmother's news, and equally upset that she was not having a child yet. But she would. Of that he was quite certain. They would have children if he could but make love to her again.

It was a beautiful spring day. The air held a hint of

warmth. The flowers bloomed on the roadside. The meadows were filled with lambs who gamboled and chased one another while their dams baaed fretfully. It was the kind of spring day that poets wrote odes about, he thought. He reached Pickford Hall in midmorning, was shown into a morning room, and offered wine, which he declined.

"Have you seen him?" Viscount Pickford demanded by way of greeting his oldest friend as he entered the room.

"I have only just arrived," the duke said, amused.

"Allegra said you wouldn't be coming probably for several days," Ocky said.

"I told Allegra not to come for several days," the duke replied. "Has she told you of our adventures in France?"

"*France?*" Viscount Pickford was astounded. "No. What the hell were you doing in Froggieland, Quint? And Allegra was with you?"

"And Marcus, Eunice, Adrian, and Caroline, too. And did I mention that Allegra's maid, Honor, speaks rather good French?" he concluded with a chuckle. Then he added, "But first I would see your heir."

"Damn you, sir, I cannot refuse my son's godfather his first glimpse, but then you are going to sit down and tell me everything," Viscount Pickford declared.

"Agreed," the duke answered his friend. "Where is my wife, by the way?"

"With Sirena. Allegra has cooed Georgie to death, and now is gossiping with my wife. She looks tired, not at all at her best, I fear."

The duke followed his friend up the stairs to the nursery where he was given a peek at his three-day-old godson, a plump pink and white lump of infant with a tuft of pale golden hair. The baby opened a pair of rather bright blue eyes to observe his visitor, and then closed them again, as if to say, I don't find you important to my existence right now, and so you are dismissed.

The duke chuckled with amusement.

"Who do you think he looks like?" the viscount demanded to know.

"He looks like an old gentleman right now," the duke responded, "so I suppose we could say he looks like your father. I assume the earl is pleased with your first efforts."

"Over the moon," Ocky said with a grin as they left the nursery to return to the morning room.

"And Sirena is recovering from her ordeal?"

"She carried him like a prize mare, and birthed him like a woman in the fields. It was amazing! That dainty little slip of a girl I've wed. The doctor said he had never seen anything like it. Says she can go on breeding for years to come."

"It must run in the family," the duke said as they entered the morning room again and sat down.

"What on earth do you mean?" the viscount queried.

"This is for your ears alone, Ocky. You cannot tell Sirena until her mother does. Lady Morgan is expecting a baby in May," the duke said, and then laughed aloud at the look on his friend's face.

Finally Ocky said, "You are jesting, of course."

Quinton Hunter shook his head in the negative.

"Damn me if that doesn't beat all," the viscount said. "That's why she hasn't been about in recent months, isn't it? Is she all right?"

"Other than being as big as a sow about to litter, she seems to be. Allegra, however, is very upset by this turn of events."

"Of course she would be," Ocky said. "She is now no

longer her father's heiress. She will have to share with her new sibling, and if it is a boy, her portion will be greatly cut."

"I don't care," the duke said, "but my wife does not believe that. She is now desperate to have an heir. She sees her failure to do so as some sort of flaw on her part. She is quite angry."

"Tell me about France," the viscount replied. "What the hell were you all doing in France?"

"Ahh, Ocky, you and Sirena missed a grand adventure. It was quite mad of us. I knew it before we set off, and in retrospect I realize how damned lucky we all were to get back alive." Then he went on to elucidate to his friend the tale of the Comtesse d'Aumont's plight, and how they had rescued her, her children, the fierce old Thérèse, and Céline. "If we had been caught we would have all faced the guillotine. Especially as the old cook murdered the head of the Committee for Public Safety in St. Jean Baptiste, though I doubt he'll be missed. The local priest saw to the disposal of his body, and forgave the cook her sin." He chuckled.

"I would have liked to have been with you," the viscount said.

"We thought about you the entire time," the duke teased his best friend.

"The hell you did," Ocky laughed. "You were far too busy making certain none of you were caught. Imagine Allegra's little maid taking charge like that, and pulling it off. She's a game gel, Honor is. I was never very good with French, though you certainly are."

"Is Sirena up to seeing me? And then I must collect my wife, and return home. I would imagine Sirena cannot take too much company, and is probably too nice to send Allegra away."

The Duchess of Sedgwick looked surprised to see her husband as he entered the viscountess's bedchamber. The duke went over to Sirena, kissed her upon the forehead, and said, "He is an absolutely lovely boy, my dear Sirena. You have done well for yourself, and for Ocky."

"It was an easy birth," Sirena admitted.

"So Ocky tells me," was the reply.

"I think Doctor Thatcher was rather surprised," Sirena said with a smile, and a little twinkle in her eye. "Oh, Quinton, I have had such a lovely visit with Allegra."

"But now you are ready to rest, I am certain, my dear. Allegra also needs her rest, but nothing could prevent her from coming immediately to see you. You will let us know when the baby's christening is to be set? Come, madame, we have a long ride home."

"I thought I should stay a few days with Sirena," Allegra responded surlily. "After all, Quinton, I have not seen my cousin in several months, and we have a great deal to catch up on, sir."

"Birthing an infant, no matter how quick the process, is difficult, Allegra," the duke told his wife. "Sirena needs to rest." He reached out and clamped his hand about her upper arm. "Come, my darling girl."

Her look was one of complete outrage, but she obeyed. "I shall be back," she told Sirena.

"Eventually," the duke said, and then led his wife from the room, almost forcibly.

"I should have thought to ask Allegra to remain," Sirena said. "Run after them, Ocky, and tell them."

"No, my dearest, Allegra must go home," the viscount said to his surprised wife. Then he sat down next to her. "Let me tell you what your cousin and our friends have been doing." He then proceeded to regale her with the tale of the Bellinghams' niece and her family. He finished by saying, "They have just returned from

France via London. Allegra is exhausted, but refuses to admit it. Quint wants to get her home so she may rest. You can see how washed out she is, sweetheart."

"But it was so wonderful to see her," Sirena said, "especially since Mama has not come. I do not understand it. Do you think something has happened to Mama, and Steppapa doesn't want to tell me for fear of harming our baby? Well, the baby is born and healthy, and I have sent to Mama two days ago and have no answer. You must go to Morgan Court tomorrow, Ocky, and bring my mother back to me."

"I think that is an excellent idea, sweetheart," the viscount answered his wife. "I shall start in the morning." He kissed her gently. "Go to sleep now, Sirena." Then he left her bedchamber, and hurried downstairs, just catching the duke and Allegra. "Quinton," he called. "Sirena wants to see her mama. What am I to do?"

"*You told him?*" Allegra's voice was icy.

"I thought it necessary," the duke said.

"Must the entire world know that my ancient stepmother is having a baby, and I am not?" Allegra demanded.

"You had best tell Sirena so she doesn't fret, and you do not have to take the long ride to Morgan Court," the duke advised.

"No. I shall tell her," Allegra cried, and dashed back up the stairs to her cousin's bedchamber.

Sirena was just dozing off. She sat up as Allegra slammed into her room. "Wh . . . what is it?" she said, startled. "Oh, Allegra, you have come back, dearest."

"I just came to tell you that Aunt Mama will not be coming to see you immediately. Quinton and I stopped at Morgan Court on our way back from London. Your mother is expecting a baby in May, Sirena. Isn't it awful? I didn't want you to be as embarrassed as I am over this state of affairs, but I also didn't want you to worry as to why she was not here with you and her grandson, where she should be," Allegra finished in a self-righteous tone.

"Mama is to have a baby?" Sirena's face shone with a mixture of amazement and delight. "Ohh, Allegra how wonderful! Now we shall be truly bound not just by our mother's blood, but by our little half sibling. How is she? Is she all right? What incredible news you have brought me, dearest. Ocky! Do you know? Mama is to have a baby."

"Yes," Allegra suddenly burst out bitterly. "*A baby.* A child who will take away my inheritance, and make Quinton hate me for not being the richest girl in England. But did our parents consider that when they fornicated like two dogs on the road? No. All they thought about was themselves, and not my happiness. You have a baby, Sirena. Now your mother is to have a baby, but I cannot seem to have a baby!" Then bursting into tears Allegra ran from the room and down the stairs.

Quinton Hunter followed after his wife, watching her as she dashed out the front door of Pickford Hall and mounted her horse. He watched as she kicked the beast into a canter and rode away. The groom holding his mount helped him up, and flipping a coin at the man, the duke followed after his wife. He was torn between the desire to kiss her, to comfort her, and to spank her soundly. She had sounded like nothing more than a spoiled brat, and he was frankly amazed. What had happened to the logical and practical young woman he had married? He encouraged his horse to a faster gait in order to catch up, or at least keep apace of Allegra.

Sirena had climbed from her bed, and gone to her window to watch her cousin tear off in a temper. "I did not consider that this might upset her," she said slowly. "Lord, I have been thoughtless."

"I think it is Allegra who has been inconsiderate, and heedless," the viscount said to his wife.

"No, Ocky, don't say that. You do not understand. Allegra and her brother, James Lucian, were devoted to each other. Until a few years ago she wasn't the richest girl in England, nor did she care if she was. Then her brother was killed in France. It is not the money that disturbs my cousin, but the thought that her father could replace James Lucian with another son."

"Did she not say to you that now Quinton wouldn't love her?" Ocky said stubbornly.

"Certainly she knows better than that," Sirena replied with a small smile. "But you will recall that Quinton Hunter with his bluer than blue blood made a match with Allegra first because she was the richest heiress in England. Allegra doesn't really understand the nature of true love so how can she believe, even if he says it, that her husband truly loves her, and would love her even if she were poor? And there is the matter of an heir for Sedgwick, Ocky. Suddenly that becomes most paramount for Allegra for she is faced with the loss of probably half or more of her fortune, or value. Of course she is angry and upset."

"What can we do to help?" Viscount Pickford wondered aloud.

"We can do nothing," Sirena said quietly. "It is now up to Quinton Hunter to convince his wife that no matter what happens he will love her forever and a day, and even beyond. It will not be an easy, or a simple task." Sirena watched as the duke rode after Allegra. She could but imagine how her beloved cousin felt right now. Lost. Bereft. And she was correct about one thing. It really was embarrassing that her own mother was having a baby at this time in her life, although, Sirena thought, I will never say it. I will be happy for Mama, and Steppapa. Then she giggled to herself. She would have never imagined that Olympia Abbott Morgan was still interested, and obviously if one was to believe Allegra, very interested in matters of the flesh. But she and Lord Morgan obviously were.

"What's so funny?" her husband asked Sirena.

"I thought how amusing that at their ages Mama and Steppapa would still be being naughty. I did not realize one's interest could last *that* long," Sirena answered her husband. "Do you think we shall still be interested in being naughty when we are their age, Ocky?"

"I certainly hope so, my darling girl," the viscount replied. "I certainly hope so!"

Chapter Seventeen

"I want to go up to London," Allegra told her husband.

"We have just come back from London," he replied calmly. Living with his bride of six months had not been very easy these past few weeks.

"Nevertheless, Quinton, I wish to go. I am bored here. I have nothing to do. If you do not wish to come, I will understand," she responded coldly.

A message had come this morning from Aston, he knew. "You have heard from Eunice?" he attempted to change the subject.

"Yes," she said shortly.

"She is well, and Marcus, too?" He tried to elicit more information from her than she seemed willing to share with him.

"They are both well. Why wouldn't they be? She is expecting a child. She says Caroline believes she is with child, too. I, however, am not expecting a child, and I wish to go up to London. If you really loved me you would not question my motives, Quinton. I repeat. I am bored here in the country. I may even want to go to Brighton this summer. I obviously have nothing in common with my friends any longer. Why would I? They are fertile, and I, it would appear, am barren."

"If you wish to go up to London for a few weeks," he told her, "then I see no reason why you should not. I, however, must remain here at Hunter's Lair, Allegra. I have an estate to manage. And we cannot go to Brighton this year. I want you home, Allegra. I know that you are shocked by the fact your father and his wife are expecting a baby. You need time to come to terms with it. So if going to London is what you want to do, go. You shall not conceive an heir for me if we are apart, but that is your choice, my dear."

He was angry at her. He couldn't help himself. Allegra had become a self-pitying little bitch these past few weeks. He had done everything, he thought, to reassure her of his love, but for some reason he could not fathom, she didn't believe him. It was irritating to say the least. What was the matter with her?

"I'll tell Honor to pack a trunk, and be gone tomorrow," Allegra said. "I will not need much for I intend having Madame Paul make me an entire new wardrobe."

"She made you one seven months ago," he reminded her.

Allegra shrugged. "I thought while I still have the ready, Quinton, I would have a fashionable wardrobe made. When Papa's new child comes along there will be little for me."

"You do not know that," he almost shouted. "Until a few years ago you had a brother, James Lucian, and your father denied you nothing," the duke told her.

"This will be a boy," Allegra said angrily. "I just sense it. He will become Papa's heir, and I will have little. Papa is besotted with his new wife. She will influence him, and her first interest will be for her son, and not for me. Do you not understand, Quinton? You bartered your good name, and now you have been cheated."

"I love you!" he shouted at her. "I have not been cheated, damnit! I am only cheated if you run away to London and do not stay by my side where you belong, Allegra." He caught her by her shoulders. "Do you not understand, my darling duchess. *I love you.*"

"You are kind," she said, tears welling up in her violet eyes, "but you cannot possibly want me now, Quinton."

"I have wanted you since the moment I first saw you, Allegra," he insisted. "I want you now, and I don't give a damn about your father's wealth. *I love you. I want you.*" And then he was kissing her passionately, his hands moving beneath her chamber robe to caress her slender body. His palms cupped her buttocks, and pulled her close. She moaned softly in his embrace, unable to help herself from pressing against him. His lips slid down her throat. He pushed her robe off, and kissed her breasts. He knelt before her, his mouth engraving a line of hot kisses down her torso. He could feel her trembling beneath his lips. He pulled her down upon the floor before the fireplace. His knee nudged her soft thighs open.

"Tell me you don't want me, too, my darling duchess," he murmured hotly against her kiss-swollen lips. *"Tell me!"*

"No," she replied softly. "I won't tell you that because it isn't true, and you know it. *I love you, Quinton.*" She opened herself to him, and cried out with pleasure as he entered her body. "Ahh, yes, my darling! Yes!"

She was warm, and welcoming. He buried himself as deep as he could within her luscious body. Her hips met his in rhythmic splendor. Slowly he withdrew from her, then he plunged again, and again, and again until he was dizzy with his passion for her, and she for him. When his desire for her finally burst and mushroomed into a bloom of incredible pleasure, he thought he would die from the excess of it. "I love you," he cried. "I love you, Allegra. Do not leave me."

*W*hen he awoke in the morning, still before the embers of the dying fire, she was gone, and he cursed to himself that she did not believe enough in his love to trust him. Yet she must care, he thought, noting the down coverlet had been taken from the bed and carefully tucked about him. Scrambling up he yanked at the bellpull.

"Yes, Your Grace?" Hawkins had answered his summons rather quickly, the duke thought.

"When did Her Grace leave for London?" he asked his valet.

"About an hour ago, my lord," Hawkins said grimly.

"She took Honor?" God, had she not remembered her maid's wedding was to be celebrated on Sunday?

"She did," Hawkins said sourly.

"Damnation!" the duke swore softly, and then he said to his valet, "I am sorry, Hawkins, but they'll be back."

"It had better be sooner than later," the valet told his master.

"I know," the duke said. "When does Honor believe the baby is due, Hawkins?"

"Late autumn, my lord. You would have thought that Honor would tell Her Grace now that we are to be wed," Hawkins despaired.

"Do not be angry at Honor, old friend," the duke advised his valet. "She has been with her mistress since Allegra was a child. Her loyalty to the duchess is very great as is yours to me."

"If the parson had already said the words over us I should not worry so much," Hawkins told his master. "I don't want anyone thinking my Honor a loose woman. What happens when her belly begins to show?"

"They will be back long before then, Hawkins, I am certain of it. Her Grace is frightened by her father's new child. She believes I shall not love her because she is not the richest girl in England any longer," the duke explained.

"Bloody silly, if you ask me," Hawkins muttered. "You loves Her Grace, and any fool can plainly see it."

"So I am told," Quinton Hunter said with a smile. "Her Grace will go to London, and when she has had time to consider, she will realize how ridiculous it is to believe I should not love her because she is no longer her father's only heir. They will be back quickly, for as you recall, Her Grace does not really like the city at all."

𝒩o, she didn't like London. It was dirty, and noisy, and crowded; but it wasn't Hunter's Lair. Marker was very surprised to see her, especially without her husband. Charles Trent raised an eyebrow, but made no other comment than to welcome her return to Berkley Square. The new social season was beginning, and a fresh crop of debutantes was arriving to embark on the husband hunt. She called on Lady Bellingham.

"My dear gel, I had not thought to see you back in town for some time to come," Lady Bellingham said. She was quite her old self now that her niece had been rescued.

"I should like a voucher for Almack's," Allegra told her old patroness.

Clarice Bellingham's warm gray eyes scanned Allegra's beautiful face. It was obvious that she was distressed and running away from something. It was impossible not to probe. "Will you need one for Quinton?" she asked casually.

"My husband is not in town, nor do I expect him," Allegra replied, swallowing back her tears.

"My dear gel, what has happened?" Lady Bellingham burst out, unable to restrain herself. "Surely you are not estranged?"

"My father and Aunt Mama are having a baby. I shall no longer be the richest girl in England, madame. My husband has been cheated. I could not remain at Hunter's Lair under the circumstances. Sirena has had a little boy for Pickford. Caroline and Eunice are breeding, but I am not. I have proved a bad bargain for Sedgwick. I have come to London to think."

Lady Bellingham put a hand over her mouth to stifle her cry of astonishment. "Septimius and Olympia are breeding? You are certain?"

"Madame, I saw my father and his wife but a few weeks ago. She is quite full with her child which shall come in mid-May," Allegra answered in a tight little voice.

"Gracious me," Lady Bellingham responded. "Who would have thought that Olympia and Septimius would have a child between them at their ages, bless me. And of course your father's wealth will now be divided, but has your husband said that he is disappointed, dear gel?"

"He says he loves me, and that it doesn't matter." Allegra began to sob. "But of course it matters. My wealth was offered to him in exchange for his name. It is a good name, Lady Bellingham, a proud and honorable name that even eclipses the king's lineage."

"Has your father said that he is cutting you off, dear gel?"

"No," Allegra wailed. "He says that he and my husband must renegotiate the terms of our marriage after his child is born. A boy, however, will be given the lion's portion. My worth to my husband will be nothing now." And she wept into her hands.

Lady Bellingham considered for several long moments while Allegra cried piteously. Finally she said, "I believe you are mistaken, my dear gel. I have known Quinton Hunter for his entire life. He is proud of his heritage, and it is true he sought a rich wife, but I know he loves you dearly. Your father's wealth is so great that even if you were given but a third of it, you should still be a very rich woman. But Quinton would love you nonetheless, my dear gel, even if you had nothing."

"How can you believe that?" Allegra wailed.

"Because for all his bluster last season about not falling in love, Quinton Hunter did just that. He fell in love with you. The fact that your papa settled an incredible amount on you no longer makes any difference. But Septimius Morgan will not cut you off. He will, I am certain, see you and Quinton have a most handsome allowance. Certainly far better than other young couples. You are being quite silly. Now dry your eyes. You can trust your husband. Spend a few days in London amusing yourself, and then go home, dear gel."

"You really think it will be all right?" Allegra sniffed. "Oh, dear Lady Bellingham, I do not know what is the matter with me these days!"

"Why, you are breeding, dear gel. Didn't you realize it?" the older woman replied. "You are at least two months gone, I should guess. And," she concluded quite archly, "I am very good at guessing."

"*What?*" Allegra was truly astounded. It wasn't possible!

"You are breeding, dear child," Lady Bellingham repeated. "You are going to have a baby."

"I can't be," Allegra cried.

"And why not? You do have normal relations with

your husband, don't you? Of course you do. And when was the last time you had any show of blood? Think!"

Allegra clapped a hand over her mouth. "Ohhhh!" she gasped.

"Women who are breeding are often given to foolish fancies, my dear gel," Lady Bellingham said calmly. "And more often than not they do not see the forest for the trees. It probably happened just before you went to France." She smiled a kindly smile, and reaching out, patted Allegra's hand. "Rest a few days from your journey, and then return home. I believe your husband will be very happy to learn your news."

"I should be certain," Allegra said slowly.

"I shall send Doctor Bradford to see you tomorrow morning. He has looked after me for years, and is most discreet," Lady Bellingham told her guest. "Now, shall we have some tea?"

"Yes, please," Allegra said. "And cake, too, I hope."

Lady Bellingham laughed. "Of course, dear gel. Of course."

Allegra returned to her father's house to discover she had a visitor.

"My dear duchess, I will admit to being most surprised at hearing you were back in town," George Brummell said as he kissed her hand.

"It was a whim, sir, but now that I am here, I believe I shall return home within the week. Quinton could not come. Something about the horses and a breeding schedule," she replied airily.

"Well then, if your duke is not about to escort you around, dear duchess, I hope you will allow me to be your cicisbeo while you are here. I am going to a delicious new gambling hell tonight, and while I understand you do not gamble, you must come with me, and be seen."

"Why, sir, I do believe that I shall accept your invitation, and while I do not as a rule gamble, I might join you tonight in that wicked vice," Allegra laughed. "Where are we going?"

"It is in St. James, Your Grace, and quite new. It has been opened by an Italian gentleman. He claims to have fled Venice in advance of a French general, Bony-part. The place is most cosmopolitan with émigrés from France and Italy, as well as the crème de la crème of the ton. We shall probably meet Prinny there. Shall I call for you at ten?"

"That would be perfect, Mr. Brummell. I have never before experienced the wicked life here in London," Allegra said. "Perhaps I should, just once before I return to the country." She smiled at him, and gave him her hand to kiss.

He did so, and smiling in return said, "Until tonight, Your Grace."

"*N*either your husband, nor your father would approve of you gambling, Your Grace," Charles Trent said quietly as he stepped from the door of his personal billet.

"I shall want a thousand pounds, Charles," Allegra told her father's secretary. "I shall not, I promise you, lose any more than that. I am not addicted to gambling, and have self-control."

"No one is addicted at first, Your Grace, but the lure of the games is irresistible. Go with Mr. Brummell if you will, but take your own carriage. That way you are free to return home whenever you desire."

Allegra nodded in agreement. She valued Charles

Trent's advice, but just this once she would do something impractical and wicked. *Just once*. Then she would return home to Hunter's Lair to tell her husband that she was breeding, and would deliver him an heir before year's end. *If* Dr. Bradford confirmed Lady Bellingham's conclusion. She hurried upstairs.

She wore black and silver, and carried an ermine muff that had a ruby and diamond pin fastened to it. Her jewelry was also rubies and diamonds, including a hair ornament nestling within her smooth elegant chignon, which was not at all fashionable, but which suited her quite well as Mr. Brummell observed. At her suggestion he released his own hired coach, helping Allegra into her vehicle. Then giving the coachman directions, he joined her. Within a very short time they arrived at St. James, the carriage stopping before a well-kept house that was all alight at every window. They stepped from the coach.

"Good heavens, isn't that the Duchess of Devonshire?" Allegra asked, staring at the very beautiful woman just now entering the mansion.

"Indeed it is," Mr. Brummell replied. "I understand that she has already gone through her allowance for the year. Several hundred thousand pounds, I am told. She is not a lucky gambler, I fear."

"Where does she get the ready to gamble with then?" Allegra wondered.

"The moneylenders, friends, relations, sometimes even strangers," Mr. Brummell replied. "She is quite charming, and people tend to like her, so they indulge her terrible vice, even though most of them know they haven't a chance of regaining what they have loaned."

He escorted her up the two marble steps into Casa di Fortuna. Footmen, attired in sky blue and gold silk livery, and wearing powdered wigs, took their outer garments. Others offered them wine in exquisite Venetian crystal goblets.

"What shall we play first?" Allegra asked him. "I have never been to a gambling hell, and I am entirely in your hands, Mr. Brummell."

"I suppose you play Whist," he said.

"I do, but I have also learned a new game with dice that is called Hazard. Do they play Hazard here?"

"Perhaps later, Your Grace," he said, guiding her to a large ornate room where there were many players at many tables, playing Whist. Mr. Brummell seated her at a table that was just being opened up, and placed himself opposite her. They were quickly joined by a Lord and Lady Kenyon. They played for an hour, and to her surprise Allegra won each and every hand. Finally she grew bored, and stood up.

"I have enjoyed your company," she told Lord and Lady Kenyon. "Come Brummell, and let me see what else Casa di Fortuna has to offer us tonight." She stuffed her winnings in her muff, and moved on into another room where a wheel game was being played. "What is it called?" she asked her escort, curiously.

"Even-Odd, or E.O.," he said.

"Let's play," Allegra told him, enthusiastically.

"This is not a good game, Your Grace," he advised. "The odds in this game are usually very much in favor of the house. It is, in fact, illegal, although many of the hells have it."

"Three spins of the wheel, Mr. Brummell, and then we shall move on to the Hazard tables," Allegra promised. Then she bet on the next three turns of the wheel, and to everyone's surprise won all three turns. "How boring," she remarked, and stuffed her additional winnings into her muff once again.

Brummell was astounded. Because Allegra did not

gamble she did not realize that she was having an extremely lucky night. She wanted to play Hazard. Well, he thought, why not, and he led her into another room where the game was being played. The players stood about the green baize table watching and waiting until the caster threw crabs, and lost. Such play was a bit rich for Brummell's blood and so he stood behind the Duchess of Sedgwick as she waited her turn. Next to her stood an equally beautiful woman, who noting Allegra's rather good diamonds, smiled and said, "I am the Contessa di Lince. Do you come here often?"

"It is my first, and probably last time," Allegra said with a small smile. "I am the Duchess of Sedgwick."

"You do not like it?" the lady said.

"I do not gamble as a rule, and my husband would be very angry with me if he knew I was here. He does not approve of gambling," Allegra explained to the lady. "You are English, and yet you have an Italian title, madame."

"Yes," the contessa replied, returning Allegra's smile. "I was born in England, but my late husband was Italian. I have returned because it is impossible to live decently in *Roma* right now with those damned French overrunning the countryside. I have taken a small house in Hanover Square. Gambling is a form of amusement for me, but offers little challenge for I rarely lose. The proprietor of this place likes me to come for I make it appear that people win," the lady laughed.

The dice were now passed to the contessa, but with a smile she handed them to Allegra. "I will only win," she said shrugging her elegant shoulders.

Allegra began to play, and once again she was overcome with luck. Soon the table at which she played was surrounded by admiring gamblers watching as she won toss after toss of the dice. Finally with a laugh she said,

"I must stop. My muff will not hold all my winnings."
She handed the dice to the next players, and turned to
the contessa. "Shall we have champagne, madame?
Brummell, do be a dear and fetch some champagne for
the three of us. We shall seat ourselves in the foyer."

They found a quiet corner, and settled themselves
upon a satin striped settee.

"Are you always so lucky, Your Grace?" the contessa
asked.

"I don't know," Allegra said honestly. "I have, as I
said, never spent an evening gambling."

"But you play cards, and you knew how to play Hazard," the contessa noted.

"We all learn to play Whist. Didn't you as a girl? As
for Hazard, my friends and I cajoled their husbands into
teaching us, but I have never before played for the
ready."

"Your husband is not in town?" the contessa inquired
of Allegra.

"No," she replied. "He doesn't like London. Quinton
is a country gentleman."

"But you do like the city and its highlife?" the contessa pressed. "Ah, I was once like that, too. My first
husband was a rather dull fellow, I fear."

"No, no!" Allegra said. "I don't like London at all,
but we argued, and so I came up to town. However, after I spoke with my friend, Lady B., I realized how foolish I have been. I will go home in another day,
madame."

"Then you love him," the contessa remarked. "One
must love truly and passionately to become so angry. I
never felt that with my first husband, but with my second it was a different matter altogether." She smiled
softly. "True love is a precious commodity, Your Grace.
Treasure it. You are most fortunate."

"I was certainly lucky tonight," Allegra replied with a grin.

"You have had beginner's luck as they say," the contessa remarked smiling. "Ah, here is your friend with our champagne." She took a goblet from Mr. Brummell, and sipped thirstily. "Delicious! Carlo has exquisite taste in wines."

"Carlo?" Allegra looked puzzled.

"Carlo Bellagio, the proprietor," Mr. Brummell explained.

"*Brummell! Brummell!* Is that you? Where have you been?" The prince had arrived with his entourage of friends.

"Your Highness," Brummell said, bowing. "I am the Duchess of Sedgwick's cicisbeo this evening."

Allegra stood and curtsied. "Your Highness."

"Thought you went back to the country, duchess," Prinny said.

"I had to come back into town for a few days, Your Highness, and with the Season beginning, how could I resist? Mr. Brummell invited me to come with him tonight. As I have never been in a gambling hell, I decided I would come. You know how Quinton disapproves of gambling," she concluded with a twinkle and a smile.

Prinny chuckled. "Did you lose very much, Duchess? I promise I shall not tell on you should I see the duke," he chortled.

"She won," Brummell said. "It would seem she cannot lose, Your Highness. Damndest thing I have ever seen."

"I am not a great sport, Your Highness," Allegra said. "I came prepared to lose no more than a thousand pounds, but it would seem I have won fourteen thousand pounds."

"Zounds, madame, you are indeed lucky," the prince exclaimed. Then he caught sight of the Contessa di Lince. "Introduce us, Brummell," he said. "Who is this most fetching creature?"

"The Contessa di Lince, Your Highness, a refugee from the armies of France," Brummell said.

"How d'you do, Contessa," Prinny said, kissing her hand.

The contessa curtsied. "I am honored, Your Highness," she said.

"You are English?"

"I married an Italian," the contessa replied.

"Who are your people?" Prinny demanded.

"You would not have known them, sir," the contessa replied. "Do you play Whist? I should be delighted to be your partner. Like the duchess, I do not lose." She smiled seductively at him.

"You'll join us, Duchess?" Prinny said.

"You must excuse me, sir, but I came up to London to see Doctor Bradford. I should not have stayed out quite so late as it is. Will you forgive me?" She smiled winningly.

The prince beamed from ear to ear. "*Is it?*" he said meaningfully. "Does your husband know, madame?"

"I shall not be certain until I have consulted with Doctor Bradford," Allegra replied, "but should he confirm my suspicions, sir, you will actually be the first to know." She curtsied to him.

"Zounds, madame! I am honored," Prinny said. "Send 'round to me tomorrow with word."

"I will, Your Highness," Allegra told him. Then she turned to George Brummell. "If you would like to remain, Mr. Brummell, you are free to do so. I shall send my carriage back for you."

"No need, madame, I shall see Brummell safely home," the prince told her, "but he must escort you to the door, of course."

"Thank you, Your Highness," Allegra curtsied again, then turned to the Contessa di Lince. "I doubt we shall meet again, madame, but I thank you for your company this evening."

"Whose daughter are you, my dear?" the contessa said. "All night you have seemed very familiar to me. Your parents have raised you well."

"I am the daughter of Lord Septimius Morgan," Allegra responded. Then she curtsied a final time. "Good night," she said, and taking Mr. Brummell's arm she departed Casa di Fortuna.

Behind her the Contessa di Lince's hand went to her heart. She grew pale for a moment, but quickly recovered herself. Turning to Prinny she said softly, "She did say Septimius Morgan, sir, did she not? The very rich nabob?"

"The same, madame. It was his wealth that gained the duchess her blue-blooded husband last season, although I understand that it is quite a love match," Prinny responded. Then he smiled toothily at the contessa, and took her arm. "Come, my dear, the tables await us."

"Who is her mother?" the contessa inquired.

"She was born to Lord Morgan's first wife, Lady Pandora Moore, youngest child of the old Duke of Arley. A proper trollop that one. The wench ran off with another man when her daughter was two. Lord Morgan only recently remarried," Prinny said.

"To whom?" the contessa asked as she was seated at a newly opened Whist table.

"His widowed sister-in-law of all things. The dowager of Rowley, Lady Olympia Abbott. Helped raised her niece, I am told, and the girl is quite fond of her they say," Prinny replied. "They came up to London last season, Lord Morgan, Lady Abbott, her youngest daughter, Lady Sirena, and Miss Morgan. When it was all over young Lady Abbott had snagged herself Viscount Pickford, and Miss Morgan was to marry the Duke of Sedgwick, which she did in the autumn. But enough gossip, my dear. Let us play cards now." He smiled about the table as two other players joined them, Lord Alvaney, and Brummell.

The following morning Doctor Bradford arrived at Berkley Square to examine the Duchess of Sedgwick. When he had completed his task he said to her, "Your Grace is indeed with child. Based upon the information that both you and your maid have given me, I would reckon that your child will be born in late November or early December, madame. Your maid will have her child earlier in the autumn I observe from her form now. Is that correct, girl?" he demanded of Honor.

"Yes, sir," she replied in a little voice.

"Thank you, Doctor Bradford," Allegra responded. "I am grateful for your consultation. I know how busy a gentleman you are with your fine reputation. Lady Bellingham has spoken highly of you."

"Thank you, madame. You are both strong young women, but it is my considered opinion that you get home as soon as possible, and that neither of you travels again until after your babies are born."

"We shall certainly follow your advice, Doctor Bradford," Allegra said calmly. "Honor, please show the doctor out, and sir, render your bill to my father's secretary, Mr. Charles Trent, here at this house."

The doctor bowed. "Most grateful, Your Grace," he said, and then he followed Honor from the duchess's apartments.

When the maidservant returned and saw the questioning look on her mistress's face, she said quietly, "Well, m'lady, me and Peter Hawkins was to have been married last Sunday."

"Ohh, Honor, why didn't you tell me instead of allowing me to drag you all the way up to London?" Allegra cried. "I should never forgive myself if something happened to you."

"You needed me," Honor said bluntly. "Haven't I always been there for you since you was six? And I certainly wasn't going to tell you in the terrible mood you was in that I was having a baby, too. Not on top of the news you got from your papa, Lady Eunice, and Lady Caroline."

Allegra put her arms about her maid, and hugged her hard. "Oh, Honor, I don't deserve your kindness and your friendship."

"That's what Hawkins says, but he just don't know you like I do," Honor told her mistress with a mischievous twinkle.

Allegra laughed, and then she said, "We will start home tomorrow."

"Before we've been to Vauxhall, m'lady?" Honor sounded very disappointed. "We talked about seeing Vauxhall on our travels up from the country. We ain't likely to get back to London any time soon."

"No," Allegra agreed, "that is true. I shall send around to Mr. Brummell, and if he is willing to take us to Vauxhall tonight then we shall return home the day after tomorrow."

Mr. Brummell sent word that both he and Prinny would be delighted to escort Her Grace, and Her

Grace's maidservant to Vauxhall that evening. They would come around at four o'clock for tea, and then on to the gardens afterward. Mr. Trent, informed of Her Grace's decisions, quickly dispatched a footman to ride ahead, and make the proper reservations at the best inns for his employer's daughter.

Marker served tea with his staff of footmen as if they did it all the time with the Prince of Wales as the guest of the house. At six o'clock they set off for Vauxhall where, Prinny said, they would meet with the Countess di Lince. Prinny had taken a fancy to the elegant older woman.

Vauxhall was a marvelous pleasure garden that had opened in the year 1661, following King Charles II's restoration. At first it could only be reached from the water. Located north of Kensington Lane, it now had another entrance in addition to its original entry to the west. The admission was currently two shillings, sixpence. Its popularity had survived for over one hundred thirty-five years because of the ever-changing variety of the exciting programs it offered the public, and of course, its five graveled promenades.

Each walk was tree- and bush-lined. The Grand Walk extended nine hundred feet from the entrance. It was thirty feet wide, and bordered with elm trees. The South Walk ran parallel to it, and was distinguished by three quite realistic archways with paintings of the ruins of the ancient city of Palmyra. Many who saw them believed them to be real. On gala nights the ruins were replaced by a Gothic Temple with an artificial fountain in its center. The South Walk was the same length and width as the Grand Walk.

To the left of the Grand Walk was the Hermit's Walk. On its right was a wilderness; on its left was a rural downs. Also running parallel to the Grand Walk and the South Walk was the Dark, or Lovers' Walk. It was quite narrow, and clandestine lovers were its most frequent guests. And finally crossing the four walks was the fifth, known as the Grand Cross Walk. It cut through the center of the gardens. The portion between the Grand Walk and the South Walk that was bound by it was called The Grove.

It was a most fashionable place in which to promenade, or to meet one's lover. This evening a concert was being held in The Grove, featuring the music of Mr. Handel and Mr. Haydn. Prinny and his party were comfortably ensconced in a supper box, which was next to The Grove. From there they could comfortably listen to the music while they were treated to an outrageously expensive supper of tiny chickens, paper-thin slices of ham and beef, pastry, and wines. The supper box was decorated with paintings by Francis Hayman. In their box the painting visualized a country scene in which simple folk were dancing about a maypole that had been set in the center of a green which was surrounded by picturesque thatched cottages.

At nine o'clock a bell was rung to indicate the famed Cascade was about to begin. An intermission was called for the concert. As it only lasted for fifteen minutes each night, and was constantly changed, they hurried from their supper box to see it. Tonight they viewed snowy peaked mountains from which a great waterfall tumbled over rocks into a frothy pool below. This was followed by a display of fireworks, and then they returned to their box to enjoy the rest of their concert.

"I ain't never seen anything that grand," Honor whispered to her mistress. It was not unusual that a servant be included in such an outing. The contessa had an elderly servant named Anna with her as well. Respectable women in the company of gentlemen not their husbands frequently traveled with a female servant.

"How long will you be in London, Your Grace?" the Contessa di Lince asked Allegra.

"We shall return home on Thursday," was the reply. "I must stop at my father's house on the way to Hunter's Lair. My stepmother is expecting a baby any day now."

"*Is she?*" The contessa looked a bit surprised. "Your father had other children?"

"I had a brother, James Lucian," Allegra said. "He was murdered in Paris during the Terror. He had gone there to marry a young lady. She and her family were arrested by the authorities. My brother would not leave her to die alone. He was very brave." Tears welled up in her eyes. "If my child is a son, perhaps I shall name him for my brother."

"You are expecting a baby?" the contessa said softly.

"Yes," Allegra confided. "That is why I must hurry home. I only came up to London to confirm my suspicions, and Lady Bellingham's physician, Doctor Bradford, has done just that. I am so happy, and my husband will be happy, too. We want a large family."

"Do you? I, myself, have never really enjoyed children, but now that my husband is dead, I regret what I have missed," the contessa said frankly. Then she turned to Prinny, smiling. "I hope we shall play cards again, Your Highness. I did so enjoy last evening."

"Indeed, madame, as I did," the prince responded. "And you were quite a lucky partner for me." He lowered his voice slightly. "My luck is not always as good as it was last night."

"I am at your service, Your Highness," the contessa said.

"I am happy to hear it, madame," Prinny replied, and his glance went to her décolletage. "Very happy, madame," he murmured.

George Brummell, a clever young man, had noted when the contessa turned away from Allegra, her eyes had been filled with tears. Curious, he thought, and then determined he would learn the reason why. As they left The Grove to promenade back to where their carriages awaited them, he spoke in low tones in flawless Italian to the contessa.

"Who are you really, madame? You are English, you say by birth. Who was your sire?"

She looked at him with bleak eyes, and then she murmured so low that only he could hear. "I was the youngest daughter of the Duke of Arley, Mr. Brummell. Please, I beg of you to keep my secret."

Brummell could not have been more surprised than he now was by her revelation. "You are the duchess's mother?"

"I am. I never expected to see England again, but that the French ravaged my villa outside of *Roma*. My husband died two years ago, and we had no children of our own. I will go back one day when the French have gone, of course, but for now I had nowhere else to come but England. I am financially safe for Giancarlo placed his funds with a family of bankers named Kira, who have branches all over Europe. I thought it was unlikely that I should meet anyone who once knew me. Even the prince does not remember me, and we met when he was a young boy. He attempted to put his hand down my dress even then. I slapped him. I will not slap him if he again attempts it." She gave him a rueful shrug. "I need friends, you understand."

He nodded. "Seeing her now, do you regret your actions, madame?" Brummell asked the contessa.

"No," she shrugged. "I fear I do not. I did not love my first husband. I did love my second. I wanted no one, nothing to come between us. I was fortunate he felt the same way. It is odd, however, to see my daughter grown. To know I am to be a grandmother. To realize my sister has taken my place. Still, I have lived my life the way I wanted to live it. Don't most people if they can? Yet, it saddens me that I have lost my only son. But how gallant he was, wasn't he? And as for my only surviving child, she is a lovely young woman, with beautiful manners, and an obvious intelligence. She has found love the first time, and I wish that she may always have it."

"You will not tell her who you are?" Brummell said.

"Of course not," the contessa explained. "While I did not want her, I nonetheless bore her, making her father happy, who for all my own feelings, is a good man. Even if she knew my identity, sir, all it could do would be to upset her. I am nothing to her, nor do I wish to be at this late date. Nonetheless, I am pleased to see what a fine young woman she has turned out to be."

"You are a realist, madame," Brummell said in English.

"Yes," she responded in the same language. "I have always known when to cut my losses. Now, if I can but teach that to your prince," she finished with a smile.

Brummell laughed.

They had reached the end of The Grand Walk, and were at its entrance. Prinny handed Allegra and Honor into her carriage. He bowed.

"I think I shall go to Casa di Fortuna with Brummell and the contessa, m'dear. You do not mind. You will give my regards to both your husband and your father."

"I will, Your Highness," Allegra said graciously. Then she pulled up the window of her carriage door, and the vehicle pulled away.

Chapter Eighteen

Alighting from her traveling coach, Allegra ran through the front door of her father's house, Morgan Court. "Papa! Papa!" she called excitedly.

The foyer was deserted. How odd, she thought. Then a young housemaid carrying two steaming kettles of water hurried by, followed by a footman carrying an armful of white clothes.

"*Stop,*" Allegra called to them, and, startled, they did. "Where is my father?" she demanded.

"Yer father?" The footman looked confused, but the housemaid said, "Dolt, 'tis his lordship's daughter."

Then the young woman turned to Allegra. "Lord Morgan is upstairs with his wife, Your Grace. Her ladyship is having her baby."

Allegra pushed past them both, and raced upstairs, going directly to the apartment she knew belonged to her aunt mama. Entering the salon she moved quickly into the bedchamber where Olympia was ensconced in her bed, looking pale, her forehead beaded with dots of moisture.

Seeing Allegra her face lit up with relief and surprise. "Darling girl, please take your father out of here so I may get on with the business of bearing our child. He will not leave me."

"I came to apologize, Aunt Mama," Allegra began.

"It is all right, Allegra. We will speak later after I have delivered your sibling," Olympia said. "Now please calm your papa."

"I will not leave you," Septimius Morgan said. He was too pale, and looked as if he had not slept in several nights. He wore no coat, and his shirt was half-unbuttoned, having no neckcloth. He ran an impatient hand through his thinning hair. "*I cannot leave you.*" He turned to his daughter. "Allegra, please explain to your stepmother that I will not go. That I love her, and must be by her side."

"But Papa, she doesn't want you here," Allegra said quietly. "Besides, how can you help her? You are more a distraction, I think."

"Very sensible," another male voice spoke. A gentleman of middle years came forward. He, too, was in his shirtsleeves. "Doctor Horace Pritchard, Your Grace. I believe your father could do with a good whiskey, and the equally comforting company of his daughter."

"Come, Papa." Allegra took her father's arm.

He pulled away, saying pleadingly, "But she will need me."

"*Septimius!* I have borne four children before this one, and all without the help of a husband," Olympia Morgan said humorously. "I love you, but in the name of God go away so I may have this child in peace. We will send down to you when we need you."

"Come along, Papa," Allegra gently cajoled him. "I have a great deal of news for you. I have just come from London."

"Allegra," the laboring woman called out. "Thank you, my dear. I do love you, even as I love your papa."

Allegra turned, and flashed her stepmother a warm smile. Then she escorted her father downstairs to his library. "Will you have a whiskey, Papa, or would you prefer wine?" she asked him.

He waved a hand at her. "Whatever is nearest to hand, my child," he told her. "Damnit, I want to be with Olympia."

"Papa, she is having a baby, and she is uncomfortable having you there in the room with her. You must accept her decision in the matter, and make it easier for her." She poured him a smoky dollop of whiskey into a Waterford glass, and handed it to him. "Here, Papa. This will, I am certain, calm your nerves."

Lord Morgan swallowed down half the whiskey in the glass. It roared into his stomach like molten lead, but then it spread its warmth through his limbs, and he decided that he felt better. He looked at his daughter who sat across from him in a matching wing chair sipping a tiny glass of sherry. "*London?* What were you doing in London, Allegra?"

"Running away," she told him frankly. "When I learned several weeks ago that Aunt Mama was having a child, I was quite astounded, and not just a little distressed. You had married me to Quinton Hunter on the basis that I was the richest girl in England. Now I was not to be, and worse, I could not seem to conceive a child. Sirena had had her little boy. Then I received word that Eunice and Caroline were expecting babies. I felt suddenly worthless. My fortune was apparently gone, and I could not even give my husband a child. I felt Quinton had been cheated by us all, Papa, and so I ran away to London."

"Does Quinton feel he has been cheated, Allegra?" Lord Morgan asked.

"He says he does not. He says if you never gave us another penny we would still live more than comfortably for the rest of our days. We have hardly touched what we have received to date, Papa. But it just didn't seem reasonable to me that he wouldn't feel cozened. He had bartered his blue blood for a fortune that was no longer there. I am afraid I was very foolish, Papa."

"What has made you change your mind, my dear?" Lord Morgan asked his daughter.

"Lady Bellingham. Dear Lady Bellingham. When I cried upon her shoulder she scolded me quite roundly for doubting Quinton, whom she has known his entire life. She said any fool could see that he loved me, Papa. And then she said that breeding women were given to vagaries and fancies. I was utterly shocked, but then . . ." Here Allegra stopped and blushed. "Well, she sent her doctor around the following day, and Papa! She was right. *I am having a baby!* It was then I realized what a fool I had been, and decided that I would stop on my way home to tell you and Aunt Mama the happy news, and to beg your forgiveness for my terrible words. Quinton is right, Papa. We do not need any more of your monies. Hunter's Lair is restored. The Kira Bank holds our funds safely. I have my investments. My husband loves me, and I love him. That, Papa, is the greatest gift we could receive." Then she began to weep happily as her father smiled, amused, having just a few months prior gone through the same sort of histrionics with his wife.

"You had best remain the night," Lord Morgan said. "I will send a footman over to Hunter's Lair to tell your husband that you are safe with us, Allegra."

"Yes, Papa." She sniveled happily.

*F*our days later the Duke of Sedgwick arrived at his father-in-law's home. He had been astounded when a footman had arrived at his home from Morgan Court. "Come along, Hawkins," he told his valet. "It would appear that our wives are back from London sooner than later as I predicted."

His wife ran to greet him as if they had not parted so oddly. "Quinton! Ohh, Quinton, I have the most wonderful news," she cried. Reaching him she flung her arms about him and kissed him soundly.

He had meant to be stern. A man could not allow his wife to behave as Allegra had behaved, but at the touch of her lips he melted. He kissed her back. "I am a fool," he said, looking down into her eyes. "You have acted badly, and I should exercise my husbandly rights and punish you, Allegra."

"Ohh, yes, my darling, you should," she agreed.

"Did you even get as far as London?" he demanded, suspicious of her charming and adorable mood.

"Oh, I did. I went to a gambling house with Prinny and Mr. Brummell, and then the next night I went to Vauxhall with them. It was lovely, Quinton. I couldn't do those things as a debutante, and we didn't do them when we were all in London last winter. It was very exciting, my darling, but that is not the best thing of all."

"How much did you lose, Allegra?" he demanded, his gray eyes suddenly icy.

She laughed. "Oh, Quinton, I am not such a turnip-head as that. I took a thousand pounds with me, and decided that when I had lost it I should come home. After all, I have no desire or passion for gambling. But the oddest thing happened. I could not lose. Whether it was at Hazard, or Whist, or E.O., I could not lose. I won over fourteen thousand pounds in a very short time. I think the proprietor of Casa di Fortuna was happy to see me leave," she finished, giggling.

"And what did you do with the monies you won, Allegra?" he asked, but his tone and his manner had softened.

"I gave it to Charles Trent to invest. When our eldest son is of age he shall have half of it for himself, and the other half we shall use for our eldest daughter's season and marriage portion," she told him with a smile. "I think the first son and the first daughter are always the most special. Oh," she said suddenly. "I have a new brother. He was born two days ago. They are calling him William Septimius James, and he is absolutely gorgeous! He looks just like Papa. My brother, James Lucian, never did you know. He favored our mother."

She was like a fountain, the words pouring forth from between her pretty lips. He felt his anger and suspicion dissolving.

"My marriage portion, of course, will be considerably constrained," she chattered on at him. "After all, Willy is the heir now, and I am just his elder sister. We shall not have five hundred thousand pounds a year anymore, Quinton. But did you not tell me it didn't matter?"

She was testing him, he knew. "It does not matter," he told her firmly. "The only thing I want of Lord Morgan is his daughter," he said.

"You are very sweet, my darling," she told him, "but not very practical. You shall receive one hundred thousand pounds each year, and I shall inherit a quarter of Papa's estate when he dies, which, God willing, will not be for many years. You will, however, have to give me my pin money out of that, Quinton, for I shall receive no other stipend. I do not need it as I have my own monies, and I have you for my husband." She smiled up at him proudly. "Have I made us a good bargain, husband?"

He nodded, slowly, surprised at how efficiently she had managed everything once again. Then he shook his head. Why was he surprised? From the moment he had agreed to marry her, Allegra had managed everything, and she was far more adept at it than he ever was. She would probably manage him for the rest of their days, although he would never admit it to his friends. He took her hand in his, and together they walked into the house. "Having won all those monies, are you still of a mind not to gamble?" he asked her.

"It was beginner's luck, or so the Italian contessa I met that night said. No, I do not believe I shall ever gamble again, sir," Allegra told him sincerely.

"And you liked Vauxhall?" he queried.

"It was interesting, especially the Cascade, but there are far more beauties of a natural sort in the countryside. I suppose it is fine for city folk, Quinton. I did enjoy the concert in The Grove, but the supper. It was shockingly expensive! Why Mr. Brummell said that the carver at Vauxhall has been known to slice a whole ham so thin you could paper the entire gardens with it! And the cheese was dry, I fear, and the Arrack punch they served was quite nasty. I do not need to go back again," Allegra told her husband.

"I am relieved to hear it as we shall have to scrimp to get by on one hundred thousand pounds a year," he teased her, and then he lifted her up, and kissed her happily. "I thought you might not come back to me, Allegra," he told her.

"You thought no such thing, flatterer," she laughed, but his bald-faced lie had sent a thrill through her right down to her toes.

He set her down on her feet again. "I love you, Duchess."

"I am glad," she responded, "for it is important that children come from love, Quinton."

"Then you are ready to resume our efforts?" he said softly, kissing her lips once more.

"It is not necessary, sir," she told him, smiling happily

into his eyes. "Lady Bellingham, our dear guardian angel, saw at once that my moods and crotchets were because I was ripening with your . . . *our child*, Quinton. Her own doctor has confirmed it. By year's end we shall have a son or a daughter, and Hunter's Lair will again ring with the laughter of children. I might even forgive Melinda and let her bring George's boy to play."

He felt as if his heart had suddenly swollen up, and when it burst his happiness was like a shower of stars. "Ohh, Allegra! You have made me the happiest of men." He lifted her up carefully, and then kissed her lips tenderly.

As he lowered her to the floor again she slipped her arms about him, and smiled into his eyes. "I love you, and after we have paid our respect to Papa and Aunt Mama, and you have admired Willy, I want to start our journey home, Quinton. And, my darling duke, I promise never to run away from you, or from our life together, again."

Both Lord and Lady Morgan were delighted to see Allegra and Quinton had reunited without difficulty. William Septimius James, a healthy, plump, pink infant with mild blue eyes, observed his elder half sister and his brother-in-law from the comfort of his mother's arms. As Allegra had told her husband, he was a miniature of his father, even to the shape of his head, which was covered in a dark down.

"I cannot wait until Sirena sees him," Allegra chuckled. "Now we are truly sisters."

"He'll make a fine playmate for his nephew," the duke observed with a broad smile. "What fun it will be in a few years' time to see all of our children playing together at family gatherings."

"If Gussie and his silly wife will allow my grandson to join us all, but Charlotte has wrapped the lad in cotton wool from the moment of his birth. Heaven knows what will become of him unless my son takes a stand. They need more children to take Charlotte's mind from the lad," Lady Morgan said firmly.

"I am going to take Allegra home now," the duke told his in-laws. "I think it is time she returned, and Hawkins is eager to have Honor home as well, you will understand. They'll be married on Sunday."

"Indeed, sir," Lord Morgan agreed.

Kisses and handshakes were exchanged all around. Then the Duke and Duchess of Sedgwick departed for their home. They made the trip a leisurely one, traveling through the bright May countryside. The orchards, just hinting at bloom when Allegra had left, had now burst into a pink, peach, and white glory. Cattle and calves grazed contentedly in the meadows. Sheep and lambs browsed upon the hillsides. Everywhere there were signs of burgeoning life, new life. This time the sight did not hurt Allegra's heart, for beneath it the heir to Sedgwick slept as he or she waited for the proper time to be born.

Hunter's Lair looked to her, as it had from the beginning, like home. Crofts greeted her smiling, as did the other servants. They quickly learned the duchess's happy news and celebrated it. Summer came, and the fields were green with the growing grain. Sirena and Ocky brought little Georgie to Hunter's Lair so he might be christened in the duke's own church as his godmother was not of a mind to travel now in her delicate condition.

Sirena had already traveled to Morgan Court, leaving Georgie behind with a wet nurse. "What do you think of our brother?" she asked Allegra. "He is quite your papa's image, isn't he? There seems to be nothing of mama in him at all, except perhaps his eyes, but only the color. The look is pure Morgan," she laughed. "Quite like you, Allegra."

Allegra laughed too. "I have not seen him in two months," she said, "but he did indeed look like Papa."

"They are so happy," Sirena noted. "They were before, but they are even more so now. I think it is having something they created and share together. I know Ocky and I feel that way about Georgie."

"I felt *it* move today," Allegra said to her cousin. "It was like a butterfly fluttering in my belly."

Sirena smiled. "Soon he will be like a horse, kicking and demanding to be let out of his confinement. At least that was how Georgie was with me. I want another."

The autumn came, and Allegra began to grow rounder and rounder as the season deepened. Indeed she was larger than Honor, or even Lady Morgan had been, yet she seemed quite healthy. On the twenty-eighth of November, several weeks before she had believed the baby would be born, the Duchess of Sedgwick went into labor. The duke sent for Doctor Thatcher to come immediately.

Looking at herself in the full-length mirror, Allegra said, "I look like one of your mares about to foal. I will admit to being glad to be rid of this enormous burden. These last weeks have been awful. Why do not women speak on this instead of nattering on about all the delights of motherhood? So far I find no delight in it at all." She winced as a wave of pain swept over her, almost doubling her over, an accomplishment in itself given the size of her belly.

"You don't make me feel like giving up my burden none too soon," Honor said, gazing down at her own girth.

The birthing room was well prepared with plenty of

clean linens. The fireplace steamed with kettles of hot water ready for use when called for by the doctor. The ducal cradle adorned in satin and lace was ready for its occupant along with the proper amount of swaddling clothes for the baby. There was a basin set aside for cleaning the infant of blood. All waited upon the Duchess of Sedgwick to give up her baby.

"Ohhhh!" Allegra moaned, as another wave of pain washed over her body. "Damnit! Why does it hurt so, Doctor Thatcher?"

"It is a woman's lot, Your Grace," he answered.

"*That,*" Allegra replied, "is a most stupid answer."

The doctor looked startled at such a bold exclamation. He was used to birthing women either weeping piteously, or cursing out their husbands, or bearing their lot with dignity and stoicism.

"I believe, doctor, that my wife desires a more practical answer to her question," the duke said, close to laughter.

"Of course I do," Allegra said. "What causes the pain I am enduring now? Is the baby all right?"

"The pain, Your Grace, is caused by the spasms your body is making to help you expel your infant," Doctor Thatcher explained. "If they become too unbearable I can give you some laudanum."

"Would that not drug the child as well?" Allegra said.

"Well, yes, but . . ." He got no further.

"I will bear the pains," Allegra said. "Ohh hell, and damnation!"

Quinton Hunter burst out laughing, unable to help himself.

"Get out!" Allegra shouted at him. "*You* are responsible for my state, and I will not have you howling like a hyena at my distress. I will have them call you back when the child is born. *Get out!*"

"Duchess, I beg your pardon, but let me remain," he said.

"No," she said implacably. "You are banished, sir, and take poor Honor with you. She doesn't need to see this in her state."

Honor did not argue with her mistress. She hurried along after her master, saying as she went, "I'll wait in the salon, my lady."

"There, there, my lady," the housekeeper, Mrs. Crofts, said soothingly. "What do men understand? It'll all be over soon."

"Not soon enough," Allegra grumbled as her labors began in earnest.

After several hours the doctor saw the infant's head crowning, and so informed the duchess that her labors would shortly be at an end. The child's head and shoulders were born, and then as its little torso began to slip from its mother's body Doctor Thatcher gave a muffled cry of amazement.

"Zounds!"

"Well, bless my soul," Mrs. Crofts gasped, surprised, for as the baby was being born they could plainly see a tiny hand firmly grasping its right ankle.

"Get out of my way, woman," the doctor roared. "Take this infant while I attend to the other one."

"*Other one?*" Allegra shrieked. "What do you mean the *other one?*"

Mrs. Crofts took up the first child, a little girl, and hurried over to the table to clean her off. The baby was howling angrily as it was wiped free of the birthing blood with warmed oil, then carefully wrapped in the swaddling clothes. "I'll need more cloths," the housekeeper said to the goggle-eyed maid standing at her side. Then she thrust the baby at the girl. "Here, I'll get them. Put her ladyship in the cradle at once, you dolt."

"Come on, woman, I have the other one almost born!" the doctor yelled at the housekeeper.

Mrs. Crofts fairly flew across the room with more swaddling clothes, hastily made up. She set them on the table, and said to the maidservant, "More fresh water, Mary, and do not delay." Then her face lit up with delight. "Ahh," she said, "here is his little lordship."

"There are *two*?" Allegra said. "I have two babies?"

"A daughter first, Your Grace," Doctor Thatcher said, "and now a son. A fine lusty son. Just listen to those cries."

Allegra, unable to help herself, burst into tears. "Let me see my babies," she begged them. "Let me see my children."

"Give me just a few minutes to complete your birthing, madame," the doctor said in kindly tones. "Then you may have your babies. Just a few moments' more business we have."

Allegra hardly noticed expelling the afterbirths, or the doctor and the little maidservant cleaning her up from her labors. She only knew she could hear the cries of her children, and those cries were music to her ears. Finally they brought the two infants to her, and put them in her arms. A great wave of emotion swept over her at the sight of the tiny faces. Unbidden, tears of happiness continued to slip down her cheeks. Then the door to her bedchamber burst open, and the duke dashed in.

He looked to his wife. He saw the two infants, one nestled in each of her arms. His mouth fell open. *"Two?"* His voice was filled with emotion. *"We have two?"* he said.

"Two," she replied, smiling.

"Boys?" he ventured.

"Charles," she said, indicating the infant on her right, *"and Vanessa,"* she told him, her gaze marking their daughter on her left. "I would like to name them after your parents, my lord, with your permission, of course." Then Allegra smiled brightly at him. "Is it not wonderful, my darling Quinton. We have at one stroke outdone everyone. Ocky and Sirena. Marcus and Eunice. Dree and Caroline, and Papa and Aunt Mama."

"And why shouldn't we?" he demanded with a grin. "Are you not the daughter of the richest man in England?"

"And you," she replied, "the duke with the bluest blood?"

Then he bent and kissed her, causing her to involuntarily squeeze her twins just a touch too tightly. Charles and Vanessa Hunter howled with their outrage, which only caused their parents to burst into a fit of happy laughter.

"Do you still want more?" he demanded of her.

She nodded. "I do, my dearest duke."

"Then so it shall be, Duchess, for I cannot deny the daughter of the richest man in England anything!"

Part Four

Spring 1813
Hunter's Lair

$\mathcal{E}pilogue$

"*B*ut, Vanessa, I do not understand why you want a season in London," George, Viscount Pickford, said pettishly. "Hasn't it always been assumed that you and I would marry one day?"

Lady Vanessa Hunter smiled sweetly at her suitor. "There is no contract between us, Georgie," she said. "And if you mean our parents' fond hopes, put it from your mind. And even if I do decide to marry you one day, I would still want my season in London like every girl of good breeding does. To not go to London for a season would imply that I wasn't good enough to join the yearly husband hunt. People would wonder what was the matter with me that I was married off to my childhood friend so quickly, and without even the tiniest foray into polite society. No. I am going to London."

"Haven't you learned not to argue with her yet?" Lord Charles Hunter asked his best friend. "You won't win anyways. She is very much like Mama, Papa says. Bound and determined to have her own way in all things. I'm certain you can find a nicer girl to marry, Georgie." He grinned at his twin sister wickedly, and when she stuck her tongue out at him he chuckled. "Better start practicing your London manners, miss," he teased her.

"Just remember who was born first," she mocked him. "You wouldn't even be here if you hadn't grabbed onto my ankle."

"But remember who will be the fifth Duke of Sedgwick one day," he countered. "You're just a girl."

"A very rich girl," she snapped.

"Don't be vulgar," he told her.

"There is nothing vulgar about money," she replied.

"Mama!" Lord James Lucian Hunter called to his parent. "Charlie and Vannie are fighting again."

"Telltale!" Vanessa growled threateningly at him.

The Duchess of Sedgwick smiled benignly as she looked out over the lawns of Hunter's Lair. She had wanted a large family, and she had certainly gotten her wish. Her twins had been followed by a second son, named after her late brother. He had been followed by a third son, Henry, a second daughter, Theora, and finally six years ago, another boy, Nigel. It was at six that she and Quinton decided to stop, for they had an heir, a son for the army, one for the navy, and one for the church. Each boy would have a comfortable living, and their girls would be well dowered.

Their friends had been equally fecund. Young George Baird, now Viscount Pickford, had three sisters, and a younger brother. Eunice and Marcus had three children, and Caroline and Dree four. Her father and stepmother had produced no more children after William. Her half brother was a delightful young man, every bit as charming as her father, and unlike so many of his generation William Morgan was industrious. He would take over his father's holdings sooner than later, but at his mother's request he would do two years at Oxford.

They had so much to be thankful for, but in particular that their children had not been affected by the wars England waged with both France and the United States.

With luck there would be peace soon on both fronts, although Allegra knew that would greatly disappoint her third son, Harry, who desperately wanted to be a soldier. "You can go out to India," she had told him.

"You are looking quite smug and contented," Allegra heard her husband say as he came to stand by her side.

"I enjoy watching our progeny," she told him with a smile.

"I heard Jamie say Charlie and Vannie were fighting again. What is it about this time?" he chuckled.

"I haven't the faintest idea," Allegra told him. "I find it best to allow our twins to settle their own disputes now that they are almost grown."

"Sixteen going on seventeen is hardly grown," the duke remarked.

"They were probably arguing about Vanessa's season next year," the duchess told her husband. "She wants one. George Baird doesn't want her to have one, but to stay home and marry him, and of course Charlie takes his best friend's part every time. But both my daughters shall have their season in London. I agree with Vanessa."

"Vannie doesn't love George," their about-to-be-ten-year-old daughter said. "She won't marry him, but I will one day."

"Will you, Theora," the duke said with an indulgent smile.

"Yes, Papa, I will," Theora responded. "Vannie will marry someone dark and dangerous who is as stubborn as she is." Then the young girl turned to her seven-year-old brother. "Come on, Nigel. Let's go to the stables and see if Marvelette has foaled yet." She took her littlest brother's hand, and together they strolled off.

"If that don't beat all," the duke said, slapping his knee. "And I believe the little minx will have George

Baird one day if she really wants him." He laughed. "But you're right, Duchess, both our girls will have their seasons. A gel is better for it, I believe."

"Ohh, yes," Allegra agreed. "Just look how well I did in my season when the richest girl in England married the lord with the bluest blood."

"And they lived happily ever after," the duke said softly, bending to kiss the top of her head.

"They did," Allegra agreed, standing up and slipping her arms about his neck to kiss his lips. "Indeed they did, my darling duke. They lived happily ever after forever and a day."

"Even beyond that," he told her.

"I like that better," Allegra said softly.

"So do I," Quinton Hunter said, kissing his wife to show her how very much he meant it. *And he did.*

Don't miss this wonderful
novel from Bertrice Small

A MEMORY OF
LOVE

A tale of stunning passion, reckless danger,
and the fierce will of a remarkable woman
who can wield a sword as powerfully as any
man—and who dares to fight for her most
uninhibited desires. . . .

"SMALL CREATES COVER-TO-COVER
PASSION, A KEEN SENSE OF HISTORY
AND SUSPENSE."
—*Publishers Weekly*

*She would ride the fiery passions of
her troubled past to forge a
magnificent destiny. . . .*

TO LOVE AGAIN
by Bertrice Small

Legendary for her exotic novels of faraway
places teeming with adventure and intrigue,
Bertrice Small has written an extraordinary
tale of passion and history, sweeping readers
back to fifth-century Britain and
Constantinople, where battles of love and
war are fought with abandon—and victory is
savored with sweetest pleasure.

**"Small continues to prove herself
worthy of the title Queen of
Sensuality!"**
—*Literary Times*

Published by Ivy Books
Available wherever books are sold

*She lived within convent walls—
until destiny thrust her into the
arms of a passionate man. . . .*

THE INNOCENT
by Bertrice Small

Eleanore of Ashlin had promised her life to
God—until fate intervened. With her brother's untimely death, Eleanore becomes the
heiress of an estate vital to England's defens-
es. Now she is ordered by royal command to
wed one of the king's knights rather than
take her final vows. With resistant heart, but
ever obedient to King Stephen's will, she
complies.

Ranulf de Glandeville is all too aware that his
innocent bride wants no man; yet his
patience, gentle hand, and growing love for
his spirited young wife soon awaken
Eleanore to passions she never knew. But
their love will soon be threatened by a
depraved woman who will put Eleanore's life
in jeopardy—and the young bride's love to
its greatest test. . . .

Published by Ivy Books
Available wherever books are sold

*Subscribe to the new Pillow Talk
e-newsletter—and receive all these
fabulous online features directly in
your e-mail inbox:*

♥ Exclusive essays and other features by major romance
writers like Linda Howard, Kristin Hannah,
Julie Garwood, and Suzanne Brockmann

♥ Exciting behind-the-scenes news from
our romance editors

♥ Special offers, including contests to win signed
romance books and other prizes

♥ Author tour information, and monthly announce-
ments about the newest books on sale

♥ A Pillow Talk readers forum, featuring feedback
from romance fans...like you!

Two easy ways to subscribe:
Go to **www.ballantinebooks.com/PillowTalk**
or send a blank e-mail to
join-PillowTalk@list.randomhouse.com.

Pillow Talk—
the romance e-newsletter brought to you by
Ballantine Books